Binding Beth

Portsmouth Paranormal Romance #3

By

David H. Barnette

Published by Piscataqua Press
An imprint of RiverRun Bookstore Inc.
142 Fleet Street | Portsmouth, NH | 03801
www.riverrunbookstore.com
www.piscataquapress.com

ISBN: 978-1-944393-83-0

Printed in the United States of America

Visit https://www.facebook.com/d.h.barnette for more information

1

Attack on the Elf Friends (*The Recent Past*)

Even paranoids have real enemies.
- 1967 graffito

It was a graceful old building in downtown Boston. Its classic nineteenth-century design had come back into fashion. Two years ago it was remodeled from basement mechanical and storage rooms to top-floor C-suite offices. Architects and contractors updated the interior and restored the exterior in stages and at considerable expense. The firm's employees kept working despite the disruption. It would have been easier and less costly to move to a new building in an exurban office park. The partners believed good corporate citizens should invest what it took to bring their headquarters into the new century.

Money had never been the Elf Friends' first priority.

The building now sat alone in a city block whose other buildings had been torn down in an orgy of urban renewal. The block was clear of rubble. Foundation work would begin once the developers completed negotiations and the city issued building permits. As yet the rest of the block held nothing, not even construction trailers. Temporary chain link fence kept the curious and the homeless out of the area.

That mostly-empty block was the only good news. The bad news was that most of the firm's lawyers, accountants, and support staff were still at work when disaster struck.

Because of their mission, the firm had serious, expensive, discreetly-armed security in and around their building. The partners had powerful enemies. They thought they were prepared for any emergency; their crisis plan was first-rate. They'd never been attacked, had they?

A young paralegal named Maura was taking a late-day coffee break. She stared out a top-floor window, daydreaming, wondering if she should tell her boyfriend about the Elf Friends. Would he join her, or would he panic and leave her? It was a big secret to keep from a guy she was getting serious with. She was thinking they could drive up to Hampton Beach this weekend. She'd bought a new bikini. She thought he might enjoy seeing her wear it during the day. She knew he'd enjoy taking it off her at night.

She looked down at the empty block outside the building, idly noticing dust on the glass. Canyons of tall buildings focused the wind flow. Fine dirt flew off bare ground into the air. The window cleaners had trouble keeping up with the grit; they worked at it diligently, around and around the building twice a week. Except for a bit of dust, nothing interfered with her view.

Maura saw a man standing in the middle of the now-empty lot, inside the security fence. A short man in dark clothes. She hadn't seen him walk in. How had he gotten there?

With a rapid movement her mind couldn't interpret, a shining gold object *arrived* right outside the window and hovered in the empty air.

On the other side of the thick glass she saw a motionless statue. A sitting gold man with a shining skull face. Its gaping mouth bared golden teeth in an endless silent scream.

It—he—stared at her out of empty sockets.

Holy shit, she thought, *he sees me.*

Maura dropped her coffee cup in the sink (coffee splashed onto the counter) and ran to the door. Like every office area in the building, the break room had a panic button to alert security, the police, and the fire department. She hit the button like she'd been trained to do.

The statue smashed through the window.

Loud electronic alarms blared throughout the building. Deafening, scary.

Sounding the alarm sent the elevators into fire service mode. Maura raced down the stairs, followed by a river of colleagues. She knew a few of them, but there were more she hadn't met. There was haste in the stairwell, but no panic. Lawyers prize composure and hope for grace under pressure. The staff practiced evacuating the building twice a month.

From the upper stories came deep intermittent crashing and grinding sounds. It was louder than the din of heavy construction had been.

Along with the earthquake noises, Maura thought she heard shrieking. Just outside the range of human hearing, someone screamed and screamed and never paused for breath.

2

Reader, I Married Him *(Beth, the Recent Past)*

She would refuse love safe with wealth and honor!
The lovely shall be choosers, shall they?
Then let them choose!
  - (Robert Frost, "The Lovely Shall Be Choosers")

Beth was having a bad day, but it was no worse than yesterday. Bad days were the new normal. The effort it took to smile for her husband made her face hurt. She owed him a positive attitude. Hadn't he given her what she wanted?

For example, they had a beautiful house in an upscale Texas community, an easy drive to Andrew's new job. Location, location, location, *and* curb appeal.

Beth had decorated the place more or less to her taste. Actually less. Andrew hired a decorator to assist her. He did this, Beth understood, because their preliminary discussions about home furnishings pitted her thrifty working-class concern with comfort against his extravagant *haut bourgeois* concern with appearances. There had been polite disagreements between Beth and the decorator and then, separately, between Beth and Andrew. In the end, the decorator prevailed.

The house, Beth was forced to agree, reflected Andrew's status as an up-and-coming vice president of an up-and-coming enterprise. His boss and his colleagues lived nearby; they and their wives would be visiting. Only it didn't look like anyone's home in particular now. The house looked ready for a real estate agent to show to prospective buyers. *Staged*, with all homey personal touches safely hidden out of sight.

Looking around the place, Beth knew what Janjan would say: *Jesus, Beth, nice fuckin' McMansion.* She smiled a real, effortless smile. Janjan had been a real friend. Janjan had never lied to her. Janjan had even saved her life.

They'd survived something so frightening that Beth couldn't bear to think about it.

Last time they'd talked, Janjan had offered Beth safe haven with the elves who aren't really elves. Beth had declined the invitation. *Too weird.*

Instead, Beth had chosen such safety as could be found in moving to Texas and marrying Mr. Right.

Neither Texas nor the Protestant wedding had much impressed Beth's very Catholic mother. Mom managed to be polite, but it was an effort.

Seeing what kind of new life Beth was getting into, her mother had said, "*This* is what ya want, Liz'beth?" in her flat Rhode Island accent. Mom couldn't imagine why anyone would want to live among wannabe-cowboys and loud drunks who shouted about Jesus.

"I *think* so, Mom," Beth had said, on the verge of tears with wedding jitters.

Mom tried to make her feel better and, as mothers do, ended up making her feel worse. "I wish you every happiness, dear. Andrew seems nice enough. If I'm wrong about that, if he doesn't treat you right and you can't work things out, my house will always be your house." Mom patted Beth's arm.

Unable to face the humiliation of leaving Andrew at the altar, Beth had ignored her own doubts and her mother's backhanded reassurance. She couldn't bring herself to go back to Providence.

Providence was too close to Portsmouth.

To her credit, Mom had never been the *You made your bed, now lie in it* type—except concerning pregnancy. She was very Catholic in that regard. So was Beth.

It was pregnancy, or its absence, that was the cause of Beth's most recent bad day. The people she and Andrew socialized with, mostly employees or customers of Andrew's company, seemed to believe her lack of offspring was a fitting topic for general conversation. She and Andrew hadn't exactly been *trying* to conceive a child, but she'd agreed to stop taking birth control pills and see what happened. She wasn't about to talk about *that* with people she wasn't close to.

So far nothing had happened on the baby front, which was nobody else's damn business. When people inquired, Beth had to struggle not to go full-Janjan on them: "Are you asking how well I'm *fucking my husband?*" She'd never said it out loud, but the thought was reflected in her pretty face.

The other intimate area people felt entitled to pry into was the state of her *soul*, for Christ's sake. "Are you *saved*, Beth?" "Have you accepted *Jesus*, Beth?" "You should come to *Bible study*, Beth."

Beth wanted to say, "Hey, I'm Catholic. If I need to know about the Bible, I'll ask a priest." But everyone was so damn *friendly*, she didn't want to hurt their feelings.

It was in this intimate area that Andrew, who asked so little of his wife (except to go along with the interior designer), expressed the wish that Beth *would* go to Bible study with the CEO's wife. In an effort to be as good a wife as she could stand to be, Beth went.

She learned a few things in the class, sure, but some of what the pastor taught made her think: *That can't possibly be right.* She'd gotten a thorough religious education attending parochial schools in Providence. Say what you will about the Roman Catholic Church, they do theology with obsessive attention to detail. These Texas Protestants she'd fallen in with just made things up to justify their right-wing politics.

Beth's Bible study group had very strong opinions, backed by possibly-relevant scripture, about how women should conduct themselves. The group spent an inordinate amount of time fussing about what women ought to do with their ladyparts. *A woman's place*, and all that.

Beth had thought she'd enjoy being a homemaker. She didn't like it at all. She couldn't bring herself to drink during the day or to have lunch with the Ladies Who Lunch. She missed the routine of going to work. She missed assignments and deadlines and accomplishing things for her clients. She missed being told she'd done a good job. She missed being part of a work group where people made jokes and helped each other. Now she had *duties* and *goals:* she was failing at what she'd been told was a woman's most important *role* in life.

Not conceiving became a problem between her and Andrew. Off they went to the doctor. No physical impediments to their fertility were found. Off they went home to have intercourse. Again.

"Should we pray first?" Andrew said as they undressed in the master bedroom.

Beth saw that he was absolutely sincere. Despite that, or maybe because of it, she said, "Are you fuckin' *kiddin'* me?" Channeling sarcastic Janjan, and not in any helpful way. She didn't want a threesome with God. Being Catholic means you don't have to think about God at all unless you're in church or dying. Maybe not even then.

They didn't have sex that day or for several days thereafter. Then they made up, and the sex was very passionate, more like their first time together.

Months passed. She still didn't conceive, not for lack of effort. The problem didn't appear to be one the medical profession could do anything about.

Beth was afraid she knew what had caused this infertility. She'd been pregnant before, but not with a human child. She'd delivered the child, but not on Earth.

Her ex-boyfriend Bobby had been the father. They'd somehow conceived an infant made only of green fae-light. As soon as the baby left her body, he shone himself back into the fae-path, the road the Fae walk around all the human worlds forever.

Her heart had no way to understand what her eyes had seen.

Bobby wanted to marry Beth when they returned to Earth. Instead, she sent him away and broke his heart. Bobby had gone off to help Janjan. He'd met (and possibly married) someone else.

All that old, sad, *weird* mystery made Beth want to weep.

She hadn't told her mother that she'd given birth last year. She wouldn't have known how to talk to Mom about the immortal travelers wrapped in light. Nor had she gone back to church and unburdened herself in the confessional. Some days she almost managed to forget she'd ever walked with the Fae.

When Beth and Bobby were walking the fae-road, she'd forgotten her baby. She'd forgotten everything but the moment. She'd still be walking there if Janjan hadn't led her back to Portsmouth. Janjan had saved her.

She hadn't shared the weird part of her history with Andrew. He knew she wasn't a virgin, of course; nobody got through her twenties with her V-card anymore, not even in Texas. (The Bible study group did a lot of tut-tutting about that.) Drew didn't know about her time walking the road around the World Mountain with Bobby, Janjan, and Jackson, now Janjan's husband. Drew didn't know they'd all had to escape Simon, Jackson's scary old Materialist Magician master. She kept those adventures with elves and magicians out of her thoughts. She tried to convince herself those things hadn't happened.

Beth thought her infertility was *metaphysical*, not physical. It was nothing medical doctors or Protestant ministers could help with. The problem had something to do with the nimbus of faint green light Beth sometimes saw shining around her reflection in the mirror. This fae-light was a souvenir of the time she'd been the subject of King Coran and Queen Maeve, may they rest in peace.

Janjan could help, Beth thought. Janjan *would* help. All she had to do was ask. Suddenly she missed her friend so much her heart hurt in her chest.

Her wallet still held the business card Janjan had given her. The card with the name of a Boston law firm. In parting Janjan told her, *If you ever need my help, these people will know how to get in touch with me.*

Beth held the card between her palms. She really wanted to talk to Janjan, but what would a phone call to the Elf Friends commit her to?

There was also a little matter of her and Janjan's having had sex one cold winter night. Another thing she'd never tell Andrew about. He thought all homosexuality, male and female, was pathological. He said there was a Gay Political Agenda that went far beyond the legal right to have sex with or marry a person of your own gender, disgusting as those things were in and of themselves. Beth thought that was a harmless belief and never called him on it. She was straight, but had once had sex with a woman, so what? Hadn't Andrew ever given another boy a handjob at prep school or gotten one? *That* was a conversation they'd never had time tor, what with all their roles and goals and missions in life.

Things were more complicated than they seemed. What would happen to her comfortable life if she invited Janjan back into it? Life in Texas might be irritating, but it was also safe and secure. Zero weirdness.

She put the card back in her wallet.

3

Staind Sings "Everything Changes" *(Janjan, Nonlinear Time)*

> *Emily:* Oh, Earth, you are too wonderful for anybody to realize you. Do any human beings ever realize life while they live it—every, every minute?
> *Stage Manager:* No. (pause) The saints and poets, maybe they do some.
> - (Thornton Wilder, *Our Town*)

So where was Janjan when her friend Beth was dithering about calling the Elf Friends, before they got attacked? I was at home in the best of all possible worlds having a wonderful time.

If you live in the present moment, you don't worry much about the future. Naturally you still remember your past, and the process of cause and effect continues invisibly in every thought and action. I mean, even among the elves who aren't really elves, things change. Sometimes dramatically.

Fairy tales end with *And they lived happily ever after*. "Ever after" is the tricky part. *Forever* means different things in different time streams.

Jackson and I were *very* happy together for a *very* long time in the next world over from Earth, where time is nonlinear. I can't tell you how many Earth years our happiness lasted.

We were married. We had wonderful sex. It wasn't just sex, we *made love*. We were *spoken for*, as the elves say, body and spirit, heart and mind.

Together we explored the great, green forests. We walked on top of the ocean to the offshore islands. Naked, barefoot, and laughing, we rode waves as they broke on the reef. We hiked along a tropical coast no glaciers had ever scarred. We lay on warm grass at night and watched the stars. We slept as close together as couples do on Earth, and our honeymoon never ended.

But something was pulling at Jackson that wasn't pulling at me. He heard something *calling* him. The call made him want to walk into the high country to see what he could see. He knew he wanted whatever was there, even though he didn't know exactly what it was.

He used his free will and stayed with me. But our minds were joined. We hid nothing from each other. I knew what he was feeling. He knew what I wasn't feeling. I knew he was almost ready to go. He knew I wasn't ready to go with him. In me the call was just a whisper.

I knew I was going to lose him, but not yet, I hoped. Not yet.

I didn't pray for him to become what I thought he should be instead of being what he was. I'm not stupid. We who are miscalled "elves" don't pray like that. That prayer wouldn't deserve an answer. Life never stands still, and I didn't want it to. Before I came to this world, I'd walked the fae-road with the travelers wrapped in light. I saw their unchanging life become weary, stale, flat, and unprofitable.

Our friends Jerry and Leda August, more in sync than we were, had walked into the highlands *together*. Intuition told me they'd be coming back, but not when. We'd been friends on Earth. They came to this world first and I followed them. I missed them *and* I was happy for their happiness.

In the absence of Jerry and Leda, Jackson and I grew closer to Daniel and Aimee Ryun. Daniel and Jackson were in the same boat, wanting to stay in the lowlands, but needing to walk higher up the World Mountain. Daniel's predicament was more acute than Jackson's. Much as he loved Aimee, his spirit kept wanting to fall out of his physical body.

Jackson had been studying with the Healer in the Groves of Healing, not far from the little village we called Nextworld Portsmouth. The gift of healing had lain dormant and unsuspected in him the whole time he was working for the Materialist Magicians on Earth. He'd learned enough about healing to know it was Daniel's time to leave. He saw it in the man's spirit.

The four of us sat on the bank of the great river in the twilight, watching the tide go out. Daniel's spirit flickered around his body like half-visible fireflies.

"You should go, my brother," Jackson told Daniel. "Now, tonight. I'll go with you."

We all spoke the only language anyone can speak in that world, Elvish, in which only truth can be thought or spoken.

Daniel nodded. Jackson was telling him something he already knew. Time to accept it.

Sudden and swift and light as that the ties gave, the poet said.

Daniel hugged Aimee. They were crying. They were happy for all they'd had together. They didn't want to accept the natural end of their marriage.

I'd expected that to happen to Daniel and Aimee. I didn't expect it would happen to Jackson and me.

Not so soon. Not now. *Not tonight.*

Jackson and I embraced, also crying. How could we help it? We kissed deeply. We shared an ecstatic inner orgasm: *Oh, my God.*

We were so close. I'd never been closer to anybody, never been so *intimate* with anyone. I'd had lots of lovers and any number of crushes before I met Jackson. Before him, "love" was just a word that soured my stomach.

Elves don't do long goodbyes. Jackson just *left*.

He walked alongside Daniel, headed toward the true north. They followed their hearts. I knew the direction they were going because the same map was inside me. I heard the same call, but I wasn't ready to answer it. Not yet. *Please.*

One minute I was married, *spoken for*, the next minute I wasn't. Boom, done.

I was going to have to find a way to feel grateful for this. In the moment I just felt empty. I had no wisdom to make it look like anything but a loss—even here in this world where there *is* no bad news.

Aimee had seen the end of her marriage coming for quite some time. She was more prepared than I was. Not that I envied her. She'd had a lot of adventures in her life and all her loves had ended in sadness. I'd say her life was touched by tragedy, but none of us believe that's a real thing.

We watched the men who had been ours walk off into the night. We looked at each other.

Our husbands might return to us. They probably wouldn't. There was no way to know.

"I know what I *should* do," I said. "I *should* sit here and meditate. I don't feel like doing that, not even a little." Yes, I was feeling restless and rebellious. I've never been a patient woman.

"We could go back to Earth," Aimee offered. "Get our perspective back, maybe do something good for somebody else?"

Sure, there was always somebody in the world of our birth who needed help, but she was rationalizing. We'd been taught a better way to face an inevitable change like this. We didn't want to let go of a love that had been so sweet for both of us. Not just yet.

Baldly stated, she wanted to go to Earth because it's impossible to suffer properly in the next world over. There's too much love for your real self and no support for your ego. I was on to her. I wanted the same thing.

Do something good for somebody else. When Aimee said that, an intuition arrived right in the middle of my chest where Leda had once painted an elvish *mandala.*

"I think my friend Beth needs me," I said. "Or she's going to need me soon." It's hard to translate that kind of perception into the language of Earth time. Jackson and I had made enemies on Earth, before we came to the elves and afterward. Our enemies couldn't touch us in the next world over, but they might try to hurt our friends.

They couldn't lure Jackson back from wherever he and Daniel had gone, that was for sure. Even *I* couldn't do that.

I *suppose* I could have got naked and sat on his face when he tried to leave, but Jackson would just have laughed, picked me up in his strong arms, and carried me with him. Someplace I was unprepared to go, even if my husband was kissing my ladygarden while he took me there.

Something else I knew for sure was that the Materialist Magicians wanted vengeance. The MMs served the Claimant, who wanted vengeance with extreme prejudice. The Claimant wanted to pull down the whole of creation and all the creatures in it, even those who served him. Speaking of self-centered ego.

That had always seemed short-sighted to me, like sawing off the branch you're sitting on. Free will with extreme prejudice, I guess. Anyway.

"Let's go back to Portsmouth, then," Aimee said.

"Just to see what's going on," I agreed.

Distracting ourselves with motion looked more appealing than sitting still and facing facts right now. Maybe we were just kidding ourselves and looking to indulge a temporary madness for two. Earth was the place to go for *folie à deux*.

We headed down the World Mountain toward Earth. We could have traveled elf-style in an instant, but sometimes it's better to walk out of the next world over. You get acclimated gradually that way. Both Aimee and I had been at home for a long, long time, however little Earth time had passed since we left.

In the past, Aimee had worked as a guide, bringing dozens of elf-seekers home through Portsmouth. The walls between the worlds are thinner there.

In the borderland we encountered the angel who guards humankind's own true home. We'd met him before, but every meeting with the angel was awesome in the original sense: awe-inspiring. If elves are sunlight on the surface of the sea, angels are light that shines into the depths.

Hello, angel, I thought to him.

Hello, Janjan, thought the angel. *Hello, Aimee. I see that your hearts are troubled.*

There's no lying in the Unfallen Tongue.

Our marriages have ended, Aimee thought. *Some people on Earth need our help, so we're going back to see what we can do.*

The angel seemed to nod. He understood what she meant—and also understood the motives she hid even from herself.

Remember who you are, the angel thought. *Remember whose you are.* It was a gentle warning.

We nodded to the angel in return. *We'll be careful out there,* I thought.

The angel's smile felt like sun on our backs as we walked out of the borderland and onto the lower slopes of the Invisible Mountain.

From the Invisible Mountain that is also rightly known as the World Mountain we stepped onto the black water of the Atlantic Ocean outside Portsmouth Harbor. We stood atop the cold ocean's surface, whispering an Elvish spell that made the water temporarily solid and kept our boots a feather's thickness above it. We bobbed slowly up and down with the swell.

It was a clear summer night with no moon. We saw the lights of Portsmouth ahead of us upriver in the distance. The faint yellow lights of our old lives. We could walk the streets of the city, but there was no returning to what we used to be.

We looked at each other in the quiet darkness. I thought to Aimee, *Now what?*

"I know a place," she said. She'd been back to Earth more often than I had in the interval since Jackson and I left the world of our birth behind.

"Lead on, my sister."

I was happy to follow her. She'd spent longer among the elves than I had and accomplished far more on Earth and in the next world over. I'd rescued a few people. Aimee and Daniel had saved all of Portsmouth and helped save all of Earth. Kind of a long story.

Instead of walking into the mouth of the Piscataqua River whose current separates New Hampshire from Maine, we skated south-southwest to the Odiorne Point State Park.

We stepped off the water onto a high granite breakwater.

"This is where I first met Jerry August," Aimee said.

Jerry was still married to Leda, the great love of his life, but Aimee was single again. So was I. We *envied* Jerry and Leda that they still had each other. Envy hurt more here than it would have at home where the thought never arose.

We scampered up huge stones to the top of the jetty. A light land breeze blew warm out to sea. We saw distant house lights on the far side of the water. On Earth the starlight was dimmed by dust and worse than dust. Smoke from distant forest fires. Poison from factories, power plants, cars, and trucks. This world was a burning house.

Like our world, this world could also be an Eden. We could see traces of paradise around the edges of land, sea, and sky. We also saw that Eden was never going to happen as long as Earth's people kept choosing something else for themselves. Free will.

"So where are we going, again?" I said.

Aimee looked at me for a moment, making up her mind. What I saw of her in the ambient light was breathtaking.

She held out a hand. "Travel with me," she said. "It's not far, but I doubt you've ever been there." I heard her voice in my mind: *Will you trust me?*

I took her hand and answered in the mind space we shared, *I trust you with my life.*

It was a good thing I did trust her. Less than a second later I found myself underground in total darkness. I wasn't afraid. My perceptions registered no threat. I smelled old cement. Echoes told me we were in an enclosed room with a low ceiling.

Aimee let go of my hand. I heard her cautious footsteps "If I remember right, there's a light switch right... over here!"

Click. Fluorescents flickered on over our heads.

"Ta-da!"

I knew where we were. Long before it became a state park, Odiorne Point had been part of Portsmouth's Second World War harbor defenses. Later a coalition of very bad people commandeered the man-made caves and tunnels and vastly expanded them. The New World Order turned the place into an internment camp for political prisoners and a staging area for an invasion of the United States from the Agharti underworld. Another long story.

I looked at Aimee. "Why are we *here*?" I meant: why this place with all its bad memories?

Aimee gave me a level look right back. "*Donita Danton* brought me here."

I looked at the empty hall: concrete pillars, concrete walls, maybe fifty yards across. "Aren't Donita and Jean-Paul married?"

"Yes." Still looking me right in the eye. She wanted me to figure this out for myself.

"But...?" I mean, I *thought* I knew what she was getting at. I kinda didn't want to say it. Elves don't pretend to be perfect, but I guess I thought the high elves were above mere cravings of the flesh. And Donita Danton-Herold, who'd been the New World Order's political officer back when these concrete bunkers were in daily use, had become the kind of being who could call her husband Jean-Paul back from death. She'd become the kind of companion who walked with her man right out of the body. She'd only returned to the flesh because the human worlds had needed her—and needed the child she chose to bear.

Annoyed at my slowness, Aimee turned, made a *follow me* hand gesture above one shoulder, and walked down a long, dark corridor. Outside the auditorium or whatever it was the lights came on as we walked. Motion detectors?

I followed her. I was born curious.

4

Carly Rae Jepson Sings "Call Me Maybe" *(Beth, the Recent Past)*

Andrew came home all brisk and managerial, saying he wanted to "work on our marriage tonight." Without consulting Beth, he'd scheduled a counseling session with the pastor of their church. After all, she didn't work outside their beautiful home. What else did she have to do after she made him dinner? He didn't *say* it, but that's how she took his words.

First Beth said No. Then she said *Hell, no.*

Once she got rolling, she went on to add that she wasn't going back to *that* church, where the ladyfolk said "heck" instead of "hell" and "oh, my gosh" instead of "oh, my God." And if she ever *did* decide to go to some boring-ass church again, it would be a proper *Catholic* church, if they even had such a thing here in Cow City, USA.

Thinking about calling Janjan got Beth thinking *WWJD*, where the "J" was not *Jesus*, but *Janjan: What Would Janjan Do?* Janjan never let anyone abuse her; being an elf wouldn't change that. She'd always known what she wanted.

The last time they talked back in Providence, Janjan gently asked Beth if this marriage was what *she* wanted. Beth said she *thought* so.

Beth had been kidding herself. Janjan had known, but hadn't pushed. Beth hoped they were still friends. She was going to ask Janjan to forgive her.

To Andrew's credit, he wasn't angry, just disappointed. He called the minister to cancel their counseling session. He made himself a sandwich and took himself off to one of the guestrooms for the night.

Beth felt liberated at the prospect of an evening alone: *Yay, school's out.* Her relief was so profound she felt guilty about it. Not guilty enough to go find Andrew in the guestroom, take his sandwich away, and sit on his face, though. Reading *The Rules* didn't tell her what she was supposed to do to keep a husband once she'd landed one. Beth found she couldn't read *The Rules for Marriage* without gagging.

She found the card in her wallet and called the law firm.

The number rang. No one answered. No recorded message. No voicemail, either. She'd expected *this* firm would have an answering service, day or night. They weren't just any old lawyers, they were *Elf Friends.*

Beth hung up and checked: yes, she'd called the right number. She called again. Again the phone rang and rang. Finally, there were some crackling noises in her ear—call forwarding, maybe?

"Hello, yes?" A man's voice.

An oddly unprofessional greeting. In the sea of cell phone static, it sounded like the man had an accent, not American or English, either.

"Is this...?" Beth named the law firm.

"Yes," the man said, rather unhelpfully. He pronounced it *yais.*

His reticence unnerved Beth. She needed Janjan's advice; maybe this time she'd even accept it. The only way to contact her friend was through the law firm; this guy answered their phone. She gave her name and said, "Um, I was trying to reach Janjan Javorski?"

"Ah," said the man. "She is known here."

Odd phrasing, Beth thought, but at least I can understand his English. "Can you ask her to call me?"

"I will see her in two days. I shall ask her then."

"Oh, thank you!" Beth said. "That's very kind of you."

"Or *you* might come to California and speak to her when I do. Some things are best *not* said on the telephone."

It was a warning: *be discreet.* Some Elf Friends had been injured or killed this year, just because of who they were friends with. Beth knew more behind-the-headlines stuff than she wanted to know. Something else she couldn't talk about with Drew.

The still-unnamed man gave Beth the information she'd need to find Janjan. Beth made notes and confirmed she had the details correct. They hung up.

Beth felt proud of herself and a little frightened. Being scared was better than being stuck in Drew's empty house in sandland, getting browbeaten by well-meaning sanctimommies, waiting to conceive and thinking maybe she shouldn't. Getting out of town seemed like a great idea. Maybe she *could* run away from her troubles.

Beth stuck her head in the guestroom door and told Andrew she'd be flying to California for a few days to see an old friend.

He frowned. "Man or woman?"

Had they begun to mistrust each other? One more thing Beth blamed herself for. Yay, Catholic guilt.

She said, "It's *Janjan*, for God's sake. You've heard me talk about her. We were housemates up in Portsmouth." She hadn't told him the whole story. She'd married him to *forget* the whole story.

Andrew looked at her closely. Finally he shook his head. "I'm sorry, gorgeous. Things are crazy at work. Then I bring the pressure home and dump it on you. We'll have kids when we have them. Let's quit worrying about it, okay?"

"Okay," Beth said.

She put her arms around him. He put his arms around her. Then they were kissing like horny teenagers.

—

Beth leaned back in her first-class seat and closed her eyes as the plane leaped off the runway into the air. She was always pleasantly surprised when an aircraft got aloft and remained there.

As Andrew had been pleasantly surprised—and shocked—when she'd swallowed his seed last night, something she'd never done before. Men really appreciate the hell out of *that*, Beth thought, Janjan was right. And it didn't taste bad at all. I thought Drew was gonna *cry* or something.

Not that oral sex was the straight and narrow road to pregnancy, or anything. Beth had been deeply grateful for the orgasm her husband had then given her with his lips and tongue. But after they were both satisfied and she wanted to kiss him deeply, he'd turned away, not wanting to taste his own semen in her mouth or not wanting her taste to linger on his tongue. With a quick awkward smile, he hurried into their ensuite bathroom, and quietly brushed his teeth. Did he think she couldn't hear him?

Thinking about this private rejection made Beth consult the secret scorecard women keep in their thoughts. For the first time since they'd parted ways, she thought about having sex with Bobby. She'd sent him away. He hadn't come back to her; why would he?

Bobby who couldn't believe his luck in having an intimate relationship with an Earth girl who would take him in her mouth and who would let him explore her with his mouth. Bobby who would kiss her deeply and ecstatically afterward like he couldn't get enough of the taste of her, even mingled with his. Because he loved *her*. Bobby who, because of the years he'd spent walking with the Fae, could couple with her all night long without release of semen. Oh, the multifold interior orgasms they'd shared.

Bobby who she'd rejected when he asked her to marry him.

Janjan, Beth's go-to source in these matters, said sexual chemistry was the main thing and that "marrying up" was bullshit. There was even a word for it: *hypergamy*. Beth was starting to think that was another thing Janjan had been right about.

Poor Bobby, she'd done him wrong so she could escape their shared history. That was a mistake. Actions bring consequences.

Janjan never said where Bobby went, but Beth thought she might know. If he'd returned to the Fae, she'd never see him again. There was no way in hell *she* was going back to the fae-road. She'd left Portsmouth to get away from the paranormal stuff. Besides, Janjan told her that Bobby had met someone who had children from a prior marriage. Beth figured if he'd found a woman to love, he'd marry her and be a good stepfather to her grown sons. In many ways, Bobby was the most traditional man she'd ever met—maybe because he was born before the Civil War.

Beth hoped she and Bobby weren't done with each other yet. Or was that just wishful thinking?

5

Iram of the Pillars *(Louis, the Recent Past)*

Cruelty has a Human Heart
And Jealousy a Human Face
Terror the Human Form Divine
And Secrecy, the Human Dress

The Human Dress, is forged Iron
The Human Form, a fiery Forge.
The Human Face, a Furnace seal'd
The Human Heart, its hungry Gorge.

- (William Blake, "A Divine Image")

There are places on Earth it is better not to go. An ordinary man who enters such a place finds himself urgently wanting to leave. Something whispers in his heart, *this is a bad place, best left quickly, best forgotten forever.*

In the *Rub' al Khali*, the Empty Quarter of the Arabian Desert, was a place known by reputation to adepts of the Order of Materialist Magicians. For thousands of years bad people had sought assistance here to do such terrible deeds that, according to the Quran, Allah smote Iram of the Pillars for its iniquity.

Most of the city lay in ruins, but H.P. Lovecraft's *Nameless City* wasn't empty. Rumors leaked into the wider world. People talk, even those who should know better.

To this God-blasted place in the dark of night came Louis the Walloon, master of such Materialist Magician masters as still survived on Earth. The Walloon traveled wherever he wished in most of the human worlds. He traveled wrapped in the shadow of the companion demon that had possessed his spirit.

After a misadventure among the Fae, the Walloon had become a man of coherent black smoke. This presented difficulties in commanding subordinates and dominating allies. People had trouble attending to what Louis told them; they had to fight a natural instinct to run away. They could not persuade themselves that Louis was a living human being.

Having no tongue or throat of flesh reduced the Walloon's voice to a faint whisper, a hiss of words as smoke particles collided. No one wanted to get close enough to hear him clearly. Misunderstandings multiplied.

The Order had once been governed by Archmages for whom a return to the flesh from temporary disembodiment was child's play. Thanks to the elves, there were no more Archmages. The Walloon believed himself to be the Order's most powerful surviving magician.

If the Fallen were capable of intervening to restore the flesh and bone of Louis' human body, they had not done so.

There were still many who served the materialist side of the Order, but they needed leadership and personal guidance. The magician faction of the Order needed to recruit and train postulants. Times were hard; the old ways were in decline.

The Walloon had come to the Nameless City in search of the oldest ways of all.

His demon set him down and vanished into a shadow. The Walloon walked forward on two legs of shifting smoke, on smoky feet that hardly felt the stony ground.

Shrill keening came to his psychic hearing from inside a ruined building. The Walloon entered. His psychic vision registered sand, rock rubble, and broken building stones in the darkness. At Louis' approach, the keening became a shriek, avid with lust, consumed with rage.

A vestige of natural human feeling told him this was a bad place, but his previous choices had left him no better alternative. To serve the Fallen

Archangel known as the Claimant, the Walloon needed a *human* body, not an animated carbon cloud that frightened everyone who saw it. He walked toward the shrieking.

A neatly-swept area had been cleared amidst piles of rubble. Louis saw broom marks in the surrounding sand. Acolytes? Hope stirred within him. Had pure ancient magic truly survived here in the Empty Quarter since before the Prophet's birth?

In the center of the swept space the statue of a small sitting man, carved or cast in smooth metal, shone in the starlight. From inside the statue came a keening sound with never a pause for breath.

Before priests of ancient Egypt sought symbolic immortality by mummifying the bodies of departed pharaohs, those who built the Nameless City had given dying magi *real* immortality. Through torment and dark alchemy the ancient sorcerers attained eternal life in physical bodies of nameless power.

The shrieking statue was nothing so primitive as a mummy, desiccated with natron, wrapped in linen, body cavities emptied out and then filled with herbs and spices like a Christmas goose. Louis perceived that it was *a whole human body* whose organs, bones, and flesh had been transformed into gold, cell for cell, molecule for molecule, atom for atom. *Like King Midas*, thought the Walloon. The ancient sorcerer himself had become the alchemical stone of the philosophers.

The man's mind still lived inside the statue. Was it trapped there or was the statue its refuge? Better an eternal life in a body of gold, Louis thought, than uncertain human rebirth in a new body of flesh. Better to be an immortal gold magus, beholden to none, than to be a mere human being on evil's Dark Path, enslaved by demons.

Long, dry, dead years sitting in one square meter of this fallen temple had driven all sane humanity out of the golden magician. He screamed a high-pitched psychic scream empty of everything but desolation and hatred for all life not his own. *And the Empty Quarter was made gold, and dwelt among us.*

The Walloon thought the statue had entered a state like the eternal one the Fallen occupied by their own act of will. *Why this is Hell, nor am I out of it.* Louis had spent considerable time in the company of demons, sharing their experience. No human being could become inured to it.

At least the Claimant sought to *do* something about the realm he fell into when he rebelled against the High Enemy. This creature just sat on its gold hindquarters broadcasting madness. It took no notice of the smoke-being who stood before it.

Uncertain how to proceed, the Walloon remained outside the gold mummy's circle. The guardian demon that possessed Louis provided no guidance. It would have allowed Louis to submit himself to a Dark Path rebirth, but that humiliation would have cost the Walloon the dark magical power he'd spent years accumulating. Reborn, he would still be himself, but much diminished. The Fallen loathed human flesh and all its necessities and works.

Louis had remembered the Nameless City. The demon had instantly brought him here. Had the Fallen prompted his memory? How to tell the possessor from the possessed? How was Louis to find his own way back to the flesh? The demon said nothing further.

The Walloon cursed the elves for all they'd cost him.

Whoever the gold statue had been as a human being, he was a magician of great power. Louis sensed enormous crackling thunderbolts leashed and ready, barely restrained inside the motionless metal. Humble submission was the sorcerer's due. The Walloon lowered his body of smoke to the floor of the temple in a full ritual prostration. With both arms stretched out in front of him, he lay face-down before the screaming magus, quite prepared to remain on his face until his obeisance was acknowledged.

The Walloon remained alert inside streaming black smoke. His particulate body communicated no pain or pleasure and little sense of temperature or pressure from the world around it. Louis remembered the human man and the elf woman who had done this to him and for the thousandth time vowed revenge against them for defending themselves.

He kept his mind and his magic to himself. He was the supplicant here.

At first the mummy took no notice of him. The screaming continued unvarying and unabated for many long minutes. Then came several bursts of louder shrieks. Then silence.

Finally:

The statue: ...?

A sense of the creature's puzzlement arose in the Walloon's mind. An entirely mental conversation ensued.

The Walloon: Greetings, O shining ancient master. I come from the Brotherhood of Materialist Magicians to do you honor.

The statue: No one has come before me for centuries thinking thoughts in the language of the *djinn*. Never have I seen a man thus half embodied. How are you called, O child of smoke?

The Walloon: I am Louis, O master. How shall I call you?

The statue: [A long pause] Ha! I had quite forgotten my own name. I will not tell you my true name and give you power over me. You may call me *Gold*. Does it not suit me? You may arise and sit facing me.

The Walloon sat up. Having done magical business in the East and in the Middle East, he was careful not to show the soles of his smoky feet, a gesture of disrespect. There was no need to answer Gold aloud. The statue's old, cold, powerful mind brushed past his will, looking into him, examining his memories, and judging him by the standards of the ancient magi. The Walloon had lived in the agony of demonic possession long enough to become accustomed to such intimate violation.

The statue: Now I see what you are and how you have attained to power. I see also why you do not simply die as other men do. You serve *Shaytan*. He is pleased to keep you alive in this form to serve his will, for so little will of your own remains to you.

The Walloon resented the statue's tone, but had to accept the blunt assessment. In these ruins, as in the world of men, having no real body meant having no real influence.

The Walloon: Master Gold, it is clear to me that you do not serve the High Enemy any more than I do myself, or my own master among the Fallen would not have brought me here. How is it that the one we call *the Claimant*—and you call *Shaytan*—has not taken you for his own?

The statue: [Another long pause] I am the last of my order. Those who helped me enter this form left Earth soon after my transformation, during the years my thoughts were lost and wandering. Years! When I returned to myself from the shock of this new mode of being, their minds were lost to me. The magic my order wrought was of a kind separate from the High God and also separate from the *djinn* who defied him. My power comes from a time before the Earth ... changed. Within this body of gold is perhaps the last place in all the human worlds that older, stronger power still abides.

The Walloon: Then... you can help me regain my human body?

The statue: Of course I can! But why should I?

The Walloon: Perhaps there is something you want that I could bring you?

The statue: Look at me! What is it you think I need? I do not breathe or eat. I never sleep. I neither marry nor am given in marriage. In an hour I can travel anywhere on Earth in this body. Or my body can sit here forever if I wish, and my mind will go wherever I send it.

The Walloon: Forgive my presumption, Master Gold, but when I entered your temple, I thought I heard you crying out in pain.

The statue: Pain? *Boredom!* For all that my thoughts travel wherever I like in many human worlds, no one sees or hears me. At most, a sensitive child will feel the chill of my presence and run screaming to its mother. If I travel in this body, those who see me are terrified. Frightening mere mortals is tedious. Eventually the tedium makes me scream. You are the first person I have talked to in … a hundred years? The mortal men who guard these ruins and sweep my temple floor are dullards. They have no thoughts worthy of my attention and scant capacity to understand my words. The Old Gods have departed this world and there is little true magic left in it. The worshipers of the High God and you who obey the *djinn* have ruined the Earth.

The Walloon: Would a companion please you, Master? I need but order it and one of my disciples will travel here to learn from you, or to entertain you, if that is your pleasure.

The statue: For now I think *you* are the only companion I want. I discern that we are much alike, you and I. There is much for you to learn from me, if you are willing. And when you leave this temple, it would amuse me to travel with you.

The alchemy that had replaced the statue's human body with molten gold so long ago had burned away the skin and reduced the ancient magician's face to skull; the golden jawbone gaped wide in an endless silent shriek. The Walloon found himself looking into the hollow eye sockets, trying to interpret an expression that never changed. The horror of the statue's final agony mirrored the suffering in which Louis chose to live—in exchange for power.

Gold was right. Appearances aside, he and Louis were more alike than not.

Gold withdrew his mind from the Walloon's. Their interaction became more like the back-and-forth of human speech. Louis did not deceive himself that he was in the presence of an ordinary human mind.

It was a quandary. How was Louis to serve two masters? The Fallen would sooner see Louis reborn as a murderous lackey on the Dark Path than have him become Gold's *permanent* companion. The Brotherhood would founder without Louis' leadership. Since an elf killed Master Simon, there was no one to teach postulants in the Order's Caucasus monastery. And worse, there were no postulants ready to be taught. The Order was disintegrating.

The situation was impossible. Louis' demon kept its distance and provided no direction. There was only one acceptable answer: failure to find it meant the Walloon's death—followed by ignominious human rebirth and loss of power. He had no cards to play in this game with Gold.

The Walloon: I would be honored to be your companion and your pupil, O Master Gold. I seek to learn something that will swell the ranks of my followers, something that will help me take vengeance against my enemies.

The statue: Metaphysical problems require metaphysical solutions. Before the world changed, Old Gods once walked the Earth. Have you any knowledge of where they might have gone?

The Walloon: Alas, Master Gold, at every turn you show me how ignorant I am.

6

Bloodhound Gang Performs "The Bad Touch" *(Janjan)*

Aimee stayed well ahead of me. Longer legs. She just kept walking, kept her hips rocking, kept her cute little ass talking. Yes, I noticed; she meant me to notice. She never looked back. She knew I'd be following along behind her, hoping to have my curiosity satisfied. Not to mention. Knowing me, she could have known that without reading my mind.

Aimee stopped. I caught up. Together we examined the closed oak door. *D. Danton, Site Manager* it said on the frosted glass window.

"Okay...?" I still didn't quite understand what we were doing here.

Aimee opened the unlocked door. I followed her inside. She turned on the lights. They shone softer here, more like natural daylight. Some kind of special bulb?

It didn't look like the place Jean-Paul Herold had described being interviewed by Donita at their first meeting. There was still a leather couch, but no desk or filing cabinet or computer. No flags of any nation from Earth or from the human world below it.

There was also a bed. Actually two folding cots pushed together and made up as one. Two pillows, sheets, and a plain olive drab blanket.

Aimee looked at me with her eyebrows raised.

"Oh," I said. "Ohhhh. So you and Donita..."

"That's right. *Me* and Donita." She sounded like she expected me to judge her harshly. Maybe that's what she wanted.

"And now?" I wondered about the status of their relationship. It's not like elves announce that stuff on Facebook or wherever.

Aimee's face softened. "We're not *spoken for*, if that's what you mean, not together. Until today *Dan and I* were spoken for. As far as I know, Donita and Jean-Paul are still married, spoken for, and happily roaming the fucking highlands *naked* together again." A few tears ran down her cheeks, and she just let them run.

I continued looking right into her eyes. I stepped close to her, put an arm around her waist, and brushed her tears off with my free hand.

"Tell me the rest of it." I spoke as gently as I could. Of course I wanted her, who wouldn't? She was beautiful. She was a free woman again, I guess, and so was I.

Aimee slowly turned away from me. She was ashamed, like by coming here willingly with a willing elf gal she'd betrayed Team Elf, or something.

"I started wanting to be *punished* again," she said. "Right about the time I knew Daniel was going to have to leave for the high country. I knew I wasn't ready to go with him."

"And what about Donita?"

Aimee shrugged, a graceful, eloquent gesture. Her back was still to me. I wanted to touch her. Hey, I wanted to take her clothes off and touch her all over, but that's just my normal day. This was kind of a delicate transaction. I noticed we were hashing things out aloud in English to *avoid* speaking mind-to-mind in Elvish.

She turned back to me. "*You* know how desire works, Janjan. I started wanting ... *that*. My desire sparked Donita's desire to give me what I wanted."

"So you guys came here."

Aimee grinned. "Yes, we did. In every possible way."

I grinned back. Now we were getting somewhere. But.

"So what about Daniel and Jean-Paul?"

"Daniel knew," Aimee said. "I made sure of it. But Jean-Paul? Probably yes, but who knows what elflords know or think about?

Nobody's more transparent than the high elves, but I let that go. "Wasn't Dan hurt? Or jealous?" I couldn't imagine Jackson being okay with his wife doing anything like this. I couldn't imagine he'd ever leave me, either. More things in heaven and earth, blah blah blah.

She shook her head. "He knew I wanted to be hurt, but he could never hurt me. He just isn't made that way. And he had to stay alert so his spirit didn't fall out of his body. So if Lady Donita could give me what I wanted and give me some pleasure along with it, he thought, where's the harm?"

I stepped in and took her hands. "You brought me here to punish you."

She searched my face and found no judgment in it.

"Only if you want," she said. "I also brought you here because I want to give *you* a little pain ... to give you a lot pleasure."

"*Teach me tonight*. Isn't that an old song?"

We were smiling together. This was going to work out fine, at least for the moment, which is as far ahead as I ever think.

I've always been bi and curious, never bi-curious.

—

You may have heard about all the weird stuff that happened that finally brought me to the next world over where everybody becomes what people back in Portsmouth call an "elf," if they dare to talk about us at all. You'll remember that in my checkered sexual past I've generally let the man take charge in bed, but taken the lead myself when I sleep with a woman.

Tonight was different. Aimee was older than me in Earth years and God knows how much older still in nextworld years. She, too, had slept with both men and women. She had once been married to Magdalena, Queen of Agharti. Like the queen, Aimee had also given birth to a half-human bioengineered child, got on her by medical rape. It's an even longer story than mine, and you can find both our stories on the Elf Friends' website, *When Is an Elf Not an Elf?*

When it came to matters of pleasure and pain, Aimee was amply qualified to be my teacher. The next world over taught me how much I still had to learn. Earth was the only place I felt even a little enlightened, and only in comparison to my less-fortunate brothers and sisters. Even Jackson understood more than me, and he'd come to the elves from the Materialist Magicians, the bad guys.

The other thing was that I hadn't made love with anyone but Jackson since we came home to the next world over. We were married, we were *spoken for*. The elves have a code of conduct that you start absorbing right from the start of your education. In a manner of speaking, Aimee would be my first time with a woman since I went to the elves and basically became a new person.

If you think I'm rationalizing, consider this. Jackson and I could have orgasms together on the inside while holding hands—or while not in the same place or not even in the same world. The very first part of an elvish education requires mapping your own inner energy network, both the simplest and the most complex thing in all creation. Elves have a more thorough understanding of their minds and bodies than people get on Earth.

I had a different relationship to mind and body now. Pain was as much a part of my past as menstrual cramps. Elf women don't have periods—unless they're going to conceive. See, for example, Donita and Jean-Paul, who'd had to *return* to the body to become parents—from wherever they went when they walked out of those bodies together. Hey, I don't claim to understand how that works, I'm just reporting what I was told by people who don't freaking *lie*. I'd learned to heal: first myself and then others. I had no deep gift for healing, but pain was only *information* to me now, something to be quickly turned into healing.

Before she became an elf, Aimee had learned how to magick pain into transcendent sexual pleasure. Donita had taught her that to save her life. Aimee was going to pass along Donita's dangerous teaching to little me. Gulp.

To set the mood, Aimee turned on a small light in the corner of the room, turned off the overhead light, and turned to me. We undressed each other. There was none of that silly master-slave role-playing. I'd once been the pierced, submissive sex slave of a guy who told me that's what he wanted. That arrangement lasted until I learned that he *despised* me for giving him everything he asked for. Dude had *issues*, yo.

Aimee was sleek and of course beautiful, as all elf women are beautiful. She found me beautiful, too. If you like a big ass and strong thighs, I'm the girl for you.

We kissed. Kissing a woman is different from kissing a man. I'd almost forgotten, perfect elf memory or not. Aimee was a very good kisser, and I gave back as good as I got. We grew more and more aroused.

She led me to the bed. She touch touch touched me here and there gently all over. Following her lead, I touched her the same way. Our inner energies lit up in harmony. Elves are caring and sensitive lovers, another happy effect of their education.

"Do you want me to come? I'm about to." My voice was unsteady.

"Not yet," she said. "I want to spank you there."

That sounded very interesting indeed.

She positioned me on the bed on my hands and knees. She stood next to me with one hand on the small of my back and the other hand on my bottom.

Slowly at first, then more forcefully, she began to spank my ass, no longer white but tan like the rest of me. That was what happened on the outside. On the inside, her mind showed me what to *do* with the flood of stinging sensation. I was a quick learner. And oh oh *oh*, in just a few minutes I came. Varying the pace and intensity, sometimes holding one or the other of my erect nipples in a firm grip, she continued to spank me. I continued to come. All of that feeling on the backside radiated to the front side and up into the inside.

I'm sure I was quite a spectacle. In the altered sexual state of consciousness I made a lot of sounds that made no sense at all. She enjoyed inducing all that pleasure and watching what it did to me.

I stood up and shook myself. I wasn't done yet. I wanted something very much, but didn't exactly know what it was. Aimee did, though.

"Where have you been all my life?" I said.

"Waiting for you, silly girl," she said.

I put my arms around her and kissed her neck. "What can I do to repay you for that?"

For answer, she gently disengaged from me and padded over to the closed door. Hanging on the back of it was a thin cane with a strap. I hadn't seen it when we came in because I was concentrating on her ass.

Aimee took the cane in her two hands. With downcast eyes, she handed it to me in an oddly formal bow of submission. Like I was supposed to know what to do with it. I mean, I kind of did know what she wanted, but hitting somebody with a stick is a long way from slapping her hot ass with your bare hand.

I looked at her closely. She had tears on her face again.

"Will this help?" I said.

She nodded, still not looking me in the eye. "It's the only thing that *does* help. You have no idea."

For all that our inner lights were blazing in harmony, for all that we smelled deliciously of arousal, I was more frightened about doing this to her than I'd been about letting her spank me. Which, let's face it, was delicious. You don't miss pizza at all in the next world over, but when you come back to Earth, you really start craving pizza again, if you follow me.

"I don't want to hurt you," I said.

Aimee looked up, annoyed that I was wrecking the mood. "Janjan, go look at your ass in that mirror over there."

I looked into the full-length mirror. My rear end was still tingling and burning. She'd really been whacking me toward the end of the proceedings. I'd expected to see bruises. Nope, just a wide expanse of smooth golden-tan Janjan ass. I looked pretty good, actually. Elves become lean and fit without making a big deal of it. I had more muscle than I remembered having. My waist was narrower and my back and arm muscles were more defined. My hair was a darker red than I ever remembered it being.

"Huh."

"Sweetie, we're *elves*. My *intention* was not about causing you harm. Not even a little."

Thus reassured, I led her where she wanted to be led, not to the bed or the couch, but to the wall, which she leaned against on her palms and forearms. She arched her back so her buttocks were presented to me for whatever I would like to do.

I touched her all over, of course I did. I stood to one side and touched the cane to her ass. Then I hit her with it, not too hard.

She made a little sound of disappointment. She wanted me to hit her harder.

Which I did. The cane made a whistling sound and landed right across the fat part (relatively speaking) of her butt.

It stung. I could tell by the way she sucked in her breath and made a little wincing motion. I felt the pain with her. I watched what she did with it.

A welt appeared across Aimee's ass where the cane had hit her skin. Almost instantly the weal disappeared as she magicked the pain into pleasure. A secret of the breath.

After that it was easy to give her what she wanted exactly the way she wanted it. I watched how she reacted to each stroke. I watched the welts and bruises disappear as she danced slowly through the sting and hurt and then presented her sweet golden ass to me, unmarked once again.

Something else, too. Something I'd never seen shone through her. Not the clear light of the next world over, but a rosy light from a place in Aimee's mind that was hidden from her and therefore hidden from me. This light subtly *prompted* me to strike Aimee *thus* but not otherwise, to strike her *here* but not there. I put it down to the novelty of giving her penetrating pleasure by employing intermittent sharp pain.

Finally, she was practically collapsing from the intensity of feeling. She was coming and coming with no interval in between waves of orgasm; I was coming with her because our minds were connected.

Even if she did want more, she'd had enough for now. That much elvish wisdom, at least, remained to us.

She began to sob. I led her to the bed, crying along with her. We had a lot to cry about.

7

The Sisterhood of the Traveling Chants *(Louis, the Recent Past)*

Much have I travell'd in the realms of gold,
And many goodly states and kingdoms seen;
Round many western islands have I been
Which bards in fealty to Apollo hold.
- (John Keats, "On First Looking into Chapman's Homer")

The Order of Materialist Magicians includes both materialists (men and women) and magicians (all men). The magicians are the priests and the materialists are the laity. Materialists concern themselves with multiplying the Order's vast wealth and increasing its sphere of influence. Magicians use wealth, political power, and dark magic to reshape the world in the name of the Fallen Archangel. Information is closely held in the Order. Materialists know little of the magicians whose orders they obey. The remaining magicians know little beyond their assignments. Only the Walloon, master of masters, knows everything.

Only Louis knows that the Order's nuns, the Sisterhood of the Dark Path, are more than mere materialists. The Sisters chant a magical invocation to accomplish an essential material result.

To a high-walled compound in the American West came the Walloon in the dark of night. He came with newly-solid arms and legs wrapped around the golden statue that was Master Gold's immortal body. Gold effortlessly lifted Louis over the wall and deposited him inside the Sisterhood's gate.

Gold's magical propulsion generated sound just outside the range of human hearing. (Louis' psyche heard the shining magus screaming louder than the engines of a commercial jet.) They flew through the air at high speed (*like a magic carpet!* Louis thought) for short periods while Gold took a bearing from the stars. They disappeared into a dark, airless, non-material tunnel, only to reappear in the air again seconds later, thousands of miles closer to their destination. Traveling this way required a rigorous mathematics quite alien to the Walloon.

The mathematics of antediluvian magic had returned Louis to human flesh in an instant. A few harsh words in an ancient tongue echoed through the stillness of the Nameless City. The air around the two magicians grew solid with sand, as if the sand had been awaiting Gold's command to awaken. The command was an equation Louis' mind couldn't grasp.

The sand found itself embodying the Walloon, remade out of silica and calcium carbonate from the desert floor. This perfect replica looked and functioned like a human body. It ate and drank and eliminated. It breathed in and out.

Louis opened and closed hands identical to those of flesh, tendon, and bone. His new body obeyed his will.

Louis felt obscurely different. Time spent away from the flesh stood like a wall between him and his ordinary human experience.

The Fallen objected neither to Louis' new alliance nor to his new body. His guardian demon had completely possessed the magician years ago, but now seemed content to let its conquest act without interference. Perhaps, as Gold had said, because Louis now had so little will of his own, having sworn himself to the One Will.

Louis grimly soldiered on, the words of *Li Tchant des Walons,* echoing in the thoughts he shared with Master Gold:

Et nos avans les tchveas foirt près del tiesse:/ Vola pocwè k'on-z est fir d'esse Walon!

(Who dare arouse our anger? / That is why we are proud to be Walloons!)

Master Gold heard the song through without comment. He failed to understand the emotion the Walloon put into it.

Gold: You cling to your birth-tribe still? Have you not abandoned them for the service of the *djinn*?

Louis: The Brotherhood of Materialist Magicians has no song, Master. The Fallen care nothing for music.

Gold: To me, all music is mathematics. The yearning I once felt for my home is long gone from this golden body; desert has buried my land. But the vibration of sound can be used against our enemies. Perhaps that should be our next lesson.

Louis: I look forward to it, Master. Er, may I leave you concealed in the deeper shadow of this cottonwood tree? I fear the sight of you may so frighten the foolish women here that they will forget my orders.

Gold: I will need no protection when the sunrise comes, child. But I will sit in the darkness and learn whatever the tree may have to tell me. Come back soon from your errand. I find your company most engaging!

Louis: And I, yours, Master Gold.

In darkness Louis walked the driveway to the main house. The building was a massive structure of giant rammed-earth blocks backed up to a cliff. He stepped onto the stone landing, banged the iron door knocker loudly three times, and waited.

He heard nothing through the thick walls and the oak door, but in less than twenty seconds the door swung open. There were security cameras in the portico above. Someone was standing the night watch to monitor the compound's video feed.

A young woman opened the door. Not a Sister yet, but a postulant who'd been shown his photograph.

As it should be, thought the Walloon. They keep the gate locked. Who else could have gotten over that wall to knock on this door?

"I've awakened Mother Mariah, sir," the young woman said. "She'll join you presently. I'll show you to her office. May I bring you some cold water or perhaps some wine? We make it ourselves."

"Some water would be lovely, thank you, child. You are most kind."

Louis sat in a green leather guest chair sipping water from a stoneware mug. Mother Mariah's office could have been an abbess' work space in a Catholic convent in the Southwest. Yellow ceramic tiles on the floor. Crucifix behind the mother superior's desk. The desk was clear except for a computer monitor, a phone, and a teleconferencing unit. On the wall hung tastefully-framed reproductions of paintings featuring Mary the mother of Jesus holding her infant son. One bookcase was devoted to Christian theology and popular treatments of Catholic piety. The Walloon thought these things vulgar but necessary camouflage.

The Sisterhood appeared to be a Catholic charity. In fact, it was the instrument for providing new human bodies to the Order's bondservants.

The Sisterhood shared certain political positions with the Catholic Church. Both opposed artificial birth control and abortion. The decline in the American teenage birthrate was a greater scandal to the Sisterhood than it was to the Vatican. Unlike the Church, the Sisterhood was neutral on such assisted reproductive technology as *in vitro* fertilization. The Materialist Magicians had abandoned biological experiments. Even here in the desert the Sisters had heard about the Order's biotechnological calamities in Tibet and elsewhere.

The Sisterhood used shell corporations to contribute to anti-abortion causes and to politicians who called themselves "pro-life" but opposed universal health insurance. The Sisters needed a steady throughput of pregnant girls for their gated communities. Troubled Dark Path spirits must take new human bodies without delay.

Mother Mariah entered her office quietly on rubber-soled shoes. The modest prairie dress swirled around her. There was no need to disguise herself in the nun's habit the Sisterhood wore outside the convent. Louis knew what she was.

She nodded formally to the Walloon and sat behind her desk, seeking its protection. She normally wore a cross pin at her chest, but had removed it in deference to her visitor. There had been no time to remove the trappings of Catholicism from the office. The Walloon was unperturbed. Her faith was in the Order's mission, not in the Church. She was the last person who would ever seek the High Enemy's protection.

"It's good to see you again, Master Louis," she said.

"And you, Mariah."

Awkward silence descended. Asking Louis what prompted his visit was presumptuous. Commenting about his health was problematic. She had heard rumors about his disembodied condition. But here he sat in the flesh.

Not for the first time, the Walloon thought, *She has the face of a man.*

He was nominally heterosexual, but his upbringing had encouraged a distaste for women. The debacle the Order experienced in Tibet had reinforced his conviction that women were flawed, inferior to men, but regrettably necessary. He let none of these thoughts show in his smooth, carefully neutral face. And Mariah had been born Catholic, as Louis had. Like him, she was celibate. She would not have looked out of place in a real convent.

Mariah liked the Walloon no more than he liked her, but her place in the hierarchy was one step below the dullest *male* materialist who served the magicians. Theirs was a professional relationship.

She was careful to keep impatience out of her voice. "How can the Sisterhood be of service to you, Master Louis?" Obedience was vital in dealing with magicians. That she had been summoned from her bed in the middle of the night was irrelevant.

The Walloon smiled, or thought he did. The muscles were slow to answer his command. Still, it was clear enough what he was trying to accomplish with his face.

"I seek your assistance in ... *compromising* a female friend of the elves—to draw her friends from their world into ours."

Mariah nodded. "The elves are beyond our reach. It might be easier to hurt them through their friends."

Impressed, the Walloon sat back in his chair. It was obvious! The Order had attacked Elf Friends as tactics required. They had never thought to annihilate the enemy's servants.

As an apéritif before that total war, Louis would have his revenge against Jackson the murderous traitor and Javorski the red-haired whore.

Credit where due. "The Order is grateful for your service and your wisdom," the Walloon said.

Mother Mariah's eyes filled with tears at this unexpected praise. She bowed her head.

What was in Mariah's heart didn't matter to Louis. He said, "How should we proceed against a woman we wish to use as elf-bait?"

She looked at him directly. "Is she an American woman?" The Walloon nodded Yes. She continued, "What do young women want? *Beauty and love*, Master Louis, or at least admiration and sex."

The Walloon raised his eyebrows in polite skepticism.

Mariah smiled. "I don't blame you for doubting this. You're too busy leading the Order to trouble yourself with popular entertainment. Western culture—*American* culture in particular—worships youth. I can show you what I mean if you'll permit me...?" She didn't say that she'd been preparing this presentation for months. In these desperate times, the Sisterhood required desperate measures to encourage pregnancy among the poor.

A remote control turned on the television in the corner of Mariah's office; her computer connected to it. She showed a video that sampled commercials with young women who were either already beautiful or sought to become so. Feminine hygiene (disgusting). Body hair removal (ugh). Cosmetics, shampoos, hair dyes. The women dressed immodestly. The video included clips of so-called comedies with loutish, stupid men cast opposite improbably beautiful young women as their wives and girlfriends. Mariah's video sampled movies with gratuitous female nudity. Feminism very much aside, the Sisterhood understood how American taste pandered to to the male gaze.

As the video cut from program to commercial to program to movie and back again, she watched Louis' face. It showed nothing.

As a European, American television made the Walloon impatient. "I'm afraid your point escapes me, Mariah."

She held Louis' gaze and spoke with conviction. "Master Louis, I have dealt with American girls month in, month out, for years. They give lip service to our High Enemy, but the deity they really worship is the goddess of love and beauty. To use young American women against the elves, we must bind one of them in service to Aphrodite, the Lady of Cyprus."

Old Gods once walked the Earth. Have you any knowledge of where they might have gone? Master Gold had asked. Now his subordinate Mariah spoke as if the power of such a deity were still accessible.

Louis felt distant stars impelling his terrible purpose. Or perhaps what he felt was a sandstorm of powerful emotion borne by a hot wind inside the hard-packed dunes of the body Gold had given him.

Louis knew that the Order's last alliance with an Old God had ended badly. The being called *Saturn*, hidden deep within the World Mountain, was entirely alien to normal human experience. In the end, the ungovernable creature had abandoned Earth altogether.

But Mother Mariah was talking about a deity with command of the deepest human weakness. It was meant to be!

All power and all beings high and low, the Magicians believed, would come to serve the One Will. The Walloon felt the inescapability of his revenge, the inevitability of the Claimant's triumph over the invisible High Enemy and all visible creation.

Why should Venus not also serve the Fallen Archangel?

As women will, Mother Mariah continued making her case in detail. The Walloon mastered his feelings and interrupted her with an impatient chopping gesture: *Enough!*

Mariah managed not to smile.

"You have persuaded me of the rightness of your views," he said. "Let us therefore invent options for mutual gain. What is required to bring this Old God back to Earth?"

"The Sisterhood's funds are enough for normal operations, but summoning the goddess will require research into the ancient rites. There will be gifts to those who understand these things. We must use a shadow organization with no obvious ties to the Order. There will be travel expenses..." She didn't say that she'd already set some of these things in motion.

"Of course," said the Walloon. "Whatever you need will be provided. We have a new financial manager, you know." He gave her the man's name and Washington phone number.

"We'll need another sort of assistance as well, sir. Perhaps a man on the Dark Path who works for you? Someone who is indebted to the Sisterhood for his human body and who is dedicated to our cause. The whore-goddess may answer a man's prayer where she would ignore a woman's invocation." It pained Mariah that men were necessary for anything but the production of sperm.

"I have just the fellow for you, raised in our European crèche."

—

Mother Mariah escorted the Walloon to the front door. At the threshold she nodded to him formally, almost a bow.

Louis inclined his head. "Get some rest, Mariah. You have much to do."

"Of course, Master Louis." Obediently, she shut the door behind him. He didn't see her smile. She didn't see him walk to the cottonwood tree where Gold sat silent in the dark.

The elves are beyond our reach; it might be easier to hurt them through their friends, Louis thought as he approached Master Gold. The Walloon knew which Elf Friends he wanted to strike first. He outlined his plans.

Gold saw the merit of Mariah's idea. At worst, the invocations would fail. At best, the Old God would be a powerful ally in the war against their enemies, the elves.

The Walloon's mind worked faster in his new mineral body than it had in his body of flesh and blood. It may also be that the Fallen patrolled the borders of his thoughts and, as they used to do, gave him glimpses of possible futures.

He was vouchsafed a vision: the nexus of American Elf Friend activity and communication in Boston. The hated attorneys and accountants who had mulcted the Order of so much treasure on the elves' behalf. It was time to destroy the friends of his enemies.

Louis had recent intelligence on the firm from his agents in government. His agents tracked the whereabouts of Javorski's and Jackson's known associates. Those who came seeking the elves would contact the Elf Friends' law firm. The firm and its voice and internet communications were under discreet surveillance. The lawyers occupied a solitary building that would be difficult to defend. (Louis didn't care about collateral damage.)

The Walloon shared high-speed thoughts with Gold. Louis considered arranging an Islamist commando raid. Perhaps a suicide bomber or two when the soft targets fled their hardened building?

Gold had a better idea.

In the darkness, Louis was too absorbed in battle planning to notice the tree where Gold sat. The cottonwood had begun to discolor, droop, and die like the timberland near the Chernobyl Nuclear Power Plant now known as the Red Forest.

8

Defeat of the Elf Friends *(The Recent Past)*

The alarm was so loud in the stairwell it hurt Maura's ears. Moving fast, she caught up with the firm's managing partner on the ground floor. He and the head of security were about to send people out the rear fire doors into the vacant lot, the normal evacuation route.

This wasn't an ordinary fire. From an upper floor came a silent shriek. *This is a bad place, best left quickly.* The endless screaming hurt Maura's psyche. She thought, *Hail, Mary, full of grace...*

She grabbed the managing partner's arm and said, "No, we should go out the *street doors*. I *saw* something back there I can't explain. It smashed right through the window and *I* hit the alarm."

The partner might have resented her interference, but the elves had taught him to listen and change his mind when the facts changed.

He said "Thanks, kid." He had the head of security start directing people out the front.

Using two-way radios to stay in touch, security staff swept quickly down though the building to get everyone out. They were the last people out the front doors.

The office manager counted heads. Everyone had escaped. The managing partner told the junior employees to head for the subway a block away: *Go home, you're done for today. We'll call you about tomorrow.* Badly frightened, Maura obeyed and ran for the T stop.

The partners, the lawyers, the office manager, and the accountants clustered together on the sidewalk considering case status and documentation. The office manager sent the firm's calls to their answering service. Alert, armed security men and women surrounded the group.

The security team led everyone through light traffic, thinking the wide city street provided enough distance to keep people safe from whatever was happening.

They reached the other side just as the building imploded.

Floor by floor, the beautiful old structure collapsed slowly inward as if explosive charges had taken out the support columns. The security chief had been in New York when the World Trade Center towers fell. He thought, *Oh, my God, it's 9/11 again.*

There was a lot of noise, no airborne debris, and little dust. Just before the building settled into its basement, a shining gold object smashed out the blast-resistant glass front doors. The security chief saw the skull-faced gold statue. He aimed his weapon thinking, *How can* that *be?* He didn't fire; the thing flew too fast, three feet above the street.

The screaming statue flew at the firm's employees and their guards; its scream entered a higher pitch. As it passed, people sank to the sidewalk, unconscious. Nobody fired a shot; there wasn't time.

The statue flew toward the subway where the rest of the firm's employees had gone. At the street entrance the thing hovered in the air, waiting.

Maura came walking up the subway steps, intent on going back and talking to the managing partner. Her panic had ebbed. She really didn't know much more than what she'd already told him, but would it help to know that *a freaking gold statue* had flown in the window? Maybe it would help now, even if it sounded too crazy to mention before. And what about that man who just *showed up* in the empty block behind her building? It was her duty as an Elf Friend to tell the boss everything she knew, even if he fired her for disobeying a direct order.

As Maura reached the top step, she came face to face with the golden statue a second time. The mind behind the horrible skull face recognized her: she was the only living witness.

She heard its shriek in her mind and thought, *Mother of God, pray for us sinners now and at the hour of our death.*

The invisible force blasting out of the statue struck Maura full in the chest. She collapsed slowly onto the sidewalk.

Having done what it had set out to do in Boston, the statue disappeared. It didn't descend into the subway to continue its reign of terror. Nor did it rise up into the air. It vanished as if it had never been there.

9

Darnand *(The Recent Past)*

I have just the fellow for you, the Walloon told Mother Mariah, *raised in our European crèche.* Mariah knew what sort of men grew up among the Sisterhood of the Dark Path.

—

10 October 1945 meant more to Joseph Darnand than his birthday in 1897. In 1945 he died to the world of men (as far as the world knew) to be reborn in the Brotherhood (as only the Materialist Magicians knew). Here he found the power he had been seeking.

On that October Wednesday the Order smuggled Darnand out of the Fort de Châtillon, after replacing him with a drugged member of the French Resistance. Powerful magic made the *maquisard* look exactly like the escaped prisoner. Believing the poor fellow was Darnand, the French mistakenly executed him for collaboration with the Nazis and buried him before the spell dispersed.

Darnand's fellow Vichy French and the men he served with in the Waffen SS were surprised when Germany began to lose the war. Their *Führer* had proven fallible. Why, oh why, did Hitler insist on attacking the

Russians? Was the real enemy *not* the Allies? But it seemed that the Jews were the hidden hand behind the Russian Revolution and therefore must be destroyed by any means necessary.

Well, the Second War was all water under the bridge now. *The real enemy* was not the international communist or even the international Jew, as Darnand had believed. The adversary was those who'd shown themselves traitors to the Earth by going to live in the world of the elves, thereby becoming elves themselves. Judaism and Christianity were masks the elves wore to disguise imperial ambitions. So the Materialist Magicians taught.

Assisting the elves on Earth was a network of fellow travelers, the Elf Friends. Darnand had never given them a thought. But when the Walloon proposed a campaign against the collaborators, Joseph saw the wisdom of it. How would the elves conduct operations against the Brotherhood with no support on Earth? Without money and materiel, how could the elves oppose the Claimant's glorious revolution against the High Enemy?

Still, Darnand abhorred the idea of having to work directly with the Sisterhood of the Dark Path. After decades of consorting with demons, he had come to share their contempt for human flesh. He loathed the biological necessities of fully-conscious rebirth.

His ego burned bright from body to body, and that was all that mattered. He had a continuous memory of this life and the one before it. The humiliation of passing through infancy and childhood with an adult consciousness was almost too much to bear. But what choice was there? He could never become an immortal Archmage. (He shuddered, remembering *how* the Fallen had once provided contingent immortality.)

He had last been re-embodied in 1965. His new body was aging rapidly. Darnand dreaded submitting himself to the Sisterhood again. Although, like a hermit crab, he rather relished the prospect of evicting the spirit of another rape child or incest baby from its human shell. As one did one's duty for the Claimant, the darker enjoyments were encouraged.

Really, "spirit" was just another word for a temporary bundle of nascent thoughts and feelings, was it not? Surely *matter* was the only reality? Matter and the energetic mind-magic that manipulated it.

Once all matter was again abolished, there would be only the Claimant's pure, dark magic. Speed the day, thought Darnand. *Si Satan le veut,* speed the day.

Darnand's previous assignment involved expanding the Order's European network. Not that those he recruited knew it was the Order they served. Many in the Brotherhood of Materialist Magicians pretended to embrace fundamentalist Islam. New recruits thought they were fighting the Crusaders in the Christian heretics' homelands. Mullahs and sheikhs in the Middle East who indoctrinated, trained, and armed the recruits, believed their operations were funded by Saudi Wahhabist corruption.

When the United States and other western powers attacked their supposed enemies in the Middle East, Darnand smiled to himself. *War on Terror*, indeed. The Western Enlightenment was tearing itself to bits. No one outside the Order knew who the real enemy was—except the elves who were seldom seen on Earth.

Darnand would rather have used the familiar hierarchy of the Catholic Church against the West, as the Order had done before the 1980s. (Metaphysical politics makes strange bedfellows.) But the poor Muslims the Order employed were easier to manipulate and less trouble to subvert than educated churchmen. The Fallen had ceased attacking the Church directly and now allowed the Order to employ whatever means seemed most likely to destroy human civilization, starting in the West.

When the West collapsed, the Church would soon follow.

Darnand resigned himself to working with Mother Mariah on Operation Aphrodite. The Walloon's strategy was brilliantly designed to undermine all worship of the High Enemy. Human sexuality had always been a weak point for religions, East and West. Who better to attack that weakness than the so-called goddess of sex?

10

The Eagles Sing "Hotel California" *(Beth, the Recent Past)*

Beth preferred not to let the airline lose her baggage. Her small carry-on fit easily into the overhead storage bin when she boarded the plane. Once the plane landed, a smiling male passenger fetched the bag down for her. Being tall and blonde had always gotten Beth extra attention. It was good to be a beautiful woman.

San Diego International Airport was big, bright, noisy, and crowded. She got a shock during the walk to the car rental counter. She wasn't the prettiest girl in the airport, not even close. Like a magnet, California attracted beautiful women from all over the country and all over the world.

She wasn't competitive about her looks; beauty contests were the last thing she was interested in. Still, flying to California had downgraded her appearance from pretty to merely attractive. By the time she hit her forties, Beth thought sourly, she'd sink all the way to California-TV-ugly.

There were plenty of good-looking married women in her part of Texas, but they all had a certain Stepford Wife look to them: breast implants (*no thank you!*) and lip plumping injections (*maybe when I'm older*). Not to mention big Texas hair on special occasions.

Wanting to fit in with the other wives in her circle, Beth had passed through a Basic Bitch phase, up to and including French fingernails and the wearing of a superfluous infinity scarf indoors. She blamed a book called *The Rules: Time-tested Secrets for Capturing the Heart of Mr. Right.* Remembering that she'd told *Janjan* about the book made her ashamed of herself. Janjan hadn't even teased her, seeing how committed Beth was to marrying up. These days she'd gone back to a more comfortable, slightly less girly look and stopped ordering anything with pumpkin spice.

Beth thought about the cruelties women visit upon themselves because of the American beauty scale. When she'd shared the Portsmouth house with Leda and Janjan, they'd talked about that stuff. They all believed in equality, even though none of them were *political* feminists or anything. Janjan had serious doubts about a woman's place in the world. Leda had kept her own counsel, worked with the Elf Friends the whole time she was Beth's housemate, and had finally *gone* to the elves with her boyfriend Jerry and married him there. The following year, Janjan went to the next world over and became an elf.

She figured elves didn't worry much about feminism. Janjan was married now, too. Beth wondered if her friends' marriages were anything like hers.

Elves, for God's sake. They weren't really elves, how could they be?

Thinking about the elves and their world made Beth queasy. *Too weird.*

Her rental car was ready. It took only a swipe of her credit card to get the keys. Drew's credit card with her name on it, strictly speaking.

Thank God the car had GPS. Beth had only a vague idea where she was and where she was going, even though it wasn't far from the airport.

The traffic was terrible. But she'd honed her crazy-driving skills in Rhode Island and Massachusetts. The GPS got her out of the airport and onto the right road heading in the right direction. She settled back in the driver's seat, both hands on the steering wheel, sunglasses on, like everybody else on the highway, and kept all her attention on staying alive, staying alive.

———

Beth had seen the Hotel del Coronado in movies. It was more impressive in real life. The hotel had opened in the 1880s, bankrolled by visionary money men and built by Chinese immigrants. Beth was too busy taking in the swooping red roofs and blinding white exterior to worry about Victorian-era social injustice. Things were better these days. Weren't they?

Beth remembered what she—actually Drew—was paying for a night's lodging. Her mother would have been shocked. Beth had stopped sharing every detail of her life with Mom. She could tell when her mother was biting her tongue to keep from speaking her mind. The tongue-biting happened every time they talked.

The Elf Friends treat themselves pretty well if they have their conferences in *this* place, Beth thought. She wasn't sure it was a conference; that idea might have been her own invention. The guy she spoke to said he'd be seeing Janjan here. In this grand hotel it might be a banquet or a destination wedding.

She didn't know anything about Janjan's life now. *That* was a sad thought. When Leda came back to Earth to tell Janjan her story, Beth had avoided the Portsmouth house they'd shared.

The hotel had quite a history. Presidents, princes, and film stars had slept here. Beth could only imagine what life was like before two world wars spoiled rich people's happy times. Her idea of the past was contaminated by sentimental, watery images of Leonardo DiCaprio from the movies *Titanic* and *The Great Gatsby*. She imagined she would soon be too old to date Mr. DiCaprio and had probably never been attractive enough by California standards.

It seemed to Beth that "the golden age" was either receding into the past or was scheduled to arrive at some point in the future. The golden age was like marriage that way. The reality you settled for didn't make you as happy as you used to be. The bliss you were expecting never showed up. *That* was a grim thought.

She drove around looking for the hotel's valet parking; no luck. Going up in a plane, coming back down, and driving around a strange city made her feel slightly drunk and disoriented. So much of American life is spent driving a car somewhere and then searching for someplace to park it. Beth felt almost at home in California, despite her travel weariness. Providence was a small city, after all, and Rhode Island was a very small state. Texas was huge and still alien to her.

She finally located what looked like the hotel's self-parking area. Her bag was light and the underground lot was within sight of the hotel, so whatever. She took a ticket from a machine at the entrance, drove down one floor and found a spot. Yay! Two other cars drove into the garage behind her; she hardly noticed.

She was getting her bag out of the trunk when a thick arm went around her body and a hand went over her mouth. The hand held a cloth with a strong, sweet chemical odor.

Beth remembered the old joke: "Does this smell like chloroform to you?" Then she was unconscious and not thinking anything coherent.

11

The Lady of Cyprus *(Aside)*

Aside in time and space the Lady slept, distantly aware of events outside the grotto that Nereids had cleft for her so long ago. She had surged into life fully-grown, beautiful beyond human imagining. She was immortal, but even Old Gods have needs that must be fulfilled if they are to remain among us.

She had been born. She had loved and been loved, worshiped and been worshiped. Something had changed our world so profoundly that she had to leave it.

She wasn't the only immortal who left. Within a few hundred years, all the elder gods and goddesses abandoned their homes in sea and sky, on the Earth's surface and beneath it. They went wherever they would, as their nature bade them go, one by one and two by two.

Those who ruled the Earth had always known the day of scattering would come. She remembered the divine diaspora with sadness.

She remembered lying in her grotto not long ago, smiling faintly as the worship of a long-neglected elder brother began. They were all linked, the Old Gods. Thoughts and deeds of one reached the others as rain soaks drop by drop into soil. Her brother had answered his worshipers' prayers until he learned they played him false to do evil deeds. Betrayed by men, her brother left the Earth with a race of beings who resembled men but were descended from insects. He whose realm had been deep in the rock of the World Mountain now sailed the empyrean with the not-men and the steelbody-men, journeyed out into the stars faster than starlight. A fitting fate for an immortal.

The Lady was glad her brother had found friendship after ages of loneliness. For her it was enough to sleep until the world changed once again and she was needed.

Then the winged sky god and the beautiful earth goddess of the Other World came back to Earth. Had a new time of gods and goddesses returned with them? But no. Soon they freed their worshipers and also departed. Deep in the Lady's mind she perceived the lovers further away from Earth now than even her elder brother. Unlike every human being who had obeyed and worshiped them, the Lady knew their secret names. If she wished, she could follow where they'd gone. The gods of Olympus are bound by nothing so prosaic as the speed of light.

A time would come when she would walk the Earth again. Men and women need love and beauty. The Lady embodied those things.

Remembering what it was like to be worshiped, to have hymns sung to her, to have women invite her into their hearts and loins, to have men offer her salt seed, the Lady slowly stroked her own smooth thighs in her sleep.

Waves formed in the blue water of the grotto where no wind ever blew.

She dreamed again, dreamed of love and desire. All the Lady's dreams were wet.

12

Invocation of the Goddess

Possessing all the memories of two lives, Darnand found it easy to acquire new languages. He had grown up speaking French, of course, and also Arpitan and Occitan, the other tongues of Rhône-Alpes. His military career had him speaking German like a native.

Unlike the ignorant American Mariah, Darnand seized the opportunity to learn the goddess' summoning hymns. Naïve female scholars had resurrected the ancient words from a Mediterranean archaeological excavation. His feel for language helped him perfect their pronunciation. Academics, pfaugh!

Darnand was glad this mission allowed him to avoid using Mariah's title. He hated calling anyone "Mother." He had bad memories of the crèche and the celibate, *lesbienne* women who had supervised his childhood. The Sisterhood were a hateful lot.

Even more than in the Third Reich, following orders and observing formal courtesies was integral to success and survival in the Brotherhood. Darnand soldiered on, leading the chanting in rehearsal after rehearsal until each separate part of the invocation sounded as perfect to his ear as the women's chorus could make it.

The women's accents in that ancient tongue remained barbarous, but their sincerity was genuine. *Yearning* powered the ceremony. If they worshiped anything besides having their own selfish way, these American women worshiped the queen of love and beauty. They believed if she shared her power with them the world would be theirs to command.

In darkness Darnand and his hirelings brought the chosen vessel to a ceremonial space they had prepared by the Pacific. The chorus was convened to chant and sing the *complete* invocation; perhaps the goddess would answer. If the invocation failed, Darnand was prepared to blame the women who chanted, the scholars of ancient languages, and even the unconscious subject of this tedious, shamefully expensive experiment. Darnand would quietly kill the girl if the "goddess" did not accept her tonight. Simpler that way.

—

When the invocation first reached her hearing, the Lady's eyes flickered. Mutual obligations were created by the heartfelt act of worship. Worshiping an Old God bound the worshiper's human nature to the god's immortal nature. Yes, the Lady was part of the All, the Everything, but she was a unique, essential, *individual* part.

Was a new age finally dawning after so long, or was the invocation just another dream? It was so pleasant to lie here and speculate drowsily. Her long sleep had profound inertia.

The Lady dreamed of a time when she had removed her clothing, slowly, as if shyly, that she might have her beauty judged by a mortal man. Yes, he was beautiful as only mortals can be beautiful, but someday his beauty would fade and he would wither and die. (Surely, he had long been dust in the waking world.) Still, she remembered how it felt to feel his ardent gaze upon her nakedness like the lightest, warmest touch. She returned to her dream's sweet wetness.

She dreamed of the times she came to her priestess, a beautiful woman who walked naked into the sea to invite the immortal divine into her mortal self, to raise her up out of the water, to be reborn with the Lady in sea foam. She remembered the hymns and chants of her worshipers as the gaze of an entire city exalted the shining body she shared with her priestess. She felt the living current of human yearning like a perigean tide.

The old hymns persisted in the Lady's ears. The accents were strange but the words were familiar. Neither accents nor words mattered to the goddess who functioned at the level before thought. *Desire* was the force that drew her.

Human beings wanted the Lady; they *needed* her. If she could believe the invocation, one particular woman offered her body to be the goddess' earthly vehicle. This most secret ceremony was rarely performed even when gods and goddesses of Olympus appeared, variously disguised, to men and women they wished to bed.

The Lady's eyes opened in response to the ceremony of innocence. She left the grotto *aside* in time and space, eager to meet the woman who begged to be her priestess.

13

Hue and Cry *(Janjan)*

Our crying went on for a while, along with the usual sexual stuff women find to do with and for each other. (Leda calls sex *comfort and joy*.) I took the lead, although Aimee didn't need much direction. Like I said, she had more experience than I did.

It wasn't just physical. Our minds were joined, like the minds of all elves. The words we shared were all English, though, not Elvish. A slight distance between people is still a distance. We didn't misrepresent ourselves or seek to deceive, but we weren't diving too deep into the truth of the situation, either.

Despite all that shared sensual affection, we weren't in love. I don't love easily. Many nextworld years ago, it surprised me to discover that *Jackson and I* loved each other. We'd been *spoken for*, as the elves see things—and as I'd come to see things.

Dammit, I *still* loved Jackson. I still felt *spoken for*, even though he'd left me.

He *had* to leave me to help Daniel. He *had* to answer the call within himself. He'd done the right thing, but still.

What did Aimee feel about Daniel? He *had* to leave her to go upcountry, no question about it. The poor man had stayed with her longer than he should have. Even I knew that.

We paused for a breather in the midst of the proceedings. Sex is about rhythm and pacing, getting in harmony with your lover. I stopped satisfying myself and her for a moment to satisfy my curiosity.

"Do you still feel *married* to Daniel? Because I still feel like Jackson and I are *spoken for*, even though he's gone."

Annoyed, Aimee looked away from me. "You're kinda busting my bubble here, babycakes. *Our* bubble."

"But...?"

She looked back at me. "But yes, I do still feel married to him. He was ... the one, you know?"

I didn't quite know what she meant by *the one*, but I nodded so she'd continue.

Her tone turned less sentimental. Appearances aside, women are tough and realistic, elf girls even more so. "Losing Dan is hard, but losing Magdalena was harder. At least I know *he's* safe in the next world over, somewhere up in the high country. I loved Magdalena and she loved me. But after we first went to the elves, she couldn't ever bring herself to go home with me again. Then everything went to hell. Literally."

I knew the story. Magdalena became an elf when Aimee did, but then sought *unchanging* immortality in a cyborg steelbody so she could claim the throne of Agharti forever. Courtesy of an Old God, the Materialist Magicians, and the Claimant. To put it mildly, Aimee's marriage had ended badly. When Magdalena laid that steelbody down, Aimee showed her the way to her next human birth. Elflady or not, I guess Aimee still wasn't over it. We don't hunt our exes down and stalk them in their new lives.

"Everybody *leaves*," Aimee said. "Everybody leaves *me*." She started crying again and pushed my hands away when I tried to comfort her.

Aimee hadn't brought me to Odiorne Point just to pleasure her, something I would have happily done in the next world over. She'd brought me here to beat her ass, something we don't do at home. She hadn't brought me here to help her get through her pain or to figure it out, but *to feel sorry for herself* and to encourage *me* to feel sorry for her, too. And to feel sorry for *my*self if I had any emotional wattage left over.

She thought something was wrong with her, that she was damaged goods and that her lovers could only want her for their own selfish gratification. So there was probably something wrong with *me* that *I* should feel bad about. Look how much I enjoyed punishing and pleasuring her, for example. She was trapped in a vicious cycle of guilt and punishment and remorse. She luxuriated in the forbidden ache and sting of pointless suffering.

I saw an odd formation in Aimee's mind, an old memory of desire, hurt, and loss she'd surrounded with forgetfulness. She was placating it with pain and feeding it with pleasure.

Self-pity is another thing we don't do at home. We look at our wounds directly and heal them, for God's sake.

I was about to remind Aimee of that when a shock of direct perception hit me. Jagged images out of intuition:

Arms wrap around her, unbidden. She is drugged and captured.

Long intervals of blankness and nightmare semi-consciousness.

She lies (underground?) on cold sand. Women's voices raised in an invocation.

A sense of imminent arrival. Something *(someone?) is coming for her.*

"Oh, crap," I said, "Beth really *is* in trouble."

Elves see their friends' troubles as their own. I'd come back to Earth with Aimee to help the two of us, sure, but I'd known it was *Beth* who'd eventually need me.

What the hell had she gotten into?

The images were random jigsaw puzzle pieces. I couldn't see where they came from or how they fit together.

It seemed to matter that *I* was underground in Odiorne Point right now; I didn't see why. Bad things had happened here until the elves intervened. Elves don't fight unless they have to, and they don't stick around after the war for nation-building.

Nothing was happening here now except for Aimee and me.

And why was the electricity on? Maybe new bad guys were getting ready to bring the bad old days back to Odiorne Point.

This was Portsmouth, after all.

14

King Robert and Queen Moira

The king and queen of the Fae were having a spat. As the royal couple led their people along the fae-road around the human worlds, His Majesty's affection for one pretty blonde Fae girl had irked Her Majesty beyond endurance. This trivial disagreement prompted the king and queen to spend the evening in separate beds in separate bedchambers in separate castles.

"Go sleep elsewhere with your little blonde whore, then, and be damned to you!" said Moira.

Robert didn't try to argue the queen out of her anger. She'd be in a better mood tomorrow. They would reconcile; they always had.

His beautiful red-haired queen had herself slept with other Fae men. The king didn't bother pointing that out. There was no reasoning with Moira once her blood was up.

Giving and receiving pleasure was essential to the well-being of the fae-path, and therefore a duty of state, said the Morrigna. The king and queen rarely saw their tutelary deities anymore, though the three sisters were always at work, invisibly helping the realm function and prosper.

From their first days together, the king and queen had swived often.

Their multiple mutual climaxes shook the whole of the fae-road like earthquake tremors. Many fae-children were the happy product of their coupling. The children were birthed by Moira, not in agony as bloody, slippery flesh, but in ecstasy, shining from the royal thighs as coherent beams of green light. This *light of other days* gathered matter to itself as the children grew to physical maturity in a single day. The Morrigna educated them on their second day of new life; on the third they joined the growing host of Robert and Moira's subjects.

As time passed, Moira's Earth sons Brad and Chad (now Prince Bradley and Prince Chadwick) became enamored of this or that girl; those unions were also blessed with issue. It had been a little weird at first, more transgressive than dating first cousins, but the comely new Fae weren't the young men's sisters in any real biological sense.

"What happens on the fae-path stays on the fae-path," Chad said to Brad.

"Nobody's left the road yet," Brad said. "Who's going to talk about us if they leave? And who'd believe them if they did?"

They exchanged princely fist bumps.

Accountability meant something different among the Fae, who were accountable for their actions only to one another, to the king and queen, and to the Morrigna. The Morrigna, still known in certain parts of Earth as the Nightmare Queens, caused no nightmares on the fae-road. Few dreams came; life itself was dreamlike. The three ancient creatures (they looked young when they wished) tutored the princes in all they'd need to know to be Fae royalty. The weird sisters were gratified with their pupils' progress.

There was little awkwardness between Moira and her sons once they'd settled into this very odd life. The king and queen normally slept in one castle along the endless road, while the princes slept in another. Moira understood that *the lads*, as she'd come to call them, would be coupling with girls who'd been born to her and her putative husband the king. Moira knew her fae-daughters and fae-sons had lived many lives before their green life energy was reborn through her. She and the king were only a channel for fae-light.

When the Fae grew weary and their bodies and spirits sank into the road, they knew another fortunate new birth would come their way in time. Whoever they were, however they'd come here, the Fae remembered little of what they'd been and done in their past lives. In this the travelers wrapped in light resembled those who are born and reborn on Earth.

As the Fae population grew, Robert's misgivings multiplied.

Moira entered into the role of queen with great relish. Life on Earth seemed the dream of a dream, not worth the effort to recall. She lived out Irish ancestral memories that bubbled up from the collective unconscious. She believed she was born to be queen of the Fae.

But Robert remembered exactly who he was and how he'd gotten here. In the privacy of his mind, he didn't think of himself as *His Majesty* or even *Robert*, but as *Bobby*.

Bobby had first left the Earth to walk with the Fae during the long, long reign of King Coran. Near the end of the American Civil War that was. Not long afterward, dissatisfied with life on the fae-path, Bobby returned to Earth—and fought for his country again in the Second World War.

Bobby had accepted the invitation of the Fae a second time. He'd walked and danced and ridden with them till he could bear their changeless immortality no more. Once again he walked off the fae-road into New Hampshire.

Homeless in Portsmouth during a cruel polar vortex winter, unable to accept a third invitation to return to the Fae, Bobby prepared for his own death. Instead, Janjan Javorski had persuaded him to postpone dying and come back to her house.

Janjan gave Bobby a second chance at life on Earth. He'd immediately fallen in love—and fallen into bed—with Janjan's housemate Beth. Beth, it seemed, had only been in lust with Bobby, not in love with him. The twenty-first century had much to recommend it. Young Americans were as lusty as the Fae, if less accomplished in the bedroom. But after walking the fae-road with him and bearing his short-lived fae-child, Beth broke Bobby's heart when Janjan led them back to Earth.

He missed Beth. He wondered what they might have been to each other if she'd let herself love and marry him. Bobby knew he was no American girl's idea of the perfect husband. In the United States, Bobby was nothing like a king, being limited by education and experience to a life of whatever manual labor he could get. Unless, of course, he fell back on the bitter skill set he'd acquired in war: enduring hardship; killing the enemy with a bullet, a knife, an arrow, or even a rock.

Janjan had offered Bobby something better than living a human life on Earth and dying there. She'd offered to take him to the next world over from Earth where he could find rest and peace among the elves. All he'd found on the fae-path was pleasant distraction. His world-weariness followed him from world to world.

Bobby had only returned to the fae-road because Moira had to flee Earth. The Walloon, her former employer, was waiting to kill her for betraying the Materialist Magicians to the Elf Friends.

Moira had needed Bobby. Bobby needed to be needed.

Before being exiled from the fae-road, the Walloon had unwittingly killed everyone mortal. The fae-born had no defense against evil. Under Moira's and Bobby's royal guidance, the green *light of other days* began the work of restoration. Directed by the Morrigna, that same light, embodied in ectoplasmic proto-Fae, grew, harvested, and prepared food and wine, cooked and cleaned, and sewed clothing for all who walked the road. With their toil done, the mindless creatures melted back into the living road to await the day of rebirth and the return to mind and body. A lot happened backstage on the fae-path.

Moira was happy in her warrior queen identity, living out imaginings of her ancient Irish ancestors. Now that she and her sons were safe, it seemed to Bobby that she no longer needed *him*. She kept busy birthing new Fae and overseeing the restoration of the castles along the long, long road a-winding.

The obligation he'd felt was gone; his duty to the lady was done.

Also this: the sharp and slippery thing so visible in the faces of those Fae born on the road around the worlds, the shapeshifting power conferred by *the light of other days*, was creeping also into the faces and the bodies of the king, the queen, and the princes. This power came at the price of a person's humanity. Bit by bit Bobby felt a mysterious, essential human quality waning in him. Humanity was worth preserving. Why else had he fought in two wars in two different centuries?

He remembered sitting in a snowy thicket in Portsmouth's deep-frozen Great Bog. He remembered when the decision to die *arrived*, like it had gotten off a train just to shake his hand. It wasn't death he'd wanted, but *something more* than the life he was stuck in. Life with the Fae, even as their king, wasn't *more* than life on Earth, it was just *different*, with the potential to last for centuries upon centuries. The Fae said they breathed in for half of forever and breathed out for the other half.

Another decision arrived in Bobby's heart. Bobby decided, not for death, but for life. Real life. It was time to find the next world over. Janjan would help him.

If he could find Janjan.

15

Notes from Underground *(Beth)*

The Voice said, "Hurl her down!"
The Voices, "How far down?"
"Seven levels of the world."
- (Robert Frost, "The Lovely Shall Be Choosers")

Beth couldn't understand what the voices were saying. Her thoughts drifted. She was moving, *being* moved, really. Sight and hearing came and went in flashes. The desire to make sense of things had gone missing along with the ability. There were people around her. She heard the sibilance of feet on sand and the sound of fabric when they moved. No one spoke to her.

She'd forgotten being abducted. She didn't know she'd gone missing from her life.

Vivid smells fought through the chemical taste that filled her sinuses. Salt water, sand, and seaweed. Human sweat, not great but not stale and disgusting, either. Traces of perfume and cologne. Laundry detergent and sun-dried clothes. (Her Texas neighborhood association, those boojy snobs, had a covenant forbidding backyard clotheslines.)

Something stung her arm. The sting faded quickly. You're going to feel a little prick, she thought, another old joke.

The arms that carried her set her down on something that was soft on top and hard underneath. The unmistakable feeling of cool packed sand. Her hair was freed from its ties and smoothed away from her face, her clothing (a flowing robe—what the hell?) was arranged in graceful folds around her body. Her feet were bare. A pillow of folded cloths was gently placed under her head.

Chanting commenced, softly at first. Women's voices, prompted by a single male voice that led them. Beth's mind drifted, unable to make sense of a language she didn't speak. The chanting continued and grew louder. There was an odd kind of singing mixed into it, very old music with a scale different from anything she'd ever heard. It echoed back from a rock ceiling above and rock walls around. She felt she was outdoors, lying in a partially-enclosed place like a cave mouth.

It dawned upon half-conscious Beth that something was being *invoked*, and not in any Catholic sacrament. Someone was being *invited* here to meet her. In her odd condition of mind, she was content to wait for whoever might come. She felt as lonely as if she'd slept for ages somewhere far from the human race.

There came a sense of imminent *arrival*. The chanting faded. That which had been invoked was here. Faint sounds of feet on sand. The people who had surrounded her were leaving.

Someone new was with her now. It was as if the full moon rose and cast its reflected light upon Beth's closed eyelids. How such a thing might be possible inside this rock-walled place did not concern her.

She became aware of her loins in a way she had not experienced since the night she welcomed Janjan into her bed. She had the sense of another female presence that understood and appreciated her deeply. Beth's nipples erected and she began to breathe deep into her lower abdomen. She felt a warmth between her legs like the lightest of touches.

Could *Janjan* have come to her aid while she was in this strange state of mind and body? For the first time since that night, Beth *wanted* the comfort of her friend's embrace, to feel Janjan's hands on her and to taste her mouth. The drug her captors had given Beth had disconnected her inhibitions.

Beth's eyes opened slowly. She blinked to clear her drug-clouded vision, but it was hopeless. The darkness was broken only by a single candle behind distorting antique lantern glass. The flame flickered in a wind that smelled like the sea; its light refused to remain still.

The figure of a woman stood before her. The other woman wore a simple white dress that shone in the darkness. The woman's hair looked as light as Beth's. She observed Beth with great interest.

There commenced the strangest conversation of Beth's life. She wanted to believe she was hallucinating, but there was no way to dismiss an experience so compelling.

This was no human woman. Her thoughts and ideas *arrived* in Beth's mind fully formed. Although the woman's lips moved in the dim and flickering light, they formed no English words.

WHO ARE YOU TO INVITE ME TO ABIDE IN YOU, O DAUGHTER OF EARTH?

Beth didn't recall sending out an invitation. Had she organized a party and then forgotten about it? One of the recurrent nightmares that troubled her sleep in Andrew's big, echoing Texas house. Beth mumbled broken phrases aloud, but her every thought was received and understood. "Hi," she said as she thought, *I'm Elizabeth, but everybody calls me Beth. I'm happy to meet you, ma'am. Have we met?*

The other woman looked at, around, and *inside* her. The sensation was odd, but not unpleasant. She was too disconnected from her ordinary self to be afraid.

I SEE YOU HAVE BEEN AMONG THE TRAVELERS WRAPPED IN LIGHT. YOU CARRY THEIR *LIGHT OF OTHER DAYS* INSIDE YOU STILL.

Tears began flowing down Beth's cheeks. She felt no shame. "Baby..." she said as she thought, *I bore a child of light in a world to one side of the fae-road. The child floated away from me, swam back into that road, and I saw him no more.*

Beth had been afraid to mourn her loss. Now that she'd been hauled back into what Janjan called *the weirdness,* her memories came back in a rush. She had no defense against the past.

AH, DAUGHTER, WHOSOEVER WEARS A WOMAN'S FORM CARRIES A WOMAN'S BURDEN ALSO.

There came to Beth a sense of great strength and deep sorrow, as if this woman-shaped creature understood human life and loss from her own bodily experience.

Because Beth's social inhibitions were offline, she thought, *I think I was kidnapped by strangers. Have you come to kill me?*

There was a smile in the thought: I AM *LOVE*. IF OTHERS KILL OR PLUNDER IN MY NAME, THEY DO THE WRONG, NOT I.

Beth thought, *I came here to talk to my friend Janjan. She got married and went to live with those people we call elves...*

The woman interrupted: DAUGHTER, THE PEOPLE OF OUR NEIGHBOR WORLD HAVE NO MORE TO DO WITH ME THAN DO THE SHADOW CREATURES WHO SEEK TO UNMAKE THE WHOLE EARTH. NOW: *LOOK AT ME...*

Beth's eyes opened wide. She looked directly at the other woman. For the first time in her life, her vision became completely clear and whole. She saw the world inside herself as a living part of the world outside her.

Those waiting and watching so avidly just outside the cave heard a voice filled with religious awe and human desire: *"O Aphrodite...!"*

After that there were only the night sounds of sea and air. Having accomplished what they came to do, those who waited outside left quickly.

There was among them a man who returned to the cave. Seeing the place was empty, he blew out the candle, carried the lantern away, and left the place to the night and the ocean.

16

Whom She Loveth She Chasteneth *(Before the Common Era)*

When the gods and goddesses of Olympus still walked the Earth, they often took human lovers; stories of those liaisons survive in our skeptical age as myths and legends. Few accounts remain of those who officiated, not at pious temple ceremonies, but in the unfettered rites of mystery cults when divine nature touched human nature and raised it up.

She was not the most conventionally beautiful woman of her time, but she was easily the most striking. Men and women turned and stared in wonder as she walked about the city with her retainers. Objectively speaking, she was attractive, taller than most women, with dark eyes full of intelligence and kindness. Like other women's, her long, curly dark-blonde hair was elaborately braided and caught up on her head. To that she added flowers whose scent went everywhere with her. She wore modest clothing of the finest material, sewn in the local fashion with layers of cloth gathered here and there. The fabric of her garments came from far to the east of the city she now called home.

Because of her light golden complexion, the envious and frightened called her *Phryne* behind her back: *Toad*. With great good humor she took the sobriquet as her own. Rumor said Phryne's mother was a woman of the Levant who met her lover in a grove sacred to those who visit Earth but do not live here. After giving birth, the Levantine left the baby with her parents, followed her husband into the grove, and was heard of no more.

Like the modern world, the ancient world was full of such stories.

Unlike the married women of the city, Phryne read, wrote, and conversed with educated men on their own level. She had her own fortune; how she might have acquired it was the subject of speculation. She lived in a society of rigid social classes, each with its confining code of behavior.

Hetaira was her station. There is no English equivalent in our world where there are few kings, few royal courts, and few "courtesans" who are not simply prostitutes. It is no exaggeration to say that Phryne would recognize independent sexually-active Western women as her sisters, educated people who see the world much as she did.

Another part of her life has no contemporary equivalent. On ritual days, Phryne and her attendants walked in silence from her house down to the shore of the Aegean Sea; a hushed crowd joined the procession. By the time they reached the water's edge, a chorus of worshipers had assembled, Most of the city's population followed Phryne, breathless with the wonder of what was about to happen.

At the water's edge her servants helped her remove all the graceful layers of clothing. They helped Phryne unbind her hair so that it fell loose and thick down her back.

Whatever they might feel after the secret ceremony, those who beheld her could only find her splendid. Something shone through her golden flesh as the chorus sang and chanted, the clear voices of many women prompted by deeper male voices.

As Phryne entered the sea, the light in her grew brighter until it illuminated the water around her. She walked fearlessly seaward until salt water covered even the top of her head.

"O Aphrodite..." she would say as the goddess came to her out of the depths to be reborn.

When Phryne rose from the sea, it was the goddess who raised her up until she walked upon the foaming surface of the water. The sight of her— the sight of them both—was a sacred blessing to all who beheld, one that filled them with the sweet pain of unquenchable desire.

There came a time when the envious and frightened wished to end all the city's anarchic ritual. To restore the barrier of propriety between human and divine. To put an end also to the scandal of public nakedness and the powerful, confusing feelings thereby engendered.

Phryne's enemies lodged accusations against her before the aristocratic council. *The foreign-born woman*, they said, *has impiously claimed to be more than a priestess of the Lady of Cyprus.* In feigning theophany, they charged, Phryne had blasphemously claimed to *be* the goddess.

The council had grave doubts about what motivated these charges, but they were duty-bound to address them. A long political show trial ensued. Phryne's patrons on the council argued for her against the patrons of her accusers. Most of the council were neutral but willing to listen to reason.

Stories (hotly disputed by scholars) have come down to us about the rhetorical champion who spoke so eloquently for Phryne that the council found her innocent.

In one story, the champion bared Phryne's breasts that she might beg each council member for her life until the entire council was moved to dismiss the charges.

In another story, at the high point of his peroration, Phryne's defender stripped her naked before the council, whereupon they took pity upon her trembling femininity and acquitted her.

The true story of Phryne's trial was so shameful that none of the council ever spoke of it.

Even to the rational atheists among them, an accusation of impiety was a serious matter: the offense undermined civic virtue. The aristocratic council resolved to test the proud woman by humbling her. They felt justified in this because they regarded women as fundamentally less than men. Property, like cattle or sheep, with no rights that could not easily be revoked.

Masked priestesses would chasten Phryne on the goddess' behalf. She was not to be injured. The council would observe her words and actions and render judgment as she was goaded and provoked.

Torches were lit. Guards were posted at all entrances and ordered to face outward. Naked and blindfolded, the prisoner was brought to a windowless chamber within the temple of Aphrodite.

The masked priestesses restrained Phryne with ropes. They set about alternately chastening and provoking her with canes and dog whips, with fingers and tongues, with soothing oils and unguents, with phalluses small and large. Again and again, she was brought to the peak of provocation, her body striped and welted front and back from shoulders to knees, from proud breasts to golden-haired mound.

Under the priestesses' ministrations, Phyrne often cried out in pain, but more often in pleasure, until finally her pain turned to pleasure the instant it was inflicted.

Some of the witnesses saw the goddess herself enter into one and then another of her priestesses to wield a loving whip and to inflict the sternest of pleasures upon Phryne: punishment for some past transgression of which the council was ignorant.

Thus entered, the priestess who punished or pleasured Phryne spoke words in an archaic dialect that mystified the council: *"Hast thou dared to seduce my son? Where has he has gone, then? Tell me!"*

Phryne's only answer was, *"O Aphrodite...!"* And whether her shuddering bliss was sacred or profane none of the council could discern.

In the end, Phryne was unbound and her blindfold removed. She stood still naked before the men, uninjured but whipped raw, shining with sweat, her face wet with tears. Still smiling a faint, mysterious smile, she breathed deeply into her belly. So compelling was she in her ecstasy that no one could look away.

She was put to the question: "Who art thou?"

"If it please the court," said the splendid woman, the cynosure of all eyes, "I am only Phryne, priestess to the Lady of Cyprus. Why have I been thus abused and dishonored?"

The head of the council said to his brethren, "I can find no fault in this woman." He did not trouble to answer her question. Men were not accountable to women.

Though the woman had passed victorious through this most degrading of trials, the council, in their wisdom and concern for the public good, banished her from the city forever. Unable to banish the memory of what they had witnessed, they returned to their homes in silent shame and troubled the sleep of their wives and female slaves.

A traveler from an antique land saw Phryne enter a sacred grove far to the east of the city. Curious, he peered inside and found the place green and silent and empty.

After many tellings, Phryne's story became conflated with that of her mother, she who had disappeared into that same sacred grove. The priestess' name came down to our disenchanted age as *Psyche*. In the myth as we have it, after passing through trials and punishments great and small, Psyche was ultimately made immortal and united with Eros, son of Aphrodite, in a sacred marriage blessed by all the gods of Olympus. Storytellers love happy endings where love conquers all.

In reality, Psyche and Eros, known to the ancient Roman world as Psyche and Cupid, were the first to abandon the Earth when the world changed around the Old Gods.

Aphrodite, whom the Romans called Venus, never learned what became of her son and his lover.

17

Bi-Coastal *(Janjan)*

Let us go then, you and I,
When the evening is spread out against the sky
Like a patient etherized upon a table
- (T.S. Eliot, "The Love Song of J. Alfred Prufrock")

Aimee and I exchanged parting thoughts. She saw my point about delighting in being hurt. I saw her point about delighting in hurting her. *Was* I more interested in her pain than her pleasure? Uncomfortable thought.

She knew she had to go home. Go directly to the Groves of Healing, do not pass Go, do not collect $200.

For once in my life, something wasn't all about the pleasure. Eventually I'd have to go into the Groves to examine the part of myself that gloried in making Aimee writhe and weep and climax under the cane.

Aimee and I felt *spoken for* by others. It was a mystery. Our husbands had gone upcountry, but our marriages didn't *feel* over. We weren't fully available to each other.

We parted ways reluctantly. We weren't done with each other yet. Maybe there were more good things to come, ho ho ho.

Aimee vanished from Donita Danton's old underground office in

Odiorne Point. She returned home before I thought to ask about the electricity.

The office had a lacquered wood cabinet with an electrical control panel for the whole complex. Inside, I found a neatly-labeled circuit breaker and turned all the lights off, waste not, want not.

I left New Hampshire, also traveling elf-style. I homed in on Beth's fragmentary thoughts. I used the natural law expressed in the Elvish language to navigate the ship of myself to a place I'd never been. It took all my concentration. Beth was in trouble; she needed me.

I forgot about Odiorne Point as new sensory information came flooding in. I left in pitch dark and arrived in partial dark. Somewhere on the West Coast, I thought.

The salt smell of ocean. There was the varied smell of a crowd, mostly women, but a few men. There was a lingering smell of female arousal that was different from whatever scents I brought with me from having sex with Aimee. Mmm, Aimee.

Elf girls smell different from Earth girls. It's partly the food we eat. It's partly that elf women don't have periods unless they're going to conceive. But it's mainly that the physical processes of illness and aging don't happen in the next world over. Our minds and bodies come into harmony and stay there.

Psychic traces said everyone had just left the dark place. The party was over before I got here. I wondered if I should follow the partygoers.

But I was here for Beth. Even though she hadn't exactly reached out to me, shared adventures bound us together: karma. Not to mention that I'd shared her bed one winter night, so I remembered exactly what Beth smelled like from those intimate hours. There was a faint trace of Beth's human scent and a fainter hint of the perfume she wore. There was no mental sign of Beth herself, or not much of one.

Strong emotion leaves a trail in the fine-material world. I reached out and found signs of Beth. She hadn't been in her right mind. Drugs?

She was just here, or I couldn't have traveled to her. She'd been awake and alert briefly. Then what?

She must have just left. It was like Longfellow's *Evangeline.* I knew I was close, but I couldn't find her. *Where the hell did she go?*

Echoes of shock lingered. People had witnessed something too overwhelming for their minds to accept. They'd scattered quickly back to their cars.

I found a trace of another mind, cold and male. A mind touched by evil. I'd seen this before when Jackson and I confronted the Walloon in his Virginia mansion. It was an evil stain on the fine-material part of the world. The Mark of Cain made me want to run away.

And I sensed someone ancient, more than humanly powerful. A being whose physical bounds were nothing I'd ever encountered. Someone older than humankind, like the Morrigna, guardians of the Fae.

Someone aside from good and evil. Like the Nightmare Queens, yet different.

I longed to see this transcendent being with my own eyes. Had it—*she,* almost certainly—taken Beth away from here? I needed a second opinion.

I reached out to my friends, currently on walkabout in the nextworld highlands. I felt their minds in mine as soon as I formed the intention to talk to them.

Jerry? Leda? I thought.

A flood of light as Leda dazzled me from within.

Leda thought: *Hello, dear Janjan.* I felt her smile. The joy she lived in touched me.

Jerry's thought: *Janjan, my sister, are you well?* He *knew* I was well, but what I said would tell him a lot. A world-class listener, my friend Jerry.

You guys, I thought, *feel this with me, okay?* With my mind wide open, I sent them the exact impression the mysterious being had left on me, erotic yearning and all:

[...]

Together Jerry and Leda thought *Oh!* The shock of recognition.

You've found a trace of an Old God, Jerry thought.

They're very ... loud, Leda thought. *They can't help it. They suck up all the air in the room and overwhelm an ordinary human mind. Even now we'd have to take special measures to keep our composure.*

Even now. Jerry and Leda had gone somewhere I couldn't bring myself to go. They'd become *high elves,* people I didn't fully understand.

If you try to go where Beth went, you'll have to take special measures, too, Janjan, Jerry thought. *You know what I mean?*

Of course I know what you mean, I thought. My irritation made Jerry smile. In my thoughts he saw the sexual desire the Old God had left in its—*her*—wake.

And here we were at my weakest point. Yes, elves have weaknesses. Even though I'd gone to the next world over in a moment of crisis, even though I'd become what people on Earth call an "elf," I was still more comfortable with the life of the body than the life of the spirit. This is why I heard the call to the highlands as a whisper. This is why I'd never explored much further upcountry than Nextworld Portsmouth. I simply wasn't ready. Yes, I sometimes got a glimpse of how much else there was to this wonderful universe I'd been born into. But mostly I was just in the elf business for the world-shaking sex and the deep, true pleasure it gave me and those I swived with. Okay, that had mostly been Jackson many, many times and Aimee only once, but still.

Jerry and Leda had more to teach me, but I had to be willing to learn it. Hell, I had to make an effort to learn it. An effort I found uncongenial.

Elf or not, committed to truth-telling or not, I didn't want to continue this conversation.

And lucky me, I was saved from further need to *inquire within* by an unmistakable intuitive perception: another old friend was reaching out to me.

You guys? I thought, *I have to go back to Portsmouth. It's not just Beth who's in trouble. Bobby has come back from the Fae.*

And—pop!—I was out of there with a quick see-ya-later-bye.

18

King Robert and Great Bog Bobby

It's good to be the king. - (Mel Brooks, *History of the World, Part 1*)

King Robert walked the fae-path alone. He wanted no horse between him and the road tonight. Though evening was not the usual time for the Fae to go a-roving, the wind still blew briskly at his back and the road rose to meet his feet.

Its surface looked like water-bound macadam, but the fae-road was actually a living thing. Underneath the path shone a dense liquid light like green mercury where uncounted almost-sentient creatures swam. These beings had once walked on top of the road and now yearned for mind and human incarnation again. Even among the Fae, the great wheel of birth and death goes round and round.

Mystics of Earth perceive mind dwelling in all things. Bobby's perception of the road was immediate and practical, not mystical. The same focus that made him a deadly sniper in two very different wars had made him a quick study of all the Morrigna had to teach.

He learned to make the fae-road move as he willed. He learned to lead the Fae on that road around the World Mountain. He learned to beget new

Fae with Moira and with others.

He learned to recruit susceptible people from Earth. Whenever the fae-road came near his home world, the king of the Fae greeted the surprised earthlings he met. He invited the lost, the desperate, and the merely bored to follow him along the long, long trail a-winding. That, too, was a duty of state.

Bobby's focused intention penetrated the path. The proto-Fae whirled the living road under his feet at a dizzying pace as they swam toward someone they could never touch. They longed for him to lead them back to mind: here was mind walking just above their reach.

Bobby double-timed along the moving road. The path glowed green with *the light of other days,* so bright with velocity that he almost missed his destination. As he slowed to get his bearings, the road grew dimmer. Beneath him he felt the disappointment of the once and future Fae who had given up their old human forms and now, with all weary memory washed away, wanted only to resume endless embodied lives on the road again. They would have to wait.

He saw the familiar hills, fields and wetlands of Great Bog, Portsmouth, New Hampshire, USA, North America, Western Hemisphere, Earth, and thought: *This is where Janjan helped Moira and her sons leave Earth. We hoped to find safety among the Fae where the Materialist Magicians couldn't go. Safety has a price.*

He stepped off the pleasantly-cool fae-path and into warm darkness. He gasped and started breathing again. For all the times he'd gone back and forth between Earth and the Fae, he'd never gotten used to the transition. Really, how could anyone get used to *breathing in for half of forever and breathing out for the other half,* as the Fae said? You either accepted your condition or went mad resisting it. And how could anyone get used to the sudden impact of mortality on an ageless body that had been free from death just a moment before?

In two heartbeats, he'd left the realm where he was a king clad in fine clothing and entered a different reality where he looked like an escaped mental patient.

Life, death, mortal, immortal: Bobby was tired of it all; his world-weariness went deep.

He looked around in the darkness. Lights from the highway reflected off wispy clouds. Stars, but no moon. Peripheral vision revealed more than looking directly. He smelled green things growing wild around him, throwing scent into the night air of New Hampshire's short summer. Bushes and long grass and distant trees. A sudden odor of blueberries. He heard crickets or maybe cicadas. Mosquitoes whined around his ears. A tick attached itself to his bare ankle; he ignored it.

Now what? That question never arose for the king of the Fae. There was only the next duty to attend to and the next pleasure to savor.

He'd made a bargain. He helped Janjan find the fae-path after she became an elf and could no longer see it. She promised to take him home with her whenever he asked.

But how would he find her? He hadn't thought this through. Janjan wouldn't still be living in the Portsmouth house he'd shared with her and Beth for a short, happy time last year. She didn't live on Earth anymore.

How could he contact her? He didn't know where to start. The police? They might want to question him about the deaths of King Coran and Queen Moira. The only human remains to be found in Great Bog would have belonged to the old king and queen. Last year's paranormal chaos had drawn the civilian and military authorities into these fields.

Bobby's conscience was troubled. If the *Army* learned who he was, they'd court-martial him for leaving the battlefield in the Second World War; they'd execute or imprison him. (No one now living would know he'd also deserted the Union Army and escaped to the Fae in the dead of night.)

His guard went up, an old soldier's instinctive alertness. There was nothing to see in the dark. He listened. He heard only the sound of highway traffic, like surf. Small night-hunting creatures scuttled through tall grass and brush. He heard frogs in the marsh a few hundred yards away. He felt no sense of other people. Surely by now the authorities were leaving Great Bog unguarded...

A disturbance in the air in front of him: *pop*. And there was Janjan, dressed in black like before, but surrounded by a sphere of clear light. From inside the light she smiled at him.

"*Bobby!*" she said and reached out her arms.

He hugged her and found himself inside the light she carried with her. And yes, he was crying, why should he not? The thing he wanted most was within reach if he had the courage to grasp it.

Elves don't lie, he thought. *They're honorable people who keep their promises.*

"Are you ready to come home with me?" she said.

"Maybe," Bobby said.

King Robert never had a doubt, but Great Bog Bobby was full of them.

19

Back in the Great Bog Groove *(Janjan)*

I said a quick goodbye to Leda and Jerry and left the dark, empty, sea-smelling hollow in the California rock.

When I popped into nighttime Great Bog in Portsmouth, there was Bobby, back on Earth again.

I hugged him and asked if he was ready for the next world over. He said he might be. He was scared. I didn't blame him. I mean, becoming an elf basically exchanges everything you know for a new life where you know nothing except that you're in good hands. It takes a lot of trust.

Which reminded me. "Um, how's Moira?"

Bobby shook his head. "The *queen*," he said in a cold, bitter, adult tone, "is happier on the fae-path than she ever was on Earth. She has found herself by pretending to be someone else."

That sounded nothing like the happy, carefree Bobby I remembered. Being king of the Fae wasn't all drinking and dancing with pretty girls in the great hall and swiving with them all night in the royal bedchamber. It was also leading a whole race of people along the fae-road and keeping personal differences with your co-regent to yourself. I knew something about the loneliness of command.

"Forgive me, but it sounds like you weren't happy together."

"I don't mean to complain, Janjan. She asked you to take her and her sons to safety with the Fae; I was glad to help you do that. I stayed with Moira longer than I should have. At first she needed me. And my fae-children needed me to guide them, like I needed the Morrigna to guide me. At first everything was fine. *Strange*, but fine—you know what I mean?"

I nodded. "The fae-road is a weird way to live. But you got tired of it again?"

A long pause. "I was tired when we went over there."

"I remember." Before we took Moira and her boys to the fae-path, I sat with Bobby in a Providence coffee house. When I touched him, I felt how weary he was of everything life had to offer. *Weltschmerz*, the Germans call it: world-pain.

We went quiet. The bugs were having a battle of the bands. A hot wind blew from inland. I heard traffic from the southbound highways that converge in Portsmouth from the north and west.

We were surrounded by plant and animal life. I sensed the ticks on Bobby's bare ankles. Ticks get worse every year, thanks, global warming. I extended the light around me to encourage the little critters to stop sucking his blood and go elsewhere. One of the best things about coming back to Earth from the next world over is that the bugs leave you alone. I made them leave Bobby alone, too.

Bobby ignored the mosquitoes, gnats, and ticks, something he must have learned in the American Civil War. He looked away from me, scanning the field. He didn't want to be overheard.

We were the only human beings out here tonight. The hobo camp had never been rebuilt after they went a-roving with the Fae. Word must have gone out through the homeless-American community: *If you like Earth, stay away from Portsmouth—and stay* far *away from Great Bog.*

"There's another reason I stayed on the fae-road with Moira so long," Bobby said into the night. "I kept hoping that Beth's child—*my son*— would be reborn—to Moira or someone else."

I had so many questions. "But no?"

Bobby turned back to me. "I hoped that once our fae-child was reborn and grown, *he and I* could come back to Earth to meet his mother. Beth,

I mean."

Oh, my God, *Bobby had never gotten over Beth.* He'd never gotten over losing the child of fae-light they conceived. I couldn't help being impressed by that display of nineteenth-century romantic and paternal devotion. Once it would have made me all cynical and sarcastic, but I had my own relationship problems, didn't I? I didn't think beating Aimee's round, ripe little ass was exactly helping me get over Jackson; sexing Aimee up was a distraction.

"You miss Beth," I said.

"Sure I do, I know it's stupid because she doesn't want me, but I'd still like to see her again."

Jesus, the poor guy. "I'd take you to her if I could, Bobby. Actually, I just came back to Earth because I knew Beth needed me. Now she's gone somewhere, but I don't know where."

His war face was visible even in the low, diffuse light. I'd last seen that bleak, determined expression when he put an arrow through the head of the Walloon, master of Materialist Magician masters—an arrow that disembodied the magician but didn't kill him. Bobby's whole aspect changed. "What do you mean? Have the magicians taken her?"

"*Someone's* taken her," I said. "My nextworld friends think it was one of the Old Gods of Earth."

"Did you go looking for her?" The question was an accusation that meant: *You guys are the elves, why can't you just fix what's wrong with the world?* Nobody likes our answer to that.

He was upset for a lot of reasons, some he wasn't aware of. I spoke gently. "I was in California a minute ago. I just missed Beth. I found a faint trace. I don't know how to follow it, and I don't know what I'd be getting into if I did. I was asking Jerry and Leda what to do about Beth when I realized *you* were back on Earth. You came looking for me because *you* needed me, too. And here we are."

Bobby, war face and all, looked at me intently, thinking about what I said.

"I'd like to go looking for Beth right this minute. Can you show me how?"

Greater love hath no man. Not the first time I'd thought that about Bobby. He was an admirable human being. Beth was stupid to send him away. Moira was stupid to let him go. His question deserved an answer.

"Maybe I can, Bobby," I said. "If I can't figure out how to go after her, I know people who can."

"That's good enough for me," Bobby said. "Do I have to go to your world?"

"I'd love to take you. Are you ready to go with me?"

He pondered that one. A king doesn't act without thinking, and the habits of his brief reign were still with him. "*I'd* like to go, sure. But what if we find Beth and *she* doesn't want to be an elf?"

Bobby was as obstinate as Jackson. I think that kind of stubbornness is a guy thing. "Why can't this one decision be about *you*, Bobby?"

"Beth and I should go together—like you and Jackson did."

"Okay, I'm convinced. Let's see if we can find somebody around here to make us a sandwich and find you some clothes first. You can't walk around Portsmouth dressed like the king of the Fae."

Bobby's smile turned his face young and innocent in the dim light. "If I could get a cup of coffee with cream and sugar, I'd be in heaven," he said. "I've had nothing but water and imaginary wine all year."

20

Big Two-Hearted Jackson *(Nonlinear Time)*

Jackson and Daniel hiked up the World Mountain. Daniel fought to keep body and soul together until they got wherever they were going. He leaned on Jackson, who was glad to share his strength. Answering the heart's call took more courage than they'd imagined. *If you could have whatever you wanted...*

Jackson wanted Janjan; she couldn't come with him. He missed her; he still felt her mind in his. Fresh water flows invisibly down the big two-hearted river to the ocean even when a resistless salt tide floods in.

They walked uphill for hours. Away from everything they knew. Away from the women they loved and desired. Into a light where only the present is utterly clear.

Around them the scenery changed. The sun rose. They walked out of savanna into forests, green and cool. However high they climbed, they never reached the timberline. They ate fruits they'd never tasted from trees they'd never seen. The Mountain seemed to welcome them.

They hiked in ringing silence, letting go of memories good and bad. They stopped thinking about the future.

They climbed through bands of forest. Feeling a sudden impulse to rest, they looked at each other and thought, *Is this the place?*

They looked over the tops of clouds drifting below them. The true sun warmed but never burned their golden skin.

A trickle of cool water emerged from the rock. They cupped palms and drank from it. The water of life, it seemed to be, that conferred deeper peace and wisdom.

They'd been called here.

Daniel sat down against a rock face that the wind had uncovered. Flowers grew all around the rock. He said simply, "It's my time, brother."

All that was required was to be present. Jackson sat beside his teacher and held his hand.

They saw how it is that mind and body are one. As Jackson watched, all the atoms of Daniel's body went quietly away in all directions.

His hand was empty. There was no sign of Daniel but the clothes he'd been wearing.

It was Jackson's time. He let go of everything he'd learned about natural law, everything the Unfallen Tongue had taught him about matter and energy. He abandoned every idea of magic or manipulation or control.

Knowing he was free of death, he found the courage to release his body; its atoms gently went a-glimmering.

Jackson's clothes lay next to Daniel's in front of the rock face.

21

Aside in Time and Space

She was like a forest, like the dark interlacing of the oakwood, humming inaudibly with myriad unfolding buds. Meanwhile the birds of desire were asleep in the vast interlaced intricacy of her body.
- (D.H. Lawrence, *Lady Chatterley's Lover*)

The Lady brought the young woman to the grotto where the goddess had lain dreaming for so long. She had only to will the thing and it became so.

Now it was her guest's time to lie dreaming while the Lady read the book of the girl's life. The Lady read quickly. Mortal lives provide little the Old Gods have not seen before.

Still, the woman named Beth taught the Lady about this new Earth where the goddess had awakened. Beth's own short story revealed how these new women thought of themselves and how they thought of the men who loved them.

And surprise! Beth had once allowed another woman to love her. The Lady approved. Women could offer one another much delight that men seldom bothered to give them. Let her sister goddesses fret themselves about hearth, husband, and progeny; those were not the bounds of the Lady's domain. She inspired deep sexual passion that engendered brave deeds among men and profound pleasure among women.

She was confused by the girl's guilt. What had she done but be beautiful and give pleasure by accepting the bliss that is beauty's due? *Shame*, the Lady understood; without it there could be no honor among men or gods. But *guilt* was something new and pernicious in her sight. The girl believed something unforgivable had blighted her essential worth.

Also new was the way this woman had been brought to her attention. The girl herself had not truly offered to become the Lady's priestess and earthly vehicle.

As she examined Beth's memories (and removed the white robe that covered Beth's beauty), she saw that the woman (not long out of girlhood) was no worshiper of Aphrodite, although she had called out the Lady's name. In this strange new Earth, the Old Gods were only stories. But a bitter herb known to the ancient world had given Beth sudden ingress of ancestral memory.

The Lady read further. Someone sought to use this woman against his (it was always men who committed such sacrilege) enemies. The girl had been brought against her will to a place where the Lady was then drawn by an invocation, sung by women and prompted by a man, as was the ancient custom. None of the women were the Lady's avowed priestesses, though their yearning was raw and heartfelt.

Plots and plans and schemes the Lady understood. Those who had power wanted more of it. Those who had beauty wanted riches. Those who hated wanted vengeance. Those who had nothing sought to take what belonged to those they envied. Around and around it went. The Old Gods had once participated in the human tragicomedy, taking on the desires and emotional coloration of their worshipers.

Yet there was the world's sea change to consider; over time it had eroded the worship of the Lady and her kin. That one change was a river fed by four tributaries. The change took an enchanted Earth, shining with wonder, and disenchanted it, turned it dismal and dull. This change turned natural shame into unnatural guilt.

An old story. Those who feigned worship of the one god believed they had the right to destroy the world in his name. The magicians who opposed the one god, hoping to please the Claimant to his throne, believed they had the right to destroy the world their High Enemy had created.

Weary of a disenchanted Earth, the Lady had retired to her grotto. Mere materialists ignored their human nature; beholding their bleak spirits was like gazing into desert. It was worse to see magicians embrace the shadow creatures who loathe all embodied life.

The Lady saw that this young woman had fled the magicians and walked with the Fae.

Who could blame people for letting demigoddesses take them off the Earth wrapped in green light to travel in endless festival around the World Mountain? The Lady understood the desire for eternal life, even one so limited.

It was a puzzle. The girl Beth was a friend of those who dwelt one world over from Earth as they always had. *Elves*, Beth called them, a good name for those who only returned to Earth to help others. The Lady remembered the sacred groves of that land which loved her and worshiped her so passionately. Those who went in and out of the groves had never worshiped any Old God. It was hard for them to see the Lady. She found it hard to see them, to think about where they went, or to imagine who they worshiped. The elves were emissaries of the new thing in the world, a good thing that went wrong in the cults that poisoned people till the Earth was dead to them.

These imponderables aside, the Lady would do for Beth what she had done for so many other women. Beth would become the Lady's High Priestess. She would reflect as much of the Lady's beauty and power as her human body and soul could bear.

She would become the Lady in human form.

The Lady would return her priestess to those who worshiped the goddess. When the worshipers enacted the ancient ceremony of summoning, she would watch them through Beth's eyes. Were the summoners' purposes good or ill?

Human nature kept few secrets from the Lady. Her being sprang from that secret place deep within the greater Nature that is always naturing itself in women, in the world around them, and in the men they love.

22

Bobby Meets Bobbi

I know what you're thinking.

Janjan and Bobby are out in the middle of Great Bog. She's an elf, but he isn't. Neither of them has a car, American money, or a phone. How the hell do they manage in twenty-first century Portsmouth?

We could have walked to a payphone and called a friend. I could have traveled instantly to that friend's house and asked him to drive back and pick Bobby up.

I hate to put my friends at risk.

Instead, I skimmed across the minds of all the elves on Earth. A lot of people had come to the next world over recently. Those new elves signed up for missions back here. Given Portsmouth's strategic location between the human worlds, surely one or two of those elves would be in the area?

The mind of every elf echoes in the mind of every other elf in every world. My earliest training was in dealing with that ceaseless information flow without going crazy. I tuned in, listened, and learned.

There'd been escalating attacks on Elf Friends in the United States; too many had been killed before the *seek shelter* warning went out. The new elves were busy taking our friends home with them step by step, walking on top of the Atlantic Ocean out of Portsmouth Harbor to the foothills of the Invisible Mountain.

There's scarcely an Elf Friend left in Portsmouth tonight, one elf told me. *There is one stubborn girl, though. I think you know her.*

She'd been waiting in hiding, said the elf. She was hoping that Janjan Javorski-Jackson, of all the elves everywhere, would come and save her. Bobbi, the little (a whole inch shorter than me) intern had helped me finish Jerry and Leda's story and post it to the Elf Friends' website, *When Is an Elf Not an Elf?* She'd stuck around to help me organize my notes about how I'd traveled with the Fae and gone to the elves myself. We got my story posted, too.

The Elf Friends' website had gone dark, the least of our problems. My brother elf traveled to Bobbi's hiding place in person and asked for her help. Bobbi said *Oh boy* and hopped into her car. The stubborn girl was now on her way to a nearby park-and-ride lot.

I thanked him. It may be good to be the king, but it's great to be an elf.

–

A car pulled into the little parking lot. Bobbi got out of the car and stretched like a cat. That was the all-clear signal.

Bobby and I were hiding in some trees thirty yards from the pavement. I whispered to him to stay put until I made sure everything was cool. I didn't want to frighten Bobbi by having a guy she didn't know show up with me.

As soon as she saw me, Bobbi threw herself into my arms and hugged me really hard. She was crying.

"I *knew* you'd come back. I knew it," she said. She kissed my cheek. Then her lips moved to mine. Her mouth opened and her tongue gently touched mine. She was trembling so hard I practically had to hold her up.

She broke the kiss first. "Oh, Janjan, I'm sorry, I'm sorry, I'm sorry!"

She was a good kisser. I knew from our time working together (last year to her on Earth, but God knows how many years for me among the elves) that she'd had a thing for me. I guess she still did. Her mouth tasted of desire.

I reassured her, "It's okay, Bobbi. Jackson and I are… Well, I'm not sure what our status is right now. Our marriage, I mean. Anyway. Shouldn't we get out of here?"

"Totally," she said. "Um, our mutual friend said you'd be with a guy?"

I'd forgotten for a moment. The girl was a *very* good kisser. I turned toward the trees, solid black outside the dim solar light fixtures around the parking area.

"Hey, Bobby? Everything's fine. C'mon over."

Bobby came walking out of the trees and joined us next to Bobbi's car.

I made the introductions. "King Robert of the Fae, allow me to present Bobbi, Elf friend and my friend."

Bobbi gave me a look, wondering what kind of friends the king and I were, exactly.

Bobby smiled. "It's very kind of you to pick us up, Little One." He'd mastered the royal style. The late Coran, the last king of the Fae, used to call *me* "Little One."

Bobbi looked at Bobby in his Renaissance Faire glad rags. "I'm happy to help. Um, what should I call you? We don't get many royals in Portsmouth."

"*Bobby's* fine," he said. "Or to avoid confusion, since your name sounds the same as mine, call me *Rob*." He turned my way. "That's what Queen Moira called me when we made the whole fae-road shake, if you follow me."

When the king and queen of the Fae reached a simultaneous sexual climax, I remembered, the whole fae-path convulsed along with them. *Goodness,* I thought, *is Bobby flirting with us, or is he just venting?*

"Perhaps we should be going ... Rob?" I said.

He nodded sadly. He was venting, not flirting. He still felt some obligation to Moira and resented it.

Rob and his long legs sat up front next to Bobbi. She drove. I sat in the back and used my elf perceptions. I wasn't picking up any bad guys anywhere around us. I didn't see any cars following us, either. Bobbi drove us from road to road. Rural New Hampshire and Maine are terrible places for nighttime surveillance.

I felt no malign intent. No other drivers with their minds focused on us. No sad, scary Dark Path slaves hungering to kill us. Not many other vehicles at all, as we drove all around Robin Hood's barn.

It was a lovely summer evening. Warm night air blew into the open car windows. It didn't smell as good as my new home, but such comparisons are unhelpful at best and odious at worst. The Earth was slowly dying; I could smell that, too. I had no idea how long its death would take, and nobody was going to take my word for it. All I could do is take people home with me.

We didn't talk much. Bobbi was too keyed up. King Robert was weary and sad, but always hopeful. Rob wanted Beth: he had his mind set on her; he'd do whatever it took to find her. Bobbi wanted me: she'd do whatever I wanted. It was going to be an interesting visit.

I won't say which side of the Piscataqua we finally ended up on. We drove slowly off a narrow, paved country road and down a dirt track. At the end of this long driveway was an old house showing no house lights, no porch lights, and no For Sale sign. To one side of the house and downhill was an old barn, tall and dark. Bobbi backed her car carefully through the open barn door. She grabbed a flashlight from the glove box, jumped out of the car and pulled the old doors closed behind us. She barred the doors by dropping a thick board into two brackets. She switched on the flashlight and led us up a stairway on one side of the barn. The stairs smelled of new lumber.

Instead of a hayloft at the top of the stairs, we walked into a small, functional apartment. All the necessities, bunk beds, bathroom, and kitchen area. Even a television. Bobbi shut the door and turned on the lights, none of which would be visible from outside the barn because there were no windows. The apartment was hot but bearable; clever hidden venting kept air moving up and out.

"This is very nice," I said. "How'd you end up here?"

I saw her thoughts. The bad guys had come too close. Except for elves, her contact with other people was bounded by burner cell phones and painstaking internet security. She couldn't talk about it without crying.

She sniffled, took a deep breath, and changed the subject; tough girl. "You guys want to clean up before we eat? We've got a closet full of clean clothes in different sizes over there." She pointed to a big old piece of dark wood furniture I guess was an armoire.

Rob and I followed our hostess' suggestion. He showered first and emerged from the bathroom wearing a pair of old pleated khakis, a plaid shirt, and a pair of running shoes. Everything fit him. I kept my mouth shut about ironic hipster-nerd fashion.

I found some jeans and a t-shirt that fit just fine. I took a quick shower, dried off, and put the clothes on. I kept my own soft-soled elf boots. No, they don't have pointy toes; I'm not that kind of elf.

Knowing what nextworld visitors could and couldn't eat, Bobbi made a salad and whipped up grilled cheese sandwiches on the little stove. All she had in the apartment was instant coffee and tea bags, so she boiled some water for us.

"Thank you, Bobbi," I said when we sat down together at the table. Then translating from the Elvish, "Bless this food and all who share it. Amen."

"Amen," Rob said. I didn't imagine the Fae had taken to saying grace during the year of his reign, but nineteenth-century manners helped him fit in wherever he went.

Bobbi gave me a crooked grin and shook her head. "*That* was a surprise." She'd dyed her hair magenta and gotten it cut short. She kind of looked like me. My hair had darkened during my time in the next world over, but still had a few reddish highlights. Deliberate imitation, the sincerest form of flattery.

Some people really resent anything that sounds like God talk. God knows I used to. I looked her directly in the eye. "I meant no offense."

"Oh, no," she said quickly, "of course not. I forget that I really don't know anything about your world. When one of you guys says something heartfelt and unguarded, it throws me every time." Her eyes were wet.

"Bobbi, after we eat, would you like to come home with me?"

It was a small table. While he ate, King Robert of the pleated khakis watched us kindly and with interest over his sugary coffee.

Bobbi reached out and took my hand.

"Yes, please, Janjan," she said. "I'm scared, but I'm finally ready."

23

Rosemary Clooney Sings "C'mon-a My House" *(Janjan)*

We finished our dinner. King Rob offered to wash the dishes. He thanked Bobbi for the food and for the chance to clean up. He said he hadn't done any real work in a year.

"We'll be right back," I told him. "As far as I know, I mean."

I held out my hand to Bobbi. She took it. I touched her mind gently and thought, *Do you trust me with your life?*

Her eyes filled up again. It's very intimate to encounter someone else inside the one place you thought you were always alone. She thought back, *I trust you, Janjan. I'd go anywhere with you.*

Like most people who live on Earth, Bobbi's feelings were strong and mixed. Her heart was in her throat. She had doubts, but she wanted to go with me. On top of all that, she was sexually aroused. So was I. Arousal is contagious.

I knew exactly how she felt; I had so been there. A year ago, I'd stepped off the fae-path into frozen Great Bog, wanting nothing more than to go home to the rented house I'd once shared with Leda and Beth. But there was Leda (naked!) beckoning to me from the other side of the thin wall between our old world and her new one. And there standing next to Leda, was Jackson (clothed!), the man I loved. Talk about strong mixed feelings. I was on the wrong side of the thin wall, but I had the power to walk through it. Leda helped me.

Tonight I helped Bobbi. One minute we were sitting at the battered table in her temporary quarters. The next minute we stood on a surface I couldn't see in a place where no human being could see clearly, the borderlands of the next world over.

It's simple enough, but it's not *easy*. Meeting the angel who protects the next world over shatters your preconceptions about what kinds of creatures you might meet and talk to.

Bobbi's reaction was sweet, sad, and funny, all at once.

Oh, my God, she thought.

Only one of his messengers, thought the smiling angel. *Welcome home, little sister.*

—

We stepped out of cloud into savanna. Our walk through the nextworld grasslands didn't take long. For most of us, it's a long journey of purification. Bobbi, the horny lesbian civil libertarian feminist, was one of those pure souls who could have kept walking all the way to the high country.

I saw her heart. She wanted to keep walking. She also knew everything has its time.

She asked to be educated in the ways of the elves who aren't elves. I left her in the hands of others who are wiser than me. There are lots of people like that over here.

Bobbi asked, *Are you coming back? Will I see you again?* She adapted quickly to speaking mind-to-mind in Elvish. Like I said, she was a natural.

"You and I have things to do on Earth," I said. I wasn't flirting, I needed her help.

We hugged. She wanted me, which made me want her. Elves can't help what we feel.

Bobbi's training near the borderland left me with time on my hands. Nonlinear time in which I could do whatever I liked for as long as I needed to.

If you could have whatever you wanted, what would you want? I thought I knew, but Aimee had made me doubt myself.

The Healer greeted me at the leafy entrance of the Groves of Healing. She knew I was on my way, of course she did. You can't sneak up on an elflady. The Healer is addressed by her function, not her name. It seemed presumptuous to ask. Her own name never crossed her mind.

The light in the Healer's mind was almost too bright to look at. She was a high elf, but there were differences of appearance. First (and strangest in a world where almost no one looked more than middle aged), she'd assumed the aspect of an aged white-haired woman, though her beautiful face was mostly unlined and her body was straight and strong. Second (and less strange), she wore a white robe. The rest of us dress in earthen colors or go naked.

As I approached her, I saw that the Healer, of all people, would enjoy seeing me naked. She smiled and wrapped her arms around me, not denying her desire but not needing to do anything about it. I hugged her back.

She thought: *Will you trust me in your thoughts, Janjan?*

I thought: *I will.*

I started to cry. I wasn't sad, but *pressure* was escaping from me as tears. Something I didn't understand was happening.

She held me while I cried. We looked at my thoughts together. You know how most people on Earth are stuck in their own heads? It's not like that here.

"You should come inside," she said aloud.

I wanted to say *No thanks* and go back to Earth to avoid whatever was generating all the pressure. Instead, I followed her into the grove.

It was a living building. A few dozen leafy rooms were separated by walls of hedges. The floors were green grass. Taller trees arched overhead like a roof.

The Healer led me into a room. Aimee was sitting naked on the grass with her eyes shut. I looked at the Healer. She smiled and thought, *Go sit with her.*

I felt a little self-conscious about undressing in front of the Healer, but not very. For one thing, the next world over is the best of all possible worlds to bare it all. For another thing, the Healer looked *right through* me. She didn't worry much about the physical body; to her it was only the vehicle. But seeing Aimee naked aroused me. Sorry, that's just how I am. Beautiful naked women and beautiful naked men make me want them. I think that's how God made me. I don't think it's wrong.

Once I got naked, I sat on the grass facing Aimee. I shut my eyes and opened my mind.

Aimee's mind was all light. So was the Healer's. It was the angel's first gift: *Remember love and light.*

I swam in light in the mind space we shared. The energy centers inside me lit up, as Aimee's were alight; as she lit me up, the lights within her burned brighter. I began to understand things I'd resisted learning. I faced what I'd tried to deny.

The Healer left the two of us alone together.

24

Operation Aphrodite *(Darnand)*

After the ceremony of binding in California, Darnand flew back to New Hampshire by private jet. Mariah and her new converts would follow by road.

The Old God had answered the worshipers' invitation. It—she—had accepted their human offering. In an instant the girl became high priestess to the gaggle of fools who were already calling themselves *Children of Venus*.

Invoked by an ancient chant, the goddess appeared and *took* the girl; they vanished together. Darnand witnessed real magic, uncontaminated by demons.

The scholars who unearthed the ancient texts had earned their extortionate fee. If they kept the discovery secret, they would live to spend the money.

When the Children of Venus next invoked Aphrodite, the esoteric teaching said, it would be *the priestess* through whose body the goddess appeared on Earth. The ceremony established a permanent channel of communication between Earth and ... wherever a so-called deity could be said to live.

The language of the summoning was obscure. Had the girl died in the sacrifice, or did she survive as part of the goddess?

The woman was an Elf Friend, fair game for the Order. (Really, who was not?) If young Elizabeth proved immune to magical recall, the Walloon would assign blame to Darnand, the team leader, and also to Mariah and the Sisterhood.

Darnand arranged to meet Louis in the empty Odiorne Point tunnels. The Materialist Magicians had never relinquished control of the complex. The tide of fortune might once have turned against the Order, but the tide always turns again.

Darnand had the key to a hidden door. The lock turned and the door opened.

He walked the dusty corridor, following the beam of his flashlight, and flicking light switches as he went. Nothing happened. He cursed under his breath. Was the power off? A materialist shell corporation was supposed to be paying the bill.

He opened the door to the quarters of the traitor Donita Danton, the last Officer in Charge. Rumpled sheets. Disgusting. The place had been used as a love nest. He would have the Sisterhood clean it. But at last he found a breaker box on the wall. He threw a switch and the lights came on.

He explored underground rooms, cells, and corridors until he found the large, echoing amphitheater. Thick rock walls and heavy columns supported tons of rock and earth above him.

Darnand felt the welling dread that signaled Louis' approach, though there was no physical sign of him. Would the Walloon approve of what Darnand had accomplished? Perhaps the last thing he heard in this body would be a death sentence hissing from the restless demon smoke of his master's face.

Through yards of New Hampshire granite came a shrieking noise like a mining drill, as native rock and reinforced concrete slabs shook themselves to bits. The din grew unbearable, then stopped abruptly. Clouds of concrete dust settled in silence, revealing a ground-level hole in the wall.

The golden statue of a seated skull-faced man flew through the hole. It stopped, hovering motionless above the floor.

Darnand was unnerved, but held his ground. It was resignation, not courage. Where could a man on the Dark Path run?

Salt water flowed in through the hole in the wall. Walking through the shallow water came the Walloon, miraculously re-embodied, no longer limited to swirling smoke.

To hide his shameful tears, Darnand bowed to his master. He gave Louis the good news: Aphrodite herself was now the Order's ally.

Louis was jubilant. He informed Darnand that Gold, a mighty ancient sorcerer, had joined their just war against the elves.

Darnand bowed to Master Gold.

Silent and unfathomable, Gold hovered in midair. Why would he speak to the Walloon's servant?

Darnand took no offense. He was relieved to have his death sentence commuted once again.

25

Me and Aimee-O Up in the Schoolyard *(Janjan, Nonlinear Time)*

> *The great question that has never been answered, and which I have*
> *not yet been able to answer, despite my thirty years of research into the*
> *feminine soul, is* What does a woman want?
> - (Sigmund Freud, letter to Marie Bonaparte)

I was surrounded by Aimee's light and she was surrounded by mine. The same light shone through us both. We'd gone to Earth to play with pain, but this was the place to come for pleasure. I wondered why anybody would ever leave.

Of course I knew why. As long as anyone suffers from life to ignorant life on Earth and the other human worlds, the elves will offer help.

We should just have done this in the first place, I thought.

I felt Aimee's inner smile. *You gave me what I needed*, she thought.

Did I, though?

Well, some of it.

What else do you need that I didn't give you? I asked.

It was a real question. What did *I* need, for example? I mean, there were a lot of things that I wouldn't mind having, but I didn't actually *need* all that much. Air to breathe, food and water, love and sex: those things are free and abundant among the elves without my even having to ask. It's only polite to ask if you want to have sex with someone, but still.

I want to be the cynosure of all eyes, Aimee thought. *I know it's egotistical, stupid, and wrong.* Something in me *wants to be the queen of love and beauty.*

You're not talking about Game of Thrones, *are you?* Aimee had never read the books or seen the TV show.

Janjan, I'm talking about walking naked into the ocean while a whole city watches with their mouths open because they all want me. I'm talking about the Judgment of Paris, where a group of women undress for a man, we all stand before him, and he judges me *the fairest.*

I thought, *Does it have to be a man?* I know, I know, nobody can be everything to anybody, but I still have fruitless desires of my own. I wouldn't be human if I didn't.

C'mon, she thought, *don't kid yourself. Didn't you love displaying your naked body to Jackson?*

She had me there. I liked nothing better than showing myself to my husband and watching his penis stand up. Woof. I'm not entirely sure about the whole spanking and caning thing, but exciting your lover is a lawful pleasure in any human world.

Would I enjoy showing myself to strangers who were judging me? Yeah, I guess I would. It gives you pleasure to be naked for the pleasure of others. Seeing how they want you gives you power over them but also makes you want them. There's no end to desire.

We sat quietly and thought about desire together. Aimee was hiding an old memory of hurt from herself, but she was getting closer to recognizing what compelled her to take pleasure from pain. I had no right to push her.

Power and pleasure were why Jackson and I had come to this world. Okay, we did it to save our lives, sure. But he'd come here seeking his deepest, truest power. I'd followed him here looking for my deepest, truest pleasure.

While Aimee and I were thinking about the paradox of pleasure and, yes, getting more aroused, the Healer returned to the little leafy room we shared. Her presence shone like sunrise on our closed eyelids.

"You might consider following me," the Healer said. "It's your choice, of course. Clothing is also optional."

She didn't laugh at us, but she did find our romantic difficulties kind of adorable. She wanted to help us get past them.

Did I *want* to join her in clarity and give up my sweet erotic confusion?

I looked at Aimee. She looked at me. We got to our feet. I think her blood was up; I know mine was. We left our clothes where they were and followed the Healer out of the Groves.

We felt uncertain because we were walking *up* the World Mountain. I held out my hand; Aimee took it.

We weren't afraid. Nothing in the next world over will ever hurt you. The ground won't even hurt your feet. When I first came here, running around during the initial elf training made my feet tough enough to walk anywhere on this world (and most places on Earth) without shoes. It happened naturally, without struggle or pain.

It didn't take long to climb higher than I'd ever dared go before. Who better to journey into the unknown with than the Healer, wisest of elfladies, and Aimee Amory-Ryun, the very touch of whose long-fingered hand made me tingle from head to toe?

I won't lie. It's exciting walking around naked, even if nobody notices. Somebody might. Our eyes might meet at a distance and he might be drawn to me. Jackson was drawn from one side of a crowded Portsmouth club to where I sat alone on the other side. Okay, all I was showing that night was a bit of cleavage and most of my then-chubby legs, but he still came to me like a bee to a fat little flower. I'd known he was a bad boy. It wasn't his badness that made me want him, it was how much he wanted me. I was always the cynosure of *his* eyes. Until he left me.

God, I miss Jackson, I thought. She'd been following my thoughts. We were in each other's thoughts because we'd been intimate. Because we were still intimate.

I miss Daniel the same way, she thought. *He wants me so much it makes me want him even more. He loved me first, you know. He loved me so much that I couldn't help loving him back.*

Huh, I thought. *Back on Earth when Leda was telling me her story, she said nobody had ever responded to her like Jerry does.*

That's what it means to be spoken for. You suit each other right down to the ground.

Aimee and I exchanged sexual imagery involving many things we'd like to do to each other right that minute if we weren't walking ten paces behind the Healer like good girls. We were humming and buzzing and vibrating with desire. Throbbing with it until it lit up the world around us. At the edge of our sensual bubble, I felt the Healer's mind, smiling, full of love, deeply aware.

The Mountain sloped up gradually. It was hard to tell we were climbing, except for a slight increase of pleasant exertion. We walked into a forest of widely-spaced trees, some with leaves and others with needles. Like in the grasslands far below, here too the green grass grew all around, all around. The earth was soft enough under our feet. Our joined perception saw into the ground down to the living rock of the World Mountain. A single cloud took its sweet time crossing the high blue sky. The nextworld rains fall most often on the highest highlands. Rainwater comes down to us in streams and rivers like the great salty tidal river that separates Nextworld Portsmouth from the other shore.

From the moment I accepted passage here, I'd felt a quiet invitation to the high country. The higher we climbed, the clearer I heard the call.

When I was living in Portsmouth, still an Elf Friend but not yet an elf, Leda had painted a *mandala* into my chest so I could travel with the Fae without forgetting who I was. The *mandala* was a dynamic, moving symbol that invited me to *inquire within*. It showed me I loved Jackson and wanted to be with him. It prompted me to follow him to the elves.

The *mandala* was gone now that I'd absorbed its message. Gone with my nipple piercings and my naughty-bits piercing. Gone with my lower-back tattoo. The holes where my piercings had been were healed up like they'd never been there; I couldn't wear earrings anymore. My teeth had been healthy before I came to this world, but now the two with white ceramic fillings were whole, natural teeth. Back on Earth I'd gained some weight, lost it, and gained it back, which gave me stretch marks. Jackson told me he thought they were hot, but he said that to me a lot. Anyway. I still had a solid Eastern European woman's build, but I had more muscle shaping my body than ever before. The stretch marks which had made me secretly hate myself were gone.

We are made new in this world, is my point. I don't know now why I was so afraid to come here. I don't know why everybody doesn't want to join us.

Well, yes I do. They're *scared*, just like I was. But now I knew what I was supposed to be doing with my life in this human body.

Whatever I was doing with Aimee whose hot hand I was holding.

Ahead of us, the Healer stopped walking. And stupid me, I thought to Aimee, *She's tired.* Like she was some poor old Portsmouth lady, instead of a profoundly enlightened being here for a limited engagement in a human body.

But no, the Healer wasn't tired from the climb, or no more than Aimee and I were. She paused to drink from a little rivulet that flowed out of the rock. We joined her and drank, too.

The Healer grinned like we were wayward, stupid girls. That's when I noticed two piles of clothing.

I reached down and touched a gray shirt. It was Jackson's, I could tell from the psychic traces. It took all my willpower not to pick the old shirt up, bury my face in it, and sob like a grieving widow in a Lifetime movie. Elves have a stiff-upper-lip code of conduct that you absorb before you know it. Not that emotion is bad, more that excessive emotional display is stupid.

Aimee touched the other pile of clothes. "It's Daniel's!" she said. She was having trouble not getting all weepy. If your husband decides to go walking the highlands to talk with Josh of Nazareth, there's not much you can do if you're not ready to go along. Maybe wish him Godspeed.

"You didn't bring us up here just to collect their personal effects," I said to the Healer.

"That's true," she said. "Where do you think Jackson and Daniel *are?*"

Aimee and I looked at each other. We had an idea, but it was intuitive knowledge, unconfirmed by the senses. *Uncomfortable* knowledge.

The Healer watched us gravely and kindly.

"I'm going back to the Groves now," she said.

"Thank you for bringing us here, sister," Aimee said. She sounded as lost and uncertain as I felt.

The Healer smiled. She had complete confidence that we'd figure this out. She had more confidence than we did; she'd *inquired within* more deeply than we'd ever dared to.

"God be with you, sisters," the Healer said.

And also with you, Aimee and I answered in our thoughts.

26

Do Not Inquire Within *(Janjan, Nonlinear Time)*

The Healer headed downhill smiling and shaking her head at our young-elf problems. There wasn't much that needed healing; we had something to *know*, not something to *do*.

When I lived on Earth and commuted to work at Portsmouth Naval Shipyard, I saw House for Sale signs that said *Do Not Inquire Within*. I thought they were hilarious. The owners wanted potential buyers to call the broker and *not* ring the doorbell while the owners were having dinner or having sex or whatever homeowners do. While Jackson and I were adventuring among the Fae (so the MMs wouldn't kill us), we had to get past the human reluctance to *inquire within* ourselves. That wasn't funny at all.

Do not inquire within, a Portsmouth secret hiding in plain sight.

Anyway. Aimee and I were higher on the World Mountain than we'd ever been. We drank handfuls of cool, sweet mountain water. It was like drinking wine, but without the buzz. We'd brought the buzz uphill with us. We were vibrating with sexual desire from holding hands and sharing what-I'd-like-to-do-to-you ideas the whole hike up here. Plus, we were both naked and sweating. Elf girls smell good when they're exercising, but we still get sticky. The next world over is nothing like the fae-road, where breathing is too slow to be detectable and nobody sweats.

We needed a bath, is my point. We soon found ourselves washing each other with cool water from the little streamlet. It felt wonderful, but didn't cool us off, exploring each other's bodies that way. By the time we were rinsed off and air-dried, we were on the verge of enjoying each other in every possible way.

But.

Along with the sexual desire we'd brought to the highlands with us, I still had this *pressure* within me. There was something I wanted more than sex, imagine that.

Aimee and I looked at each other. I touched the area between my breasts with the palm of my hand; she mirrored the movement: *You too?*

Yeah, me too. Aimee was feeling the same pressure, like she'd caught it from me.

What was it, then? Even if she'd stuck around to watch us bathe like two barefoot, short-haired, makeup-free porn goddesses, the Healer would not have presumed to explain what was going on with us.

You see where I'm going with this, right? Aimee and I had to *inquire within.* If the next world over had real estate signs, they'd read *Please Inquire Within.*

Instead of falling on each other like a couple of slooty drunk girls at a wedding, we arranged our husbands' clothing on the ground so we could put our bare asses down on something other than soft grass. We'd hiked into a new part of the world and we were inquiring within a new part of ourselves. We didn't know how long we'd be sitting there.

I sat cross-legged on the worn, soft cloth of the shirt and pants Jackson had abandoned when he went ... wherever he'd gone. Aimee sat in the same posture, facing me with her knees touching mine.

Normally we'd leave our hands nested one atop the other in our laps, but intuition told me this would be a team effort. Normally we'd have our eyes lowered or closed altogether, depending. Intuition told me our eyes should stay open.

I took the initiative, of course I did. I reached out my left hand and stroked Aimee's face. Tears started in her eyes, but she mirrored my action and cupped my face with her left hand.

I'm glad it's you here with me right now, I thought.

I'm glad you're with me today, Janjan.

My hand traveled slowly down her neck and cupped one of her breasts. She didn't need a bra. I may have mentioned that I'm still on the thick side despite being a very fit elf girl. Aimee had always been sleek, but the training we all go through had given her strong muscles to shape that sleekness.

She was beautiful, is what I'm getting at. Aimee found me beautiful, too. Now it was my turn to have tears in my eyes. Still some unhealed stuff left over from my time on Earth, I guess, traces of belief on the inside that I was fat and ugly on the outside. But no, Aimee cupped my slightly-larger breast and found it—and me—very much to her liking. I didn't need a bra, either. Believe me, nobody's manufacturing them in this world.

In case you're thinking *What a couple of sloots*, it wasn't just sex. All the lights within us, the shining beacons lit in our first, mysterious creation that supported our physical being, shone in unison. The lights began signaling each other. Our hands moved on each other's bodies in accord with the signals, gently, barely touching the flesh. Together we entered a vast space where what lies beyond the sexual climax paints the boundless sky in rippling bands of color like Earth's northern lights.

I knew what was happening. Daniel had taught me how to take my mind on a test flight out of my body. The vertigo was less this time, maybe because Aimee was with me. I wasn't ready to lay this body down—or let it dissolve, which it hovered on the verge of doing. This was unfamiliar territory to Aimee.

I don't want to go voyaging after Jackson, I want him to come back to me, I thought. *If we stay like this in the high country, we'll fall out of these bodies like Daniel and Jackson did.*

She nodded agreement. *I love you, Janjan,* and *I want Daniel back, too.*

We needed something to bind us closer to our bodies. I took my hands off the center line of Aimee's body and took hold of one of her nipples; it stiffened. With the other hand, I reached down and cupped her mound.

Aimee said, "Oh!" Her belly began rippling with wave after wave of orgasms. Curious, I increased the strength of my grip on her hard nipple. She liked that very much. Girl juice sprang into my hand in hot intermittent spurts. *"Ah!"*

I saw a flash of that old memory-formation in her mind, her hidden desire, hurt, and loss. I fed it with pleasure. I won't lie, having power over her gave *me* pleasure.

"Oh!" Aimee said again. Her hands found me, breast and mound. She began to give me exactly what I was giving her.

"Oh!" I said back to her as the physical orgasms began coursing through me, too. That single word seems like a profound statement when your blood is up and all your naughty bits are engorged and waves of climax break upon your inner reef. *"Ah!"*

We might have remained there until we were exhausted and dehydrated, but I felt the touch of another mind I recognized.

[...]?

I patted Aimee's sweet, hot, wet body tenderly and got my feet. She stood up beside me. There's nothing to fear in the nextworld high country. There are no illusions, either.

Our eyes opened wide and our thoughts went still.

27

Lifehouse Sings "Hanging by a Moment" *(Janjan, Nonlinear Time)*

And it came to pass, when men began to multiply on the face of the earth, and daughters were born unto them, That the sons of God saw the daughters of men that they were fair; and they took them wives of all which they chose.

- (Genesis)

It's quite a thing to see a human being come back to a human body from, what—the All, the Everything? The Tao? The Mind of God?

I knew *who* was condensing from spirit into matter. Jackson's mind dawned in mine before his body appeared.

Aimee felt Daniel's mind as his body began to appear. She was aroused, full of hope, and hesitant to believe her eyes.

None of the movies I'd seen on Earth could have prepared me. What I saw through my tears was nothing like a Hollywood special effect. Too undramatic. Light turned quietly into the object illuminated with no surge of hokey background music to dictate how I should feel. One minute transparent fluid, next minute completely solid. All at once: boom, done.

The elements of this unfallen world rose up in silent cyclones to clothe the men again in muscle, bone, and sinew. The human day was waiting for the chance to dawn in the exact shape of those we loved. It was *they* who did this new thing they'd just learned to do.

It was the Judgment of Paris, with no golden apple of discord. They looked at our naked bodies, found us beautiful to look upon, and loved us. To Daniel and Jackson, *Aimee and I* were the fairest.

We were all naked, all in the same mind space, hiding nothing. Aimee and I were crying and our husbands felt our feelings with us.

The men had more reason to cry than we did. If you love your mate, leaving her behind is like abandoning your own body. If you love your freedom, going back to the flesh curtails that freedom dramatically. So: good news for Aimee and me; good news *and* bad news for Daniel and Jackson.

Jackson was solid again and there we were in each other's arms, still married, still *spoken for*. I wanted him so much and he wanted me as much as always. He needed our hot sexual connection to bind him to me and to the warm nextworld earth again. Part of him had yearned for more than he could find on Earth; it still yearned for what he had when he dropped his body off and found himself still alive without it. Thank God he yearned for me, too.

We left Aimee and Daniel in each other's arms, kissing with all the passion inside them, dropping slowly to the soft grass. As much as I felt for Aimee, as much as she excited me, I wanted her to have happiness with Daniel more.

Jackson and I walked around the mountain till we found a likely spot where we could be as private as anyone ever is in a world where everyone's minds are joined. He drew me gently down to the soft grass beside him and caressed my familiar flesh with his new flesh that soon felt familiar to him too. And he was inside my body with his body that I loved and we were each inside each other's loving minds.

Jackson was the same, yet different. If he found differences in me, they were minor in comparison. There was a new light in him. He rejoiced in it as we swived and I rejoiced in his joy. *On with the dance! let joy be unconfin'd*, the poet said. And so we danced and so it was.

Baldly stated, I was pretty much the same, but he was much more than he'd been when he left for the high country. Not that I was analyzing anything at the moment. We weren't in a competition, nothing like it, but I wondered in passing as we pleasured each other what a mighty being like Jackson was doing with an ordinary elf girl like me—if it hadn't been perfectly obvious that he was making me come again and again and again as much for his pleasure as for mine. There's no power over others in the next world over. When I came, he came, too. We were in each other's power.

No, Jackson was fully human. It was just that I'd had no idea what that meant till my hot little body came up against his hotter bigger body and he held me tight and we cried out together, something he'd never done on Earth, and we laughed at the delight in that simple new thing we'd found. *Oh. Ah.*

Before he and Jackson walked out of the body together, Daniel had been a new thing among the elves. I thought his difficulty remaining in the body was over now. There was a new thing I intuited in Jackson, an enormous power, an overwhelming strength like deep water behind a dam. Daniel would have brought the same power back with him.

I started coming again with each breath and Jackson matched me breath for breath, orgasm for orgasm as waves of eternity broke upon the shore of our small human bodies in moment after moment of nonlinear time.

We looked into each other's eyes without clinging, without grasping. He was above me now, smiling inside and out, so happy for me, so happy with me, so happy for himself. He lifted himself up on his two strong arms to see me better, and his happy tears fell unnoticed on my breasts.

Welcome back, my love, I thought

Instead of responding in thought or spoken word, Jackson opened his mind and showed me what he found when he *inquired within* so deeply that his body fell away.

28

Base Camp *(Janjan, Nonlinear Time)*

We wandered blissfully back to where we'd left our friends blissfully entwined. They were gone.

We reached out our minds and found them as happy as we were. We agreed to meet down in Nextworld Portsmouth. They wanted time alone to talk and to touch each other's bare skin, like we did. Daniel was just carrying his clothes.

With arms around each other's waists, my husband and I wandered slowly downhill. I'd missed him. I felt more complete now. It was odd. We didn't need each other, but having each other made this wonderful world even better. That's the way the place was from the borderlands and the grasslands and the forests on up to the high country, more wonderful the higher you went. And wonderful when you went back to share what you'd learned. I mean, that was the theory.

Speaking of theory. "Does it bother you that I've been swiving with Aimee?" I said, just to get the conversation going. I saw no resentment in Jackson's mind, but I wanted reassurance. Aimee and I had been in the middle of a highly-charged erotic interlude when our husbands showed up.

Maybe I wanted forgiveness. I was probably the horniest, least-enlightened person in the highlands, with Aimee right behind me, as it were.

Jackson grinned and held up his clothes. "I *wondered* how you got my shirt wet." Then seriously, "Of course it doesn't bother me. When I ... came back to the body just now, I thought we might still be spoken for. I *hoped* we were. But *I* ended our marriage when I came up here. I had to do it. I didn't know I'd be coming back. It was a mystery to me. Hey, it's *still* a mystery, you know?" He trailed off, remembering how it felt to walk into the Great Way beyond birth and death. Then, "Look, if you'd remarried while I was gone, I'd find a way to be happy for you. But you and Aimee don't seem to be more than lovers. Or did I miss something?"

My turn to hunt for words. He didn't push me. We ambled down a gentle slope, headed to the great river. I felt high in every sense of the word, like I might be stepping out into the bluest sky I'd ever seen. I knew how to walk on air, but the earth was so kind to my feet that I kept walking there. The grass was a bluer green at this altitude than in the grasslands, a different species. The trees around us were conifers, widely spaced so none were crowded out; their cones were edible, faintly spiced. I discovered I was hungry, and Jackson had feasted upon nothing but me for a long time. We stopped for a naked lunch and drank from a spring in the midst of a stand of trees. *Le Déjeuner sur l'herbe*, if you remember the Manet painting, Picnic on the Grass.

I finally answered his question. "I think *I* missed something." We were sitting next to the spring. I saw so much love in his face and so much compassion. I kissed him. His mouth tasted like cinnamon.

I opened my mind. We relived everything that happened to me from the night he and Daniel left until today.

I saw my life through his eyes that saw so much more than mine. I saw things I'd missed while I was living in the moment. I saw how elflords see things. Jackson had inquired deeper within than I had. He'd gone higher and further in search of the true power that was his alone.

And he'd come back because we needed him. He'd come back to me because he loved me and wanted me. I didn't know what I could ever do to deserve that.

We finished the review of little Janjan's little life and doings. Jackson saw what I'd missed. We had an idea what had happened to Beth and the start of a plan to find her and to help the Elf Friends who helped us on Earth.

—

We strolled into Nextworld Portsmouth. He put his clothes on, such a shame. I recovered my clothes and got dressed. Sigh.

Bobbi came to see me. She'd finished her elf initial training. Nonlinear time flows differently in different parts of our world.

We hugged. Bobbi swallowed hard when I introduced Jackson, but she hugged him, too. Just as well he was dressed. Women who only sleep with women generally prefer not to be hugged by naked men. And Jackson had become *impressive*. Bobbi felt his spirit's impact.

She felt something different in me. Her eyes got wet as she looked directly into mine. She shook her head. "How could I ever be worthy of you? Look what you've become. Look what kind of person loves you." She meant Jackson. She was trying to let go of her crush on me. There's so much more in heaven and earth than little Janjan.

"It's not about being worthy, sweetie," I told her. "You can't earn worth if you're born with it—and all of us are." I couldn't have said that in Elvish if it wasn't true. I was still talking myself into accepting it.

—

A group assembled on the grass down by the great river to watch the tide change. The rhythm of the water encouraged decision making. A tide in the affairs of men and so on.

The elves are very deliberate in matters of deliberation. They'd drive you crazy if they weren't so wise, smart, and funny. There's enough time to do whatever needs doing. If you're impatient, you're missing something.

Daniel and Aimee were there, along with Jerry and Leda, who'd come back from the high country, knowing they were needed, too.

The question was what to do about Beth's disappearance, the attacks on Elf Friends, and another Old God manifesting on Earth.

Not to mention the Fae. What should we do now that we knew about the road they walked—and dissolved into? I'd vowed to help them, no matter how long it took.

We don't talk much about the Great Vows, but they're real to us. Yes, I'd been screwing around here in the next world over from Earth, but the Fae lived in a time whose duration, though it somehow lasted forever, was the same as Earth's. I hadn't wasted a second of linear time.

Bobbi listened while the rest of us shared thoughts and talked aloud. She asked good questions. It struck me that I might have underestimated her just because she was shorter and cuter than me.

It developed that there were, let's say, technical difficulties involved in Daniel's, Jackson's, Jerry's and Leda's return to Earth, that were not involved in Aimee's, Bobbi's, or mine. The four of them had crossed the invisible threshold that separates high elves from the rest of us. They had to be careful what they did on Earth. A kind of self-emptying was required before they returned. We don't go to Earth to create new religions, ugh. Elflords and elfladies have to undertake a discipline that hides their light under a bushel, as the Bible has it. They have to be extra careful on Earth. Consider what happened to Jesus of Nazareth in Roman-occupied Judea: mostly good news, but also a lot of bad news.

So the elves have a usually-no-martyrdom, generally-no-paranormal phenomena rule. It's a matter of general agreement, like the Great Vows.

Around and around the talk went. Finally, Bobbi had had enough.

"Why don't we go back to Earth, *find* the bad guys, and just fucking *kill* them?" she said. "We can't let them keep killing our friends, can we?" In Elvish her words were more elegant but just as emphatic.

"She has a point," I said. "Why not keep it simple?"

Glances among Jackson, Daniel, Jerry, and Leda.

Daniel spoke for the high elves. "It's not just Materialist Magicians. There's another enemy on the battlefield," he told Bobbi, "one we've never encountered. Someone's using dark magic from the ancient world to attack the Elf Friends. The four of us have never seen anything like it."

He left unsaid what we all knew. Anyone who *had* seen that enemy and that kind of magic had long since gone upcountry and walked out of human form altogether.

Oh, wait: *the Healer.* She was older than anyone outside the highlands. Nobody knew how long she'd lived here. It's silly to ask, because there's no clear answer to the question. Nonlinear time, remember?

Jackson said, "I'll go talk to her." He left in a flash of thought.

I said, "Honestly, the Healer almost scares me."

"She's the highest of the high elves," Leda said. "She heals those of us who come here and then go back to try to heal the Earth."

To heal the Earth. Jerry gave his wife a multilayered look, leaned closer, and kissed her ear. She really did suit him right down to the ground. Leda smiled at him. She knew what he wanted; she wanted the same thing.

Bobbi's eyes got wet again. The kid was a bundle of emotion. New elves start out that way. Suddenly you burst into tears because you're so happy, or because some old hurt lets you go. Bobbi was beginning to understand the scope of what she'd gotten involved in. *To heal the Earth.*

It's only daunting if you think it's all on you, I reminded her.

Like that *helps,* she thought. I'd made her smile, though.

Then Jackson came back with the Healer and it was my turn to get teary-eyed.

Jackson was dressed all in white. He looked beautiful. Yes, I wanted to undress him, thanks for asking, but he was looking at his mentor, not at me.

The Healer, smiling broadly at my husband, said, "We have a new Healer."

"What happens now?" Jerry said.

Jackson said, "I'll work in the Groves with Leah until she thinks I'm ready."

I had not known her name was Leah. She had only confided her name to Jackson. Their relationship was both personal and spiritual: master (or mistress) and disciple. I was more confused than jealous.

"And then?" I said.

I don't think very far ahead. I never did on Earth, either. That's no handicap among the elves who do things with gentle persistence, one step at a time, until they accomplish the goal.

Jackson was made of different stuff now. What he'd done in the high country—while he was out of the body and not in any country at all—gave him a glimpse of the future. His future and mine. He never mentioned any of this on our way back down the mountain while we were celebrating our love and our marriage. Should my feelings be hurt?

Leah *knew* Jackson and Daniel would be coming back to the body when she led Aimee and me up the Mountain. She knew because she'd done the same thing long ago before becoming the Healer. That was the entrance exam.

She said, "We're all given the gift of healing when we come to this world. There's not much knowledge to acquire. Few of us are called to the work—the way we're all called to the highlands. Jackson was called back to the body for *you*, dear." She nodded to me. "And he came back because healing is his power and his calling. Once he's ready to take over the Groves, I'll go up the Mountain and see what's next for me. Maybe build a hut and live alone for a while. Or find a lover. I've been celibate too long." She looked dreamy with memory.

I thought: she's just a human being. Deep, wise, strong, powerful, but still a woman. It gave me hope to see her. And did she look *younger* all of a sudden? The thought of passing her duties to Jackson had lightened her burden.

The Healer saw my undisguised thought and smiled. *We're all just people,* she thought to me. *It's a good thing to be a human being. God is great.*

I wasn't going to argue about that. Not today.

I smiled at her and we got back to practical matters.

29

Practical Matters *(Janjan)*

King Rob was drying the dishes when Bobbi and I popped back into the hidden apartment. Seeing someone just *appear* shocks most people into immobility. Rob had been in two wars and witnessed part of another. Our reappearance shocked him into motion.

He left the dishtowel and the plate on the little kitchen counter. In an uninterrupted flow of movement, he took a heavy steak knife from the drawer and turned, ready to fight or flee, sunk deep in fighting mind.

He realized who we were and relaxed.

"I'm glad you're on *our* side, brother," I said.

He grinned, put the knife away, and came over to hug us.

"*That* was fast," he said. "But is my imagination is playing tricks on me?"

Bobbi said, "What do you mean, Rob?"

He looked at her closely. "There's so much *light* around you both. Especially you, Janjan. I almost didn't know you. Even your eyes look different."

I stuck my arm out and looked at it. Yup, there it was, the full-golden skin color of the elves. You don't notice these things at home. I'd never been obsessed with my appearance and now I didn't need to be.

Suddenly curious, I ducked into the little bathroom, switched on the light over the tiny sink, and looked at my reflection in the mirror. Sure enough, my eyes did look sort of East Asian, which happens to everybody who spends enough time with the elves. Nobody knows why; one of God's little jokes, maybe. I turned around and looked over my own shoulder. Yup, my big ass was still there, more lean muscle now than when Jackson and I first went to the next world over, but still my best feature. Elves come in all shapes and sizes. So to speak.

Rob had noticed something in me because he'd been ready for battle and looking with the eye of the spirit. I looked past my image in the mirror and *inquired within.*

My time in the high country had left its mark. Rob's time with the Fae had sensitized him to life energy, whether it was the green fae-road kind or the clear nextworld kind.

Within I saw the vast sea of clear light Jackson had shown me. My little personal consciousness sat quietly on its shore.

Yikes.

I rejoined the others.

"Thanks, Rob," I said. "I didn't realize how different I look. While I'm back here, I don't want to scare people who used to know me."

Bobbi gave me a sad look. "*Back here?*"

I thought to her, *We just visit, we don't live here now.*

She nodded and thought, *I know. It's a shock to hear you say it.*

I'm sorry you had to travel here with a person of such little wisdom.

She wiped a couple of errant tears with the back of one little hand. *I love you, Janjan,* she thought. *I know we can't be lovers, but I'm glad you're my sister elf.*

I felt a sudden shock of desire for Bobbi and shared it with her. *Desire's a good thing,* I thought. *We just have to be mindful what we do about it.*

Rob had been watching us. "Funny, I can see you two talking real fast on the inside, like, but I have no idea what you're saying."

Man, he *was* sensitive to energy. Maybe I could do for Rob what Leda had done for me before I went walking with the Fae.

"Bobbi and I can communicate easily," I told him, "but you and I can't.

If you're willing, I'll give you a way to call me."

"Sure!" he said. Rob was quite a guy. Not my type, but I was *spoken for*, wasn't I? I wondered if he was too good for Beth. Well, one step at a time.

I looked at him steadily. "If you agree, I'll paint a *mandala* into your flesh. It hurts like hell at first, then it only flares up when it prompts you to do something. The symbol is tied to your intuition, into your deep mind." I was talking myself into this. I knew how it was done, but I hadn't done it before.

Rob looked steadily back at me, equal to equal. "Janjan, I'm not afraid. Do what you have to do, so we can go save Beth."

He had no piercings, no earrings, no rings, no chains for me to paint with. I reached into the drawer where he'd dropped the knife. I found a tarnished old spoon; I had him hold it in front of his breastbone.

Careful not to frighten him, I reached gently into his mind and asked, *Do you trust me in your thoughts?*

He thought *Yes;* the spoon melted. He winced in pain, but held onto the handle until it evaporated. Intuition guided me step by step as I painted Rob's *mandala* into his body with invisible silver vapor in three dimensions and more.

All Rob's light turned clear. His green fae-light shined out the crown of his head, right through the ceiling, through the roof, and away into the universe. Typically, I'd forgotten that would happen. I hoped nobody was watching the barn.

–

When they brought in water and electricity, the Elf Friends had cabled the little apartment for internet. Rob, who had minimal computer skills, watched me scan the online news outlets to study the battlefield. As always, things were happening in the United States and in the wider world. Elf Friends who would have seen the connections between those things were keeping their heads down.

A faction in the U.S. House of Representatives once again attempted to repeal the Affordable Care Act. They argued that the government's regulating insurance companies and requiring everyone to have health insurance was worse than slavery and the Holocaust. Don't try to make sense of it.

Another congressional faction once again attempted to stop the government from paying the Planned Parenthood Federation of America for providing health services to poor women, in the belief that driving Planned Parenthood out of business would stop them from providing abortions—that the government already didn't pay for. Don't try to make sense of that, either.

Four women's health clinics were targets of vandalism and several people were shot at another clinic, in the belief that shooting the already-born would save the unborn. The anti-abortion congressional faction disclaimed all responsibility for these illegal and intemperate acts, but added in a pious published statement that unfortunate things would continue to happen as long as anyone anywhere had the legal right to terminate her unwanted pregnancy. *Nice little clinic ya got here; be a shame if anything happened to it.*

Immediately after the last clinic shooting, Congress again attempted to repeal the law that gave Americans the right to purchase affordable healthcare. The faction responsible, being immune to irony, again compared both universal healthcare and Planned Parenthood to the Holocaust and to slavery.

A nominally-Christian nonprofit organization spent millions of dollars to "help American families"—by preventing people of the same gender from getting married, adopting children, and *becoming* families.

Nobody bothered to pretend this agitprop had anything to do with the health of actual women or the welfare of actual children. There was a war against women—and men, too. I knew who was behind it.

The Elf Friends' website, *When Is an Elf Not an Elf,* came back on line. Denial-of-service attacks took it down two hours later. That night, the building that housed the site's servers was destroyed in what Canadian authorities ultimately ruled to be "an accidental natural gas explosion."

The Elf Friends had mirror sites in Europe and Asia. For now, our contacts told us, they'd keep the site offline to let the attackers think they'd won.

Several clergymen around the country were arrested on child sexual abuse charges. High bail amounts were paid by anonymous well-wishers. Family Values at work.

Rival religious factions in the Middle East continued killing each other. Some of them deployed poison gas against their heretical enemies and against unarmed civilian coreligionists. None of these groups acknowledged the Geneva Conventions forbidding the use of gas, a horror not seen on the battlefield since the First World War.

An Islamic State militant group threatened Russia; Russia threatened back. North Korea developed and tested nuclear weapons; China raised mild objections.

The United States budgeted more for its Defense Department than anyone, anywhere, ever. Congress then cut marginal tax rates for the wealthy and adjourned, surprising no one.

There were also some unusual developments.

Groups of clergymen publicly denounced the heresy of "the new paganism" evidenced by the worship of "the false goddess Aphrodite, also known as Venus." These denunciations took the view that such deities were actually demons disguised as gods to snare the souls of the ignorant.

No formal response to the Christian outcry emerged from the Neopagan community, whose members had no idea what the Protestants and Catholics were upset about. The Wiccans have no hierarchy or Pope. Who has anything bad to say about the goddess of love?

TMZ published sketchy third-hand accounts of a Hollywood fringe group calling itself "The Children of Venus."

Salon published an interview with a woman whose life was forever changed by a single theophany of Aphrodite. Lurid details of a secret cave ceremony emerged. Website reader comments on the interview were mostly of the *"LOL your stupid"* or *"STFU moran"* variety.

I knew we shouldn't ignore it.

Bobbi caught my thought and looked a question at me.

I reminded her what Jerry August told me about my California excursion: *You've found a trace of an Old God.* Jackson confirmed it.

"But *Venus?*" Bobbi said. *"Really?"*

"*Aphrodite* is just a name. They call us 'elves'. They call the Fae 'fairies'. People give names they understand to things they don't understand."

"Maybe there's a Portsmouth connection," she said. "I know some Neopagans. Want me to talk to them?"

"Yeah, and find out if somebody's using the old tunnels at Odiorne Point."

"*That* came out of left field," she said.

"I've got a feeling we should check the place out. It's complicated." I didn't want to tell that story right now.

And there were rumors of war.

The Boston news carried a story about what looked like an ordinary disaster. That's what you'd think if you didn't know the background (and didn't suffer from paranoia). Good luck getting the real story from anybody in the U.S. Naturally, the authorities were explaining things away (*"Likely natural gas explosion, tragic accident"*) and issuing bland reassurances (*"No continuing threat to the public"*).

It was no accident. It was a deliberate attack on the Elf Friends' law firm.

When it came to those who live in the next world over, the government had three heads, like the guard dog at the entrance of the Greek underworld. The first head was rabidly anti-elf (materialist apparatchiks and agents of influence), the second head was quietly pro-elf (Elf Friends and neutral allies), and the third head wanted only to pretend nothing scary was happening. In Portsmouth people used denial to manage their psychic unease. In Washington people used denial to augment their political power.

This three-part division produced isolated news stories that didn't connect. News aggregator sites published nothing about the bigger picture. Nobody saw a signal in the noise.

The wire services carried generalities about the explosion, but no details about who was hurt, who was killed, and who escaped. Details were *promised*, but never produced. Information delayed is information denied. The news media's moving finger writes, and having writ, moves on. The public forgets quickly.

The explosion site was a crime scene that only the authorities were allowed to enter. What we didn't read anywhere, because nobody had written it down or said it for the cameras, was anything the subsequent investigation might have revealed. We didn't even know which authorities were involved.

We didn't learn until later about lingering high levels of radiation that would require everything from the building to be excavated with enormous care at enormous expense and buried as nuclear waste. Before that happened, a whole containment shell would be built around the ruins.

Nobody knew these key details because the story fell out of the twenty-four-hour news cycle and down George Orwell's memory hole. The Elf

Friends were wisely saying nothing. The anti-elf and elf-denial heads of the government dog were deny, deny, denying everything and putting out half-truths. Who was going to challenge them? Nobody was doing investigative reporting anymore. And who'd believe the reports? Welcome to post-factual America.

A thought nagged at me. The last time I saw Beth face-to-face back in Providence, I handed her a business card from the Elf Friends' Boston law firm. The one that just blew up.

"I have to head out pretty soon," I told her before I went home to Jackson in the next world over. *"If you ever need my help, these people will know how to get in touch with me."*

What if Beth had called the law firm?

30

Secret Ceremony *(Darnand)*

When the stars threw down their spears
And water'd heaven with their tears:
Did he smile his work to see?
Did he who made the Lamb make thee?

- (William Blake, "The Tyger")

If you want to enslave a generation, start with their desires, Darnand thought. Basic human needs never change. Today the masculine warrior ideal took a distant second place to the feminine principle of love and beauty. Women wanted it. Men wanted to possess women who had it. The eternal polarity.

It made Darnand sick, the whole repulsive enterprise of physical bodies in a physical world. The Claimant was right. It all deserved to be undone, starting with the human religions that celebrated embodied life in the world, rather than embracing the inevitable end of everything with the Fallen.

The women who served the Dark Path were useless at strong-arm tactics like kidnapping, and armed assault. But the Sisterhood had found a way to access one of the Old Gods. The *soi-disant* goddess was only a

manifestation of impersonal, *material* odylic force, of course, but she—
it—possessed real power.

Mariah relocated a gaggle of Venus-worshipers from California to
New Hampshire, where they began recruiting more devotees. The women
followed Darnand's orders because they feared him; this gave him a sexual
frisson.

To his astonishment, the blasphemous incantations of his female
chorus succeeded again in New Hampshire. Mariah had been right!

The Walloon sent Mother Mariah back to her desert compound and
left Darnand in charge of the Children of Venus. Darnand understood the
workings of power. Like Mariah, he went where the Walloon ordered him
to go and did as he was told. Orders must be followed without question.
Louis was master of masters for good reason.

Did the ceremony require flowing salt water? The Walloon provided
it, thanks to his new ally, an ancient magician in an immortal body of
gold. The magus blasted a tidal passage into the Odiorne Point cavern and
magically shored it up with granite.

Louis was pleased with Darnand's work. Therefore Darnand was also
pleased. He would lay the trap. Louis would get his revenge on the elves.

Ultimately the Fallen would take revenge on the whole body of the
Earth and unbody all its people.

A wicked and adulterous generation seeketh after a sign, Darnand
thought, *and there shall no sign be given unto it, but the sign of Venus, the
evening star.*

He got to work, following his orders.

31

Return to Odiorne Point *(Janjan)*

Rob didn't just sit around the apartment watching TV. Bobbi taught him to search the internet. He learned what happened on Earth while he was fighting in one war or another and walking with the Fae around the World Mountain.

The Elf Friends' website came back up. Rob learned the *secret* history of the world while he waited to help us rescue Beth—assuming she wanted to be rescued. He thought of himself as a king. It was in his mind that kings should never stop learning. He hadn't been worthy of Beth last year when he was still mired in ignorance. His native intelligence was waking up, thanks to the elf *mandala* in his chest.

Bobbi and I had been popping in and out of the little apartment to meet with people around the area. Rob drove Bobbi's car to buy groceries and run errands. When we came back to the barn, he made simple meals. He was glad to do what he could.

"You'll be okay?" I asked him.

He smiled. "You girls are better scouts than I am. I'd just slow you down."

He was a good man. He was as determined to find Beth as I was.

Traveling as the elves do, Bobbi and I returned to Odiorne Point and the rocky little beach between the inlet and the man-made hills. We found only darkness and the sound and smell of the ocean.

I knew now why the electricity was still on in the tunnels and in the underground office with Donita Danton's name on the door. Someone *was* using the place, and it wasn't just horny elf girls sneaking in for a romp where the pleasure was spiced with pain. I'd have figured that out when Aimee and I first came here if I hadn't been concentrating on her ass.

From the outer air, I took us inside in a flash of thought, right to Donita's door. I wasn't ready to tour the complex yet. Bobbi and I needed to talk. I opened the door and turned on the lights.

Huh. Somebody had changed the bedding. I looked in the bathroom: fresh towels. The bad guys' housekeeping was exemplary. More than Aimee and I could say. We'd used the place (had we ever) and then left without cleaning up after ourselves. Exigent circumstances, harrumph harrumph.

When Aimee and I visited, the place hadn't been used for years, except by Aimee and Donita. The office had new psychic traces: preoccupied worker bees and the faint, cold touch of a mind devoted to evil. Once you meet someone on the Dark Path, you never forget it. Shudder.

Bobbi wrinkled her nose like the office smelled bad. "Is somebody living here? And is this where Aimee brought you? Or was it you who brought her?"

Uh-oh, hey jealousy. "Well, she brought me here because I'd never been before. Just like I brought you. The place was all sealed up then. We thought nobody but elves could get in."

"And you came here so you could *have* each other?" She was making herself angry.

"Yes." I shared the memory of what Aimee and I had done to, with, and for each other here on Earth and later in the next world over.

"Janjan, I want you so much I can fucking *taste* it," Bobbi said. "And you bring me *here* and tell me *that?*"

I saw her point. And being a new elf and a hot girl, she thought everything was about her. It takes a while to get over that. I wasn't altogether over it myself.

But.

I touched Jackson's mind with mine. He was asleep in the Groves. He woke up instantly.

I'm still on Earth, I thought to him. *Bobbi wants me and I want her. You see my problem?*

I felt his smile in my mind. *We're still* spoken for, *my love,* he thought. *Will she mind that my thoughts abide with you while you swive with her?*

I'll ask, I thought. *I love you, Jackson.*

I love you Janjan. God be with you.

And also with you.

I hid none of that conversation from Bobbi. "You see how it is. You know Jackson and I are *spoken for.* Do you still want me?"

"Oh, my God, Janjan, of course I do."

I held up one finger: *Wait a minute.* Bobbi watched, fascinated as I took off my boots, shirt, and pants and laid them to one side. It wasn't a striptease. I wasn't coquettish or flirtatious. It was more, *This is what I look like naked.*

The naked body has something to teach if we're willing to look directly. Leda and Jerry and a bunch of other elves standing in the next world over had once shown themselves naked to Jackson and me: *This is what we are. Come to us and be accepted as* you *are.* I showed Bobbi myself.

I said, "Your turn." I stood there naked, watching her.

She hesitated. "I'm afraid," she said. Words you never hear in the next world over.

"Afraid of what?"

"I'm afraid once you see me you won't want me." She wasn't crying, though, brave girl.

"This isn't about your body, is it?" I said.

Reluctantly, Bobbi inquired within herself. "I guess it isn't," she finally said.

I said, "Let me help." I began undressing her. She cooperated fully, like she was grateful for the assistance. She was nervous, trembling.

We stood naked facing each other. The red color she'd added to her hair was all gone now, but she still looked like a slimmer, shorter, brunette version of me. I thought I was attractive enough and that she was even more so. Everybody—or at least every healthy young-looking person—

has some external beauty which is unique to them.

"You're prettier than I am," I told her. It was only the truth. I wasn't blowing sunshine up her skirt, and it wasn't just because she wasn't wearing a skirt.

"What? No!" she said.

"Look through my eyes." I shared my visual impression of her.

She wasn't interested in seeing her reflection in my thoughts. She felt she lacked substance and worth. Instead of enjoying the sight of herself the way I enjoyed it, she shared her visual impression of me.

It was greatly exaggerated. In her eyes, my waist, hips, and thighs were thinner, my ass was less pronounced, and my breasts were bigger. In her mind, even my lips were fuller and poutier, for God's sake, like she'd given me imaginary lip injections. Pornstar Janjan.

She was looking at me through beer goggles, and neither of us had been drinking.

That wouldn't do. "C'mon, look again," I said. Touching her mind gently, I guided her perception back to accuracy. I look pretty good naked, but I'm not physically perfect by the impossible contemporary American standards of appearance. I helped her correct her perception. Was it really me she wanted? What did she think would happen?

Bobbi made a wry face. "You're kinda busting my bubble here, Janjan." Where had I heard that before?

I decided to be blunt. We were on Earth and embarking upon physical intimacy here in enemy territory.

"Do you want to fuck the real me or the imaginary me you were creating in your own head?" I said.

"I have extensive experience *making love* to the imaginary you," she said. She imagined that once we enjoyed each other we'd live together happily ever after.

We laughed. Bobbi was a smart girl. I can't imagine being attracted to a dull woman or a dull man, however beautiful they are.

When Leda told me what had happened to her and Jerry, she said, *You see what Jerry is, what we've both become. We're the same people we always were, not perfect, but all grown up now.*

I was also *all grown up now.* Well, mostly. Which meant I'd started looking *through* the body. Human birth is a Great, Good Thing and the beginning of something even more wonderful. Like sex, love, and marriage, the body is a good thing, but not the best thing.

Jackson had *seen* the best thing. He'd dropped his body off and been *part* of the best thing. He came back to the flesh for the same reason I came back to Earth. He was all grown up now and he was needed.

I held out my arms to Bobbi. "Come here."

She walked into my embrace and hugged me back, hard. "This isn't gonna happen, is it?" she said into my shoulder. She meant the two of us having sex. She kissed the skin above my breast, regretfully.

"Do you want it to?" I said.

She held me out at arm's length and looked at me directly. The classic Elf Look. "What I thought I wanted doesn't exist." Then in Elvish she thought, *I thank you for this teaching, my sister.*

We put our clothes back on a little regretfully. Like grownups.

We left the office and took a quiet walking tour of the entire underground complex. I could have done it alone, but Bobbi was new to this elf business. How are you going to learn if nobody teaches you? She'd never been inside Odiorne Point before. I had to take her through all the tunnels.

She'd be coming back without me.

Last trip, the main entrance had been sealed up with concrete and covered with dirt. That was no longer true. Bobbi and I walked as quietly as only elves can, casting our perceptions about us, alert for signs of danger. We didn't find any immediate threat, but we did find two new ways into the maze of tunnels and living quarters. Two entrances that weren't there when Aimee and I took a tour of the place—and a tour of each other.

The first entrance was a solid metal door that led to the state park outside. The door looked new. It was locked from outside. I zipped out, examined the big shiny new padlock, and zipped back inside.

Across from the new door, in the deepest part of the tunnels we found a hundred-yard stretch of curving wall with interior doors at regular intervals. All the doors were unlocked. Behind the doors we found an amphitheater that sloped down to a stage. There we found the second entrance. A new access tunnel led to the stage from the river. The floor of the tunnel was full of salt water that would flow in and out with the tide. Somebody had recently blasted their way from the outside until the water came in. All around the opening was freshly-broken concrete with pieces of rusty rebar sticking out.

Bobbi and I looked at each other. *Do you feel that?* A trace of radiation above background levels. New Hampshire is rightfully known as the Granite State, and the opening was shored up with piled stone piers. Our elf senses might be picking up radon gas from the granite. The radiation made us jumpy, like we should complete our business quickly and get out of there.

People were using the underground part of Odiorne Point again. They were using it regularly for some organized purpose. A lot of effort went into that new tunnel.

Except for the office and the amphitheater, the rest of the complex was dusty and empty, unused for years since the defeat of an alliance of magicians and materialists who called themselves the New World Order.

The *Second* Portsmouth War nobody in Portsmouth ever talks about.

Bobbi looked at me uneasily. She knew what had happened in this massive echoing space. She didn't like the vibrations any more than I did. This was where Jean-Paul Herold had left for Agharti. It had been the New World Order's train station. It wasn't human beings who made the trains run on time, and they were more like spaceships than trains. The unease we felt was partly caused by old traces of the nonhuman intelligence that had traveled in and out of this chamber.

There were a lot of overlapping psychic scents. At first we found only old spoor, nothing useful.

We wandered down to the edge of the little streambed. The tide had gone almost all the way out, reducing the flow to a trickle. On the other side of the stream was the stage, a raised area where fitted granite blocks sat on top of the rock floor. A covering of beige New Hampshire sand made the islet smooth and round.

We shared a thought: *That's interesting.*

Something about the little island tried to *deflect* our attention. If we hadn't been looking for clues with our senses joined, we would have ignored the innocent-looking sand the way it was encouraging us to do: *Nothing to see here, move along, people, just a pile of sand.*

It was a sophisticated spell of concealment. It had not been placed here by elves.

"The Walloon's back in town," I said. There might be other Materialist Magicians who had this power, but my money was on Louis, up to no good again.

Close-woven spell fabric covered the sandy islet like a net, reaching magical tendrils up the support pillars and all over the ceiling like grapevines.

If we dispersed the spell, the bad guys would know elves had been here. We gently lifted one corner of the spell to see what the magic was meant to conceal:

Distant chanting, mostly women, and a few men.

Leading the chanting, a cold, dark mind trapped on the Dark Path.

A shining power. A mind that was human-like, but not human.

A mind that was Beth-like, but not Beth as I knew her.

A naked woman—no, a naked crowd—and free-floating clouds of sexual feeling.

We gently lowered the spell-net.

When we lifted a last spell tendril near the newly-blasted entrance, we saw that something ancient and terrible had done this.

No Old God left that trail of radiation behind. It was *dark magic from the ancient world.*

32

Run-D.M.C. & Aerosmith Perform "Walk This Way" *(Janjan)*

And the people asked him, saying, What shall we do then? - (Luke's Gospel)

I thought we could handle the Walloon, but there was an enemy on the battlefield we had no answer for.

Bad things had happened in Odiorne Point. Worse things were on the way. *What shall we do then?*

We could have called the police, but a new padlocked door and a tunnel to Little Harbor didn't look like much of a crime. If you deny Materialist Magicians exist, you can ignore most of what they do. The authorities liked to pretend nothing bad had happened around here since the Treaty of Portsmouth ended the Russo-Japanese war in 1905.

Odiorne Point could wait. The bad guys had started systematically attacking the Elf Friends.

Sometimes it's hard not to hate your enemies.

Materialist Magicians keep trying to inaugurate the Claimant's rule on Earth. Along the way. they'll settle for making the Earth as horrible as it can be. You know, plagues of frogs and locusts, slaughter of adults and children, bloody wars, overpopulation, famine, and dread diseases. Don't try to make sense of it.

Nuclear weapons hold a special place in their hearts. Radiation is an elf repellent.

They try to turn people away from us. They don't want anyone to hear about the next world over. They attack the Elf Friends' website. They even steal books from libraries.

Obedience serves them better than knowledge. They cultivate fundamentalists of every religion, fanatics who place blind faith in a creed above personal experience: *I believe because it is absurd.*

Bad things had happened to the Boston Elf Friends. The Portsmouth Elf Friends had gone to ground. People around the country would get hurt without our help. Bobbi and I signed up to travel from group to group in North America.

Our sales pitch was blunt: *Bad things are happening to our friends on Earth. In all the human worlds there's only one safe place for you now.*

We didn't mention the Fae; walking with them was a dead end. Beautiful travelers wrapped in light ended up as blobs of mindless green ectoplasm swimming inside the fae-road.

I was born with a gift for leadership; I guess we both were. "God, you're such a *bossy* little bitch," I told Bobbi. She laughed. We disagreed about details, not the big picture.

What helped in dealing with Elf Friends who were older, taller, and had serious Earth careers was the fact that I was short and (arguably) cute and Bobbi was even shorter and definitely cuter. If you've been listening to me about the elves I've met, you know that some of us are sort of *daunting* at first meeting. Sometimes it's helpful to be less impressive than Daniel and Jackson. Lawyers, accountants, executives, soldiers, civil servants, and suchlike, Elf Friends though they were, saw us as smiling flight attendants welcoming them aboard.

Party girls don't threaten anybody's ego. Maybe we were underdressed for the party in the way of elf gals visiting Earth, but still.

"I'll be damned if I'm gonna run around Earth in a short dress," I said, putting on a pair of clean jeans. Rob had just made a run to the laundromat.

"You are such a lesbo," Bobbi said, as she put on a pair of cargo shorts.

"You wish. I don't have to show people my ass to get them to follow me."

"I wouldn't mind seeing your ass again."

And so on.

Some people were able to trust us with their lives. They traveled with us to our world in flashes of thought. Ten people in the basement of a Chicago safe house would be gone in twenty seconds, quick, safe, and easy.

The other trips were more dangerous because they took longer to organize. You can't even see the World Mountain until you decide to walk it. But some people can only approach the end of every familiar thing one step at a time. After Elf Friends traveled to Portsmouth, we led them out of the harbor in the middle of the night. We walked together on top of the Atlantic Ocean.

Whispering Elvish spells, we herded groups of frightened people down the river out of Portsmouth. Like childcare workers, we dried their tears and helped them find their courage. Like sheepdogs, we nipped at their heels to keep them moving together on top of the waves. They were exposed and vulnerable till we reached the foothills of the Invisible Mountain.

It took us a couple of anxious weeks to get everybody safely home. We saw no sign of the bad guys, but maybe their attention was elsewhere. The Elf Friends were diligent about secure communications, but maybe we got lucky.

Some of our friends told us what was and wasn't happening in government. While we were running the Elf Friend Underground Railroad, we learned more about the Boston disaster.

The Friends became new elves and began coming back to Earth. Once they learned how to elf, they saw what we saw.

The bad guys were mobilizing for another Portsmouth War.

33

Andrew Agonistes

Andrew was having a bad month. Beth hadn't called or texted since she left. His calls went straight to voicemail; he stopped leaving anxious messages. She didn't answer his texts; he quit texting her.

He couldn't stop worrying. He checked her computer. She'd booked a flight to California, reserved a rental car, and made hotel reservations just like she'd told him.

He called the Hotel del Coronado. A desk clerk said she'd had a reservation but had never checked in. Could the hotel be of further assistance? Andrew said No thanks and hung up.

He checked their credit card statements. Beth's charges stopped after she paid for round-trip airfare with an open return date. The car rental charge wouldn't show up until she returned the car to the airport.

Now what? He wasn't going on social media to tell the world about his problems.

Not knowing where else to turn, he went to the police station. He spoke to a detective sergeant who'd been assigned desk duty because he was retiring at the end of the month. The sergeant asked questions and filled out a missing person report on Beth. It didn't take long. There wasn't much to tell.

The detective gave Andrew a pitying look "I'll put her info into the national database," he said. "Wives leave husbands all the time, Andy." Andrew hated being called *Andy*, but he let it go; he needed the guy's help. "Husbands leave wives, too." the cop continued. "Most 'missing persons' aren't really missing, they just want to get away. People find out the grass isn't greener wherever they wandered off to, so they come home."

"Does that happen often?" Andrew wondered if he could forgive Beth for straying. If that's what she'd done.

"Happens a lot," the detective said. "Couples get back together and make it work. You know, counseling, blah blah blah." He made a yakety-yak gesture with one hand.

"What would you do if you were me?"

The detective looked at him wearily. "Son, if *my* wife took off and didn't say where she was going, I'd cancel her credit cards and wish her godspeed."

"That's it? Just give up?"

The detective made a palms-up weighing gesture. "*Or* if I was worried about her and the police out there didn't find her right away, I might hire a private investigator to track her down in California."

"I hadn't thought of that," Andrew said. "Thank you."

Andrew's company retained a law firm with contacts in California. The lawyer he spoke to was happy to recommend a discreet West Coast private investigation firm. Andrew signed a short-term contract (and paid a shocking amount of money) to have an investigator look into Beth's disappearance for no longer than three days. He emailed them Beth's personal details and everything he'd already learned.

He said a prayer and went back to work.

A private investigator named Benjamin Dee called him back the next day. Andrew was impressed. Quick response is vital when you're worried about someone you love.

"We located your wife's rental car, sir," Dee told him. "We haven't found your wife yet, but we're hopeful." He didn't sound hopeful.

"Any idea where she went, Mr. Dee?"

A pause on the other end of the line. "Let me brief you on what we've learned so far. You said you want to hear what we learn as soon as we learn it?"

"I did say that," Andrew said. "This sounds bad." He'd been standing up, pacing while he used the phone. He sat down. He was having trouble catching his breath.

"We got her phone records and locations from your wireless carrier. You paid us for expedited service and we paid someone who works for the carrier for the information. They'll deny they ever did such a thing and so will we. Anyhow, the last number she called from your location belongs to a Boston law firm." The investigator named the firm and paused again.

Andrew was frightened for Beth and it made him impatient. "Is that supposed to mean something to me?"

"I thought you might have heard. It was in all the news. There was an explosion and a fire in their office building. People were hurt, but no details have been released yet. Everybody I talked to says 'the investigation is ongoing'. That means law enforcement is sitting on information."

Andrew had been too preoccupied to follow the news. "I'll pray for the victims, of course. But what does an explosion in Boston have to do with my wife disappearing in California?"

"Sir, it appears that your wife was talking to someone through that law firm's main switchboard—*after* their building blew up. The phone number for their switchboard is no longer in service and the firm isn't doing business from anywhere else."

Andrew saw that the investigator was leading him somewhere. "So she called these lawyers, but couldn't have been talking to anyone in their building. Wouldn't they have forwarded their calls somewhere electronically? And who *was* she talking to?"

"That's the question. Who was she talking to, where, and why? If the lawyers always forward their calls off site after normal business hours, why is their number disconnected now? Big law firms do *not* just go out of business and disappear without notice to the public. There's been no official word from the firm. Even the Massachusetts Bar Association refuses to discuss this. Another part of the *ongoing investigation* nobody will talk about."

Dee was suggesting something, but wouldn't just come out with it.

"Well, why would Beth call a law firm in *Massachusetts*, not Texas?"

Andrew said. "Divorce? *I* thought we were doing great together. If she ever wanted to end our marriage, I'd try to talk her out of it, but I wouldn't stand in her way."

After a moment of silence, he said, "Okay." Like Andrew had said something helpful. "*Okay,*" he repeated, "we need to talk face to face."

"Sounds expensive," Andrew said, thinking how much money he'd given the guy's firm.

"You've already paid for my trip. Some things shouldn't be discussed on the phone."

—

One day later Benjamin ("call me Ben") and Andrew ("call me Drew") shook hands in a hotel cocktail lounge near the airport. Dee had chosen the meeting place. It was too bright and noisy, nowhere Andrew would entertain visitors. It had all the atmosphere of a cafeteria. Andrew felt he bar was telling him *Finish thy demon drink and get thee hence, miserable sinner.* The lounge only existed because the conservative Christian hotel corporation thought a hotel should have a bar. Mornings, the chain thriftily used it as a complimentary breakfast room. All signs of adult beverages had to be hidden away from innocent eyes while breakfast was served. Andrew was glad *his* church didn't frown on a man having a beer on a hot afternoon.

"I've got my car outside," Andrew said. "We'd be more comfortable at the country club. I'll be happy to drive."

"I'm sure your club is very nice, Drew, but I'd rather talk here. Look around. Nobody who looks like Homeland Security. More importantly, I don't see any cameras. This hotel has cameras around the entrance and above the front desk. Maybe in the hallways, too, but not here. They don't care about the bar."

Andrew had no idea why that was important, but whatever, he'd paid for Ben's expertise and discretion. He had plenty of drinking buddies.

After discussion with the young woman at the bar, the men got two bottles of Lone Star Beer and found a corner table where they could talk privately.

Saying, "To happier days," Ben clinked bottles with Andrew. He took a drink and made a face. "Guess I can take Lone Star off my bucket list now."

Andrew grinned. "Not the best beer I've ever had, but it's far from the worst. All part of the authentic Texas experience. Hell, you already look more like a cowboy than I do. All you need is the hat."

Ben was two inches taller than Andrew and maybe ten years older. He had short graying hair and a lined face that had spent a lot of time outdoors. He was the kind of man who didn't fret much about his appearance. He wore a gray suit that was tailored to his lean, tough frame, a white shirt with no necktie, and a pair of lace-up dress boots, footwear Andrew rarely saw in Texas. Golf kept Andrew lean enough, but he'd never needed to be tough. Away from the office this afternoon, he wore a green golf shirt, tan chinos, and boat shoes with no socks.

"Okay, look," Ben said, "I'm sure you're busy and I know I am. I'd like to catch a five o'clock flight if that's how things shake out. Let me tell you what I know, and we'll figure out what to do next."

"Sure." Andrew's hands started to shake. He set the beer carefully down on the table top. "Go ahead."

"First off, your wife is friends with Janjan Javorski?"

"Like I told you, that's the friend Beth flew out to California to see. I figured 'Janjan' was a nickname; I don't know her last name. Beth kind of made new friends when we moved down here. I don't think Janjan came to our wedding."

"It is a nickname. Her real first name is Jadwiga," Ben said. A pause. "Ms. Javorski is on the No-Fly List."

"What, she's a *terrorist*?"

Ben shrugged. "Probably not. Almost certainly not. Let's just say that she left the country under ambiguous circumstances. Homeland Security, among others, really wants to talk to her."

"Huh. Talk to her about what?" Andrew had lost the plot.

Ben sat back in his chair, took a drink, and regarded Andrew closely. "Now we get to the issues I didn't want to discuss on the phone. You're an East Coast guy who's moved to Texas. You look comfortable here. I'm a West Coast guy, born and bred, who doesn't feel at home anywhere. Military service does that to you. Point is, my firm hears *a lot* of unlikely-sounding things. We don't automatically dismiss unexplained phenomena as bullshit."

"You're going to tell me something unlikely," Andrew said. "You'd like me to keep an open mind."

Ben nodded. "Yup. That law firm your wife called before she flew to California? They have enemies in government. They also have powerful *allies* in government—and elsewhere—who look out for them."

Andrew shook his head. "Help me out here. Is this about money?" Money was the prime mover in his world, the first thing he thought of.

"Well, sort of. It's about politics, too, just not the usual liberal-conservative kind. Mostly it's about Portsmouth, New Hampshire and everything that's happened there since the Eighties."

Andrew's eyebrows went up. "*Beth* lived in Portsmouth. She shared a house with Janjan and another girl. *Leda*, I think her name was. *She* didn't come to the wedding, either."

One step at a time, Ben led Andrew through a forest of unlikelihoods. Portsmouth's troubled history: elves, Elf Friends, Materialist Magicians, other worlds. How government and citizens joined forces to explain paranormal disasters away and deny they ever happened. How two of the three former housemates had gotten involved in what Janjan Javorski called "the old Portsmouth weirdness." The Elf Friends even had a website; Leda's and Janjan's stories were on it. Ben said the website was now offline. He didn't say why his firm was interested.

Ben suggested that Beth, who'd kept herself out of all the weirdness, had gotten pulled into it because of her friend Janjan.

"The law firm Beth called? They're *all* Elf Friends. They handle people's financial affairs after those people leave Earth. They provide aid and comfort to the elves when they come back here to do ... whatever the hell they do."

"So why blow up their offices?" It was a feeble protest. Ben could have told him this cock-and-bull story over the phone, terminated the investigation, saved the cost of airfare, and kept the rest of the fee. Despite himself, Andrew was starting to think Ben's theory was plausible.

"You're having a hard time buying this," Ben said. "I don't blame you. To answer your question, the magicians have had no luck attacking the elves. They can't touch the elves in their world, so they're attacking the elves' support system, the Elf Friends. It's a textbook counterinsurgency campaign."

"If I understand what you're telling me, Leda was an Elf Friend. She and her husband went to the elves—*became* elves, whatever that means.

They helped Janjan, who also joined the elves and ... left the country. You think Beth called the Elf Friends' law firm, hoping they'd put her in touch with Janjan."

Ben nodded. "Beth's call would have gone through the law firm's switchboard if their building hadn't been buried in smoking rubble. I think the bad guys temporarily hijacked the number *because* they were looking for known Elf Friend associates. Looking for Ms. Javorski in particular."

"So Beth talked to these ... *magicians*? What did they tell her?"

Ben looked sad. "We know she flew to San Diego. They may have told her she could meet Janjan somewhere nearby, like the Hotel del Coronado."

"You think these crazy people *kidnapped* her?" Andrew didn't want to believe it.

"Sorry, Drew, that's exactly what I think."

"*Why?*" Andrew only realized he was shouting when the barkeep looked over at him, alarmed. "Why?" he repeated quietly. "We're not *rich*. There's been no call about ransom."

"It's not *you* these Materialist Magicians want to hurt. It's not about money, either. The elves have hurt them. The magicians are looking for payback; they're worse than *Daesh*. Beth may be a hostage, a prisoner of war, really. These are very bad people, Drew. They're quite capable of using your wife as bait to draw in Janjan Javorski and as many other elves as possible—so they can kill them."

Andrew sat back in his chair. His hands shook. He wanted a drink, but picking up the bottle seemed impossible. He clutched his knees until the pain made his head stop spinning. "That's crazy," he said.

Ben took a drink of Lone Star and managed not to make a face; at least the beer was cold. "You haven't heard the craziest part yet. Ever hear of the Children of Venus?"

—

Andrew shook Ben's hand. He watched the investigator climb into his rental car and drive back into the airport. Renting a car for a two-mile trip seemed stupid to Andrew, but Ben had needed to stay mobile. And Andrew was paying for the rental, wasn't he?

He sat in his own car and considered his options.

Thinking only made him angry. The situation was totally unfair. *It was all Beth's fault.* All he wanted was a wife to love him, bear his children, and go to church with him on Sundays. Family Values, his pastor called it: you could hear the capital letters.

Now he discovered that Beth's past and old friendships still meant something to her. She'd let her carefree single life interfere with her new serious married life. His jealousy was painful.

Was she in danger—wherever she was? Ben seemed to think so. Beth had flown into the war zone. She'd been taken hostage in a conflict that was none of her damn business.

Andrew thought about Ben. How reliable was he? He knew about the war between the "Materialist Magicians" (ridiculous name) and the "elves" (even more ridiculous), but remained on the sidelines observing a conflict few Americans ever heard about. Ben didn't say what he'd done in the Army. Some kind of special operations seemed likely, given his level of access to government people with compartmented information.

Ben had mentioned serving in the Middle East with a man named Jean-Paul Herold. Another name that meant nothing to Andrew. Ben had given Andrew a website where he could read Herold's story for himself. *And* Leda's story. *And* Janjan's story. *If* Andrew wanted more background on this mess Beth had jumped into with both feet. Big "if." The site with the ridiculous name *When Is an Elf Not an Elf?* was only occasionally available: "the bad guys" attacked it when it came back online.

Ben had offered Andrew information, not advice. Ben's sources told him that the Venus worshipers (*really?*) who'd kidnapped Beth were no longer operating near the California-Mexico border. Now these lunatics had moved house to Portsmouth, New Hampshire. Where else?

Ben had shared none of this confidential information with the San Diego police. Having seen no sign of Beth and no sign of foul play in the rental car, the police had shrugged and notified the rental company to reclaim the vehicle. Andrew would be receiving a bill.

Ben suggested that he and Andrew leave for the airport now in Ben's rental car, fly to Portsmouth and search for Beth. Once they found her, Andrew could persuade her to come home with him.

Being an expert in upselling services to clients, Andrew believed Ben was trying to upsell him. It might even be some kind of scam.

How much more time could he afford to take away from his career before the CEO realized he didn't *need* Andrew? How many more thousands of dollars would he have to invest in this pointless quest? Perhaps a second mortgage on the house? Borrow from his retirement 401(K)?

No way. No fucking way.

Andrew spoke to himself in the air conditioned car. "*Seriously?* Fuck this. And fuck you, Beth. I'm done with you."

Anger felt better than the fear that lay underneath it.

There was a whole world out there he wanted no part of. Beth had walked into that world—and away from him—of her own free will. Good luck to her. Why should *he* follow *her*? A wife should follow her husband.

Andrew had embraced his church's traditional ideas about marriage. The man was head of the household. The woman, the homemaker, raised the children with the advice and consent of her husband, the breadwinner. Jesus was head of the Church. Patriarchy was the will of God the Father. Andrew was a little vague on the Holy Ghost.

Andrew called his company's law firm a second time. The attorney who had happily recommended Ben's California detective firm was equally happy to recommend a local divorce lawyer. Serial monogamy was not unusual among his clients.

34

Covert Operations *(Janjan)*

I didn't like sending Rob among our enemies, but I couldn't go with him. I didn't look quite like an earthling anymore.

Bobbi looked like a girl with a healthy summer tan. An initiated Materialist Magician would know what she was, but she was going to meet ordinary human beings. We hoped.

Bobbi could protect Rob as well as I could. And he had the *mandala* I'd given him over his heart, invisible to anyone except an elf or someone who loved him. No green fae-light flickered around him; no one would guess he was King of the Fae.

I hugged Bobbi for good luck. Every elf is in touch with every other elf. Bobbi and I were even closer because this mission was ours together and we were friends.

I hugged King Robert of the Fae. "You know what to do if you get in trouble?"

He put his hand over his breastbone where the *mandala* danced. "I put my mind *here* and call you." He smiled at the thought of his big, strong self asking little Janjan to rescue him. But he knew what I was; I had powers he didn't have. He'd fought for me. He knew I'd fight for him.

This was about rescuing Beth.

Bobbi and Rob drove out of the barn in her car and headed off to Portsmouth. I pulled the doors closed behind them.

—

Friends in the gay community had told Bobbi about the Odiorne Point ceremonies. One of Bobbi's exes talked about turning over a new spiritual leaf. Bobbi showed interest.

There's a commonality of interest among outsiders. In this case, it was people in flight from the Abrahamic religions. Wiccans and other pagans. Practitioners of alternative medicine. Seekers of ecstasy. Devotees of sexual magic. These groups overlap. Americans are always trying something new from the spiritual supermarket.

Now Bobbi was getting naked in the moonlight, leaving her workaday clothes folded neatly on top of her shoes, watched over by a formidable, silent woman in a robe. Bobbi put on her own clean white robe and joined a queue of barefoot women. She walked through the open door that had been padlocked when she first visited Odiorne Point.

A grassy hillside with a thick door set in concrete was far from the strangest place Rob had ever been, but he didn't like dark, enclosed spaces. Walking through the door made the moving symbol burn in his chest.

Janjan warned me I might start having intuitions, visions, and memories and not be able to tell them apart, he thought.

He'd never felt fear on the fae-road. He was more afraid tonight than he'd been in the Civil War or the Second World War. He wanted to turn back.

He thought, *Beth!* and took command of himself. He kept walking into the half-dark cave, three feet behind the woman in front of him. Frightened or not, his long-ago upbringing kept him a polite distance from a female stranger.

35

Mystery Cult *(Beth)*

O Venus, beauty of the skies,
To whom a thousand temples rise,
Gaily false in gentle smiles,
Full of love-perplexing wiles;
O goddess, from my heart remove
The wasting cares and pains of love.
- (Sappho's "A Hymn to Venus,"
    translated by Ambrose Philips)

Beth had never felt more pleasure or power. The Lady didn't overwhelm and possess Beth's spirit like a demon, she touched something elemental in the depths of Beth's being. To be in the Lady's presence was to reflect her rosy light; it disconnected Beth's doubting, reasoning mind. She functioned on the level of instinct and intuition moment by moment with little thought of past or future.

Was she happy? The question never arose. What she was doing was *necessary*. A dying Earth *needed* what was shining into the world *through her*. Being the goddess' human face, welcoming the goddess' worshipers to a closer walk with her, gave Beth almost as much pleasure as the half-forgotten nights when she and Bobby had gloried in each other's bodies.

Back then Beth had been full of misgivings, second thoughts, and inhibitions, while Bobby had been the pure one, full of love for her, giving her orgasm after orgasm. She hadn't understood how a man could have orgasms inside himself with no release of semen. She would think, *Has he still not come yet? Oh well, one more climax won't kill me.* And come again. And then again.

Beth's qualms and guilt had been worse the night she and Janjan had slept together, her orgasms astonishing in their intensity. Beth would think, *Is she coming again? Oh, my God, so am I.*

But the Lady entered the lovely tropical land of orgasm with each breath. While Beth served as chief priestess, she dwelt in that country with the Lady. To serve the Lady was to pleasure her. She welcomed the goddess' most intimate touch.

At the same time, Beth was aware that something was very wrong with all this and the wrongness wasn't just Catholic guilt about how she was deploying her ladyparts. She'd felt the same pervasive sense of something awry when she walked the fae-path.

She *and* Bobby. Not to mention Jackson and Janjan who'd saved them all, first from the Materialist Magicians and then from the seductions of a nearly-eternal life among the Fae. Beth remembered few details, but the unease was familiar.

Being so deep in uneasy bliss pushed Beth's memories aside. The memories were irrelevant to the intensity of what was happening. The ultimate price of the unbalanced passion she lived in would be the annihilation of her human nature, followed by the death of her human body. It was the fae condition all over again, without immortality.

She felt the Lady's wordless reassurance: there would be no pain in her final extinction and the body she laid down would remain beautiful, a tribute to the goddess she had served with her whole self. Being a modern American woman and a lapsed Catholic, Beth found that oddly comforting.

Beth's task as the Lady's priestess was ceremonial on the surface and spiritual beneath. The goddess was the human-shaped manifestation of a real power in the world. Her secret ceremonies were powered by *desire*, by men who desired Beth and by women who wanted to be her. Who they wanted and wanted to be was the Lady, whose power and beauty beckoned them closer, promising that in her embrace would come all they desired, beyond words.

Worshipers saw Beth's body appear during the ceremony, seemingly out of thin air. But in Beth's arms it was the Lady they encountered. There was no penetration in the ceremony, only a prolonged, shared sexual climax that persisted after Beth released them. No one could doubt the power of the goddess' sacrament: they left her grotto shaking with it.

The ceremonies disturbed Beth at the level of feeling and intuition. As one of Nature's eternal absolutes, the Lady had nothing to fear and little empathy for the human condition beyond romantic disappointment. She mourned her lovers lost to old age and death, as any woman would do, and then moved on.

Along with the admiration and desire of the worshipers in the cave, Beth sensed a dark current, a threat she'd encountered before. Contemptuous eyes observed the Lady's ceremony: the singing women, the robed men, the call and the response, the dropping of robes to stand naked before the goddess. The watcher remained scornfully apart from the ceremony.

As if, Beth thought, the ceremony, the worshipers, and even the Lady herself (and Beth through whom the goddess favored those who came to her temple) were meant to draw the attention of someone else.

The watcher awaited his prey with the coldblooded patience of a snake. Like Beth, he was not alone in his mind. Behind him were others who sometimes used his eyes.

36

The Cave of Mystery *(Rob. Beth, Bobbi, Janjan)*

> *Sea-born goddess, let me be*
> *By thy son thus graced, and thee,*
> *That whene'er I woo, I find*
> *Virgins coy, but not unkind.*
> *Let me, when I kiss a maid,*
> *Taste her lips, so overlaid*
> *With love's sirop, that I may*
> *In your temple, when I pray,*
> *Kiss the altar, and confess*
> *There's in love no bitterness.*
> - (Robert Herrick, "A Hymn To
> Venus And Cupid")

Rob stood patiently on cold sand at the water's edge. Women, dressed as he was in white robes and nothing else, looked at him shyly or boldly in admiration; he didn't notice. During his time leading the Fae along the endless road, King Robert had acquired dignity and commanding presence.

He was one of a few men scattered throughout the crowd. People observed the rule of silence as best they could. Nobody spoke, but there were still human noises: sighing, throat-clearing, a cough.

Little Bobbi stood between two taller, wider women twenty yards from Rob. The cave was lit by the flickering light of scattered candle lanterns that filled the echoing dark with moving shadows. Rob's gaze passed over Bobbi. She looked different from when they spoke an hour ago. It wasn't just the robe she wore. Like many of the worshipers here tonight, Bobbi kept her eyes on the ground. Inward-focused attention made her inconspicuous.

Bobbi knew exactly where Rob was. She perceived the sparkling, moving *mandala* in his chest.

Her attention was centered. Her mind was connected to Janjan's. Bobbi got a bad feeling from one of the robed men. He stood guard at the door and gave each robed celebrant a searching, contemptuous look as they walked past him into the sloping amphitheater.

His gaze clung to Bobbi as she passed. With her gaze lowered and her breathing quiet, Bobbi looked nothing like a threat. Did he know what she was? Something was very wrong with him. She knew better than to investigate.

Wordlessly, Janjan reminded her not to use expanded perception, work magic, or speak Elvish. Bobbi prayed for courage.

The Children of Venus took their places in ragged, curving rows. Dark salt water separated them from the sacred islet: *Thus far and no further.* The tide flowed in. Ranks of worshipers filled the space from the high tide line in the sand all the way up to the entrances. They waited as patiently as they could.

—

And where was Janjan, exactly? My body was miles away, in the barn apartment sitting on a folded blanket on the old wide-plank floor. My mind was just above that body, faintly aware of its discomforts and desires, and vividly aware of what was happening to my friends at Odiorne Point.

I saw the man whose gaze troubled Bobbi. He was a tunnel of shadow. I'd seen that concentrated darkness at the Walloon's house last year when Louis' bodyguard bent his whole mind and will on killing me. The man with the flat killer's eyes had chosen to be reborn on the Dark Path; the dark beings of that path had taken him for their own.

People on the Dark Path help Materialist Magicians like Elf Friends help the elves. Their motives are different. Seeking power over others, magicians hoard their secrets. Elves have no secrets; they share what they know with everyone who asks. Elf Friends become elves simply by asking. Did people on the Dark Path ever become magicians?

Anyway. I had to control my own mind right now. I went into passive sonar mode. I became the night sky. Whatever passed across my awareness was allowed to go its own way. I still had an ego, an experiencing self, but it mattered less once I took one baby step outside my body.

Darkness. Many stars, light filtered by Earth's atmosphere. And there in the west was the Evening Star, better known as the planet Venus. I was in no condition to appreciate the irony.

In the distance two very different evil minds appeared. Those who walk about seeking whom they may devour. I let the dark seekers go flying across the firmament without reacting to them.

I'd encountered one of them in his Virginia mansion. It was Louis, master of Materialist Magician masters. King Robert of the Fae had shot an arrow through the Walloon's head, reducing him to a coherent statue of greasy black smoke. The Walloon had regained physical solidity. Cunning magic had made him a body of minerals.

A demon shadowed Louis' bent spirit. Rather than moving him and talking through Louis as it once had, the demon only watched him with its unblinking eternal gaze. They didn't notice my silent awareness.

The Walloon's new body was the product of dark magic from a time when the Earth's physical laws were still fluid. From a time when those who became the Fae followed the Morrigna off the Earth onto the fae-path around the human worlds. From a time when Old Gods appeared to their worshipers in person.

This ancient magic was embodied in a being who'd survived the Great Flood. This creature was more powerful and further removed from the human condition than the Walloon. A vast spirit was trapped in a small metal space, a thundercloud filled with lightning inside a gold wine amphora. It had rapidly-moving equations instead of DNA, ever-evolving sigils that made no sense to me. Its power was barely contained, like a flow of molten rock seeking to erupt from beneath the Earth.

That spirit was no fallen angel; it had once been human. Now, immeasurably powerful, a gyroscope of pure energy spun inside its container like the genie in the lamp. It left a faint radioactive trail across the sky.

This was the ancient and terrible thing Bobbi and I sensed when we scouted Odiorne Point. The creature left radioactive traces behind when it blasted a channel from the river into the tunnels. Its primeval magic had exploded into the Elf Friends in Boston, killing and poisoning them, collapsing a multi-story office building like a house of cards.

At one remove from my body, I was as unremarkable as the trees and grass outside the barn. Like the birds looking upward from their nests under the eaves. Like a cloud sailing unseen across the dark in a faint breeze.

But the ancient magician detected my presence. There came a stirring of awareness as something invisible saw my invisible mind. Then came a quick pulse of darkness.

Then nothing. All sign of the magician and the Walloon vanished.

That sudden surge of darkness felt like a lure.

I whispered inside Bobbi's thoughts: *Don't respond, just listen. The Walloon is headed your way, along with something even worse than he is. And by worse, I mean more powerful.* I sent her images of what I'd seen.

Bobbi stayed cool. I felt her wordless assent.

I reminded her: *This whole ceremony's a trap. It's aimed at all of us* (I meant the elves)—*me and Jackson, in particular. And the Walloon wouldn't mind killing Rob for shooting an arrow through his head.*

Bobbi's question was a nonverbal *Now what?*

I thought: *Keep an eye on Rob. Stay there as long as you can. If you have to leave, meet me at your place.*

Leading elves is different from leading earthlings. With elves, you don't have to pretend you know what you're doing.

I was just improvising. I had no idea what our next move should be.

—

The tide came into the cave in little wavelets, almost silent. No perceptible wind blew into the huge domed space, but the lantern candles flickered. The night outside was quiet and warm. Inside, the cave smelled of salt water and seaweed and a crowd of human beings. Rob had forgotten what people smelled like during his year on the fae-path where breathing was so slow.

In the center of the widening water between the shore and the opening to the river was a small island made of artfully-placed stone covered with natural sand. The sand had been smoothed by reverent hands.

The chanting of the women's chorus went on and on. Rob felt the chant in the bones of his arms and legs, at the base of his spine, and if he was honest with himself, in his groin. He was no nineteenth-century sexual innocent, not after detouring into this century by way of the fae-road. Deliberately (and dutifully) begetting children as king of the Fae made him distrust desire prompted by the green *light of other days,* or by anything but love. Dismayed, he thought, *Not this again.*

The ceremony was designed to manipulate its participants. Rob was having none of that. In accepting Janjan's *mandala* in his chest, he'd embraced his own free will.

He wasn't here for his own pleasure. Beth was in trouble. He was here for her and for his other friends. The *mandala* burned over his heart and inside it.

Rob breathed deeply and exhaled slowly. He watched the little island like he was looking through the scope of a sniper rifle. Inside, the *mandala* showed him the mysterious lights of his being, and as he watched they began to shine more brightly.

In his own lights he saw Bobbi's lights reflected. He didn't turn to confirm the perception with his eyes. It was enough to change the course of a man's life. He thought, *How long have I lived and never seen this before?*

His life was asking something of him: not defense, not attack, but *awareness.*

The external light began to change on the little island; it grew brighter like candles in the chandeliers of the great hall hoisted above the king and queen of the Fae. But this was a human-shaped light the color of roses. In its center he saw a woman wearing a simple white garment.

Rob held his peace and watched the island from inside the indestructible tree of lights that had been lit in his unimaginable first creation.

–

For Beth the trip with the Lady from *aside* in time and space (wherever they'd been) to here (wherever *here* was) was the work of a paradoxical slow instant. This travel employed the pathways of early sexual arousal. At first it was merely pleasant, but the tide of desire would soon flood her. There was no hurry; there was enough time to desire and to be desired, to give pleasure and to accept it.

Beth had no sense of her body condensing out of mist into solidity; that's what others saw. The Lady taught her a paradox: her body mattered infinitely and mattered not at all. The Lady embodied the light of erotic love between man and woman or the love between woman and woman or man and man; bodies were incidental. That light had the pink-rose color of a bridal bouquet or of the flesh inside Beth's mouth.

In these ceremonies Beth received worship on behalf of the Lady and let the Lady touch her devotees through Beth's naked body. Worshipers waded through the shallow water to her simple ceremonial island and into her complex embrace.

Tonight something was different.

Inside herself where the Lady's power had fixed her attention Beth saw reflected lights of a different frequency than the worshipers'. There were arrays of the strange lights in two different parts of the cave. Who had come to the ceremony with *clear* light shining through their flesh?

And why did she feel she knew one of them?

—

A woman's form appeared lying alone in the sand of the little island. She wore a robe that left her arms bare. Rob knew instantly whose body it was. He had dreamed only of her while he was king of the Fae and able to swive with Moira his lovely consort and with any fae woman who took his fancy. For the ranks of the Fae had yet to reach full strength, and whose green light-seed was more puissant than that which shone through him who ruled the fae-road?

The woman looked like Beth, but not as he remembered her. King Robert had spent time in the company of the Morrigna, powerful ancient creatures whose being was sunk so deep in the fae condition that there was no telling where Morrigan ended and fae-path began. Beth was not entirely Beth. Another entity shone through her, perhaps with Beth's consent.

Beth! He waded into the shallow salt water.

—

On the islet the woman slowly sat up on one elbow. She looked at the man approaching through the water. His face looked familiar. She had not been in her ordinary mind since her first meeting with the Lady.

The Lady, fully present to Beth and always in her mind, looked out Beth's eyes. This man was different from those who worshiped her in the body of her priestess. Worshipers, male or female, entered an exalted state as they approached theophany. This man saw past the Lady's aspect to the human person she'd taken as her earthly vehicle.

Still, love was love. And was she not love's goddess? The Lady felt the approach of a great conjunction where distant stars align and things happen on Earth for the first time. Even a goddess can be curious; the source of her own being was hidden from her.

She spoke in Beth's mind: BE NAKED FOR THIS MAN, DAUGHTER. THOU ART FAIR. BLESS HIM WITH THE SIGHT OF THEE.

Beth's social inhibitions were asleep next to the memory of her ordinary life. She got gracefully to her feet and let the white garment fall to the sand.

From the other side of the water came an intake of breath from the worshipers: *Oh!* What the Lady did to Beth's aspect made it impossible to look away from her.

The man in the wet robe held Beth's gaze calmly. He walked out of the water and stood on the sandy island facing her.

His smile was wide and genuine. "Hello, Beth. Are you well?"

Beth didn't understand the question. She didn't understand why the man she almost recognized called her "Beth." The proper form of address these days was "my lady." As the Lady's earthly vehicle, Beth no longer needed the name she'd grown up with. Her lips parted to answer the worshiper's question, but no words came.

Rob saw her blank expression and shook his head. "You don't remember me." King Robert knew the volatility of fae memory. Queen Moira, for example, claimed to remember little of her life on Earth. She also claimed to remember other lives in which she and her Irish ancestors fought alongside the Fae and went to walk around the worlds with them forever. Rob had lost all interest in Moira's game. It was a relief to sleep apart from her.

But Beth didn't seem to be playing a game or salving her guilty conscience with denial and forgetfulness. Rob had never stopped wanting her. There was unfinished business between them.

Rob said, "Do you remember our child, Beth?"

Her mouth opened in a silent *Oh!* Rob's body responded to her beauty; he ignored his need.

Before she could rebuild the crumbling wall around her memory, he said, "I spent a year among the Fae looking for our son, but I never found him. I wish I could give you better news."

Her gaze sharpened. "I'd forgotten," she said. "I forgot all of that. I forgot you. I forgot we were together. I even forgot that I married somebody else." She looked down at her body, but made no move to cover herself again, what would be the point, he'd seen everything she had, kissed it, said he loved it all.

She said, *"Bobby."* A simple acknowledgment of all they'd been to each other. He smiled. "Be naked with me. I shouldn't be the only one with my ass hanging out here."

Rob was out of his robe in seconds. Before this went any further, he had things to say. "I was with Moira all year. We had dozens of Fae children together, if that matters to you. I've left her now, Beth. It's you I want. It's always been you."

She understood. "I got married, too. Andrew and I tried to have children, but it didn't happen. Something wasn't right between us. Hell, lots of things were wrong between us." She shook her head, frustrated by the volume of unhappy memories thronging back to disturb the separate peace she lived in with the Lady. She remembered why she'd left Texas. "I flew out to California to see Janjan. Then somehow I ended up here." Details were moored in fog.

"I've seen Janjan," he said. "She says you're in danger here."

Beth stepped close and threw her arms around Rob. His arms went around her like they belonged there.

"I'm in danger everywhere," she said. "Just hold me, okay?"

Was she still married? Rob had a nineteenth-century reluctance to enter an affair with a married woman, no matter how much he loved her. For the moment it was easy enough to hold her and let her hold him. That was something they both wanted. Who could damn him for giving this chaste comfort to someone, even if she was married? Sure, they were naked and he was erect, couldn't help it, but still.

—

Bobbi knew she was the canary and Aphrodite's grotto was the coal mine.

Around her, robed worshipers entered an altered mental state. They swayed to and fro. The singers intoned their hymn of invocation again and again, part song and part chant. The others joined in. Call and response, call and response.

Out on the little island, lean, sinewy, naked Rob embraced tall, thin, beautiful, blonde Beth. Bobbi identified with Rob. Jesus, she thought, no wonder Janjan has sexual feelings for Beth. Who wouldn't?

Bobbi saw a heightened state in Beth she'd seen in others: that they were fair and true and hovering on the brink of becoming extraordinary. Bobbi never knew if this was illusion projected by youth or if it was the first light of a day that never dawned before marriage, children, jealousy, work, trouble, and the thousandfold distractions of Earth enshrouded it. If it was only fertility Bobbi had seen through the eyes of her own desire, the world of Earth women was crueler than she'd known.

Unlike elves, earthlings are alone in their hearts and minds. Beth wasn't alone; *someone* was very much with her, watching with benign and proprietary interest. Bobbi kept her thoughts quietly centered and used peripheral mental vision to watch what happened.

There was Rob with his inner energy centers all lit up.

There was Beth whose energy would have pulsed in harmony with Rob's had *someone* not prevented it. Beth's spirit was masked by the mysterious presence of another watcher. *Someone* ancient, elemental, and powerful, but benevolent.

There was Janjan. Bobbi felt the touch of her mind like a sunrise or a smile, all compassion. Someday I'll be *spoken for*, Bobbi thought deep inside herself. Someday I'll teach people the way she teaches me.

There was the guard with something wrong in him. He lived in a tunnel of darkness, his thoughts bounded by the Dark Path. The guard's mind went from wary hypervigilance to wordless yearning, like a lonely dog who whimpers as he hears his master opening the door.

Who had he summoned?

Bobbi's face and demeanor remained unchanged as she entered fighting mind, ready for anything.

A static charge built in the air of the grotto. In the next world over there was no fear, but on Earth perfect love was seldom found to cast fear out.

Bobbi observed the faces of the women on either side of her. A middle-aged woman's features smoothed until she looked young. A plain young woman's face glowed with gratified desire. Around Beth, women and men too entered orgasmic breathing. Pleasure transformed them as breath soughed in and out of the body's center of gravity in the belly.

Bobbi wasn't immune to the spell of desire that filled the cave. It lit her up and filled her with yearning that focused on the shining woman who stood naked on the islet surrounded by shallow water.

Janjan had taught Bobbi something about desire, something that let her stand aside from her loins and her breasts and her throat and simply observe. Sex is the tune, but I'm the instrument, she thought. If there's beauty in me, it's nothing I created, nothing I can grasp and keep, nothing I can lose.

Looking discreetly around, Bobbi saw that the other people in the cave, swaying with desire, believed that they had been given something they were lacking. That they needed to worship or be worshiped to deserve to live in beauty.

And behind that, Bobbi discerned the dark intent of those who had brought this once-innocent secret ceremony back into the world.

37

We Have Met the Enemy *(Janjan)*

Floating just outside my body, I felt Bobbi's unease. I felt Rob's hope.

I felt lost along with Beth. Her body might have returned, but she was as far from Earth as she was from ordinary thought and feeling. She reached out to Rob while her deeper self wandered wrapped in cloud.

Spirals of cloud. The whirlwind. The double helix of DNA. The female mystery that human bodies wander through into life after life on Earth. This was the mystery the Children of Venus had come to worship.

A world away, Aimee had resonated to the power of what—*who*—had come to Odiorne Point:

I want to be the cynosure of all eyes. I know it's egotistical, stupid, and wrong. Something in me wants to be the queen of love and beauty. I'm talking about walking naked into the ocean while a whole city watches with their mouths open because they all desire me. I'm talking about the Judgment of Paris, where a group of women undress for a man, we all stand before him, and he judges me *the fairest.*

Coming Earth events cast shadows into the nonlinear time of the next world over. I'd seen what Aimee was getting at: being wanted and desired.

Not merely worthy, but deserving of admiration: *commanding* everyone's attention.

And why did she say it was wrong? The elves teach that judgment and love can't be reconciled. Love gives us peace; judgment leads to sorrow. Myth blames the very personal sexual Judgment of Paris for starting the Trojan War.

Speaking of war. Five men in boots and gray camouflage shouldered their way through the crowd of white-robed worshipers in the concrete cave. The strangers converged on the little island where naked Rob and Beth held each other. Two drew pistols from belt holsters and took aim at my friends.

Bobbi stood frozen among the other celebrants.

In through the river channel flew an abstract black-and-gold statue, hovering just above the salt water. Bobbi's first impression resolved itself into the familiar pale, moveless face of the Walloon. The master of Materialist Magician masters was dressed in black. He rode upon the golden statue of a screaming man, an obscene parody of the sitting Buddha.

I saw what Bobbi saw; she knew what I knew: the Walloon's body wasn't ordinary flesh and blood.

The Walloon's vehicle, the thing that looked like a statue, was *alive* in some way we knew nothing about. That dreadful gold sculpture contained a living soul. Horror battered Bobbi's consciousness.

That wasn't the worst of it.

The statue-creature wasn't solid gold all the way through. From inside it came a beam of radiation deadly as nuclear fallout. Everyone who stayed in that cave was going to die.

Ionizing radiation presents an acute problem to us. We can heal its effects on our own bodies, but that makes it hard to help anybody else. Helping people is why we come here.

Natural radiation is bad enough. The sorcerer's attack was deliberate: *dark magic from the ancient world.*

One second I was getting real-time updates from Bobbi at Odiorne Point. The next second she was standing next to me in the barn apartment, dressed in a white ceremonial robe, gasping, shaking, and crying. It took all her willpower to stay with me on Earth.

I snapped back into my body, kind of a shock.

I'll understand if you go home, I told Bobbi. We aren't all alike and nobody's perfect, whatever that even means.

Bobbi said she'd stay in the apartment unless our enemies attacked her. She was too shaky to fight. Earth was worse than she'd known. She'd done her best, the poor kid.

I don't know if I'll be able to do more than you did, I told her, *but I have to do what I can.*

I traveled to Odiorne Point in a flash of thought. Two sturdy women guarded the entrance to the tunnels. They were surprised to see me just *appear.* But it was dark; they told themselves I'd approached too quietly to be heard.

I took charge. "I need you to get everybody out of there," I told the women. "There's no time to fuck around. Go do it *now.*" I spoke quietly with my voice pitched low. The guards assumed I was somebody important in their chain of command. Who else would dare order them around?

One of the guards started hissing at worshipers and pulling them out the door from the back of the cave. The other guard forced her way through the crowd and began pushing everyone away from the water and toward the exit.

I have to do what I can. I popped into the middle of the little islet surrounded by salt water. Rob was still holding Beth. The armed men were walking out of the water. They didn't shoot. They'd been ordered to capture, not kill.

First, the two men with pistols drawn. They didn't expect to see someone appear in front of them. Moving quickly, I disarmed them and put them on the ground, unconscious, *one, two.* Whispering shining Elvish spells, I took down the other three guys before they got their weapons out, *three, four, five.* Yes, I am a fast woman.

Those guys weren't the main threat.

The screaming gold statue's attention turned my way. I understood how Bobbi got squeezed out of here. Toxic magical intent launched a shrieking attack on the settlements of light underlying my physical body while radiation attacked the cellular level. This felt oddly *impersonal;* there was no anger in it.

As if it weighed no more than a leaf, the statue drifted slowly, slowly across the incoming water. It flew *backwards*. The Walloon stood up on the statue's solid-gold thighs and steadied himself with one hand on the shining skull head like someone riding a golden BMX bicycle. The gold mummy was the Walloon's chariot of war, bristling with magical radioactive javelins.

The Walloon's unnaturally smooth face was twisted with rage—at me. Now *this* felt personal.

Poor Beth. She'd been cast in a melodrama staged for me and King Robert—and maybe Jackson, too. The Walloon's vengeance comeback tour at Odiorne Point, tonight only.

Last year I'd stood up against the worst Louis and his guardian demon could do. The screaming gold statue made me sicker than the demon had.

I couldn't stay here long. I had to act.

What should I do?

The Walloon had a body that looked human but wasn't. Magic aside, a physical fight with Louis alone would take more time than I had.

Louis wasn't alone.

Intuition provided no good news. The statue had been a long time gone from humanity. I couldn't challenge it directly. The spirit inside it felt male, but I had nothing he wanted. He was free of the Fallen; speaking the Unfallen Tongue wouldn't touch him.

I saw the shadow of Louis' demon. It watched events unfold and took no action.

Sunk deep in fighting mind, I retreated to the center of the sandy islet. Everything around me moved in slow motion because my body and mind moved so quickly. Rob kept one arm around Beth. Slowly they turned to face me.

Rob's face showed grief and determination. He was glad to see me. He was sad we were going to die in battle.

Beth's face was vague with confusion. She knew who Rob was, knew it deep in her body. Her memory of me was clouded and set aside.

What masked Beth's memory was the Old God who Beth had somehow incarnated. Beth had let something far older than herself manifest through her. She was bound to it by magic and by her own free will. Unbinding her would also take more time than I had. At least the Old God was shielding Beth and Rob from the statue's radiation attack.

Do what you can moment by moment.

I spoke to Rob's mind in Elvish so there would be no mistaking my meaning: *We're out of time, brother. Will you come home to the next world over with me?*

His answer (in English) was immediate: *I won't leave Beth. I came here for her. I love her.*

When the time comes, put your mind in your mandala *and ask for help,* I thought. *One of us will come for you.* I meant the elves.

I will, Janjan.

I turned to Beth. Rob stood on her left with one arm around her shoulders. I stood on her other side with one arm around her waist.

The sorcerer continued screaming in my mind, in everybody's minds, without pause for breath. It drifted in the air beaming radiation directly at me. The fallen men in camouflage were getting a lethal dose. I couldn't help them.

Across the water, the guards were evacuating the grotto like I'd told them to. Worshipers were leaving quickly. The ecstatic state kept them from panicking.

The Walloon stepped off his solid gold chariot. He looked unhappy and inclined to do something about it. I had three seconds before I had to fight or flee.

"Hi, Beth," I said. On impulse, I leaned in and kissed her neck. I mean, who doesn't like having her neck kissed?

The kiss half-awakened my beautiful naked friend's dreaming mind.

"Janjan!" she said.

She remembered the cold night I'd spent in her bed kissing her neck and everything else and happily allowing her to kiss me back. *The heart has reasons that reason cannot know.* The body has a mind of its own.

But there was somebody else in the grotto with us, someone I couldn't see. That other being, powerful, more-than-human, had laid claim to Beth and wouldn't let me draw her away. Clouds, lit from within, gathered and diffused muted rosy light through Beth's mind.

I tightened my hold on Beth's supple waist and reached out my mind to offer her safe passage to the next world over.

The Walloon advanced on us.

The last worshipers straggled out the door.

The statue screamed and screamed. My mind fogged. I grew weaker.

Rob took his arm off Beth's waist to protect us from the Walloon with his empty hands. Greater love hath no man.

The Old God reclaimed Beth's body and mind, pulling her away from Odiorne Point in a long instant. Because I was holding on to the goddess' bondservant, I went where she went.

Where they went together: *aside* in time and space.

38

The King of the Fae and the Master of Masters

Janjan blurred across Rob's vision. In seconds she danced through five uniformed men and left them alive and unconscious on the ground.

Another enemy approached, a man riding on a metal sculpture. Rob let go of Beth's bare waist to defend her with his bare fists.

Janjan spoke to Beth, kissed her—and disappeared with her.

Rob had gotten used to sudden appearances and disappearances. Ruling Fae and befriending elves had changed his ideas about what was possible.

Still, his heart sank. Beth remembered me, he thought. She recognized Janjan and then she was gone again. They're both gone. Maybe Janjan's saving her?

Suddenly too weak to stay on his feet, sweating and overcome with nausea, he dropped to his knees in the sand.

The screaming gold statue lifted off the islet and flew out an open door. Sneering, the Walloon advanced on Rob. Around him, armed men struggled to their feet and obeyed the Walloon's orders.

They handcuffed Rob's hands behind his back and led him, unresisting, through the shallow water, out of the amphitheater, and down winding concrete corridors to a cell. They uncuffed him and shoved him inside.

The Walloon stood in the cell door studying his captive in the light from the hallway. "I look forward to a long conversation with you later," he said. "We have much to discuss."

Rob studied his captor. Was the Walloon's face *blue?* "I didn't recognize you at first. You look different since I shot that arrow through your head on the fae-road last year."

"A capital crime for which you shall answer," said the Walloon. "Perhaps a small glass of molten hell as apéritif, followed by pertinent parts of yourself as entrée. Then I think a Fallen soufflé." He smirked at his own wit.

"The Morrigna crowned me king of the Fae. Harm me and you'll answer to them."

"Hah! The Nightmare Queens have no power here. They will kneel before me once again."

Piqued, Louis slammed the door and threw the bolt.

Rob felt his way around the dark cell. He'd seen a pit toilet in one corner; he could still smell it. A low steel bunk was cemented into one wall. He sat on the bunk and waited patiently for whatever would happen. He felt weak, but the nausea ebbed a bit. He had no clothes, but it was warm here.

Eventually, fluorescent lights flickered on above his head. Three men in camouflage uniforms came in and ordered him to his feet. Two of them held his arms while the third injected something into a vein on the inside of his elbow.

Rob didn't resist the needle. The men gave him another robe to wear. He put it on over his head.

He figured Janjan had gone to save Beth; he was content. Beth's safety was the main thing.

He remembered the prayer he said when he faced down the Walloon and the Morrigna in the fae castle. Back when the Walloon's evil had poisoned the whole fae-path, all the Fae died, and their *light of other days* sank into the living road. Rob prayed as he had in the Second World War: *God help us.* He knew whose creature the Walloon was. *Deliver us from evil.*

He began to feel lightheaded. His thoughts frayed and the prayer blew away with them. The uniformed men kept him on his feet and led him away.

Rob had been blessed with rugged good health since his poverty-stricken nineteenth-century childhood. His interludes of walking with the Fae and his year of ruling them were naturally free of illness. The drugs Louis' men injected into his arm brought back the memory of a high fever. He could neither awaken fully nor slip into unconsciousness. He forgot what had happened in the amphitheater. He was dizzy, weak, and feverish. His body was burned. Large areas of his legs and chest ached right down to the bone.

His enemies gave him other injections as well, augmenting his half-conscious torment. They were treating his radiation sickness to keep him alive until Master Louis could extract the information he wanted and savor his revenge.

From New Hampshire they drove Rob south in a white windowless tradesman's van. He lay on a child's thin mattress in a compartment concealed from the rear doors by hinged shelves for tools and supplies. Every two hours they stopped the van and one of his captors, now wearing work clothes, gave Rob another injection to send him spiraling away from lucidity. The trip was a succession of linear movements that seemed to last forever. A faint smell of diesel fuel made his nausea worse.

This van had a smoother ride than the Army troop carriers Rob remembered from the European Theater. The sensations of movement changed as the van left the loud constant whoosh of a major highway for quieter side roads. The sun came up and the van got hotter. There was nothing to do but lie there and think thoughts that refused to cohere.

Movement stopped. Time for another injection? Rob was thoroughly sick of them. Both front van doors opened. The vehicle jostled as the driver and his assistant got out and slammed their doors.

The rear doors opened. The shelves swung aside. Rob was grateful to see daylight, even if it made his eyes water.

One of the men said, "You still alive in there?"

Rob couldn't find words to answer with. The best he could do was clear his throat. His mouth was terribly dry.

"Get out here," said the other man, not unkindly.

Feverish and weak, Rob labored to get to his knees and crawl forward. The two men reached in, grabbed his arms, and helped him get his feet on the ground.

Wherever they were was hotter and far more humid than New Hampshire. The sky was overcast and yellowish like a thunderstorm was on the way.

Next to the van was a wall that went up and up. A huge house. There was an open door in the wall. His captors led Rob out of jaundiced tropical light into cool darkness.

They escorted him through a maze of low-lit corridors to a door with a lock on the outside. Rob knew a cell when he saw one. One man opened the door, and turned on the lights while his other guard held Rob's arm. He was too weak to run. He had no idea where he might run to.

The windowless room had a single bed with a stack of clothes on it, a bedside hospital table, and a tiny adjoining bathroom. On the table sat a plastic bottle of water and a meal replacement drink, also in a plastic container.

"Okay, Robert," said one of his captors, "you're going to want to sleep. Don't do that right away. Go take a shower, put on some clean clothes, and drink those all up." He pointed to the drinks.

"Okay. Thanks," Rob said.

The other guard said, "Master Louis is sending someone to talk to you. I recommend you tell him everything he wants to know." He waved one hand at the little prison cell. "We have much worse places to put people who refuse to get with the program, you know what I'm saying to you?"

Rob nodded. He understood completely. He was a prisoner in a secret war. He was at the mercy of people who had no mercy.

He had to get Beth back from whoever had taken her. The mission was incomplete.

The men left, locking the door behind them. As directed, Rob showered, put on the clean clothes, and drank what they'd left for him. He was terribly thirsty. The nutrition drink tasted vile, but the water washed the aftertaste away. He was brushing his teeth and thinking how nice sleep would feel, when someone knocked on the door.

An older man he didn't know unbolted the door. An armed younger man stood out in the corridor to discourage an escape attempt.

The heavyset man pushed a wheeled office chair into the room ahead of him and shut the door behind him. He sat in the chair and pointed firmly at the bed. Rob sat down.

The guy looked to be in his fifties, graying hair cut short, deep-set eyes. To Rob's eye he looked unhealthy, despite his rigid military bearing.

The man examined Rob closely, looked him up and down, demonstrating that Rob was completely in his power.

Finally he spoke. "Getting along all right?" Rob heard some sort of foreign accent.

"Yes, sir," Rob said. "Thank you."

"My name is Darnand," said the man. "*Sturm...* er, *Major* Darnand. I am here to ask you questions. Do you agree to answer them frankly?"

As a soldier in a real war, Rob would have refused to give Darnand anything but name, rank, and serial number. He had no code of conduct to guide him here, only his own judgment and the *mandala* in his chest. He felt weak and sick, but he wasn't going to hurt his friends.

"What would you like to know, Major?"

39

Old School *(Janjan)*

O body swayed to music, O brightening glance,
How can we know the dancer from the dance?
- (W.B. Yeats, "Among School Children")

Being an elf isn't all good news.

Yes, you can travel instantly from place to place, within the limits of your acquaintance and experience. If you have a teacher like Daniel Ryun, you can even travel outside your body if you dare. But learning to do these things makes it possible for you to be *pulled aside* into a place you've never seen or imagined, and would rather not go.

This happened to Jean-Paul Herold a few years back. When he rescued Aimee and her spouse Magdalena from the Mad King of Agharti, he got *pulled aside* deep into the spacetime of the World Mountain.

Now it was my turn.

The energies in play were enormous, irresistible. There really are more things in heaven and earth than we ever dream of.

The trip from Odiorne Point happened in an instant that felt a lot longer than the time it takes to inhale and exhale. The place I'd left had been warm enough by coastal New Hampshire standards. This place was warmer still, dense with tropical humidity, fragrant with flowers and fruit trees.

Like Beth's, my perceptions were clouded. On the surface, I had a pleasant illusion of knowing who I was and where I'd been, but my deeper self had entered strange halls of desire where every breath brought pleasure.

I was going to meet my lover.

Who *was* this lover? It never occurred to me to wonder. The fact that I was married and *spoken for* was clouded. The one essential person whose love would complete me was someone I had somehow always known, but had yet to meet.

This paradoxical meeting would be soon.

Another cloudy area was my connection to Jackson and to other elves. I was separated from *something* vital, but I didn't know what.

I felt the aftereffects of a battle I'd forgotten. I did a quick inventory. Dark red burns stretched from my throat to my ladygarden. I watched my body heal. The burns turned back to golden skin. Nausea vanished.

The healing generated more heat in this hot, humid place. I dropped my clothes in the sand. God, that felt good. I've never been shy; I had nothing to be ashamed of.

Warm sand kissed my bare feet. Warm air embraced me. Someone even warmer was coming to meet me.

But it was naked Beth I saw walking gracefully toward me across the sand. Her eyes looked at me in something like love, but I wasn't fooled. It wasn't *just* Beth looking out of those blue eyes.

My lover was hiding *behind* Beth.

My vision was as cloudy as my thoughts. I shook my head to clear it.

"Beth?" I said.

Beth's lips parted, but she didn't speak. She wanted to kiss me. I wouldn't have minded that, but...

Oh, yeah, *Beth is married,* I remembered. So am I.

Jackson! I thought.

No answer came, not in this place *aside* from everything I knew.

Instead of Jackson's familiar, loving thoughts, another mind spoke in mine with overwhelming force:

WHY HAVE YOU COME FROM YOUR WORLD TO MY BOWER?

I couldn't answer. My thoughts wobbled from the impact. (Had someone warned me about this?) It wasn't an attack. The words were an irresistible phenomenon that rose from my own depths. The thought-voice was female all the way down, further up and down than I could see. It—*she*—appeared to me through Beth in the form of a woman.

I shook my head again. Clarity eluded me. I needed to take *special measures*. I couldn't remember who'd told me that or what the special measures were.

All I could do was *inquire within* the shining lights of my own being where my life flowed like water, like electricity, inside the metes and bounds of my physical body and also outside it.

Somewhere within and without myself I saw a beautiful woman who was both inside Beth and outside her. *This* was the lover who was coming to meet me. *She knew me.* I didn't know her name, but I knew what she was. She was more than human. Old Gods are only human in appearance. She manifested here, but her true being lay elsewhere.

I collected my wits enough to answer. "I came here to help Beth. She's my friend."

The goddess who appeared to me in and through Beth's body and mind *stepped aside* from her, like Beth was a cape she was removing. She separated herself from Beth's side like she'd been hiding in Beth's rib cage. In the Genesis story, Eve is created out of Adam's rib while he sleeps. When I asked the angel of the borderlands about that story, he said, *It's all true.* The good angels don't lie; that doesn't mean we understand what they say.

Where there had been only one body, Beth's, now there were two. Beth stood naked and unsure, alone in her own human form next to the shining naked goddess.

Beth started swaying; she was out on her feet. I stepped forward to help, but the goddess held up one hand: *I got this.* Tenderly, she helped Beth lie down on the warm sand. The goddess stroked Beth's perfect body from cheek to breast, to belly, to thigh like they were lovers and she had every right to touch her. Beth smiled. Her eyes closed and she slept.

I was happy to see all anxiety gone from Beth's face. Separated from the goddess, she looked more like herself, but younger. She'd been born beautiful, but whatever power compelled the attention and made it impossible to look away from her belonged to the goddess.

The queen of love and beauty. Was it ... *Aimee* who'd said that?

She whom most men want and all women want to be. The deep power of desire beyond words, beyond the Earth, beyond all worlds.

The power of beauty women once exchanged for security and family and now trade for uncertain marriages and ungrateful children. None of that was the goddess' fault. She remained what she'd always been. She'd do what she'd always done for those who prayed to her and sacrificed at her altar. She was as real a force in the universe as gravity.

I looked into her beautiful eyes, brown, the color of rich soil. Long eyelashes and thick eyebrows, yum. I looked directly and hungrily, the way men stare at women they want. Her long hair was a darker gold than Beth's, the color of honey. She wore it braided and pinned up with flowers. I guess if you're a goddess, you can have fresh flowers whenever you want. Her breasts were full and high as a girl's with nipples and areolas larger than mine. Under my gaze her nipples grew hard; my own were erect and practically hurting me. I yearned for something I could put no name to.

What was *happening* here?

She was a few inches taller than me. Her arms, legs, and shoulders were strong and smooth. Her skin was lightly tanned all over. Her pubic hair was thick and blonde. And slightly wet.

My body entered the next stage of desire.

This was nothing like what the Morrigna had done on the fae-road last year. The goddess didn't alter her appearance to suit me. Whatever else she is, I thought, this is how she has always presented herself in human form. This is what healthy young women looked like in the ancient world.

To accommodate my human limitations, the goddess stepped down her communication from the overwhelming Old-God thought-barrage somebody *(Jerry and Leda!)* had told me about. Overtones of a wider realm of power in her voice said she was much more than the body that appeared before me.

She smiled and said in a human voice, "Hello, daughter. You are the first creature of the world next to Earth I have ever talked to." She spoke English, perhaps having learned it from Beth's mind and mine.

"My name is Janjan, ma'am," I said. "What should I call you?"

The question surprised her. "Surely you know who I am?"

Whom do men say that I am? I said, "We call your sort of beings Old Gods. I can guess who you are by how I feel standing face to face with you."

"Your folk have never worshiped in my temple." She smiled at this elvish waywardness. "You may call me *Cypris*, if you like. I am the Lady of Cyprus." She pronounced those words with a "K," not a "C."

"I'm honored, my Lady." Naked, I bobbed a little curtsey with one bare foot in front of the other, the way I once greeted Coran and Maeve, king and queen of the Fae.

The Lady inclined her head to acknowledge my gesture. She had more claim to nobility than the human kings and queens she'd known over the centuries.

My ladygarden was preparing itself for a night of carnal delight. She took an appreciative look in its general direction. "I see that you desire me."

I had to laugh at myself, always in search of the deepest, truest pleasure, whatever else was happening, whatever world I found myself in. "Who would *not* desire you?" I laughed aloud and felt the laughter in my loins. However strong my desire was, it wasn't going to have its way with me.

Not offended, the Lady laughed with me, and I saw that long before Jesus, it was she who'd been the joy of man's desiring. Then, more seriously, "What do you want of me?" She was eager to play her part in the great scheme of things. Like the Morrigna, the Lady *lived* her most essential self; nothing that happened to her, around her, or as a result of her could change her relation to it.

The day I left frozen Great Bog to go to the elves, I'd missed my father in a way I hadn't thought to do for years. I'd felt the piercing, bitter, painful sense of his loss in my heart: *Fucking mortality, anyway.* Another change had just rolled over me like a big wave, and the Lady saw it before I did. I was no longer the silly, slooty Earth girl I'd been before I became a woman of the next world over and left mortality behind.

I wanted the Lady, sure, but I had no desire to *be* her or to wield her power over others. I wanted something else more than I wanted her; I wanted it more than I wanted what her power could do for me. New knowledge of loss hit my heart. *Life is change and change sucks,* said

Richard Round's teacher Zenman—before he and poor Richard went looking for the doorway to the next world over. Perfect elf memory is a mixed blessing. It takes away all ability to deceive yourself.

I answered her question truthfully. "My Lady, I came here because my life is linked to Beth's as hers is now bound to yours. I came to help my friend. But I left other friends back on Earth in danger from an enemy with powers none of my folk have ever seen. Will you help us?"

The Lady stepped her communication back up to goddess mode and spoke in my mind:

LET US SHARE THOUGHTS, THEN. HUMAN SPEECH IS FOR LOVEPLAY, BUT TOO SLOW AND UNCERTAIN FOR DELIBERATION.

—

The Lady called it "deliberation," but it was loveplay, too. She couldn't help herself. The Old Gods are what they do and do what they are.

She woke Beth up gently and took us to school. The curriculum concerned the deepest secrets of womanhood.

I kept myself centered as best I could in the midst of all she did and revealed and all we did together. There were things I knew that the Lady did not. My knowledge shone with a steady light that had been lit back in the beginning of everything when, as the elves say, the One gave birth to the Many.

The Lady's origins were different from mine. When she recounted the myth of her birth, it pointed somewhere I'd never thought to look.

There's a way in which gender doesn't matter much. So the elves teach. Their lives demonstrate the truth of that teaching, but the elves are no longer from Earth.

On Earth gender matters very much indeed. So the Lady taught, and her immortal life demonstrated the truth of her teaching. The Lady was part of Earth in a way no mortal could ever be.

When you first go to the next world over, you remember most of the lives you've ever lived. I'd been born and reborn again and again, usually as a woman, but sometimes as a man. Usually on Earth, but not always.

In one life I'd been born to a human mother in the Other World of the nameless god and goddess. The god's nonhuman mind had touched me, still an embryo in my mother's womb, and made me into one of the Myrmidon warriors who served him and his mate. In that life, I'd had a penis *and* a vagina, manly muscles and womanly breasts. Until I was killed in battle at the end of that life, I had plenty of sex with other Myrmidons and with men and women, too.

I'd been born female in every rebirth after that one. I'd swived with men and women both, though I had occasionally married a man and had children by him.

In all the long ages, the Lady had been born only once in a cosmic cataclysm. It must have happened after the Big Bang of the universe's creation, right after the Earth was first formed.

It wasn't birth as human beings think about these things, a headfirst trip down the birth canal. Aphrodite shared with me a shattering memory of arising from the foam of her primal father's severed genitals. The image was vivid, appalling, incomprehensible, irrefutable. The Lady accepted this story without a second thought. She was born with many gifts, but reflection was not among them.

She had been given great powers. She used those powers to marry or swive with dozens of gods and hundreds of men. The Lady asserted her divine right to sleep with whoever took her fancy, for a night, a human lifetime, or forever.

We call these stories *myths*. I'd never thought they stood for anything *real*.

Anyway. What was left out of the stories I'd heard was how many *women* the ageless Lady had bedded in her long, long life. Sexual relations between women were accepted in the ancient world, but also ignored because no children could be born of them.

And speaking of children, the lady had given birth to many and then left them to be raised by others. Very liberated or very cold? Human categories didn't apply to her.

I was thinking her children bored her until she began, SURELY YOU HAVE HEARD OF MY SON…

I waited to hear more, but Cypris shook her head and left the thought unfinished. Even Old Gods can have thoughts that are too painful to think.

What could have happened to the goddess' son? I wasn't going to ask to hear a tale that caused her pain. Cypris, Beth, and I shared a rosy, highly-charged erotic bubble; I was determined not to bust it. Whether it was deliberation or loveplay, I needed us to continue.

Instead of telling me about the child who meant more to her than any other, she began a different story.

As the Lady spoke, I listened carefully to what she didn't think to think. Her past life was less of a concern to her than all my past lives were to me. I learned from all my lives and then let them go. The Lady had no need to learn or change. The secret hurts she carried never transformed her.

She was always and everywhere the same. I was different in every life I lived.

Elves ask "If you could have whatever you wanted, what would you want?" There's no one right answer.

Old Gods ask "Being who I am, why shouldn't I have what I want?" They plan, scheme, seduce, and fight to acquire whoever and whatever they set their hearts on.

My life's central question, distilled in my heart by the elvish *mandala* Leda had painted into my flesh and bone before I walked with the Fae, was: *What is my deepest, truest pleasure?*

The central question of the Lady's life was one she asked me with the full force of a mind distilled in the most ancient beginning, deep down in all the minds that would ever come to Earth:

BEING WHO I AM, WHY SHOULD I NOT TAKE YOU AS MY LOVER NOW?

Her question assumed I would have no objections.

Being who *I* am, I really didn't.

40

O, that this too too solid flesh would melt,
Thaw and resolve itself into a dew!
- (Shakespeare, *Hamlet*)

Everything went *almost* to plan. The elves walked into the trap.

Through Darnand's eyes Louis watched a female elf enter the Odiorne Point grotto. At the first sight of Master Gold she vanished from the amphitheater.

Then the Javorski bitch came to rescue her friend, the Old God's priestess; the elf whore was no match for Louis and Gold. She, too, fled Aphrodite's temple. Louis wanted the elves dead, but such were the fortunes of war. He had captured his enemy Robert des Fae.

Javorski tried to wrest her friend from the goddess; the elf and Aphrodite disappeared together. Was *the elf* now bound to the Old God as the priestess was? Perhaps both women would reappear when the Children of Venus next invoked the goddess.

The battle distracted Louis from his own predicament. Prolonged proximity to Gold's radiation would have killed the Walloon's organic body. His current physical form, made mostly of desert sand, still obeyed the laws of physics.

His hands had turned blue.

Radiation polarized the Walloon's atoms, changing his color. By the time Louis' men captured King Robert, the Walloon's visage was turning dark blue.

He saw irrational fear in the eyes of all who looked upon him. It was the same problem that had driven him to seek Gold's help, though less troublesome than a body of smoke. What should he do?

The Walloon's demon had stepped back from him. Louis had to think for himself. The Fallen never answered prayers. Demons *took* what they wanted in service to the One Will of the Claimant, who only spoke to human beings to mock and destroy them. The Fallen Archangel surely had plans of greater scope than he would ever reveal to the Materialist Magicians. The thought gave Louis no comfort. No one who has believed himself an *Übermensch* is happy to discover he is only one of the *Untermenschen*.

Abasing himself, the Walloon begged for clarification from his companion demon, the shadow creature whose feet could never touch the Earth. Instead of guidance, his mind received a withering stream of wordless, urine-stinking contempt. The Fallen had sent the Walloon to Gold. *Gold* would guide Louis now. It was death to question the Claimant's will.

The Walloon remembered the night Master Gold carried him to the Sisters of the Dark Path. While he met with Mother Mariah in the convent, Louis had left Gold communing with a blooming cottonwood. When he returned to Master Gold, Louis was too full of himself to accept the evidence of his senses. The tree had been healthy; now its trunk showed multiple cankers, its leaves were withered, and its branches had begun to droop.

Whatever the cottonwood might have told Master Gold, all the golden magus had to tell the tree was that its death was nigh.

What would Gold tell Louis, then? Was this alarming color change the first canker to appear in the course of his inevitable demise? He had no choice but to ask. To obey the demons, he had to commit himself to the ancient mage. To return to his mansion and savor Darnand's interrogation of the prisoner, he needed a body.

The Walloon met Gold in a quiet room in the depths of the tunnel complex. Having won the first battle, Louis thought it best to have Gold carry him away from any worshipers who might return—and away from the Order's unfortunate mercenaries, likely dying of radiation sickness. He bowed to the statue. The two communicated in flashes of thought.

Louis: I thank you for this victory over our opponents, Master Gold.

Gold: I had quite forgotten the joys of battle. I am in your debt, Master Louis. Your enemies are now my enemies. Do I perceive that becoming my companion has done you a mischief?

The Walloon found a switch and flicked on the lights. His reflection appeared in a stainless steel wall mirror. His face was the color of sapphire and his hair was darker still; this had frightened those who looked at him. And this, Louis now perceived, was the outward sign of an alarming inner condition. His flesh only looked solid. He was eroding from within.

All I need is a Phrygian cap, thought the Walloon indignantly, and I could be one of *les Schtroumpfs*. He meant the little blue cartoon characters known in English as The Smurfs.

Donning new clothes would not return the deep blue skin of his hands and face to its original pale European white. No magic he knew would restore his inner solidity.

Louis: I am forever in your debt for this solid flesh, Master Gold. That it was but a temporary return was a greater gift than I could have asked.

Gold: All flesh-and-blood bodies are fleeting, are they not? Perhaps we should return to Iram of the Pillars. My servants will help us assay a more permanent solution to this problem.

Louis could hardly decline. His cold demon masters spurned him. He saw the Fallen watching him and thought, *The lonely crowd.* All who served the Claimant had to discern his Will; they would be punished for guessing wrong.

—

Again the ancient magus carried the magician across the sky. Again the flight sewed ragged stitches of high-altitude travel in the air of Earth as Gold navigated by the stars and tunneled through the world's space-time fabric.

Once Gold flew so high that Louis became dizzy from hypoxia. Gold, who hadn't worried about human limitations for centuries, apologized and took pains to fly at a lower altitude.

—

In the Nameless City, Gold's servants made Louis comfortable in a windowless temple chamber. Light reached the stone-walled room after passing through the ruined front door down sand-covered stone hallways. Louis sat on sand so soft that he needed neither chair nor bed. Primitive accommodations were no affront to his dignity. If the inner shifting continued, the sand that embodied his spirit would simply fall out of his hiking clothes and rejoin the sand on the floor. What then?

For years the Fallen had kept Louis alive and vigorous in a magically-enhanced body that looked no older than late middle age. Louis had been content. He had always sought power rather than physical gratification. Leading the Order in this troubled age required all his time and attention.

With unwelcome time to think, he saw old causes and preoccupations shift and blow away as the *simoom* wind swept through his interior. Without his dedication to the Claimant's glorious revolution, what was the meaning of his long life and years of struggle? He could not let it all disperse. Could not!

His imagination had withered when he embraced perfect possession by the Fallen. Yet he fancied his new internal organs were flaking away. Heart, liver, lungs, and the rest all blew in storms of fine sand inside the solitary indigo mountain of his exterior.

Lust for revenge had supplanted the Walloon's sex drive. The elves Javorski and Jackson had brought him to this pass. The Elf Friend Robert des Fae had put a clothyard shaft through Louis' head, but had not killed him (thanks be to the Fallen Archangel). Louis would see his enemies suffer the torments of the damned. He would savor their agonies.

First. Darnand would extract actionable intelligence from their captive and the Walloon would dismember King Robert. The elves would seek to prevent this. Gold's directed radiation was the perfect weapon: the Javorski *putain* would die.

Next. Louis and Gold would destroy the remaining networks of Elf Friends on Earth. How could mere human beings resist them?

And then? They would invade the fae-road and conquer the Morrigna. The Order would plunder all the riches of the human worlds.

In time, worship of the goddess the Greeks called Aphrodite would subvert all worship of the High Enemy in this degenerate Western world. How right Mother Mariah had been! Faithless Western men would follow their faithless women like dogs sniffing after bitches, even as the West fell to attacks from hordes of self-righteous Middle-Eastern fanatics. As more unstable countries acquired nuclear weapons, the Order's dream of global nuclear war came closer to realization.

As a nuclear weapon himself, Master Gold was the Walloon's perfect ally.

—

Gold spent an hour conferring with his servant-priests in an archaic dialect no longer spoken outside the Empty Quarter. Louis was not required to attend, sparing Gold the trouble of translating.

Eventually, Gold floated back to the sand-floored chamber where Louis sat.

Gold: You are well, Master Louis?

Louis: Not well, Master Gold, and yet I endure. I think this body will not long cohere in its current balance.

Gold: I can of course easily restore your body's equilibrium. Perhaps after that you would welcome a *permanent* solution to this difficulty. Unless you *wish* to enter *the House of Dust where the dead drink dirt and eat stone, where they wear feathers like birds, where no light ever invades their everlasting darkness, where the door and the lock of Hell is coated with thick dust?*

Was Gold mocking him? Babylonian Hell sounded better than the burning torment Louis experienced among the Fallen. Still, the Walloon was no fool. He knew what Gold was proposing.

Louis: Are you offering the same immortality *you* enjoy, Master Gold? I have no knowledge to make me worthy of this honor.

Gold: An influx of knowledge is part of the transformation. We will have centuries together for me to teach you all I know, once you are preserved forever in your body of gold. All the powers I have acquired, you too will gain as time passes into irrelevance.

Louis listened numbly as Gold explained how his body would be made everlasting and protected by "the metal of invisible death," some sort of nuclear material. He had always left science to the materialist side of the Materialist Magician confederacy. How would Gold's followers find such a thing in this infinite, barren desert? Irrelevant. Why lie to a powerless inferior?

How would the transformation be effected?

First a wax sculpture would be created around Louis' naked body. (He couldn't help staring at Gold's lap where only a small lump remained of the ancient sorcerer's penis and testicles. Whether or not he uses his genitals for anything, a man is reluctant to bid them farewell.) Hollow reeds up the Walloon's nostrils would allow him to breathe through the wax that covered him. Once the wax sculpture dried hard, molten gold would be poured into a wax cup at the crown of Louis' head. The wax around his body would contain the burning metal as it dissolved and replaced the human flesh and bone inside the mould.

Gold would guide Louis' mind in the magical use of the body's death throes to animate his new immortal body. Gold would lead his acolytes in chanting the ancient spells.

Gold: Agony is nothing to fear. I am living evidence of that truth.

The Walloon searched the statue's empty eye sockets to discern if Gold was trying to deceive him. Would Louis simply die a tortured death for nothing?

I am the last of my order, Gold had said at their first meeting. *Those who helped me assume the form you see before you left Earth not long after my transformation, and their minds were lost to me. The magic my order wrought was of a kind separate from the High God and also separate from Iblis and the* djinn *who defied that god—from a time before the Earth changed. Within this body of gold is the last place in all the human worlds that older, stronger power exists.*

Gold had failed to restore Louis' body permanently. Was he *experimenting* on Louis for amusement?

More to the point, if Gold's "older, stronger power" existed only within the statue, why would he share it with Louis? Sharing power was anathema to the Order. *How* Gold would do such a thing was beyond any learning Louis possessed.

How far could he trust the ancient sorcerer? Gold said he wanted Louis as his companion, though the body Gold magicked up had proved only slightly more durable than human flesh. Had the magus had gone insane during long centuries of isolation? Did Gold seek some occult pleasure from torturing Louis to death with molten metal? (Louis calculated it would take two or three million Euros to fill his body with gold. Not counting the cost of whatever radioactive source material would become his core.)

And how would the death metal get into his body? Would he have to *swallow* it? Would it be somehow *forced* down the burnt-out channel from his head through his chest, ultimately to repose in his gut?

He was afraid to ask. Gold would tell him.

Fearful speculation accelerated the sandstorms that scoured his insides, wearing away the physical wall around Louis' spirit.

Gold *had* helped Louis attack the Elf Friends. It was *Gold* who reminded Louis about the Old Gods. *Gold* had helped him lure the elves to Odiorne Point where the goddess appeared. Gold had accepted the Walloon's enemies as his own.

Cui bono? What would Gold gain from helping Louis join him in a body of gold? *Purpose and companionship.*

Louis found himself reinvigorated by the threat to his survival. He reproached himself for leaving the interrogation of King Robert in Darnand's hands without monitoring his subordinate.

Louis: If you could stabilize my body for the time being, I will be better able to consider your generous offer of immortality. I only hesitate because my human followers are used to my .... more ordinary human appearance. It will take time to prepare the Order of Materialist Magicians for a dramatic change in their leader.

Gold: [An inner smile] Of course!

41

Bananarama Sings "Venus" *(Janjan)*

And it seemed she was like the sea, nothing but dark waves rising and heaving, heaving with a great swell, so that slowly her whole darkness was in motion, and she was Ocean rolling its dark, dumb mass.
- (D.H. Lawrence, *Lady Chatterley's Lover*)

Like I said, Cypris took me to school. Me *and* Beth. Beth had been at this school long enough to have learned a lot. She'd entered conscious, mature womanhood here in the Lady's bower. I'd grown up in the fields and forests of the next world over.

You may be expecting some sort of contemporary erotica here. Even if there was video of our lovemaking, you wouldn't see the important part, the experience we shared where our secret minds embraced. You wouldn't see the Lady, either. She shone with her own rose-colored light and neither sunlight nor moonlight had ever touched her. We displayed ourselves for no one's pleasure but each other's.

Beth and I had different ideas of where love and beauty come from. She'd never known a passion stronger than the one Cypris evoked. She'd never felt as lovely as she did under the golden weight of the goddess' gaze.

God is Love, the Church taught us. Beth turned that into *Love is God*, a mistake that's all too easy to make in the bedroom, or in the grotto of the goddess of love and beauty.

Only uncountable years of timeless nextworld time had taught me better.

Jerry August said that Old Gods look upon human beings with *affection*. To them we're lesser beings to be cherished as we cherish cats, dogs, and horses, whose lives are shorter and whose minds are dimmer than our own.

The Lady *loved* human beings whose bodies gave flesh to the abstract, hidden part of her that looked out her level brown eyes. She loved us without reservation or condescension. Beth and I loved Cypris in return— at least in the hot moment—as if she alone was what our eyes were made to look upon.

When the Lady touched me, my body fizzed and buzzed like bubbles breaking on the face of the waters. When I touched the Lady, she responded with exquisite sensitivity and profound gratitude: to be touched by those who desired her was what her human form was made for. Every kiss, every touch, made a profound difference to her.

For all the rosy lovelight she surrounded us with, Cypris also had a dark, irrational side. She never showed us what hid in that blind spot; we saw no petty spite or anger or old sadness.

I thought of the rosy light I'd seen where Aimee's mind that was hidden from her. This light had *prompted* me to strike Aimee *thus*, and not otherwise, to stroke her *here* but not there during our tryst at Odiorne Point.

It was an awkward time to ask if Cypris knew my friend Aimee.

Outside the dark place that was hidden from herself, the Lady recalled everything she had ever seen and done and had done to her. She never compared one moment with another or sought more than was contained in the blissful present. All her lovers, male or female, mortal or immortal, conventionally beautiful or objectively ugly, were loved equally for what she gave them and what they gave her. She felt no need to judge one against another.

The Lady was my first goddess. I was her first elf girl. We shared ourselves with each other and with Beth. We shared Beth with each other with great delight. Since the Lady and I communicated on the level just before thought, I saw Beth through Aphrodite's ancient eyes. Once an immortal goddess has seen you as beautiful, you might be forgiven for thinking your transitory beauty was the most important thing about you. You might mistakenly believe your essential worth was also fleeting. The Lady was the goddess of sex, not wisdom.

Thank God I could go home to Jackson in the next world over. After swiving with the Lady of Cyprus, no one on Earth could ever make me come like she did. And like Beth did, under the Lady's divine inspiration.

Again and again and again and again.

42

I Was Naked and You Clothed Me *(Janjan)*

First came the loveplay that was also deliberation. After the countless times Beth and the Lady and I came together, a decision came to us.

From her fragrant tropical bower aside in time and space, the Lady bore us back to the little islet in the man-made cave. It was different from elf-style travel. Elves operate according to natural law. The Lady came from *before* that law.

Cool darkness in the Odiorne Point tunnels. No scent of flowers here, only salt water, candle smoke, and fear. It was good that we were alone. I had to protect Beth and I was still shaky from our swiving.

Beth was physically shaky after swiving with the Lady, but she'd never been stronger inside. She knew who she was. Love cast out her old fear. It was thrilling to see her that way.

Beth and I were naked because it pleased the Lady to have us so. The Lady was naked with us. Sisterhood is powerful. We were all damp and glowing and languid with satisfaction. Thoughts are actions to the Old Gods, with no barrier between intention and, ahem, fulfillment.

The Lady had no more words to speak and no more thoughts to fill our minds. We'd said all we had to say with our bodies.

The Lady embraced Beth (they were the same height). They kissed deeply, deeply. The Lady gave Beth's forehead a farewell kiss.

How many times had Aphrodite done this, over how many centuries, with how many priestess-lovers?

My desire surged again, of course it did. The Lady embraced me (she was taller). We kissed deeply and sweetly. She kissed my forehead in farewell. I kissed her neck on both sides. I longed to say *I'll be your priestess*, but the call of the nextworld high country would have made a lie of the words.

Then the Lady was gone, leaving only her scent. Wildflowers and sweet, fresh punani, if you want to know.

I felt a familiar mind in mine. *Janjan? Are you okay?*

Bobbi! I'm fine and Beth's with me. Can you find us some clothes? We didn't need any where we were. Long story.

Of course I can. And oh boy! Bobbi was partially teasing me and genuinely excited about seeing me and Beth naked, the little sloot.

Beth and I waded to the concrete shore. The water was a foot deep and cold.

I didn't want to take naked, vulnerable Beth outside the tunnels. I didn't know how long we'd been absent from ordinary reality. I didn't detect anybody out there. I was worried that the bad guys might have posted distant sentries or snipers. Bobbi would warn us of danger.

Honestly, I wasn't quite myself. I felt aftershocks from all the Lady had done to me.

Bobbi showed up within the hour with loose beach cover-ups and armfuls of pants and tops and a handful of flip flops she'd found outside the big steel door. Most of the Venus worshipers had taken off barefoot, wearing their ceremonial robes.

"Something in this pile should fit," Bobbi said. She was trying not to stare at beautiful naked blonde Beth. Elves carry their own inner light; we can see in very low light, like cats. A few stray beams shone into the amphitheater from outside, all the way from the far side of the river. "You want me to find the lights?"

"Sure, thanks," I said. Bobbi quickly located the light switch. A row of fluorescent bulbs sparked into light above us.

I found some loose drawstring Capri pants that fit me, or close enough. What a stupid style. Me being short, the calf-length pants came down to my ankle bones. Beth, being elegant and skinny, kept searching till she found a pair of jeans and a sleeveless top. It was hard to find clothes that didn't stink of sweat. Were the Children of Venus dirty hippies, or what?

Anyway. Bobbi got an eyeful of Beth. Who says women aren't excited by visual stimuli? Beth saw Bobbi staring and grinned at her with sincere good nature and without embarrassment. I mean, Beth had just had *all* the sex—and with a goddess at that. *And* with an elf warrior maiden. That would be me.

Bobbi was looking for something in Beth; she didn't find it. She sent me a quick thought: *We need to talk.* I nodded agreement.

Bobbi was also perceptive enough to see that something had taken the edge off Beth's erotic appetite. Back to business, then. She told me. "Most of the radiation's gone, but not all of it. We need to get out of here."

This was still a bad place. "You're right," I said. "Beth, let's go, okay?"

Beth came along quietly. Not descending-into-shock quiet like when she half froze to death in Great Bog. This was a restful silence, like she'd awakened from a long sleep and was enjoying her thoughts. I left her to them. She deserved some peace.

We walked out of the cave into the quiet summer night. Nobody bothered us.

Bobbi's friend was parked on the coast road, waiting to give us a ride. Beth and I sat in the back seat. Bobbi sat up front and made chitchat with him. She didn't introduce us. Her friend was willing to risk his life for her, but he wanted *nothing* to do with the Elf Friends. Given their recent mortality rate, I didn't blame him.

He dropped us off in a nice neighborhood. Bobbi had parked her car at the granite curb of the long, straight street, like she lived in one of the remodeled nineteenth century houses. She thanked her friend for us. He smiled, gave her a brotherly kiss on the cheek, and drove off.

Once he was out of sight, we left in Bobbi's car.

Beth broke the silence. "What a mess." Her thoughts were right on the surface for me to read: she would've avoided a lot of trouble if she could have brought herself to come home to the elves with me instead of marrying Mr. Right and moving to Texas. "Where's Bobby?"

Bobbi gave Beth a puzzled look in the mirror.

"Beth means *Rob*, Bobbi," I told her. "She always called him Bobby. Everybody did." To Beth I said, "The Walloon's men captured him. They're holding him down south somewhere. We're sort of in touch. I'm pretty sure he's safe. He's cooperating with the bad guys."

"Can't *you* rescue him?" Beth said. She was thinking, *C'mon, you guys are the fucking* elves. *Why can't you save our bacon so we can go back to our lives?*

"It's complicated, honey." I wasn't sure how much to tell her about what the bad guys had done to the good guys who were our allies.

Bobbi drove a winding road out of Portsmouth, just to keep us moving. We weren't headed back to our hideout. How far could we trust Beth? I sat next to Bobbi in the passenger seat. I turned around to see Beth while we talked.

She was doing more feeling and intuiting than calculating. I counted that as progress.

The car windows were open. The east wind smelled of the tidal Piscataqua River and the ocean. We drove over bumpy little bridges past enormous remodeled houses. Old money and new money lived side by side, enjoying the million-dollar view. It was a scenic tourist byway the wealthy locals were too cheap to repave. We bumped over halfhearted temporary pothole repairs, the tragedy of the American commons chronically playing itself out in crumbling infrastructure.

Beth said what she was thinking. "Bobby—I mean *Rob*—wants to be with me. He came back from the fae-road and risked his life to find me. But it's impossible. We're both married to other people."

I know Catholic guilt when I see it. "What do *you* want, Beth?"

"Rob wants me for *me*. Andrew wants me for *decoration* and so I can have his *kids*. Because that's what everybody *expects*." She sounded bitter.

"You didn't answer my question, sweetie." I spoke gently. *If you could have whatever you wanted...*

"I want *Rob*," she said. "I want him as much as he wants me. If he wants to go with you, I'll go with him. I won't go *without* him." She started crying quietly. Her old familiar life on Earth was over.

Believe me, I could relate. Jackson went to the elves first. I only followed him there because I loved him.

Beth used to be a drama queen, like so many beautiful, insecure women. She'd had enough drama to last a lifetime. She knew what she wanted now. Good enough for me.

"Bobbi, you want to take us back to your place?" I said.

"Sure," she said.

I thought to her: *Beth wants to be one of us. I think we can trust her.*

43

Sturmbannführer Darnand Interviews Robert, *Roi des Fae*

Darnand had interrogated Elf Friends before. They were as mundane as shopkeepers. *We found the elves some clothes to wear and gave them some money—it's* their *money, you know. We drank tea together. They thanked us and left. They didn't say where they were going.* Bah.

Although King Robert was unlikely to have useful information, Darnand sought to gain his trust. There might be a way to exploit him in the immediate future.

There would be no long-term future for Robert des Fae. He had done violence to the Order's master of masters. The Walloon planned a prolonged and terrible revenge, insisting there be no torture until he returned to the estate. The king might be flensed, burnt, maimed, disemboweled, emasculated, blinded, slowly electrocuted, or all of these.

Not wanting to frighten the prisoner into silence or provoke him to defiance, Darnand said nothing of the endgame.

Initially, he asked general questions. Americans were an open, friendly lot, easy to manipulate if one displayed a cordial manner. Unlike Europeans, Americans were fundamentally unserious.

As promised, Rob answered his captor honestly. The questions revealed more than Darnand knew.

With rapport established, the interrogation became more pointed.

"You served in the United States Army?" Darnand asked.

"Yes, I did."

"And when was that?"

"Until 1945," Bobby said. "In Belgium."

Darnand's face showed no surprise. *He already knew that,* Rob thought.

"The Army listed you among the missing in action. But you ... deserted, then?"

Rob flushed. Strictly speaking he *had* deserted. However long ago he'd done it, whatever he'd endured on Earth in this new century, whatever he'd achieved on the fae-road this year, leaving the battlefield in wartime was a capital crime. His reasons for walking off with the Fae wouldn't matter to the United States.

Did Darnand want to recruit him? A man who deserted once might change sides again.

"I deserted, Major," Rob admitted. Sincerely ashamed, he stared at the cement floor between his running shoes.

Darnand let silence work on the prisoner's conscience,

"Let me ask you this, then," Darnand said. "Have you ever thought that you might have been fighting for the wrong side all those years ago? Are you *happy* with the direction your country has taken since the so-called Second World War?"

Rob looked up. Darnand sat still and straight, his military bearing unchanged even in the undignified secretarial chair.

"For most of the years since the War, I wasn't on Earth," Rob said. "I don't *know* much about what was happening in America." Rob's internet reading had made him hungry for more.

Darnand nodded approvingly. "We will return to that point later. If you earn my trust, I will tell you things that may surprise you. But what did you do when you left the Fae and returned to the United States?"

Rob went on to explain how he'd gone traveling with the Fae a *second* time near the end of the World War. He had first gone to the Fae much earlier, during the American Civil War.

Darnand's bushy eyebrows rose a fraction of an inch. *He didn't know that,* Rob thought.

Rob told Darnand he'd returned to the Fae a third time with Janjan Javorski. He said nothing about Moira or her sons. The Walloon would see Moira as a traitor, but how much had he told Darnand? Rob didn't mention the confrontation between Janjan and the Morrigna. Nor did he mention the Walloon, whom Rob had tried to kill. Instead, he talked about what he'd done after the Morrigna made him king of the Fae.

Darnand asked repetitive questions about military matters among the elves and the Fae. If the elves had anything like a chain of command or an order of battle, Rob knew nothing about it. And the Fae had hadn't fought on Earth for centuries. Their old swords, spears, and bows would be of little use against a modern army.

In modern times the Fae intervened in human affairs only to invite earthlings to join them. In that, the travelers were like the elves who offered to escort anyone willing to come home with them.

Rob knew about the elves from conversations overheard between Janjan and Bobbi. (He said nothing about meeting Jerry August a year ago.) Rob had heard there was no death in the next world over. He'd seen that living there *changed* the people who returned to Earth.

Darnand expressed no interest in elf biology. What captured his attention was hearing how the Fae live forever in the body—*and unchanged.* The surface of Darnand's face remained stiffly immobile, but Rob saw the passions flowing beneath.

He wants something from me, Rob thought.

Someone had always wanted something from Rob.

> Help me, Bobby, the baby's not breathing.
>
> Your country needs you, son. Come fight for the Union.
>
> Shoot that Rebel officer, soldier. Good! Now aim for the sniper up yonder tree.
>
> *Come join the Fae. We never die.*
>
> Come work for me, Bobby. You can eat with the family and bunk in the barn.
>
> Say listen, kid, your country needs ya to fight the Jerries and the Japs. Don't want to be a *slacker,* do ya?
>
> Kill every last Nazi bastard who sticks his head up, Bobby.

Come back to us, Bobby. There'll always be war down there. Come where you're welcome and study war no more.

Bobby, I have to ask for your help.

Let's make a fae baby together, my king. Come inside me now with your scepter of green light. Let's make the whole of the fae-road shake. Oh, oh, ah!

Janjan had offered to take Rob to her world. He put off accepting her gift. Because she had saved his life—and Beth's—he helped Janjan take Moira to safety on the fae-road.

Little Janjan the elf offered to help him find Beth and bring her to safety. So he could have another chance with Beth. Janjan and her folk deserved his allegiance.

Who had earned his loyalty? Not his country. Not the fae-road, his adopted land where he ruled the Fae with such wisdom as he could find within himself. Not even Moira. He'd helped her find safety; now she clung to the fae condition and its masque of eternal youth and desirability. She had what she wanted; she didn't need him. He and Moira were quits.

Moira's sons? They fulfilled their obligations as Fae princelings with evident enjoyment. Brad and Chad might grow up to be good men on Earth, but not on the fae-road where nothing ever changed and no one's choices mattered.

What about Beth? She'd rejected him like the ragged suitor he'd been. But she needed him, whether or not she knew it. He still loved her, whether or not she deserved it. He'd touched something in her she'd chosen to deny. She'd touched something in him he couldn't ignore.

Love had to count for something, or why go on living in any world?

He needed another chance with Beth. Then they'd either be together or they'd be quits, too, and Rob could go to Janjan's world and find what *he* wanted, underneath everything else.

But what was Darnand saying? His posture remained stiffly upright and military, but his gestures became more expansive.

"You were a soldier, no? As I have been myself. I know what that means. The hardships, the comradeship, the shared sacrifice. Banding together against a common enemy. What can compensate a man for risking his life? Certainly not a soldier's pay. Medals and promotions? Pah!"

Rob didn't respond to the rhetorical question.

"You fought for the United States against Germany. Then you left the battlefield of that so-called just war. You deserted to pursue what we might term *a higher calling* among the Fae, is it not so?"

"There's no honor in what I did, Major. I'd seen too much war. I wanted to live—and the Fae live a long, long time. I deserted them, too."

Darnand waved one hand in disagreement. "No one still living cares about petty misdemeanors from so long ago. For example, would it interest you to know that I, too, once fought against Germany?"

Rob's open face showed his surprise. "You don't look old enough, sir."

Darnand scowled. He worked with the Sisterhood because the Walloon ordered it. The thought of returning to the women to take a new birth nauseated him. "The Order has ways of allowing a man's life to continue. But more importantly, what ought a man to fight for? As I said, I fought *against* the Germans—until I discovered that they were right and France, my own country, was in the wrong."

"Wrong? How?"

Darnand laid one finger beside his nose: *A word to the wise.* "Jews. The so-called 'French Resistance fighters' were communists and Jews. And who has killed the most people, after all? Communists have slaughtered so many millions they make Nazis look like the Red Cross. Hitler was correct to oppose them."

"*Jews...*" Rob knew about the death camps from soldiers who'd liberated the skeletal inmates—and would never recover from what they'd seen. Poison gas. Crematoria. A word he'd never heard in the nineteenth century came into common use in the twentieth: *Holocaust.*

Darnand nodded. "Jews, communists, and traitorous Christian fellow-travelers. Does it surprise you to hear this?"

"I'm not an educated man, Major. I don't understand what you're telling me."

Darnand's smile never reached his eyes. "Your modesty does you great credit. Before he pledges his life and honor to a cause, a soldier must ask himself: *Who is my real enemy and who are my real allies?*"

Rob was honestly confused. "Who's the *real* enemy, then?"

Darnand leaned in closer and spoke confidentially. "Behind the Jews, behind those who fought to save them, behind the Catholics and the Protestants, even behind the godless communists stand *the elves. They* are the enemy of all white Western civilization. *Theirs* is the hidden hand that has so warped the modern world."

"The elves are *bad?*"

Darnand nodded. "Pure evil."

Rob sat back. "I don't believe you. It wasn't *elves* who flew airplanes into the World Trade Center." Rob had learned enough about the War on Terror to be properly horrified. *Not my war,* he'd thought. *Never again. Whatever's gone wrong in the world, killing more people won't make it right.*

Their discussion ranged over the centuries. Darnand knew things that were utterly foreign to Rob. He spoke about those things with passionate intensity.

Rob's knowledge came from his own experience. He didn't pretend to accept anything he had no way to confirm or understand.

As they talked, Rob saw that Darnand wanted something he was unable to admit to himself. Communicating indirectly was essential to life on the fae-road. King Robert let his subjects make up their own minds, rather than simply ordering them to do his will.

Rob interrupted Darnand's disquisition on the nobility of the Claimant's revolution against his own creator. "Major," he said quietly, "I'm an ordinary guy in a hell of a mess. I don't belong here, whatever year this is. Nothing you can tell me will *make* me belong here. I want to go where things make sense, you know?" Rob supported his weight on his forearms and looked at the thin rug on the cement floor. *Beth,* he thought. He'd been so close to her back in Portsmouth; he'd held her body against his. He ached from the loss of her. Tears gathered in his eyes.

Darnand watched him in cynical silence. Was this a performance? No, Darnand decided, the prisoner was sincere. "Where is it you wish to go, *soldat?*"

Rob looked up at his interrogator. "Back to the fae-road," he said. "I got restless and wanted to leave. I forgot nobody *needs* me here."

"You want to be king of the Fae once again, *soldat?*"

Rob shrugged. "I never cared about being king. I just happened to be there when the job opened up. The Morrigna *offered* it to me."

"And while you were among the Fae, you never grew older?"

Rob held out his open hands. "It's true. Hey, I can *show* you! We could go together. If you want to be king of the Fae, the job is yours. I guess you know more about commanding people than I do."

Darnand acknowledged the justice of Robert's words. The prisoner might be setting some sort of trap, trying to flatter him, but Darnand saw no sign of duplicity. The man was decades older than Darnand, but looked younger. And despite the king's youthful looks, Darnand saw the same weariness that he felt in himself. *Weltschmerz* increased each year as Darnand grew weaker.

Their shared world-weariness convinced Darnand. He wanted what Robert had abandoned: youth and immortality without the disgusting necessity of human rebirth. He shuddered at the thought of his conscious adult mind floating once again inside the suffocating prison cell of some little whore's sperm-polluted womb.

To live unchanged on his own terms. To take no more orders from the Walloon and his ilk. To escape the Sisterhood and the Dark Path they served.

To be his own man again forever.

"The Order has no current intelligence on the Fae," Darnand said. "You and I shall gather some. Make no mistake, try to escape and I will kill you instantly. Do you believe me?"

"I believe you, Major."

"You will assist me in this undertaking?"

"I won't be doing it for *you*," Rob said with perfect truthfulness.

Darnand smiled. "One of the few honest men I have ever met."

Darnand thought, Who better than I to be king of the Fae? He said, "Get some sleep, *soldat*. I will make arrangements for our reconnaissance."

44

What About Rob? *(Janjan)*

Beth was safe with us, but what about Rob? I could take him away from the Walloon, but I didn't want to fight a battle in the enemy's house. Rob might get hurt.

I touched Rob's mind through his *mandala*. Very lightly. He didn't notice me eavesdropping on his conversation.

Darnand, the Walloon's man, asked Rob questions; Rob answered them. The bad guy tried to recruit him. Rob convinced Darnand to follow *him* to Portsmouth. They were going back to the fae-road together.

I'd underestimated Rob. He'd engineered his own escape.

But where was the Walloon? And where was the living gold statue who did all the damage in Boston? They were the primary threat.

What did the enemy want to do tonight, Brain? Same thing he wanted every night, Pinky—to try to take over the world.

Oh, and revenge. The Walloon would want vengeance on Rob for knocking him out of his human body. He'd want vengeance on me for disrupting his control of the Morrigna and the fae-road. And surely he wanted vengeance on Jackson for deserting the Order and killing

Master Simon. Louis thought he was entitled to take whatever he wanted. Historians describe that mindset with words like retributionism, irredentism, and revanchism. Old, pointless grievances poison the present. *Ressentiment*, anyone?

When I wasn't slooting around, I was paying attention in college.

The interrogator left my friend alone to sleep. Rob's mind started drifting as soon as he lay down on the bed. He was exhausted and sick.

I used my lightest, faintest elf perceptions to explore the Walloon's mansion. I'd been in the entryway and the library before with Jackson. The corridors and basement rooms were unfamiliar, as were the suites on the upper floors.

I came close to stepping out of my body. Ugh. Was *I* going to have to fight to stay in my own skin now?

On the first floor Darnand was giving orders to the Walloon's other employees. He had no obvious psychic powers, but I kept my distance. He'd been the Walloon's Dark Path servant at Odiorne Point. He was a lightning rod for the Fallen.

The Walloon and the flying gold sorcerer were nowhere to be found around the estate. They'd been there, but I didn't follow their faint psychic trail. The statue had sensed me even outside my body with my thoughts like still water. Whatever he was, I wasn't ready to face his power. Not now and not alone.

But I knew people who might be equal to an enemy like that. I talked to them mind-to-mind. I'd come back to Earth with a tentative plan; we made some changes to it.

I reached out to Rob. I turned his dreams lucid so we could talk. I had to ask for his help again. He had the right to refuse. Free will.

While he came to a decision, I helped his body heal. I would have done that whatever he decided. *What goes around...* and all that.

45

Death Cab for Cutie Sings "Good Help (Is So Hard To Find)"

Master Gold worked restorative magic. A dust devil of sand flew off the temple floor, scything into the Walloon's body. His inner sandstorms ceased. Internal organs and the mineral walls around them solidified. Louis' skin returned to Caucasian white, shining with health and strength.

For now.

Thanking Gold for his help, he excused himself and returned to the sand-floored chamber to contact Darnand in Virginia. "Contact" was Louis' euphemism for seizing temporary control of an underling's mind.

The Walloon's awareness returned in an instant to the estate. Darnand was not there.

Louis' angry spirit stalked the empty halls of the mansion. He found no one. No one was in any of the basement cells. *Robert Roi des Fae*, his captive, was also missing.

Had Darnand dared disobey his master? The Walloon extended his consciousness, looking, looking, further, further, outward from the estate in concentric circles.

Ah! From his mind's height above the Earth Louis discerned the unmistakable mark of a Dark Path spirit. Darnand was speeding north away from Virginia in an automobile stolen from the Order.

Louis was unable to control the French traitor's mind or even to read it.

Darnand had acquired the protection of the Roman Catholic Church. Perhaps he wore a crucifix or a rosary. Perhaps, like an old peasant woman, he muttered the Our Father or the Hail Mary as a warding spell to protect himself from Louis and the Fallen.

Surely Darnand's sins were unforgivable in the eyes of the Church and the High Enemy it claimed to serve. Louis was no theologian. More to the point, Darnand's treason was unforgivable in the eyes of the Fallen, whose unsleeping eyes watch over the Dark Path forever.

Darnand would need a new body soon. His aging physical form was more mortal and vulnerable than the Walloon's. Why would Darnand abandon the conscious serial rebirth only the Sisterhood could give him?

Having relinquished such immortality as the Order could provide, was Darnand planning to *die* in a grand gesture of Christian sacrifice? Unlikely.

And what of Robert des Fae?

Next to Darnand's besmirched and clotted spirit in the moving vehicle was a clear light so bright that the Walloon's darkened psyche recoiled. The king was more than he appeared to be.

The answer was obvious. Having interrogated the Walloon's prisoner and learnt about Fae immortality, Darnand had co-opted King Robert. Darnand had convinced the erstwhile sovereign to take him to the fae-road where Louis was impotent. Darnand would escape the Fallen, desert the Order, and live forever. *How sharper than a serpent's tooth.*

When the Fallen sent him to Master Gold, they didn't bother to restore Louis' sense of irony.

46

Elf Friends, Come Forth! *(The Recent Past)*

It was a mass casualty; the command had trained for it. They used emergency action plan tablet computers to stay in touch and work their plan step by step, making adjustments as needed.

Controlling communications was the first step. All inquiries were directed to a single point of contact, the public information officer. No one else spoke to the news media. The PIO was ordered to refer to this unfortunate event as *the explosion* when she talked to reporters. She would tell the media that the investigation was continuing—and nothing further.

Calling this attack "the Boston explosion" shaped the media narrative. It sounded plausible. *Something* had leveled a multi-story office building. The building was in Boston. Even in Massachusetts, buildings don't just spontaneously collapse. What else but an explosion could have done such a thing?

A reporter might ask, *Could it have been a natural gas explosion?*

The spokesperson would say, *We're not ruling anything out at this point in time.* But her body language implied, *Yeah, it was probably gas.*

The reporter would feel he was getting the facts. The PIO had been hired partly because she was attractive enough to cloud men's minds.

The operations staff quickly established a perimeter. The existing fence around the entire block was reinforced. Armed guards were posted. A series of connected tents were erected.

Inside the tents out of public view the injured were triaged and given first aid by medics wearing radiation suits. The suffering were given painkillers. The dying were given last rites by a radiation-suited chaplain.

Surviving victims were stabilized and quickly transported in unmarked shielded ambulances to a nondescript medical facility outside the city. The dead were transported in unmarked shielded vans to the facility's basement.

Supposedly run by the U.S. Department of Veterans Affairs, the hospital sat at the edge of a forested area. It had been built after the Second World War and well maintained since, its technology regularly upgraded. Patients were normally few: government employees, technicians, researchers, special operations soldiers, and military contractors. Whether patients lived or died, their medical records left the facility with them.

The hospital had excellent security. It had no public emergency room, but did have a helicopter landing pad. A sick or injured patient who showed up at the hospital's doors by mistake would be flown to a civilian hospital.

The civilian medical community knew little about the facility. Some sort of government research operation? The doctors and nurses who worked there were members of the armed forces with top secret Defense Department and Q-level Energy Department clearances. They had standing orders not to discuss where they worked or what they did there. Security breaches were ruthlessly investigated and aggressively prosecuted. The staff didn't mingle with their peers in the local community; safer that way. Everyone rotated out after three-month assignments and didn't return for a year.

When a hundred people showed up at the hospital with acute radiation syndrome, the staff did what they were trained for. There's no cure for that major insult to the body. The medics focused on supportive treatment and aggressive pain management. They put a brave face on things. *You're safe with us now*, they told burned, drug-groggy patients who were already starting to lose clumps of hair.

Privately, the doctors and nurses shook their heads. Ten more patients died; their bodies were moved to the shielded part of the hospital's basement. The ward would lose another few every day. At month's end, the ward would be empty and the morgue would be full. After a dignified nonsectarian funeral service, the bodies would be respectfully packaged like radioactive waste and shipped west for eternal storage deep inside a mountain.

After dark the hospital settled into a nighttime rhythm. At the nurses station, two burly men periodically checked the victims' vital signs on monitors. They took turns entering the ward to change out slow-drip intravenous fluids, painkillers, and antibiotics. A doctor slept in her quarters, ready to respond if needed. No one thought she would be needed except to pronounce patients dead. One patient was rapidly going sour from internal burns. They kept him comfortable without prolonging his suffering. Battlefield medicine makes military doctors more realistic than their civilian counterparts.

A brighter light began to shine in the dim ambient light next to the dying man's bed. At the center of a globe of clear light appeared the figure of a dark-haired man with broad shoulders, possibly Asian. He stood at the dying man's bedside in silence.

The man in the bed felt something touch him and woke up. Unlike everything else that had happened after the explosion, this touch didn't hurt. He looked up to see, not a doctor in protective gear, but a man wearing black pants and a black shirt.

The stranger smiled down at him and whispered, "Hi."

"Hi," said the man in the bed. Although the single syllable hurt his throat, he smiled.

"Will you let me help you, Elf Friend?" said the visitor.

How did he know that? the lawyer wondered. He was drugged and not thinking clearly. But he said, "Of course I will."

The shining man held his hand on the lawyer's head. The pain that drugs had only masked vanished as if it had never been.

Overwhelmed, the lawyer fell into deep healing sleep.

The man at the center of the globe of light went around the radiation ward, from patient to patient, starting with the sickest. None of these interactions took long.

The night nurses were young Air Force lieutenants, highly-trained professionals at the top of their game. In addition to monitors for each patient, the ward had video cameras. Some patients were having a hard time dying, fighting death so fiercely that they had to be moved to separate rooms so as not to wake the others.

"Dude," one nurse said, pointing at the video display.

The other nurse took a long look at the screen. "They told us to expect *something*," he said. "But what the hell? Who is that guy and how'd he even get in here?"

"Better wake the duty doc," said the first man.

His phone call brought a tousle-haired Air Force captain in surgical scrubs to the nurses station. She looked at the monitor, shook her head, looked away, and then looked back.

The unauthorized visitor systematically made his way around the ward. The cameras were all in night-vision mode, so the man looked green. Everything in the ward looked green. The restless patients who would soon need medication. The beds and intravenous delivery systems. The green standing man touched the head of a green-faced patient. The patient smiled. Both men disappeared.

The doctor watched the screen intently. The patient in the bed stayed gone, but the visitor returned two seconds later. He moved on to the next patient.

The nurses watched the doctor watch the screen.

"Doc, should we have Security suit up and go in there?" one said.

First, do no harm, thought the doctor. Her oath had never seemed ironic before. "That man's doing more for our patients than we can, guys," she said.

"Ma'am, are we just gonna let him take people in our care away from us—away from *the U.S. Air Force?*" The second nurse was making himself indignant.

The doctor looked calmly at the burly lieutenant. "That's exactly what we're going to do. Do I need to remind you that everything that happens in and around this building is a matter of national security and never to be discussed anywhere else?"

The first nurse gave his colleague a look that meant *Stop being a fucking idiot in front of the captain.* "Even if we're summonsed to testify before Congress?" he said, hoping Mr. Steroids would get the message.

"*Especially* then," the doctor said. "Wouldn't you rather go to jail than get disappeared?"

"I'd really like to know what he's *doing* in there," the first nurse said. He was drawn to the light around the visitor, the way he touched the sick people, and the way they responded to him. His colleague looked at him in shock. "Permission to go ask him, ma'am?"

"I can't give you permission," she said, "but I can probably forgive you afterward."

It took the lieutenant a few minutes to put on his radiation suit. He entered the locked ward just as the visitor finished tending to the last patient.

The visitor looked up at the lieutenant. "I'm glad you're here," he said. I need you to show me the morgue."

The nurse thought, What could it hurt? He nodded Okay.

The two men walked out the door, down the corridor, and down the stairs to the basement. At first, the nurse was struck dumb by the impact the visitor's presence. He wished they could hang out together. This guy *knew things* the lieutenant had no words for.

Finally he said, "How'd you do ... whatever the hell you did in there?"

The visitor made a face. "It's easier to do than to explain."

The lieutenant nodded. "Okay, I'll buy that. Um, why did you want to see the morgue, then? I mean, dead is dead, right? I can't let you in there, y'know. The radiation would kill you." He was breaking security by initiating this conversation, but that didn't seem important.

The guy smiled at him. "My name's Jackson. I appreciate your help."

The nurse said, "Call me Tony. We don't use our real names in this facility."

They reached the locked morgue door. It was labeled "Containment." Jackson looked through the wire-mesh window. Low emergency lighting illuminated the walkways. Everything else was in shadow. Nothing was moving.

Everybody knew what the Containment room was for. There were no other signs, not even a radiation trefoil. There were three radiation meters mounted on the wall next to the door. The sensors that reported to the meters were all in the locked room. Tony checked the meters. All three held steady in the red. Nobody was going in there without suiting up in protective gear.

Tony turned to Jackson to convey this information. Jackson wasn't there.

What?

Tony looked through the thick window glass. Someone was moving inside the room now. It was Jackson.

How'd he do that? Tony thought. The door's locked. Did he walk through the wall? He would have notified the doc and called security, but he saw something that knocked every other thought out of his head.

Lead-lined body bags lay on steel morgue tables. Jackson walked from table to table, unzipping the bags.

Outside the morgue, all three radiation meters inched higher into the red zone.

Jackson stood over the last bag he'd opened. He spoke to the dead in a language that lit up the dark room. The words gently shook the building to its foundation, like heavy trucks were driving up the access road. Tony's ears couldn't hear words through the thick blast door; his mind heard the thought:

There is no death. God's children are forever free of it. Come back to this life or move on to the next. Choose now, brothers and sisters.

People who'd been dead an instant before started breathing, hesitated, and sat up on the steel tables. They looked around at the unfamiliar surroundings. Were they dreaming? They shook themselves.

The Walking Dead, thought Tony. He shuddered.

Jackson spoke to each person. There commenced a rapid series of flickering transitions. Jackson took the person's hand, they disappeared together, Jackson returned. This continued until only the last of the ten remained.

—

When the golden statue launched its radiation attack in Boston, Maura's spirit instantly left her body. It didn't go far. Free of the body, her mental processes attained a speed and pure objectivity she hadn't known since she was a little girl. She was, her mother often told her, too smart for her own good. *Wicked smaht.*

Maura saw she was in some kind of intermediate state between one life and the next. She had been here before. Nothing in her religious education had even hinted at such a condition as the *bardo* (where had *that* word come from?) state. She wasn't bitter. To live in a human body is to accept human limitations.

There was a lot going on. The *bardo* was like the circus or a county fair. There were thrill rides. There was a Spooky House and a Tunnel of Love. There were beings that looked like they wanted to scare her and others that looked like they wanted to help. Maura made a face at them: *Fuck off, the lot of yez.*

She was watching from outside her own body when large men in white suits with faceplates easily picked that body up and zipped it into a heavy lined body bag. She found this very interesting. Her spirit tagged along behind the ambulance that carried her body into a hospital like none she'd ever seen.

In this uncertain state, Maura was certain of only two things. First was the fact of her own continued existence. *I still think, therefore I still am.* Second was the fact that *something or someone was coming for her.* Or at least that something was going to happen that she was supposed to stick around for. There was a lot of ambient knowledge in the *bardo* that she didn't have to study to acquire.

Maura felt the elflord's approach before he passed through the thick wall of the containment room. She saw the light of his being, so like her own. His light called to hers. At a level before words, his mind spoke to her of the source of all mind.

He unzipped the lead-lined bag. His shining thoughts offered her a choice.

She chose to return to her life, with its limitations and all its constant changes.

Maura entered her body again and felt the pain of thoughts slowing down to human speed. She sat up on the steel table and looked at the shining man, the elf who wasn't really an elf, and saw what he was.

"*That* was unexpected," she said. "Thanks for bringing me back. My name's Maura, by the way."

There were tears on the elflord's face. He was exhausted and sick, but he smiled at her. "I'm Jackson. Ready to come home with me?"

"I think I am," she said. "My family and my boyfriend must think I'm dead, anyway. It's time to start over with you guys."

Jackson reached out a hand and Maura took it. In her mind she heard his voice saying in English, *Do you trust me in your thoughts?*

Abso-fucking-lutely, Maura thought back.

Jackson smiled again. Their minds joined for the brief trip to the next world over, in which he would follow the map that was written in his heart.

In that same moment, a past-life memory struck them:

A life on the Dark Path. Deep within a mile-square mill or factory on some world, not Earth, a muscular shaven-headed man with stunned eyes and a lobotomy scar is controlled by a snakelike electrical leash around his head. Holding the semi-sentient leash is an elaborately-dressed woman with cold, cruel eyes. She is his mistress. He is her devoted bodyguard and selfless sexual plaything.

"Holy shit, *I* did that to you? I am so, so sorry."

Jackson shook his head. "As I was then, I wanted that with you, Maura. But all is forgiven. We're off the Dark Path now, thank God. Ready to come home?"

"Yes please, Jackson."

Jackson and the once-dead girl disappeared from the containment room.

—

Jesus Christ, Tony thought. *Jesus Christ.* Tears burned his eyes. *Lazarus, come forth?*

Tony's eyes turned to the radiation meters. He watched the readings drop from the extreme red to the yellow early-warning zone. Even empty, the body bags and the morgue tables were still hot.

Jackson popped back into the corridor five feet away from Tony.

Jackson's face looked gaunt and his golden skin had gone gray. His short hair was damp. He breathed laboriously, supporting himself with his hands on his knees, like he'd run the Boston Marathon on a hot day.

He looks terrible, Tony thought. *He looks worse than our patients.*

"Dude," Tony said. "I ... don't know what to do for you."

With obvious effort Jackson straightened up. He grinned.

"Well, if I stay here, I'll have to lay this damaged body down," Jackson said. "If I go home right now, I'll be healed. Want to come with me?"

"Can you teach me to do what you did?"

Jackson looked at Tony like he saw into his heart and mind.

"I think I can," Jackson said.

"Then *hell yeah*, I want to go with you."

Just like that the corridor was empty.

47

The Time Traveler's Elf *(Janjan)*

Let me back up a bit.

Most of the time I was messing about on Earth, my mind was touching Jackson's, taking comfort from our silent connection.

Until something new happened.

See, Jackson had become an elflord; he'd entered a new mode of being. When his body resumed itself, its atoms vibrated at a higher frequency. It's difficult for the high elves to go back to Earth. They have to leave part of themselves behind. I don't fully understand it. Virgil of Agharti did it for his homeworld—and for his friend Daniel Ryun. Long before Virgil, Josh of Nazareth emptied himself to be born as a helpless human baby. The shock of that birth still reverberates through the human worlds.

I heard my husband think, *I am more than this. I know I am more. I set all that aside. This one thing I do.* He accepted the sorrow of the human condition. He managed not to die of it, but still he grieved.

He made travel plans. He got the coordinates from elves and people he knew in the area. He touched their minds and gladdened their hearts.

Somewhere near Boston Elf Friends were dying of radiation sickness.

That's *where* he was headed. No mystery about that

The mystery was *when* he went there.

From nonlinear time in the next world over, he traveled in an instant to a point that was in the past to me where I stood on Earth. Another thing I don't understand and can't explain.

While he was gone from the next world over and out of the Earth time stream where I stood, Jackson dropped off my radar. As if he didn't exist—or I didn't.

When he emptied himself to travel where he was needed, he also emptied himself of me. Only temporarily, but still. I felt like it was payback for dropping off *his* radar as I swived with the Lady and Beth *aside* in time and space. As if, you know, the whole freaking universe was about *me*. My head knew better, but my heart and my loins had their own ideas.

But when he flickered back from Earth to the next world over, there he was again, connected with me. I saw what he'd done for our friends, living and dead. I saw how the radiation had sickened him.

The Earth became a bad place for elflords when nuclear weapons arrived in the 1940s. The gold sorcerer's radiation had made a small part of Earth far worse. The Walloon was going to use the skull-faced mummy against the elves, starting with the Elf Friends.

Jackson would have laid down his life for our friends. It was only a little comfort to know, distantly, that he'd be able to take his life up again.

Jackson shared the raw recent memory of entering a containment room in an above-top-secret military hospital: the morgue where our friends' dead bodies lay zipped into lead-lined body bags. He showed me what he'd done there.

My mind followed him into the Groves of Healing.

He became whole again; it was more than I could take in. We saw each other face to face, my husband and I, and it was our original face before all our human births.

He stood there fully present to me for a long moment. He smiled and set about doing what Healers do.

From my temporal perspective, what he'd done in Boston was finished months ago.

That's why details about the attack and its aftermath never made the news. *Miracles, really?* Nobody wanted to talk about what happened in Boston. Best to fabricate a story for those who prefer comfortable narratives to uncomfortable facts.

When Leda came back to Portsmouth from the next world over, I didn't understand what she'd become. The fairy-tale word "elf" hints at what it was like to talk to someone so much the same but so different from the girl I'd known.

Jackson had taken another step into the human nature we shared. He'd changed more than Leda.

Riding in Bobbi's car this pleasant summer night, I knew how Aimee felt when Daniel walked into the highlands and out of his body. It was a raw, salty sexual feeling. I wanted someone to beat me and pleasure me again and again, until overtopping sensations flooded out my heartache and fear.

Elves on Earth can still be poisoned by old fears and unexamined passions. The purest of us get squeezed out of this world by radiation and preternatural evil. Our enemies knew this. They'd found a way to gain the whole Earth for *the prince of this world* again: the Midas touch that turns things dead and gold.

I knew what needed doing—if I had the courage to do it. All I wanted now was to head for the place called *there*. As in "Don't go there."

—

I touched Rob's mind and found him and the interrogator driving north. They wouldn't get to Portsmouth for hours.

Bobbi drove us back to the windowless apartment in the barn. We put together a light meal and shared it in silence. There was a lot to talk about, but we couldn't seem to get started.

Beth had been pulled into an intimate relationship with a powerful, immortal, nonhuman being born (if that's the right word) in Earth's distant past. She tried to make sense of it, but her thoughts kept hitting the weirdness barrier. And she was thinking about the practical matters involved in leaving Andrew. Her heart was made up, but her mind wasn't. She wondered if Rob would take her back, or if he was still a nineteenth-century man who'd see her as a fallen woman. Would he forsake her to pay her back for rejecting him last year? She'd gone dreamy and distant.

Bobbi had just had her first encounter with evil. Nothing prepares you for preternatural malevolence, even when you see the truth shining within you. *Remember love and light.* She wanted to go home now and be closer to the light.

Bobbi also wanted *me.*

And me? I wanted to be with Jackson. I wanted him a lot. Even though he was busy with the new elves he'd brought back from Earth, I felt his mind shining in mine. He'd done what he signed up for. All his self-emptying and journeying into the recent past was over, thank God. We were connected again.

I felt his love and he felt mine. We told each other: *Do what you have to do, my love.*

If you could have whatever you wanted, what would you want? We were married. More importantly, we were *spoken for.* Naturally we were going to have each other every which way. But there was something new awaiting us once I did what I'd signed up for on Earth—or thereabouts. Jackson had kept his promises. To keep my promises I had to see things through, no matter how scared I was.

I saw myself sitting on the shore of a vast sea of clear light and my thoughts went silent. I felt lost. I had no way to talk about it with Beth and Bobbi.

We had hours before our rendezvous with Rob. My mind was like storm winds swirling crosscurrents into the sea of light. The turbulence was making me horny, of course it was. I started remembering my time with Beth and the Lady...

Bobbi read my thought. She looked at Beth. Then she looked at me sadly. "Janjan, you've fucked practically everybody we know *except* me."

Bobbi's psychic crosscurrents were churning, too. She was as horny as I was. Her eyes were wet; so were mine. Sensitivity to the feelings of others can be a weakness or a strength. Tonight I wasn't sure which it was.

Bobbi's sarcastic tone shocked Beth out of her reverie. She reached across the table and took Bobbi's hand. Something *not-Beth* entered her aspect. She was still *connected* to the Lady because she'd agreed to that during our, um, deliberations.

"Janjan and I swived with each other and with the Lady of Cyprus," she said. *Swive* was not a word I'd ever heard Beth use before. "Janjan and I were lovers once, even before that happened. I'm not ashamed anymore." She looked at me when she said that, then looked back at Bobbi. "I can't speak for Janjan, but *I* would happily lie down with you."

Bobbi hadn't seen that coming. Neither had I. Bobbi said to Beth, "But you're *beautiful*." She meant: *You're out of my league. Why would you want me?*

"You're beautiful, too," Beth told her. She grinned. "You're one of those little hot girls who get *me* all hot. Like Janjan."

Being compared to me made Bobbi happy. "I would ruin you for men forever," she said. "But I think Janjan needs something from me tonight. Or from both of us."

Both of them turned to me expectantly. Gulp.

I walked over to the wardrobe where we'd gotten clothes. Sure enough, I found a leather belt. I closed the wardrobe doors, walked back to Bobbi and handed her the belt. I took off my clothes, just dropped them on a kitchen chair. As I undressed, I looked directly at Bobbi and Beth, like: *This is me. This is what I am. This is what I want. Do with me what you will.*

Bobbi might have had different kinds of sex with all kinds of women, but this shocked her. "Oh, Janjan. Oh, honey, no. No." She shook her head.

She thought giving me what I wanted would be bad for me.

I was showing her another difference between Real Janjan (me) and Imaginary Janjan (her dream lover).

I held out my hand to Beth. She walked me to an old armchair. I kneeled up on the chair and presented my hindquarters to Bobbi. Beth stood behind the chair. I put both my hands on the back cushion and Beth put her hands on top of mine. She bent down and began kissing me softly with an open mouth.

Bobbi stood behind me holding the belt. She thought, *Are you sure, Janjan?*

I'm sure, I thought. *Aimee taught me how to do this. Watch and learn.*

Bobbi swung the belt, not too hard. It burned. It stung. I moaned into Beth's mouth as I magicked the pain into pleasure. It was a warm night. The hayloft apartment retained the day's heat. The living area was getting hotter and so were we.

Beth stopped kissing me for as long as it took to undress. Bobbi took a break from swinging the belt at my ass and thighs to take her own clothes off.

Bobbi reached down and slapped my thighs further apart. She pushed down the small of my back so my ass stuck out further and exposed my naughty bits. She paused and thought, *Are you ready for this?*

Yes, I thought back. *Please.*

It went on and on. I rode breaking waves of pain that turned to pleasure with me inside them. I stepped into the zone of dangerous bliss that Aimee had entered when I took the cane to her beautiful backside.

Bobbi liked whipping me so much that it frightened her. She would have stopped long before I wanted her to if our minds hadn't been linked. She gloried in her power over me. The welts on my ass healed as quickly as she inflicted them. We entered bliss together.

We were connected. Everything was connected. Beth did things to me that made me come. My rolling orgasms became Bobbi's and hers became Beth's. I thought I knew everything about sex, silly me, but this was new territory.

I was breathing hard but hoping this wouldn't end, not yet, please. I loved being the center of their erotic attention, having their minds bent on me, enamored of me. *The cynosure of all eyes.*

There came a rosy light around Beth. She held out her hand for the belt. Bobbi gave it to her. Beth gestured imperiously for Bobbi to hold my hands. Then it was Beth who swung the belt again and again and again. And as she beat me, prompted by the Lady, Beth spoke words in a language neither of us understood.

Wisps of meaning arrived in Beth's mind from some wild angry grief in the Lady's shadow side, hidden from the goddess herself: *Where hast thou taken Eros, O Psyche?* (smack) *Which dost thou love more, the pleasure or the pain, my too-proud beauty?* (crack)

Yes, I came. Even in my confusion, I was still myself and no one else.

From the next world over, Jackson's mind spoke to mine in Elvish: *Remember how you came to this knowledge, my love, when you face our enemies again.* He showed me how it hurt to face our friends, dying of radiation sickness, or already dead of it, knowing that radiation was killing him, too. *The valley of the shadow.* There was no jealousy in my husband's mind. No anger and no fear. Only love.

If you were to think Jackson's teaching spoiled things for me or for Bobbi, you would be mistaken. The deepest power and pleasure flow from the same headwaters, something I'd never have learned if I'd obeyed the rule of life in Portsmouth: *Do Not Inquire Within.*

When Beth and I swived with the Lady *aside* in time and space, the goddess was physically present with us. Both of us touched her and were deeply touched by her physical body. Being an elf, I could never forget that the human-looking person I pleasured was both more than human and not exactly human. What I saw of the Lady's mind was different from what I saw of Beth's.

What I saw in Beth's mind tonight were traces of the Lady, not the overwhelming Old-God communication. To be intimate with the queen of love and beauty is in some measure to share in her being. To receive in some measure the worship that is rightly offered to her. Beth had been *raised up* by her connection to the Lady. Now she walked in beauty like the night, as the poet sang. *Apotheosis* is the old word, one too grand to ever apply to me, the sturdy peasant girl and novice elflady with the big ass, modest breastesses, and hot punani. It was the Lady's darkness Beth walked in, as big a mystery to the Lady as it was to Beth.

Giving Beth a *mandala* like I'd given Rob would end Beth's relationship to the goddess. It would force a choice she wasn't ready for. A time to every purpose, ripeness is all, and so on. I could see the time coming when Beth would have to choose and Rob would have to make a final choice if he wanted her.

By now the three of us had ended up on the old rug on the barn floor. I was worshiping at Beth's altar, if you follow me, while Bobbi kneeled next to me where she could see and touch my bare labia and do whatever took her fancy. She had me right where she'd wanted me from the first moment we met: face down, ass up.

I knew Beth was enjoying my ministrations because she was moaning and crying and coming all over the place. She shouted in that ancient language and I caught the thought behind it: *Ah! Art thou my priestess or am I thine?* The next instant, she was simply beautiful Beth again.

As she stroked me, Bobbi's thought came gently into mine: *How many fingers do you want?* She wanted me to beg.

All of them, I thought back. *Please.*

You asked for it, Janjan, she thought. Her little hand was gentle at first, then less gentle, and finally not gentle at all. *Oh, oh, ah.* If there was pain, the pleasure overcame it. I lost the ability to connect one thought with another. Bobbi came when I did, feeling what I felt where I felt it. We were in sync in every possible way, if not in love the way she'd hoped. She was learning something she'd have to go home to understand.

She learned another new thing when I turned my intention from sated, smiling, quivering, dripping Beth to devote my full attention to Bobbi. She was vibrating with desire and all the emotions that go with it.

Do you trust me to pleasure you, Bobbi?

Yes, Janjan, with all my heart.

I did something to her that Jackson and I had learned together. Instead of piling powerful sensation upon sensation until the nerves went numb, I touched her inner light with mine, lighter and lighter, evoking the most exquisite sensitivity.

You're giving me the Elflady's Gift, Bobbi thought. New elves do a lot of speculating among themselves about what kind of intimacy the elflords and elfladies might be enjoying up in the highlands. Making myths and stories is a natural thing to do, especially when your teachers will say nothing about high-country sex except *Come see for yourself.*

It's a gift you were given in your own creation, I thought.

Bobbi and I shared an inner smile and a series of rolling inner orgasms. Nothing to do but enjoy the gift, no grasping needed, no heroic efforts to control, overpower, or impress the other.

See this?

Oh, yes. Oh!

And this, too?

Yes, Janjan. Ah!

Jackson and I used to think that sex was just sex; we were only kidding ourselves. Sex is always more than a quest for physical satisfaction. There's a lot to learn if you watch what happens in yourself and in your lover. Those we call angels are messengers and created thus, but we embodied creatures also carry a message—one we receive when we share it.

Bobbi spoke in our mind-space: *How lovely are the messengers.*

48

Far Afield *(Janjan)*

After all the sex, we slept together, literally, curled up on the rug. We needed *sleep that knits up the ravell'd sleeve of care, the death of each day's life, sore labour's bath, balm of hurt minds, great nature's second course,* ho ho ho.

I don't need a lot of sleep these days. I woke up first as leaders often do. I got cleaned up, collected my wits, and reached out with my mind.

Rob's *mandala* let me see what he saw. I recognized the section of highway he was driving. The car was close, only an hour south of Portsmouth.

Darnand of the Dark Path slept a troubled sleep in the passenger seat. One fist clutched something on the chain around his neck.

What's he holding? I asked. In battle these things matter more than you think.

It's a crucifix, Rob thought back. *I guess he grew up Catholic, whatever he's done since then.*

Darnand was protecting himself from the Walloon.

A crucifix wouldn't protect him from the screaming gold mummy; nothing I knew would work against him, either. I needed to get my awareness away from that car before the sorcerer's mind could find me.

Rob, I thought, *Bobbi and I have Beth with us. We'll meet you in Great Bog. You know where.* I meant the place where the fae-road almost touched Portsmouth.

Thank you, Janjan. A pause. *Tell Beth I love her. You know, in case something happens to me before I can tell her myself?*

That was all too possible; anything can happen in battle. Rob was a war-weary soldier before he ascended to the throne of the Fae.

I'll tell her, Rob. Go with God, my brother.

He gave me a sad interior smile. He had trouble praying and he hardly dared to hope.

From the barn, Bobbi drove us to the park-and-ride near the state highway. With nobody watching, we'd have a short walk in from the main road.

Last year when everything was frozen solid and covered with four feet of snow, Great Bog had been guarded. Leda and I had to neutralize three watchers so I could take Rob, Moira, and her sons on a long hike across the hilly fields, abandoned orchards, and icy marshes to the fae-road.

This year when Rob abdicated the throne of the Fae, he and I were the only people in the Great Bog. The authorities abandoned their surveillance when people stopped coming to Portsmouth from the Fae—and stopped going to the Fae from Portsmouth.

There were no troops or police here tonight. Nobody was lying in wait for us. Traffic was light. We waited for a pause and sprinted across the road into the tall grass.

We crouched in the weeds until the next break in the traffic. Unseen, we hiked west under the power lines. We pushed through brush that had grown over the trail. People had stopped visiting Great Bog after last year's battle. The good citizens of Portsmouth wisely avoided anywhere that threatened paranormal peril. I wondered why anybody still lived in the pretty little city on the Piscataqua. Denial, I guess. People build houses on the slopes of active volcanoes.

I walked point, Beth followed, and Bobbi brought up the rear. There was no one anywhere near us. I sensed a few minds in nearby houses and in passing cars.

Well, that's not quite accurate. Mind is in every living thing, and there was a lot of animal and vegetable life around us. Bobbi and I used elf-light to keep biting insects away. A trivial use of a great gift, but we didn't have to scratch ourselves.

The spot where the fae doorway would open was practically engraved on my brain. Trying to open the door looked like a bad idea. I found us a place of concealment. We'd wait in the bushes to see who showed up.

I thought about what Leda said to me the winter Beth, Rob, Jackson and I went walking with the Fae: *Love is the answer. Duh.* If love was the answer, I still didn't understand it.

Here we had Beth, who'd been a goddess' high priestess. It's hard *not* to love Love. Beth's aspect still shone with a rose-colored erotic light that wasn't her own. A very good thing, as the elves say, but not the best thing.

Here we had Bobbi who learned she was in love with her idea of me. There was love in her and love in me, but Bobbi and I weren't *spoken for*. Even though we'd had an extraordinary sexual experience with Beth. Sex was another kind of love whose meaning I didn't understand. (How do you get to Carnegie Hall? *Practice.*)

And here we had me, still married to Jackson, still loving him, still in love with him and wanting him. Still *spoken for*: still connected to him.

There's always more to learn. Before I went looking for the higher love Steve Winwood sang about, I had to survive tonight.

I left Bobbi and Beth in the hideout and went to look at the doorway to the fae-road.

Nothing much, that's what my eyes saw. Nothing to hear but insects and the distant hum and rush of the highway. Nothing to smell but things growing in mud around the wetlands. Nothing to touch but humid air. My heightened perceptions told me exactly nothing about the doorway.

The poet Blake said *The Eye sees more than the Heart knows.* With elves it's usually the other way around. I had no sense data to work with, but memory told me where the door had to be.

I'd stepped through it twice before.

The first time was when Beth, Rob, Jackson and I escaped from Simon, Jackson's horrible old MM master.

The second time was when Rob helped me escort Moira and her sons to safety.

We approached the spot I remembered so well. The place where Coran, king of the travelers wrapped in light, first spoke to me out of the air, or seemed to speak.

"Can you not see the doorway, then?" Moira said.

"I can't see it, Moira," I said. "What do you see?"

"Ah, well, the door's plain as day to me, but I haven't the strength to open it. For that, I'll need the help of this handsome lad." Moira removed her thick glove and held out her lily-white hand not to either of her sons, but to Bobby.

The light surrounding Bobby turned a deeper green. He blushed as he took off his own glove and grasped Moira's hand.

And there as if an invisible door had opened, I saw the fae-road.

Again today I was stuck outside a door I couldn't see. A door no elf could open. Rob wasn't here yet, and there was no sign of Moira.

Frustrated, I went back to our hideaway in the bushes and crawled in next to Beth and Bobbi. I may have mentioned that I don't have a lot of patience.

49

Juice Newton Sings "Queen of Hearts" *(Beth)*

Beth sat on coarse dry grass in the hiding place. She watched the field through a screen of leaves. The fae-path was somewhere nearby, but all she could see in Great Bog tonight were innocent shadows. Janjan and Bobbi would protect her from the dangers she couldn't see.

Beth considered the things she'd done in the last two years and the things that had happened to her. Really, she was conducting what her Jesuit teachers called *the examination of conscience,* or what Alcoholics Anonymous calls *a searching and fearless moral inventory.*

Her time *aside* in time and space with the Lady gave her perspective on the rest of her life. She'd put some distance between herself and the killing anxiety that drove her out of Portsmouth and away from Bobby. *Rob,* they were calling him now.

Bobby or Rob. If he gave her another chance, she'd call him *Robert* if he liked. Fear had driven her to push him away, a man who loved her beyond reason. Every time she'd looked at Bobby, she'd remembered walking the fae-path with him and making love with him all night and birthing their fae-child of green light. Every time Bobby smiled at her, she'd remembered their smiling child drifting away from her *into the road she'd just been walking on.* She'd wanted to forget everything she couldn't make sense of.

Her mother's house in Providence was too close to Portsmouth. She'd wanted to escape from the recent past, from Janjan, and even from her own mother. *Gotta get out of here, gotta get far away from all this weirdness.* Fear drove her to Texas because it was *far away.* Fear drove her to marry Andrew because he was *suitable,* because he *proposed,* and because he was *normal.*

Beth had had a lot of different kinds of sex lately, most of it adulterous. She knew being unfaithful to her husband was wrong. She also knew this mistake could easily be corrected. She was grateful to the Lady for showing her depths of erotic response she'd been blind to. She was grateful to Janjan and Bobbi for helping her discover her own power to give and receive pleasure. She was grateful to be sitting here safe in the bushes, enjoying the afterglow that promised more joy to come.

Sex was more important than she'd thought, more than a matter of friction in the erogenous zones, more than a means of becoming a mother. Sex was connected to love. Love was different from anything she'd expected.

Deeper, stronger, wilder. Scarier.

Her place in the world (whatever world she ended up in) had to be more than just being someone's wife and becoming someone's mother. The elves knew something the Lady had no need to know. There was a war against all human beings, a war Beth could no longer deny. She'd seen the enemy's screaming skull face on a flying mummy made of gold. She'd seen the enemy's human face in the hateful magician who traveled with the statue.

She'd seen in Rob's face that he loved her. How much he still loved her—however little she deserved it. *Rob says to tell you he loves you,* Janjan said, like they were all in middle school instead of trying to survive a war. *Loves:* present tense!

Walking the fae-road with Rob was a way to escape the war and keep her youth and beauty for as much of forever as she could endure. The thought of an unending suspended life walking with the Fae oppressed her breathing. *Breathing in for half of forever* wasn't for her.

When she embraced the goddess in her sacred grotto (wherever it was, whatever world it was in), she'd shared a mode of being which belonged to the Lady alone. The goddess' mortal lovers remained mortal, helpless against the desire she evoked in them.

And what was the ancient power bargain offered to a woman on Earth? To exchange her love and youth and beauty for children and material things. It was an unfair exchange: it was a robbery.

Beth's eyes were open. It was good to have a husband and children to love, but was that the end of the story? Janjan said the primary lesson they'd learned in Catholic school was: *Be a good girl and do what you're told. Don't ask questions and don't make waves.*

What God wanted of his creatures was deeper, stronger, wilder, scarier, and more mysterious than she'd known. The thought of returning to Andrew's mealy-mouthed, authoritarian church made her angry. Obeying arbitrary human authority was another robbery; you were exchanging your life for nothing.

What about Andrew? The thought of returning to her empty air-conditioned showplace of a house—her husband's house, really—filled her with dismay. Who *cared* about tray ceilings? It wasn't her home.

The thought of returning to Drew's bed filled her with pity: his secret aversion to her body; his haste to wash away all trace of her. They'd shared their last intimacy. She'd seen him clearly. He saw her as a pretty status symbol like the house. Like his church, he saw her as a means to an end, a broodmare.

The war on all human beings included a particular war against women, Janjan said. The war looked political or maybe religious on the surface, but it was actually spiritual and magical. The elves might be weird, but they were the good guys. Janjan was *good*—even if she didn't live on Earth anymore.

Her time with the Lady revealed things she'd never been told about time and eternity. Beth's intuition ran more to numbers than to poetry. There were numerals in the universe she'd never known about, forms of mathematics she might learn that powered music she wanted to hear.

Janjan had asked: *What do you want, Beth?*

Beth wanted love and life, wherever they took her.

50

King in Play *(Rob)*

The drive north was mostly silent. Rob had nothing else to say to Darnand. They weren't friends. *Try to escape and I will kill you instantly.* The Frenchman carried an old SS dagger like he'd used it before.

There had been more going on in the European War than Rob had known. The war behind that war was still being fought in secret. The Materialist Magicians' endless war against the elves made Darnand Rob's enemy.

Darnand was deserting the battlefield for a neutral nation, the way he might have fled the Nazis into Switzerland in the 1940s. Rob was in no position to judge; he'd deserted in two different wars. It was small comfort that few living men would care what he'd done or why he'd done it. At least he could hurt his enemies now by taking Darnand to the Fae.

How much deader could I have killed the Walloon? Rob thought helplessly. He had no magic in him but the *mandala* Janjan painted into his chest.

Darnand didn't trust himself to speak. He was dreaming of freedom and steady-state immortality. He was afraid of the Brotherhood and of the Walloon who led it. He was safe while the car stayed in motion. No magician could attack a moving target, not even with a demon to carry him instantly wherever he wished to go.

How much of a threat was Master Gold? Did he serve Louis or did Louis serve him?

Darnand took the first shift behind the wheel of the Walloon's Mercedes. Despite his fear and impatience, he kept to the speed limit. He had no desire to talk to the police. Neither he nor his prisoner had ever filed a tax return or held a driver's license. The ordinary obligations of twenty-first century American life were foreign to them both.

To Rob's surprise, the Major made a quick stop at a strip mall just off the highway. (He took the car keys with him.) He came out of a jewelry store clutching a small crucifix on a silver chain. He looped the chain over his head.

"In case the Walloon tries to take over my mind," Darnand said.

Rob could only nod. He understood the words, but he didn't understand the magic. Fae magic animated the realm he and Moira had ruled, but the Morrigna's teachings only confused him.

How could magic be real? How could a religious symbol protect Darnand from the Walloon? *God help us,* Rob prayed. *God help me, I don't understand religion, either.*

After the next stop for food and fuel, captor and captive swapped seats. Rob wanted to get to Portsmouth more than the Major did. *(Beth!)* Driving in heavy traffic at highway speeds was new to him. With his superb eye-hand coordination, he found the rhythm quickly. He kept extra room between the Mercedes and the car ahead. There wasn't anything he could do about cars following too close behind him. He watched the mirrors and stayed in his own lane.

At intervals, Rob felt a brief, wordless touch of Janjan's shining mind, checking on his well-being. He felt her smile and depart.

Before they reached Portsmouth, Janjan spoke to him.

He answered her in thought.

That conversation made Rob want something he had no words for. He wanted to hold Beth in his arms again and see *her* in the light Janjan had shown him. Despite having taken a long and winding road around the World Mountain to this bleak present moment, he was a sentimental man from a more sentimental time. Sentimental and resolute. He wouldn't give Beth up until she sent him away.

He hadn't even given up searching for his son, the child of green light whom Beth had borne him. Surely that was a hopeless, sentimental search. But surely he would *know* when he beheld the face of the child who now swam inside the fae-road, dreaming of rebirth into human awareness. It had not been an ordinary birth. Nor was it an ordinary death, or even death at all as Rob understood it. It was both better and worse, like life on the fae-path was both better and worse than life on Earth. *Better* because it offered youth and virtual immortality instead of old age and death. *Worse* because the fae-road led nowhere and meant nothing.

Rob took the exit off Interstate 95 into Portsmouth's west side. Five minutes later, he drove into a park-and-ride lot next to the state highway. He got out of the driver's side. Darnand got out of the passenger's side. He handed Darnand the car keys.

Darnand hesitated, then shrugged, reached back into the car, and tucked the keys behind the sun visor.

"I have only borrowed this vehicle, *soldat*," he said. "It belongs to Master Louis. I am no thief."

Even evil men can have a code of conduct. "The doorway to the fae-path is that way, Major." He pointed across the road. "About a mile."

Darnand clutched the crucifix. His lips moved in a prayer. "Let us go quickly, then. The Walloon will soon be here. I fear that he and the gold sorcerer are right behind us."

There was nothing to see in the darkness. Yet.

51

Queen Moira Goes A-hunting

A-hunting we will go, a-hunting we will go
We'll catch a fox and put him in a box
And then we'll let him go
- (Thomas Arne, "A-Hunting We Will Go"
from John Gay's *The Beggar's Opera*, 1777)

Queen Moira missed King Robert. She could no longer remember why they'd quarreled. A silly spat about a silly girl, no doubt. Whichever girl it was had surely moved on to other lovers. Only Moira retained any memory of the affair. Fidelity was uncommon among the Fae. The queen was happy to forgive her husband. None of the lovers she'd taken in his absence were his equal.

The king wasn't her husband in the earthly legal sense. They'd exchanged no religious vows either on Earth or here among their subjects where no one felt the need to marry. They'd signed no papers and filed no joint tax returns. They'd simply slept, lived, and ruled together for more months than she could recall.

Some idea of the fitness of things nagged at her. Even here on the fae-path, the queen was more Catholic than she knew. Her life on Earth was less clear than memories that bubbled up from other long-ago lives. Not all those lives were lived before Christianity arrived in Ireland. She wanted the valid sacrament of marriage conducted by a priest of the Church to unite her life to Rob's. That would make everything come right again. Wouldn't it?

After all, the Morrigna considered them wed, and Moira had borne Rob many, many children. Granted, they were what the Fae had instead of children, born with bodies made only of *the light of other days,* but still. Nobody on the fae-road worried about "legitimacy" except the queen; she kept her worries to herself.

There was no point asking the Morrigna where the king had gone. They'd tell her and she'd be shamed into acting on impulse.

Today, like every other day, Moira led her people along the fae-path rejoicing. At day's end, the queen arrived at a castle where she would normally spend the evening dining, dancing, and intriguing with her court. She also arrived at a decision. She guided her horse to one side of the path and waited until her sons and their retinue came along.

"Mother, well met!" said Brad.

"Good eventide, my queen!" said Chad.

The young men had quickly adapted to being princes of the realm. They'd spent more time being tutored by the Morrigna than either Rob or Moira.

"Dine with me this evening, my sons," Moira said. She smiled and spoke gently, but it was no invitation Brad and Chad could decline. Their libidinous plans would have to wait a day.

Like royals everywhere, the family lived in a fishbowl. The Fae watched their leaders for social cues, fashion tips, and hints of scandal. The king's absence from the queen's bed had been thoroughly analyzed by people with little else to occupy their minds.

That evening Moira and the princes dined alone in the castle's royal bedchamber. Those who served the royals overheard only trivialities.

So it came as a surprise to all the Fae the next morning when Queen Moira failed to mount her steed and lead her people onward, ever onward with the wind at their back and the fae-path rising to meet their feet.

Instead, Prince Bradley and Prince Chadwick announced themselves as princes regent and rode at the head of their people.

The fae-folk might grow bold enough to ask, *Where is the queen?* The princes would either tell them or not; the answer didn't matter. What mattered was walking into the joys of a new day. How delicious to speculate: Did Her Majesty have a secret lover in one of the worlds next to the fae-road? Had virile King Robert and luscious Queen Moira reunited in order to tag-team some lucky young men and women as part of a new sexual recruitment drive?

—

In reality Moira had walked all night, untiring, with the wind at her back and her intention set on returning to Portsmouth, back to the spot where she'd first stepped onto the fae-path with Rob and her sons.

The living road responded to her desire. Hundreds of thousands of proto-Fae propelled her forward with their wordless hunger to return to consciousness.

The Queen was not consciously aware of the creatures beneath her feet, the tide that urged her toward her destination. Why should she not have whatever she wanted? Was she not queen of all the Fae? Wherever she wished to go, the road existed to take her there, as the Fae reborn in green light though her womb existed to follow her. Should it not please both the reborn and the unborn to make her happy?

Those thoughts led her naturally to the thought of *Bobby*, as she'd first known him, before he became *Rob* her lover and *HRH King Robert* her co-regent. He'd walked with the Fae twice before during the ages-long reign of King Coran and Queen Maeve. Had he been happy as their subject? Had he been happy ruling at her side?

Moira thought Rob had *not* been content among the Fae, not content even to sit on the throne and rule over them. Not content to become the literal father of a reborn people.

Rob had only consented to walk with the Fae again because of Moira. The fae-road was the only place she could bring herself to seek sanctuary from the magicians she'd betrayed. The Walloon sought her death and the death of her sons. Surely Master Louis still lived; surely he still wanted to destroy them. Trying to protect her, Rob had destroyed the Walloon's body of flesh and bone, but the magician fled to Earth embodied in smoke.

Janjan Javorski offered Rob and Moira passage to the world of the elves. Moira had been unwilling to seek safety that meant forsaking everything familiar. If she had the slightest appreciation of irony, she would have seen how bizarre it was to rule the Fae and help them be fruitful and multiply. She had simply accepted the fae condition; there was no making sense of it.

The fae-path and its demigoddesses *spoke* to something deep in Moira, amplified ancestral voices she confused with her own thoughts. Myths spring from something ancient within us. She understood the idea of archetypes from her own experience.

As queen she wasn't her old self anymore, but she wasn't quite her real self, either. If we examine these ancient thought-formations when they arise, won't they vanish like smoke? What will happen to us then?

Moira allowed herself to know only that she was unhappy without Rob. She wanted to be happy. Therefore she would find him and persuade him to return to his rightful place walking the fae-road with her.

He came here to please her. Did he not want to please her still?

In the privacy of her thoughts Queen Moira vowed to fuck his brains out and in future to refrain from bitching at him about the other girls he fucked. (She found her former American self unbearably prudish.) Was it not also Rob's *duty* to repopulate the road around the worlds with near-immortals? His occasional dalliance with others was a practical matter, as much a necessity as her own sexual adventures. Jealousy was pointless here, the Morrigna taught. What mattered was the fae realm and the king and queen who ruled it for as much of eternity as they could bear.

As Moira walked along the road (*her* road!), she made a plan. She knew what would happen once she stepped off the fae-path into Portsmouth and the human condition. As a (mere!) human woman she'd been enduring menopause till the Morrigna restored her fertility. She'd become the mother of their people, reborn one by one from the mindless realm beneath her feet, through the *light of other days* that animated the fae-road. Every one a child of light. Every one a creature coalescing into flesh again, eager to explore the road around the worlds and dance and drink and swive in a near-immortal body.

Like all Fae women, Moira was beautiful and fertile. Her youth would fade when she returned to Earth and resumed the mundane breathing-in-and-out of mortal existence. She dreaded the thought. The shame of age was worse than death.

Would the Walloon's servants find and kill her on Earth before

Robert could rejoin her on the throne? She'd worked for the key financial institution of the Materialist Magician confederacy. She'd dared to disobey the Walloon. Although his orders would have meant the end of her human life on Earth, the Walloon would regard her disobedience as treachery.

On Louis' orders, the Morrigna had turned Moira into a tree to create a permanent living gateway from Portsmouth to the fae-path. In retaliation, Moira betrayed the Order's financial dealings to the Elf Friends. Her defection surely cost the Order millions.

There would have been reluctant federal prosecutions in the United States. Materialist underlings would have gone to prison or (more likely) to house arrest and probation. Neither the government nor the Order's attorneys wanted publicity. *Nothing to see here.*

Moira considered Janjan's offer of safety among the elves, the only safe place in all the human worlds. Anxiety filled her mind. Why *should* she surrender everything known and knowable (at least on the surface) where she was in charge of everyone (thanks to the Morrigna) in exchange for starting over amidst elvish mysteries?

Did she *have* to wander Earth looking for her consort, her royal fae finery gone ragged, pathetic in the harsh Earthlight, her lustrous red hair gone lank, gray, and brittle?

No, she would hover on the fae-road near Portsmouth and keep her immortality and her beauty. She would tempt King Robert back to her side by offering him her garden of earthly delights. She'd done it before.

52

Something Ancient and Terrible *(Louis)*

To contemplate the extermination of the human species and the long pause that follows before some other species crops up, it calms you more than anything else.

- (D.H. Lawrence, *Lady Chatterley's Lover*)

Carrying the Walloon's reconstituted body, Master Gold stitched his way across the empty sky. He carefully maintained an altitude where Louis could breathe. Through the space and time of Earth they flew, with breathless instants *inside* that spacetime, heading for Portsmouth on the coast of North America.

The two had enjoyed deep discussions about Louis' transition to his own golden body. With, as the ancient sorcerer said, a radioactive core warming the space where his heart once beat and his stomach once took nutriment. Installing of the radiation source was a matter requiring knowledge of both natural physics and preternatural metaphysics.

It was humiliating how much Louis would have to learn before he embraced the agony of transformation. He would master arts forgotten and rediscovered many times since Master Gold was born in the civilization that withered after Allah smote Iram of the Pillars. There was more history than anyone on Earth dared guess. The Order was ignorant of most of it. Perhaps the elves knew, but they were traitors to the Earth.

———

Born in Belgium before the First World War, the Walloon grew up speaking *Walon*, German, French, and Dutch. His wealthy family's ties to the Brotherhood of Materialist Magicians dated back centuries.

Nominally Catholic in public, Louis had been sworn to the Claimant's service since puberty. During the First War and especially during the years that led up to the Second, Louis came to see the Order's interests in Europe as nearly identical to those of the German Reich.

The Order sent Louis to work for an anti-Jewish paramilitary group. From the MM perspective, the earthly ideal was a totalitarian society which brutally suppressed first Judaism and then Christianity. There would be no distinction between policeman and priest in the secret intelligence service.

A secret confined to the Order was that the *Führer* was the Claimant's proxy. This Austrian antipope held the keys to the Claimant's kingdom and sought *The Triumph of the Will*. Not free will, but the One Will.

As Master of Masters, Louis learned that the Archmage and a few powerful magicians were monitoring a magical anomaly on another human world. Like a bubble rising in a lake of lava, the anomaly would burst in the air of Earth. Even the Archmage was ignorant of its nature. Human memory is limited, even in those whom the Fallen make nearly immortal. Louis helped the Order move their enemies into the blast zone of the magical explosion.

Adolf Hitler had been a by-blow of the Old Gods' reproductive cycle, neither human nor divine. The story was documented in fallen stone and broken cities on the Other World; the human damage happened on Earth.

The elves, who weren't really elves, were the Order's primary enemy. They came and went on Earth as they pleased, undermining the Order by recruiting whom they chose. They invited people from Earth to visit their world—and become elves. Materialist Magicians, who were both those things, sought to eliminate their enemies. The Order hated and feared the elves. The elves didn't worry much about the Order.

That was an arrogant elvish mistake, thought twenty-first-century Louis as Gold bore him through the air.

The magical anomaly erupted on Earth, killing sixty million people, over three percent of the total world population. The uninitiated blamed the Second War.

Certainly the War was a great help. A flood tide of spirits left the Earth. All those military and civilian deaths provided vast odylic force the Brotherhood could harness.

The heart of the dark magic the Order set in motion was the ritual murder of Jews. The sacrifice of the Jews provided the *magical* part of the spell the Archmage and his lieutenants cast upon the Earth. The Order enticed the world's finest scientific minds into the *material* part of the enchantment. These people labored both in Germany and in the United States to create the atomic bomb.

The war against the elves had many collaborators. Key members of religious, military, scientific, and intelligence groups from every nation abetted the Claimant's revolution against his High Enemy.

In a year, Earth forgot the elves completely. The sacred groves were cut down, paved over, and built upon. The slow poisoning of the planet accelerated. Millions of deaths created a collective psychic trauma that walled off all memory of the next world over.

The Order began cultivating a fitting *corpus*. The Claimant would incarnate on Earth in the flesh and bring the world under his rule.

But the elves touched the dreams of twentieth-century Richard Round with, of all things, an obscure fairy tale they'd left in nineteenth century Germany. There was still white magic in the world and a few who understood its uses. When Round and his teacher tried to reach the next world over, the memory spell began to fade. Old Elf Friends remembered the elves and helped Round escape the Order.

Richard Round traveled to the next world over and returned to Portsmouth to defeat a magician in battle—despite the Claimant's personal intervention. In Tibet he somehow unleashed a whirlwind of lesser demonic entities that aborted the ceremony of incarnation, killed the Order's Archmage, and incinerated the Claimant *in utero*.

Now barred from Earth, the Fallen could only work through those whose spirits they possessed.

The possessed hunger to do the Claimant's will. Further down the World Mountain the Mad King of Agharti aspired to invade and despoil

Earth. With the aid of the Spacelings, a sentient nonhuman race, he bred soldiers who could survive on Earth and fight next to their earthling allies in the New World Order.

The Mad King traveled to Earth, drugged Richard Round's ex-wife, and got a child on her. That child was Jean-Paul Herold, born with a Spaceling homing device in his head that would either kill him or draw him back to Agharti to serve his father.

The elves got to Herold before he could return to the underworld. He became an elf, returned to Earth, and seduced Donita Danton, an NWO political officer. When the elf traveled to Agharti, he rescued Queen Magdalena and her lover Aimee Amory, both pregnant with the Mad King's spawn.

That rescue triggered an irruption of the World Mountain from the underworld into Portsmouth. In the end, the King fell on his sword, his invasion of Earth aborted.

Which brings us to Daniel Ryun, thought Louis as he and Gold dove inside Earth's spacetime. The Order impregnated Ryun's wife with the Antichrist. After giving birth to the Chosen One, she entered a cyborg body to become his guardian.

Ryun had friends among the elves. With their help he undertook a quest around the World Mountain to save his wife.

Deep beneath the Mountain, the magicians had persuaded an Old God they called *Saturn* to magick human beings into nuclear-powered *steelbodies*. They programmed the steelbodies for a chained nuclear explosion around the World Mountain to cut the elves off from Earth again.

Ryun stopped them. Now free of the magicians, the Spacelings left Earth and took Saturn with them. The steelbodies exploded deep underground, near the base of the Mountain. When the World Mountain subsided, it pulled most of the continental shelf away from the American East Coast. Daniel Ryun and Aimee Amory saved millions of lives by using elf magic against an onslaught of enormous seismic sea waves.

The Order had never worried about ordinary human beings.

Gold flew them ever closer to their destination. Louis caught sight of the long chain of distant lights along the East Coast.

The Order needed a radical change of direction to survive and win their war against the elves. Louis thirsted for Gold's powerful arcane knowledge. Even if the end of all his exploring would be to arrive where he started and be slowly burnt to death inside and out.

Being mostly human at heart, he dreaded the transition from a human-looking mineral body to a metal statue in which only his mind could move. When he first stepped onto the fae-path, his breath had slowed into imperceptibility. The thought of giving up both breath and heartbeat in the Ceremony of Holy Agony filled him with more fear than the proximity of his guardian demon had ever done.

If there was anything heartening in the prospect of losing his still-beating heart (or having it petrified in gold and plutonium), it was the *enthusiasm* Master Gold brought to the Walloon's war. The Materialist Magician cause had given Gold a new lease on life. After all, Louis had found Gold shrieking mindlessly in the Nameless City, driven temporarily insane by the sheer weight of time. The ancient creature was truly immortal. Perhaps only a nuclear bomb could sever Gold's spirit from his body; Gold himself was a nuclear device.

Louis thought *he* had given Gold reason to continue living. *To fight:* to have his way in the world again. *To breed:* Gold wanted to create someone like himself and to oversee the centuries of Louis' learning. Gold would be Louis' father, his mother, and the midwife at his rebirth out of the flames.

Together, Louis and Gold would destroy the Elf Friends and defeat the elves. Permanently. And if the war should happen to kill the Earth? *Enfin, c'est la guerre.*

The Walloon worried what his former masters might still want. The Fallen once held Louis close enough to look through his eyes and speak with his mouth. Why would they have let him go to Gold if this new transformation was not their will? Gold gave Louis to understand that he and the Fallen had long ago reached a separate peace. The Nameless City lay outside the Greater Demonic Co-Prosperity Sphere.

Thinking of the Fallen, their interests, and the things that repulsed them reminded Louis of Darnand. He turned his psychic attention toward the shielded mind of his subordinate.

Darnand's car had stopped moving. The twice-traitor's mind was still hidden from the Walloon, but the Frenchman's location was perfectly clear.

Darnand was back in Great Bog and headed for the fae-road.

Louis had believed King Robert defenseless against the Order. The *faux naïf* had somehow subverted Darnand and was leading him back to the Fae—where Louis could not go. Some magic innate to the Morrigna now barred him from their domain.

Barred him *alone*. Louis was not alone.

What power could forbid the magus from using primordial magic to go where he wished? Surely nothing could prevent Gold and Louis *together* from entering upon the light-wrapped road that linked the worlds.

Si Satan le veut, the Walloon thought. As the Claimant wills.

53

The Strangers *(Janjan)*

For they have sown the wind, and they shall reap the whirlwind: it hath no stalk: the bud shall yield no meal: if so be it yield, the strangers shall swallow it up.

- (Hosea)

I felt Rob's mind before I heard or saw him. I gestured for silence.

Two human-sized shadows came crashing down the path, pushing through the brush.

Darnand, Rob's captor, filled Bobbi with silent revulsion. Rebirth on the Dark Path of the Materialist Magicians had sent things wrong in the man. Even with a crucifix for protection, he was a house divided.

Religionists say: Confess your sins and God will be merciful. Obedience will make you safe.

Magicians say: Come join the Claimant's glorious revolution against the High Enemy. Safety lies in serving the One Will.

Darnand was using his childhood faith to ward off evil. The Materialist Magicians had given him serial immortality in the body. What could God to do for him? He was still at war with his own creator. Walking with the Fae looked like freedom, exchanging his old life for a new life where he wouldn't have to lay his body down for a thousand years.

Rob neglected to mention that Darnand might end up swimming in the fae-path as one of the mindless, selfless beings who want only to return to mind and flesh again.

The Fae say: Recycle yourself for a greener tomorrow.

Unseen threat grew by slow degrees, darkening the psychic atmosphere in the field. Rob and Darnand felt the predators coming for them.

The two men made their way to a place that looked no different from every other spot in Great Bog that wasn't wetland.

The *mandala's* clear light had cost Rob his fae-light. I wondered how he'd find the fae-road again without it. He looked up, down, and all around: *Where's the damn doorway?* With *the light of other days* gone from him, the king of the Fae couldn't see the fae-path any better than I could.

Darnand held his stocky body stiffly. His shoulders were up around his ears. He was badly frightened. He wanted nothing more than to leave Portsmouth far behind.

Rob gave up the futile search and shouted, *"Moira!"*

Beth reacted to the sound of Rob's voice. She wanted to run to him. I shook my head and made a patting gesture: *Stay here.*

Green fae-light illuminated the spot where the fae-road came close to Earth. A woman's hand reached out of the air like a tarot card: the Ace of Swords. The queen of the Fae had been waiting for the return of the king. I was too scared to joke about it.

Moira's hand took Rob's, and I saw the rest of her. She looked young and beautiful, the gift of the fae-path and the Morrigna who watch over it. Rob took a step onto the road.

Darnand grasped Rob's forearm; Rob pulled him up. The two men stepped out of Portsmouth. Bobbi and I couldn't see them, a consequence of becoming an elf.

Beth was still an Earth girl. *She* saw Moira, the two men, and the fae-path they stood on.

Bobbi and I compared notes. We were tempted to run through the doorway before it closed, but intuition said *Wait.*

We faced a serious power imbalance. We were no better prepared for it than we'd been at Odiorne Point. War is like rock-paper-scissors. Every power is vulnerable to something. If we were patient, maybe we could figure it out without getting killed.

We only waited twenty minutes, but it felt like forever. Upwelling dread soaked our thoughts. Fear made Beth sick. I put a hand on her arm to calm her.

The hunters appeared in a rush of displaced air.

Our minds went quiet as the thick screen of leaves around us. Every human instinct made us want to gasp, scream, throw up, run away, or all of the above. Beth's face began to work; she swallowed convulsively. I put one palm over her mouth and rubbed her back till she felt better.

The Walloon rode on the sentient golden statue, floating just above the ground. The statue levitated him across the field faster than a man could run. They ignored us. Their minds were set on bigger game. Bobbi and I let our minds soak into the life of the grass and brush and weeds around us. In the dark we were no more noticeable than the milkweeds of the field.

Beth's mind stayed quiet after her time with the Lady. And after her time with Bobbi and me. Good sex can be a lifesaver. Bobbi and I screened Beth's thoughts with ours, like, *Nothing to see here, no minds, just grass and bushes and bugs.*

Despite our best efforts, I felt a touch of the statue-sorcerer's old, powerful mind and his nonverbal amusement: *You again? No threat, then. Moving right along.*

A silent explosion shook the ground. The statue's magic breached the doorway between worlds and left it in tatters. That violent penetration made me think of my long-lost, unlamented virginity, of course it did. I was like, *How much further is that thing going in?*

It was going all the way in. We saw the ancient road that wound around the worlds. The open doorway shone with green fae-light like an invitation.

The two magicians floated onto the fae-path and out of sight.

Beth thought: *I don't want to go back there, but I will if I have to.*

Bobbi looked at me. Rob needed us. Why weren't we running toward the open door?

Something was happening. Something had *already* happened.

The first hunter, the Walloon, was surrounded by a force field of evil thoughts and evil deeds. Last time we met, I was too weak to fight him.

The second hunter was worse. I recognized his mind. The ancient and terrible sorcerer lived in a body of gold. He'd joined the Walloon's war against us and was serving as Louis' chariot. Last time we met, he'd attacked me with the radiation held within his body.

Before there were Materialist Magicians on Earth, worse things had plagued mankind. The gold statue was one of those plagues. I hoped it was the last of its kind.

What's changed?

The Walloon's body was different; I'd seen that at Odiorne Point. It retained its human form, but everything inside had been remade. The touch of Louis' spirit was *almost* the same, but something was missing.

Back at Odiorne Point, I'd been too busy fighting radiation to see what the Walloon had lost.

When I first met the Walloon, he'd been perfectly possessed by the Fallen, his will no longer his own. His companion demon overshadowed his human spirit, moved Louis' body, spoke through him, and attacked Jackson and me.

Louis' spirit still bore the mark of the Fallen, but he was alone in his mind.

Where were the Fallen now?

Strictly speaking, they always remained outside the human worlds where their mad rebellion had put them. They'd been barred from independent operations on Earth since Richard Round reopened the way to the elves back in the 1980s. One elf got himself to Tibet at exactly the right time; the demons suffered a self-inflicted cataclysm. If the Bible had predicted it, you could only tell in hindsight. But the Fallen could still poison the wills and the lives of those who sought their power. That exchange of free will for power and long life happened to Materialist Magicians in one terrible initiation after another. The last of those exchanges had made Louis the master of masters but left him almost no will but the Claimant's.

That had changed.

Why would the Fallen relinquish a prize that took so much effort to possess? Had they abandoned the whole take-over-the-world-and-destroy-it project? Had they given up on seizing and degrading human souls?

No. No, they hadn't.

Beth, exhausted by the day's activities, by fear, by weirdness, went into paranormal overload and fell sleep, like people do if they have any sense.

Bobbi and I went back into passive-sonar mode. We cloaked Beth's peaceful sleeping thoughts with ours.

Massing shadows from a vast abyss were reflected on the still waters of our quiet minds. At an enormous distance visible darkness swelled like a thunderhead full of poison rain, more ancient and terrible than the gold mummy.

Remember, the Fallen couldn't come to *Earth* anymore in person. The objective of all their preternatural power was the ragged open doorway.

The Fallen were no longer barred from the fae-road.

Back in the beginning of all beginnings, the Fae had rejected the choice of good or evil. They went a different direction when the Morrigna crafted a way to walk around the worlds forever. They traveled on a road powered by *the light of other days* and by the spirits of those who wearied of that false eternity.

The good angels accepted that human beings were created with free will and would come home to the next world over, no matter how many births and rebirths it might take.

The evil angels wanted all creation to burn the way they burned. The Claimant would have seen the fae condition as a personal insult. I mean, he thought he deserved to sit on the throne of God. He'd been insanely fighting to make that happen ever since the crazy thought occurred to him.

The Fallen, those ancient and terrible strangers, were massing, getting ready to swallow up the fae-road.

Uh-oh.

54

Go West Sings "King of Wishful Thinking" *(Rob)*

You're back, Queen Moira seemed to say. *And who's this, then?*

It was the start of a fight Rob had no time for. As he formed the intention to speak, his consort soundlessly received his meaning.

Moira, this is Major Darnand. He seeks asylum among the Fae. Moira started to argue, but Rob pressed on, *Let's seek shelter now. Magicians are pursuing us. They may find the doorway out of Portsmouth.*

Moira decided to skip the quarrel; she'd missed her king. Really, he was the most skilled and passionate lover she'd ever had, on Earth or the fae-road. Wasn't pleasuring him her *duty* as well as her delight? Her desire surged. She cast her eyes downward in feigned subservience.

The three made haste along the fae-path. The road rose to meet their feet and helped them along the way. As always, the wind was at their backs.

Darnand's mind whirled. Entering the fae mode of being slowed his breathing until he could no longer feel it. When the king and queen spoke, he felt a *pulling* on his inner self and received what they *seemed to say,* rather than hearing words in his ears. It wasn't the strangest thing that had ever happened to him and was far from the most unpleasant. He had more questions than he could frame.

He was content to follow the king and queen further into their realm and conduct reconnaissance.

As they reached the wide-open gates of a roadside castle, the universe changed around them. The fae-path stopped moving underfoot like an escalator in a power failure. The wind ceased abruptly. With a convulsion of the diaphragm they began breathing at normal human speed.

Rob gasped. He filled his lungs and spoke as loudly as he would have on an earthly battlefield: "O Morrigna, guardians of those who walk the fae-path, I ask your aid!"

At the word *Morrigna*, three black-robed women of uncertain age appeared before the three human beings.

Rob told the three demigoddesses what enemies were pursuing him. He said nothing about elves and nothing about Beth, not in front of Moira, not yet. He didn't know if the girls had followed him here. *Don't borrow trouble*, his father said back before the Civil War.

What the king told them confirmed something the sisters already knew. Handling the Walloon's dark magic would be difficult. And the flying gold magician wielded magic the Morrigna hadn't seen since the Earth *changed*.

Darnand, however, was like nothing they'd ever encountered, a different sort of creature than Louis who had so briefly ruled the sisters and the fae-road. They walked around Darnand, looking him up and down, examining the energy he'd brought with him. They *sniffed* him. Were they examining his soul?

Darnand clutched the crucifix around his neck. A Nightmare Queen grinned at him, undaunted. The Morrigna were already old when Jesus of Nazareth was born in Judea.

Having learnt what they needed to know from the Walloon's slave, the three demigoddesses went looking for his master. Even here where the physical laws were different from Earth's, it was eerie to see their feet floating just above the road's surface. Sailing at unnatural speed, they disappeared in seconds.

55

Magical Thinking *(Louis)*

Master Gold saw the dimension where the skyroad and the Earth intersected. Like a cutting torch, his narrow beam of radiation speared the invisible barrier that divided Great Bog from the fae-realm. In a silent explosion Gold smashed easily through the wall. Fine-material rags fluttered around the opening. Louis clung to his patron like the passenger on a motorcycle.

Gold's life-force and spirit were confined to his shining metal body, but his mind and perceptions were not. He could travel equally well oriented backward, forward, up, down, sideways, or upside down. Louis sat on Gold's lap with his arms and legs wrapped around Gold's back and hips. Gold assured his client no harm would come to him.

The Walloon stared into Gold's empty eye sockets out of a lifelong habit of looking at human faces. Seeking a change of expression that never came. Imagining changes of expression on Gold's face that were not there. It was supremely undignified having Gold carry him like a homosexual lover. Louis could hardly bear to think about it.

He was crushingly dependent on his patron. Louis forgot the indignities he had forced upon on countless subordinates and disciples to bend them to his will—really to the Claimant's.

The magicians found themselves alone and no longer in Portsmouth. They hovered just above the ordinary-looking surface of the road. Louis' breath slowed almost to a stop. He remembered how little he enjoyed *breathing in for half of forever*, as the Fae said. Gold had no need to breathe in any world.

Louis nodded respectfully to Gold's unmoving face. He stepped off the golden thighs. For the first time in his new mineral body, he stepped onto the fae-path, right foot, left foot.

The road shook. Greenish darkness whirled above his head. With a gasp that hurt his chest he began breathing again as he had on Earth.

Once again the Fae had lost their provisional immortality. Partly because Gold's powerful primeval sorcery had smashed open the doorway, but mainly because of Louis.

Looking out the door to Portsmouth, the Walloon saw a cloud of demons massing far from Earth. The malignant awareness of the Fallen flooded through the opening into the fae-path, more deadly to the Fae than Gold's radiation was to the elves.

The fae-born had no defense against the touch of evil. Louis felt the travelers die. The Claimant's impress, the mark of Cain on Louis' darkened spirit, poisoned those he'd thought to make his subjects.

The Walloon's second visit to the fae-road was proceeding no better than his first. He had opened the door to the source of all evil.

"Master Gold," said Louis, "it seems my presence has had ill effects on those who walk the fae-path. Would you be so kind as to join me in that world we see on the other side of the road while I find a way to address this difficulty?"

"Of course! Perhaps I can be of assistance."

The sorcerer floated next to his apprentice as he walked fifty yards off the road into a dry desert world. Louis sat down heavily on a flat-topped rock. Gold hovered in midair, his face level with the Walloon's.

The magicians soon became engrossed in the permutations of magical theory. They didn't see three young women cloaked in green darkness walk quietly past on the motionless fae-path.

56

Send in the Elves *(Janjan)*

Time to go.

Bobbi and I pulled Beth out of the bushes. We ran down the trail. Bobbi ran like she was trying to steal second base. I ran like I was heading home so Jackson could have his way with me. Beth ran like she was unfamiliar with the feeling of earth under her feet. It made me smile to see her. I guess Texas is so hot you have to be a serious athlete to run anywhere but on a treadmill in an air-conditioned gym. Beth had always been kind of a princess.

I flash-updated Jackson. He absorbed everything so fast I was a little in awe. While he was out of the body, his mind became deeper, quieter, and quicker than I remembered. That process had continued while we were worlds (or months) apart, doing what we'd signed up for.

He still loved me. I was doing my damnedest to deserve it. I wanted him. It was reassuring how much he wanted me. I wrenched my thoughts away from what I wanted to do to, with, and for Jackson. I felt him smile.

We approached the doorway and slowed down. I took the lead. I'd been among the Fae twice. This would be Bobbi's first time. Beth had been there before. She was scared to go back. I didn't blame her.

Slightly above the ground of Great Bog an old woman dressed in black stood on the shining green road. A Morrigan. Her dark eyes revealed nothing.

"Anann?" I ventured a guess. The three sisters looked more alike than not, though they could assume any female appearance they wished.

"Aye," said the Morrigan. "I did not expect to see you again, Lady Janjan. What seek ye among the Fae?"

Not knowing what kind of creature the Morrigan was, Bobbi was ready to kick ass. I thought to her, *Anann has the power to keep us out. She's asking why she should let us in.* Bobbi dialed back her impatience and let me negotiate.

"I came to talk to my friend King Robert," I said. "Our mutual enemy the Walloon has invaded your realm—along with an ancient magician who looks like a golden statue. I fear for the king's life." There was more, but I didn't want to get into it.

"You are welcome here, then," said Anann, "you *and* your friends." She gave Bobbi a searching look. Bobbi gave her a level elf look back. Bobbi found the Morrigan very interesting. Even to elves, the Morrigna are opaque.

Anann gave Beth another searching look. Did she actually move closer, lean forward, and *sniff* my friend?

"Oh, dear," Anann said to Beth, "Queen Moira will *not* be happy to see *you*." The Morrigan was smiling like she couldn't wait for Moira to meet Beth. Not for nothing were they called the Nightmare Queens. The three sisters loved trouble and conflict; they were going to get plenty of it.

Her business complete, the Morrigan vanished. More accurately, Anann grew smaller and smaller until my eyes no longer saw her. She was using another dimension to go somewhere. The Morrigna were demigoddesses. They traveled the same way the Lady took Beth and me *aside* from Earth's spacetime and brought us back again.

We stepped through the ragged portal onto the fae-path.

Beth and I took deep breaths. *Huh.* Surprised, we looked at each other. We'd expected our breathing to slow way down. *Breathing in for half of forever*, the Fae said. Tonight we were breathing like we would on Earth.

This had happened before.

"It's the Walloon," I said. "Last time he was here, he tried to take over the fae-road. All he managed to do was kill the Fae."

"So where are they?" said Bobbi.

I pointed to the road under our feet.

Bobbi's mind sank below the surface. Her awareness touched thousands upon thousands of almost-sentient beings who swam helplessly toward her. "Jesus Christ," she said. Tears came to her eyes.

Beth's perceptions were limited to the human spectrum. "Everybody's dead?" she said.

"Kind of, yeah. I don't think anybody who was born here is still above ground."

I looked back at Portsmouth. There wasn't much to see in Great Bog at night. Grass, bushes, stunted trees, cattails in the marsh. The green light shining out of the fae-path illuminated a hole in the air next to where we stood.

I turned to the other side of the road. Bobbi turned with me. We saw a rocky landscape and low mountains.

That world looked empty, but it wasn't. I sensed toxic thoughts. The Walloon and the statue-sorcerer were over in the rocks, not far from us. I didn't know why they'd killed all the Fae and then left the fae-path. I didn't plan to go ask them.

"Let's just move right along, okay?" I whispered. I started walking briskly.

Bobbi walked with me. "Let's do that," she whispered back.

We centered ourselves, ready for battle. Quiet minds are less detectable.

"Why are we whispering?" Beth whispered as she caught up.

"Bad guys," I whispered. "*Worst. Guys. Ever.* C'mon, maybe we can find somebody nice to talk to at the next castle."

No wind blew at our backs as we walked up a long, gentle slope of fae-path and (I hoped) out of the magicians' range of perception. The road wasn't rising to meet our feet like when Jackson and I walked it. I could have used focused intention to harness the power of all the proto-Fae below us, but that felt wrong. I wasn't here for myself. Better to put one foot in front of the other and keep my eyes open.

Within the hour we reached a fae castle. There were minds I recognized inside. I paused outside the open gates.

"Bobbi," I said, "would you take Beth into the castle? Maybe have her show you around? I have ... a thing to do here."

Bobbi said, "Are you *sure*, Janjan?" She saw the shape of what I had in mind; I didn't try to hide it. This time she wouldn't be standing behind me with a leather belt to give me the dangerous pleasures of pain. I'd be inflicting distress and danger on myself.

"I'm sure enough, honey," I said. "Kiss me for luck?"

Bobbi hugged me and kissed me chastely on the lips, no tongue. Just as well, I needed my wits about me.

Beth was still being Beth. She knew something was up, but didn't want to know the details. I hugged her, too.

I slapped their asses. "Get indoors, you two. I'm pretty sure that's where the action's going to be."

That was at least half true.

57

Nothing Gold Can Stay

Two very different creatures sat together in empty desert. They felt at home there. The story of the Walloon's first fae-road expedition flew from his mind to Gold's.

On his first visit, he used dark magic to turn his human body as transparent and fast-moving as air. When the doorway to the Fae was opened, Louis slipped in.

He'd claimed power over all the Fae in the name of the Claimant, though the Fallen themselves were barred from the road around the worlds. On Earth Louis had seized magical power over the Morrigna, the tutelary spirits of the place. The throne was empty. It *should* have been simple enough for Louis to become king of all the light-wrapped travelers.

Coran and Maeve, the old king and queen, had stepped off their path in Portsmouth and simply accepted their own deaths. The elves Jackson and Javorski had done something to the royal couple so that the odylic force of their green light shone off into the universe, wasted. Nothing was left for the American authorities to find but bones so ancient and fragile they turned to dust at the first forensic touch. Government functionaries in the pay of the Brotherhood removed all mention of Coran and Maeve from the classified record of that day.

There was other eyewitness testimony of that confusing night. The materialists also expunged all mention of Master Simon, Louis' lieutenant. Jackson, the ungrateful traitor, killed Simon with his bare hands. The Fallen left no trace of Simon's body behind when they swept up his spirit and carried it away. Who would believe anyone had seen such a thing?

And then Robert, *soi-disant* king of the Fae, had tried to kill the Walloon's body with *an arrow*, of all things, through Louis' head. Remembering the pain of his sudden transformation into smoke filled Louis with fury. The choice between entering death (if the Fallen released his spirit) or entering the visible darkness of demon-smoke was no choice at all.

Far away (yet always far too close) Louis heard the scornful laughter of the creature who had first seduced him and then sent him away to Gold. His companion demon. His possessor. The Fallen broke their human toys and then mocked them. At least Gold, who lived on a different spiritual frequency altogether, didn't hear the demons fleering at Louis and his *loathsome bodily problems.*

Up ahead on the fae-road Louis felt Darnand's mind. The traitor's thoughts were still veiled by an artifact of the High Enemy. Vile superstition. The Walloon thought, *What, could ye not watch with me one hour?* And *Verily I say unto thee, That this night, before the cock crow, thou shalt deny me thrice.* Of course there never had been any such person as Jesus of Nazareth and if there had been, how could he have had followers as faithless as Darnand?

Louis was distracted by a continuing pain from having his breath stop and start in a spasm. His mostly-mineral body still had absolute requirements: air, water, and nourishment. He felt an *ache* in his slippery silicate lungs, but was too vain to bother Gold with this shameful physical difficulty.

As Louis laid out a detailed analysis of the metaphysical problem, his toxicity to the Fae, Gold's attention wandered. Gold's mind wasn't distracted by anything physical. Down the light-road not far away, he sensed an enormous *presence.* It stood behind a fragile veil waiting for *him.*

Gold found himself *wanting* something, *yearning* for it more than his human body had ever craved food, drink, or sex. Surely a being who could induce such desire embodied deeper power and knowledge than even Gold possessed. Could the sorcerer add that power to the humming, vibrating, magical sun-source that sustained his life?

Louis had asked Gold to bring him to the fae-path because Louis was *in hate* with the elves, with their friends, and especially with those who had betrayed him, his faithless servant and the fugitive king of the Fae.

For the first time in thousands of Earth years, Master Gold found himself *in love*. He failed to recognize the symptoms.

Completely forgetting his protégé's quest for vengeance, Gold levitated away from Louis in the desert world. In effortless silence the magus flew above the fae-road.

The sentient *presence* drew him. He had the power to resist, but not the desire.

58

The Harrowing of the Fae-path *(Janjan)*

If you will it, it is no dream. - Theodor Herzl

Last year I stood outside a fae castle where the Morrigna and the Walloon were waiting for me. I extended my mind into the fae-path. Below the solid-looking surface were the minds of almost every Fae there had ever been. Poisoned by the Claimant's lethal image in the Walloon, the Fae died and sank into the road. They melted body and soul into the *light of other days* that powered the path and wrapped those who walked it. They were really only *almost*-minds, not Fae yet, *proto-Fae*. It was terrible to see. I'd made a spontaneous promise to the helpless beings trapped in the fae-path:

May all creatures be free from suffering. Though you are numberless, though it takes me forever, I vow to free you all. Then I added: *In the name of Jesus Christ, amen!*

Religion's shadow disappears in the light of experience, but a promise is still a promise

A mass Fae extinction had happened again.

I reached out my mind, not worrying about being detected. Above the road I sensed only the minds of Bobbi, Beth, Moira, Rob, and (more distantly) Moira's sons. The only *fully-human* minds.

I also sensed Darnand, whose humanity the Dark Path had desolated. He was nearby, but keeping his distance from us.

The Walloon was still in a world I'd tiptoed past next to the path. I felt his dark spirit's impact. His mind felt less human than Darnand's.

And I felt the impact of the ancient sorcerer mummified in gold. He'd traveled further from the human condition than the Walloon. His mind felt more alien than the cloaked minds of the Morrigna.

He was traveling this way fast.

We had no way to fight the magus when he got here. Bobbi would have to protect the living as best she could. Welcome to elfhood, dear sister.

The Fae who'd been reborn during Rob and Moira's reign were mindless and helpless inside the road. How could I help them?

All I had was my human mind, my human spirit, and my human heart. Not being a Materialist Magician, I had no power to turn myself into magical smoke. Not being fae, I had no way to dissolve my flesh in *the light of other days* as the dying Fae had done. This body couldn't pass through the fae-road.

I had to lay my body down, the thing I least wanted to do in any world. My spirit had to enter the path naked. Temporarily, I hoped.

I mean, look what happened to Daniel in the nextworld highlands. He and Jackson let their bodies completely disperse. Later they resumed physical life. The bodies that looked and felt and smelled exactly like their old bodies were made new from nextworld water, earth and air. Dust to dust: all flesh is grass. It made me dizzy to think about.

My body was an old friend; we'd been through a lot together. Maybe it wasn't *me*, but it was a *picture* of me. It was as close to my real self as I was able to venture. Even when I learned to *inquire within*, I never questioned my physical being. But Daniel had shown me how to step out of my body so I could see things other elves could not. Taking my spirit into the fae-path was just an extreme, extended version of that. Right?

I didn't *think* I'd have to die to do this.

I know what you're thinking. Does Janjan think she's *Jesus* or something? What right does she have to make a vow like that? *Harrowing Hell, really?*

Elves keep their promises as best they can, using whatever they have to work with. I was the only person here who knew how to do this. Welcome to elfhood, dear Janjan.

I rested my back against the rough stone wall of the fae castle, crossed my legs in front of me, sat up straight like a good girl, breathed deep into my belly, and took my consciousness out of my body. It was like saying goodbye to a lover.

59

This Is Awkward *(Bobbi)*

Bobbi felt a dark spirit fly into the castle. A shining gold statue spiky with invisible radiation.

She broke a cold sweat. *I don't belong here.*

It was the Odiorne Point debacle all over again. Bobbi was no better prepared than she'd been among the Children of Venus. She longed to fly home faster than light to the warmth and loving-kindness of the next world over. She fought not to fade out of this darkened realm.

Struggling to remain where she was needed, fighting her fear, Bobbi forgot that Beth was isolated in her own thoughts. She assumed Beth would feel her alarm and follow her out of danger.

Bobbi went running down a passageway. She raced deep into the castle to put tons of stone between her and the radiation. She never looked back.

Bobbi was breathing hard and sweating harder by the time her panic ebbed. She slowed to a walk and took two more turnings down shadowy corridors. She looked around.

She was alone. *Dammit, I had one job to do.*

Far behind her in the great hall, Bobbi sensed the ancient, terrible creature slow and stop. She felt his power. Now that it was too late, she felt Beth's terror and despised herself for her weakness.

A second ancient power entered the castle. It didn't fly in through the open gates. The Lady of Cyprus emerged through Beth's mind and heart in light the color of roses.

The Lady kept Beth safe. The goddess held converse with the statue.

Even at a distance, Bobbi felt the Lady's impact in her heart and loins. She began to wish Janjan was here with her. Naked.

Bobbi wasn't the only one affected by the goddess' radiant power. A murmuring came from a room across the stone-paved hallway. A man and a woman, lovers who thought themselves alone.

She would have walked past and left them in privacy, but this was an emergency. The door was ajar. Bobbi hesitated in the doorway.

It was Rob, her friend, Janjan's friend, Beth's ex. Bobbi didn't recognize his mind because it was flooded with sexual desire.

Rob was standing in the middle of the room He was still wearing his pants and shoes, but his shirt was off. His lean musculature was abstractly beautiful, but sparked no desire in Bobbi.

Standing close to Rob, holding his gaze, was a beautiful woman in the full flower of fertile maturity. Her mind was as full of desire as King Robert's. She kicked out of her shoes, pulled her dress off over her head, and dropped it on the floor. This must be Queen Moira, Bobbi thought. A natural redhead, too. Mmm...

Even at a distance, the Lady induced sexual desire in people who would normally have been preoccupied with other things.

Rob and Moira had eyes only for each other. The Lady's presence amplified the natural sexual attraction that had bound the king and queen together.

Full breasts swaying gently, Moira knelt on the stone floor before Rob.

"Moira, no," Rob said. Gently, he held her face away from him.

Bobbi was put off by the bulge in the front of the king's trousers. She'd never understood what penises had to do with sex.

Moira's voice was hoarse with lust. "How I've missed you, my king. Only let me take you in my mouth again. Share the green light with me once more and everything will come right between us. Let's make the fae-path shake!" She reached to undo his belt. Rob wasn't fighting her too hard about it, either.

Bobbi did *not* want to see what happened next.

"Um, excuse me?" she said.

60

The Lovely Shall Be Choosers (Beth)

Beth felt the approaching threat. The *thing* that had bypassed her in Great Bog was headed right for her now, making her sick and weak again. She looked around the great hall and found herself alone.

What? Where was Bobbi?

This was not how things were supposed to go.

She'd expected the elves to ride in on white horses or whatever and save the day. But she was alone with no help in sight.

She was dismayed to see everything turning to shit around her, even here on the fae-road where she'd never imagined walking again. And whose fault was it? *Hers.*

She remembered having tea with Janjan last year in a Providence coffee shop. This was after she'd broken up with Rob—*Bobby* she'd always called him. Janjan told her Bobby was okay and that he'd met somebody else, a woman with children. Beth had looked down at her tea.

"That's good," she said quickly. What she meant was, *I don't want to hear any more about this.* Then, being a selfish bitch, she asked, *"Janjan, am I in any danger still?"*

"The best I can say is *Maybe not*," Janjan said. "The worst I can say is *Maybe*."

Beth said, "I'm not stupid. I know there's only one safe place. I just don't want to go there."

Beth remembered thinking *I am too damn pretty to have to leave the Earth behind.* A thought so shameful that she immediately denied thinking it. Wasn't she *entitled* to have everything her own way while she was still young? *The lovely shall be choosers, shall they?* If you want to escape the weirdness, go someplace normal and boring. She'd hoped Janjan wouldn't hate her for running away.

Leaving Portsmouth, moving to Texas, and getting married still didn't insulate Beth from what was happening in the world. She wasn't insulated from the consequences of her own actions.

Janjan had left a business card for the Elf Friends' law firm. Beth had called them, gone off to the West Coast to talk to Janjan, and gotten kidnapped, then rescued—first by the Lady, then by Janjan. And here she was.

Where were the elves? She wasn't exactly sure where Janjan was right now.

Bobbi had tippy-toed back to peek out the front door and told Beth that Janjan's *body* was leaning against the castle wall, but Janjan wasn't *in* that body anymore. Was she dead?

And where had Bobbi gone? Had she seduced Beth only to abandon her?

Was *anybody* around who'd gone to the next world over and gotten whatever superpowers people got there? Hello? Anybody? Anybody?

Why had no one shown up to rescue Princess Beth from Castle Perilous? *Worst. Fairy tale. Ever.*

Beth knew her way around a fae castle. They were all built on the same layout. She retreated to a dark corner of the great hall. She pulled a chair in with her, sat down, hugged herself, and hoped for the best: for the elves— or *somebody*—to solve all her problems so she could just go home.

Go home and do what? Where was home? Those questions would have to wait. She had to survive today.

In through the open door of the great hall floated the living gold statue. She'd seen it through the haze of her Lady-altered consciousness when she stood on the sandy island in the Odiorne Point grotto.

Being in her right mind today was no great gift. Beth was scared sick. The face of the floating thing was twisted in an eternal mask of agony. The alchemy that gave the creature eternal life had killed the man in the process. The evidence was there for anyone to see. The golden skull mouth gaped wide in a silent golden scream. Bony hands were clenched in golden fists upon its golden thighs.

Beth sensed a restless intelligence inside the figure. That intelligence fastened upon her. The thing floated toward her, horribly stable in midair, a fever dream that made her eyes burn.

Her life was about to end. She should make a sincere Act of Contrition. She should say the Our Father or the Hail Mary, but all the religious belief she'd grown up with seemed distant and abstract. Instead, nearly paralyzed with horror, Beth thought, *Oh, Lady, what is this? I can't even...*

Her resolve grew stronger. The Lady was her only experience of the transcendent; who else should she call upon now?

O Aphrodite... she thought. As she cried out, she *inquired within* herself where she had never dared look before. *If you can save me from this thing or help me escape it, your praises will be forever on my lips in whatever world I travel.*

First there was only a hush deep within Beth, then a sense of ripples, as if a wind blew above the surface of a boundless, silent ocean.

Like the first day they met, the Lady *arrived* in Beth's mind. Cypris looked out Beth's eyes and beheld the golden statue.

Beth wanted to slip into deep and dreamless sleep. To let this cup pass from her. To escape the approaching terror. To escape the full awareness of *who* she'd asked to help her. Her mind began to fade.

STAY AWAKE WITH ME, DAUGHTER. The goddess' overwhelming mental voice shocked Beth alert.

Now commenced the full theophany Beth's will had resisted before. The Lady had not pressed her for this deepest surrender, even when they lay together and pleasured one another and pleasured Janjan. Beth needed the power closest to her own human power. The power women had always sought on Earth. The power embodied in the queen of love and beauty.

Two beings from ancient Earth faced each other across five feet of stone floor. The goddess occupied Beth's body along with her. Cypris sat in Beth's wooden chair shining through Beth's flesh and bone.

The sorcerer's mummy would remain seated for all eternity. Being part of a solid object, his arms and legs never moved. He hovered movelessly just above the floor. Unwilling to defer to anything in the universe, he rose gently upwards until his golden eye sockets were level with the Lady's.

Such different modes of being and power had difficulty taking each other in.

The Lady saw all the way into Gold, all the ages of his history. She saw where the search for power over the elements and energies of heaven and earth had brought him. What the Lady saw, Beth saw with her, though her human mind lay quiet.

The Lady saw all the names within the shining statue. The name Gold had been born with when he suckled at his mother's breast. The name the magi gave him in a secret ceremony in the days when men still farmed the Sahara. The name he had taken when he became a magus, preparing to enter an immortal body of gold in the Nameless City. The name he used now described his body, not his hidden self.

Gold saw the power that inhered in the Lady's being. He yearned for it, but also resisted, lest she engulf him and he be lost. In her he saw the history men call myth, profound and powerful, a story that springs from the root of life itself which reason cannot comprehend.

The statue spoke first. (It seemed to Beth that he spoke and that the goddess answered him.) Their mental communication was rapid with many exchanges of idea and symbol until they settled upon a mode of discourse. Far more information was exchanged than Beth understood. What follows is all she was able to remember and reconstruct in English.

"Never in all the ages have I looked upon such a one as you, O Aphrodite Pandemos."

"Nor have I ever seen your like, O Master Gold."

"Are we to be enemies? The power cloaked within this body could slay your earthly vehicle in an eyeblink, but I think that would leave you yourself untouched."

"I would be sad if you killed young Elizabeth of Earth. She has most generously shared her mind and body with me in every way. Besides, it was the servants of your protégé Louis who *offered* Beth to me and thereby invited me back to Earth. I see no need for enmity between us."

A feeling of lonely melancholy from the golden statue. "They live such a short time, the humans. I had only sixty Earth years when I became as you see me now. But tell me if you will, have you tidings of my own people who left Earth so long ago?"

The Lady was quiet for several long moments. Seeing her mind questing first into its memories and then into its vast current perceptions, Gold waited patiently. To wait cost him as little as to act, he felt so little.

Finally the Lady spoke, "Your brothers and sisters have left the human worlds, as have my kinfolk. The worlds changed around us until even I sought rest and refuge *aside* in space and time. Here is what I see..." The Lady shared her vision with Gold.

[*The ancient sorcerers, free of bodily limits, enter orbit around a far star whose energy nourishes their attenuated physical being. What they then become makes more sense to Gold than to the Lady whose perception carries the vision.*]

Beth, submerged in the Lady's mind, though not effaced, could make no sense of all she saw. The Lady perceived all dimensions of time at once. It would be more accurate to say that time was mostly irrelevant to her. She was, the multiverse was, things came and went. The Lady had been born to this mode of perception, while Gold had attained it by slow degrees in the last thousand years.

Gold finally said, "Ah!" He went silent, considering what to say about what he'd been shown and considering what to do about it.

Now it was the Lady's turn to wait patiently. Even Gold's high-speed thoughts had a long way to travel to reach a conclusion.

"Forgive me if I intrude," she said, "but does this knowledge I bring make you happier? For I would make no creature sad." The Lady knew that being herself sometimes caused suffering to those who adored her.

"Sad? No! My teachers said it is always better to know than not. To deny what one knows is to die a coward's death."

The Lady understood death only insofar as she'd mourned the loss of human lovers, husbands, and children. Being immortal, she had no need of courage, though she admired it in others. "What will you do with the news I bring of your people?"

"At first I gloried in joining Louis in his war on [*the elves*]. Now I see there is nothing to be gained. The Earth has changed time and again since

I became as you see me today. What Louis calls the High Enemy is perhaps the ground of his own being. And perhaps yours and mine as well. Ha!"

The Lady did not care to consider the foundation of her existence. Her story of birth in the foam hid something deeper that made no more sense to her than it did to Beth, who sat at a slight remove in her own body and mind, watching and listening.

The Lady asked, "What will you do now?"

Gold thought for a long moment. Finally, "I was the youngest of my people to pass through fire and agony into this body of gold. You have shown me the path my kin traveled so long ago. I am ready to follow them into the stars. The magic whose seeds they planted in me has ripened."

"Will you take that golden body with you?"

"It has been my house and my temple for so long. Now I fear I must leave this form behind and voyage in the *[fine-material]* wind between galaxies."

"And what of the killing power within your body?"

Gold's attention sharpened. "I take your meaning. I have no real enemies I need attack. Let Master Louis fight his own war! Where can I leave this body so that it will harm no one?"

The Lady said, "If you would but sit upon the road that runs past this castle, presently I shall send servants to help you unbody yourself at the most auspicious time, in the most fruitful place..."

[A rapid exchange of idea and symbol altogether beyond Beth's understanding.]

Seeing that the Lady told the truth because she had no need to lie, Gold turned in midair and said, "I thank you for all you have taught me, O Cypris." He floated out of the great hall and left the castle.

The Lady's shining power showed Gold that he yearned not for union with a female creature in the sexual embrace, but to be reunited with his own kind around their star, however long it might take to journey there.

Long before Jesus walked the Earth, the Lady taught: *Love, and do what you will.*

61

The Lady and the Morrigna

Be not too tame neither, but let your own discretion
be your tutor. Suit the action to the word, the word
to the action, with this special observance, that you
o'erstep not the modesty of nature. For any thing so
o'erdone is from the purpose of playing, whose end,
both at the first and now, was and is, to hold as 'twere,
the mirror up to nature; to show virtue her own feature,
scorn her own image, and the very age and body of
the time his form and pressure.

- (Shakespeare, *Hamlet*)

The Morrigna knew the instant the wall around their realm was breached and the sentient darkness shone through it. They felt the Walloon's feet touch the fae-path and saw his personal evil kill those who'd been born to walk it.

They had no immunity against the plague Louis carried, Fallen-magnified dark magic from far beneath the worlds. Having once succumbed to that power, the sisters would never do so again. For the moment, they evaded their enemy.

The golden statue-creature was a puzzle to them. How could an inanimate *thing* contain a human spirit? What did such a being want with the Fae and those who served them? Why did the statue fly out of the castle only to sit silent and inscrutable in the middle of their path? *The Human Form, a fiery Forge.*

The Nightmare Queens had never been human. Wondering what would be forged today on the road where the magus sat, they entered the castle and approached the Lady of Cyprus.

Like Gold, the sisters were drawn to the sentient *presence* that had entered their realm. They were not surprised that this power manifested through Beth's beautiful human form. The girl had stepped onto the fae-path smelling of the Lady's roses.

Badb, Macha, and Anann brought their outward appearance into harmony with the goddess. In the body of the Earth girl, the Lady appeared young and lovely; so now did the Morrigna. As they embodied the *light of other days* that powered the fae-road, they reflected the goddess' light back to her. They held the mirror of themselves up to the Lady's nature to show virtue her own feature.

The Lady was more their sort of creature than Master Gold was. Gold had been born human and painfully made immortal by magic. The sisters had never been children, rising full-grown from the sea as enigmatic as the Lady.

Beth bore witness to something unique in the secret history of the worlds. She struggled to translate the exchange between four nonhuman beings into English so her human memory could retain it at the meniscus between myth's extravagance and Nature's modesty.

"What do you want of me?" The Lady's tone was magisterial but not unkind.

Anann said, "We served the Fae. It seems our people and the path they walked for so long will soon be no more. To return to any of the human worlds as we are would mean our unmaking. The Earth is not as it was when first we left it. When you return to your realm, O Aphrodite, take us with you and we will ... *serve* you."

The emphasis the Morrigan gave the word "serve" made her meaning clear enough. To see the Lady was to understand the kind of service she desired. Ironically, the Morrigna had been too preoccupied overseeing fae procreation to take any pleasure from it. In the Lady's presence, they found themselves eager to embrace and be embraced once again.

The Lady grew sad. She had known so many demigoddesses, merry and bright as daylight, pretty, changeable, and amorous; where had they gone? Why had *she* remained aside from Earth's spacetime for so long with none of her own kind for comfort, company, and delight?

"Ah, well," said the Lady, "the Earth was disenchanted long ago. New philosophies replaced old certainties while I slept. The Nereids have left the oceans, along with Poseidon himself. Gone, all, to worlds more congenial than the world where first we came to life. Yes, be my nymphs, then. Share your love and beauty with me and with the mortal women of Earth. What has been disenchanted may be re-enchanted."

The Lady was a creature of the eternal present moment. But as she spoke, a painful hidden memory returned. In the mirror of the sisters she saw reflected how she had lost the one child she could never willingly let go. Wild with grief, she had enshrouded that part of her past to put him out of her mind.

Her son was older than her in the way of the primordial gods. He had only become embodied through the Lady's body. Unlike anything before or after it, his birth *changed* her.

She had loved him to distraction, sought to possess and control him, to keep him away from the woman he loved. A woman who had been something more than merely human. A woman whose roots went deeper than even the Lady's, into a sacred grove, into the clear light.

Some new bargain had been struck in the depths of creation where the Lady dared not inquire. Her son had loved the woman (Psyche was her name) and had married her. The marriage made them one flesh, one spirit. (The Lady made no distinction.)

And then?

Together had they (O unthinkable thought!) gone from Earth wherever men and women go when they lay their bodies down?

Together had they gone to walk the high country of the elves, never to return?

Never would she see her son again, never be reconciled to his bride, never dandle their children on her knee. Grief rose again, raw and new. The Lady remembered why she had hidden her own history in a blind spot. Yes, she was the queen of love and beauty. Yes, she'd married the crippled blacksmith god. Yes, she'd taken many lovers among gods and men, made even the mighty god of war cry out in ecstasy. Yet her son, the one lover she had yearned for above all others, was forbidden her, a monstrous and unnatural lust even for a goddess.

How Cypris hated the woman who took her best-loved son away. And still whenever she saw a glimmer of Psyche's beauty in one of her own priestesses, unreasoning anger would escape the Lady's blind spot. Cypris would punish and pleasure the woman to shame her for Psyche's sins against the queen of love and beauty. Secretly hoping that Eros would return to save his bride from his mother.

He had never returned in any form the Lady recognized.

She was tempted to return to the refuge of endless sleep, aside from the realms of men and gods.

Being what they were, the Morrigna mourned the Lady's old loss with her. Being what she was, the Lady quickly reached a decision.

"Come with me," she said. "If you would follow and serve me henceforth, I have a task for you now."

62

Inside the Fae-path *(Janjan)*

They cannot look out far.
They cannot look in deep.
But when was that ever a bar
To any watch they keep?
- (Robert Frost, "Neither Out Far Nor In Deep")

A pang of loss. I wanted to go back to my body. I didn't.

My ears stopped working. From the quiet path around the worlds I entered total silence.

Oh. I heard an enormous distant harmony: the Music of the Spheres, creation itself continuing in every moment, seldom noticed by us human creatures. I would have wept with joy, but emotion requires a body. What I felt was profound but *austere,* a long way from Janjan country.

Ah. I heard the high country of the next world over calling me. I'd heard it faintly when I first stepped into the land of the elves. Now there was no interference from my body's wants and needs.

I was more tempted to answer the call than I'd ever been. No one would have blamed me. I felt myself *summoned* into a freedom I could never have imagined. A freedom greater than all the love and all the sex

I'd ever had. It would *include* those things and go beyond them. I would swim out into the vast sea of clear light and find ... what Jackson found when he left me.

But I'd made a promise to free the trapped, mindless spirits of the Fae. Once I did that, my mind began to pattern energy to draw to me what I'd need to keep the promise. The vow came out of my body with me. My human heart and mind left their impress in my spirit, like making a handprint in mud.

Beneath the spirit-body, linked to it by a fine-material silver cord, I saw my physical body. Compassion woke up in me. I felt empathy for everyone who'd ever passed through the human condition or ever would. I felt sympathy for everyone now embodied on Earth or disembodied inside the fae-road.

Into the fae-road I went, like I'd sworn to do. My spirit penetrated the road's surface like sinking into a wide river. First I was out in the air, not breathing. Then I was into the depths, still not needing to draw breath.

As my body sat, unfelt, against the wall, my spirit-body sank fathom after fathom to the depths of the fae-road until I sat on the floor of the green light-sea.

I shone with the clear light of mind. The proto-Fae came to me like moths to a lamp. They needed help to rise to consciousness. With the fae life-cycle interrupted, none of them would be born as babies of fae-light on the path above.

Last time I'd been among the Fae, I'd had no help to give the glowing beings who swam below the surface of the green-glowing road. I had more to offer them this time if they were willing.

What now commenced shared the paradoxical nature of the nonlinear time we inhabit in the next world over. It took forever. It took only an instant. Or a series of instants, each extending from the moment of creation, through the living present, into the boundless future. Outside my physical body I'd lost all sense of self and duration. I didn't know what I looked like or "sounded" like to those who came before me, one by one.

I didn't know how much time was passing for my human body where it sat against the castle wall.

Thoughts came out of me in Elvish, the Unfallen Tongue, all truth and nothing else. My spirit body moved gracefully in the gestures of wisdom you see depicted in statues and paintings of every faith where the human form appears. Neither thoughts nor gestures were personal to me. They belonged to our common human heritage.

The point of those thoughts was: *Choose once again.*

Everyone who came to me had taken to the fae-road rather than choose between good and evil. I'd been given the power to help them choose differently and show them which way to go. The map had been written on my heart since Leda painted an elvish *mandala* between my breasts as we stood in the snow of Portsmouth's Catholic cemetery.

Hundreds upon hundreds upon thousands of green-lit proto-Fae came to me and chose. They touched my fingers and received the teaching. In great flocks they flew like birds out of the fae-road and back to the great wheel of human rebirth. As they were, there was no way to go to the elves. But they could be reborn as human beings and from there make the one essential choice. As King Coran and Queen Maeve of the Fae had finally done. As I had done.

That choice required these almost-mindless spirits to see what they'd done with the past human lives they'd lived. Most were strangers, but I recognized a few who came for such liberation as I had to offer. They, too, thanked me for the gift of choice.

The last of the proto-Fae waited to face me until the others had gone. I'd met him when my very good friend Beth gave birth to him in a stand of trees in an empty world next to the fae-path.

We knew each other instantly. I shared mind energy so we could talk.

Before you go on to what is next for you, will you come with me to greet your last parents? I said.

I will, he said. *It is this for which I waited to come before you.*

Spirit hand in spirit hand, we rose through the depths. Like a dying ocean, the inside of the light-road was empty of creatures but still green with the impersonal energy that held the kingdom together.

As we rose, the sorcerer's body sank past us, melting its way into the green depths of the road. It was a poisoned gold statue without a single flicker of thought. The magus himself was gone.

With Beth's child of light I passed easily through the surface of the fae-road into the air. I saw my body slumped against the castle wall, its face as gray as the stone.

The poor thing, I thought, she's stopped breathing. She's dying.

Not knowing what to hope for, spirit-body re-entered physical body. Beth's fae-child clung to my spirit hand as it put on my flesh-and-bone hand like a glove.

The glove fit. I started breathing and opened my eyes.

Holding my hand was a naked child of green light. His eyes contained more knowledge than a human baby ought to have. He had no navel, nor any need of one. Bobby and Beth's son shone with the mind reflected in me.

I stood. The glowing child floated up into the air at my side and smiled at me. Holding his hand, I walked into the castle to find his mother and father.

63

The Solid-Gold Sorcerer

*Can you paint rosy lips upon a skeleton, dress it in loveliness,
pet it and pamper it, and make it live? And can you be content
with an illusion that you are living? - (A Course in Miracles)*

The Lady led the Morrigna outside the castle. Beth's feet remained on the ground. The Morrigna floated just above it.

In the middle of the fae-road sat the unbreathing ancient sorcerer, ensouled in his deadly immortal body of shining gold. The Nightmare Queens beheld an embodied nightmare. The magus beheld three more beings from the realm of myth. A curious silence ensued.

Cypris led lengthy formal introductions, as was the custom in the ancient world. These exchanges of pedigree and history established a common language between different kinds of creatures.

Master Gold and the three sisters considered the task before them.

Gold's explosive breach of the invisible barrier around the fae-path had unwittingly shortened the lives of the fae-born. No longer immortal, they began breathing in and out as earthlings do.

The fatal blow came from Gold's ally, the Walloon. The Morrigna explained that the Fae had withered, died, and sunk into the fae-road to join the legions of proto-Fae.

What killed them? Gold inquired.

The barest touch of the Walloon's feet of hardened sand on the light-road had poisoned all the fae-folk, said the sisters. The living darkness of Louis' master, propagating itself through the doorway to Earth, blighted the *light of other days* until it no longer supported embodied life.

Gold said, *Iblis brings destruction wherever his followers go.* He told the story of the Nameless City.

What then must we do? he inquired.

The Morrigna shared their perceptions with Gold and the Lady:

Something had changed beneath their feet. Someone new was inside the fae-path. Someone the Morrigna had met (and failed to seduce) who had freed the Morrigna from the Walloon. Far below daylight and air sat the Lady Janjan in a spirit-body which was somehow also herself.

The Lady of Cyprus was shocked to learn such a splitting was possible.

Janjan's defenseless mortal flesh slumped motionless against the stone castle wall, caught between one breath and the next. Body and soul were not meant to be long apart. What Lady Janjan did for others could kill her body before her spirit returned to it.

The sisters had no capacity for tears. They shared a look and a thought:

She does this for our *people, though it mean she lay down her own life. Never have the Fae known sacrifice. Never have they needed such courage, for we protected them from birth out of the fae-path until they sank back into the pure* light of other days *to rest awhile.*

The Morrigna saw what must be done. The Lady Janjan would release the spirits of the Fae from *the light of other days.* Then the radiant death within Gold's body would expel *the light of other days* out into the cosmos.

The little ship of Gold's spirit would ride upon fae-light until he could spread his inner sails and go a-voyaging to seek his own kind, propelled by fine-material interstellar wind.

The sisters would protect young Janjan's life as she freed their people, one by one.

The Lady left her new servitors to their task. Directing Beth into the castle, the Lady withdrew her consciousness three steps from Beth's mind.

Caught between relief at the Lady's departure and loneliness at her loss, Beth walked obediently into the great hall. She was afraid for Janjan, but the Morrigna had promised to protect her friend...

Beth stopped breathing for a moment when she saw Bobbi standing in the great hall with Rob. Standing next to him was a beautiful older woman. Her hair was red and her eyes were wide with rage and fear.

64

The Baby That Wasn't a Baby *(Janjan)*

After escaping the fae-road last year, Beth couldn't stay in Portsmouth. She ran home to her mother in Providence. I didn't blame her. I might have done the same thing, but the elves showed me that *home* was nowhere near my mother's house in Buffalo. My own true home wasn't even on Earth.

I tried to get Beth to come home with me to the next world over, but she wasn't having any of that. "Janjan," she said, "I had a baby that wasn't a baby. I mean, I carried that child in my body. Where is it now? What the hell am I going to tell the priest when I go back to church? What happened to my son? I don't even know what happened to me. Other worlds? Fuck that. I am so out of here, Janjan, I can't even. I just want a normal life."

She was sobbing. I didn't blame her for that, either.

She tried to live a normal life. She pushed Bobby away so there'd be nobody to remind her of the weird stuff that had happened. She moved to Texas with Mr. Right, and did her best to become Mrs. Right.

She left me behind, too. I wasn't on Earth to get hurt feelings about missing her wedding.

Beth underestimated herself. The marriage she settled for began closing in on her. She tried to find me and got kidnapped. The illusion of normality blew away like fog. And here we were in a fae castle again, except we were breathing and talking like we would on Earth. Even the fae-path had lost its normal life. Everything changes, everywhere and always.

But love endures. King Robert had never stopped loving Beth. He set aside his immortality, abandoned his throne, left his consort Moira, and returned to Portsmouth to find his lost love.

Today he left Queen Moira's side and held out his hand. Beth took his hand like it was the place her hand belonged. They were *spoken for*.

The queen saw how things were with Beth and the king. Before Moira could go to battle stations, Bobbi drew her into another room with a soft word and a strong arm around the queen's waist. Bobbi was a smitten kitten, not that Moira cared.

Moira went with Bobbi, but she looked back at Rob. Her face was full of sadness at all she was about to lose.

"They had a *child* together, Moira," Bobbi whispered. "As a mother yourself, surely you understand?"

Moira understood. Whatever became of her fae children, she had her Earth-sons to think of. What would happen to them now that the road was no longer safe?

Came now into the great hall Badb, Macha, and Anann, guardians of the fae-road and of all who once walked it.

Came now into the great hall Janjan (that would be me), holding the hand of a shining green spirit the size of an infant.

We stopped before where Beth and Rob sat, not on thrones, but merely on the edge of a low dais. The weird sisters garbed in black whispered a spell in their ancient language, full of sibilants. The green spirit assumed the form of a young man. For modesty's sake, the Morrigna clothed him quickly with a tablecloth that covered him from shoulder to knees and left one shoulder bare. Temporary clothing: he wouldn't be staying here long. None of us would.

"Mother and Father, I thank you for my last birth," said the shining young man. "Do you know me?"

Beth said, "I only saw you for a moment as a newborn, but I see traces of that child in your face."

"Aye," Rob said. "Queen Moira and I sparked many a fae-child into life. I searched all their faces looking for you. Till now I never saw you. How shall we call you, my son?"

The young man favored his parents with a smile full of old fae mischief. "Call me *Eamonn*. I was King Coran's kinsman. When my body died on Earth, I breathed my *light of other days* into a young magician named Jackson. Being sore afraid of human birth, I took my spirit back into the fae-road, as it seems I'd done a time or two before."

This was the Fae who'd bequeathed his fae-light to Jackson last year. After which, Jackson pursued his mission in Portsmouth and among the Fae, left the magicians, and became my husband, Healer to the elves and the Elf Friends.

Being human, knowing they'd lose their child a second time, Rob and Beth were crying. Young Eamonn's face was merry on top with old, old sadness beneath, the characteristic fae expression.

"Ah, don't weep, don't weep," he said. "All is well, or well enough. You'll go where your fate takes you. And I will go back to the round of rebirth. I see there's to be no future for anyone on the fae-road or underneath it."

Rob stood up and pulled Beth up with him. Together they embraced the being they'd innocently brought back into the body.

"Ah, lad," Rob said, "how I wish it could be otherwise. But your mother and I are off to a place you've no way to go."

"I'm so sorry, Eamonn," Beth said. "But I'm grateful to have seen and talked to you today."

Under the sadness Beth's heart was at peace.

It was like the time Rob and Beth and I had hugged each another for comfort; we rocked and wept when everything changed and the two of them had to run away from Portsmouth. We were sorry for everything in our lives there was no way to undo.

These are the tears of things, said a poet who knew what he was talking about.

The Morrigna watched Eamonn's life on the fae-path end almost as soon as it began. This time he didn't dissolve back into the road. As the green fae-light shined out of him, the Morrigna directed it somewhere. This time I guided his spirit away and beyond to what was next for him. As I had done for Queen Maeve, Coran's consort. As Jackson had done for

327

King Coran, Eamonn's kinsman.

Being a rebirth tour guide takes your full attention. It wasn't till Eamonn's spirit flew beyond the range of my inner vision that I realized I had an incoming call.

Janjan, said Jackson's unmistakable mind voice, *come quickly. I need you.*

It wasn't sex talk. He was in trouble.

65

The Problem of Evil *(Janjan)*

Two seconds later I was standing next to Jackson on the dead surface of the fae-road. On the side of the path behind us was the desert world I'd tiptoed past. On the side of the path in front of us was the ragged hole the golden sorcerer had blasted from Portsmouth. Enough radiation lingered to make me sick.

Jackson had more experience with radiation than I did, but he was sick, too.

He was a Healer now. What had it cost him to come here?

We were present in each other's minds as all elves are present to one another, with the additional intimacy of being married and *spoken for*. My husband was ... not all there. The guy standing next to me wearing blue jeans, skate shoes, and a Boston Red Sox t-shirt was like a photocopy of the original Jackson. Okay, fine, a three-dimensional hologram.

It was a shock to see him so diminished, so *ordinary*. I wanted to take him back to the Groves of Healing and give him all the sex and all the love it would take to make him shining and whole again. But he'd signed up to come here and do ... whatever the hell we were doing, just like I had. The horizontal bop would have to wait.

Jackson saw my dismay. "I had to *empty myself* to come here." He shook his head. "It never gets any easier."

This being a survival situation, we spoke Elvish, that most truthful and accurate of languages. He was telling me he'd set his small self aside and surrendered completely to the source of all life and mind. *Not I, but the divine wind.* It was a mystery to both of us.

"And here I thought it was a big deal that I stepped out of my body to enter the fae-path and then put my body back on."

"That *is* a big deal, my love," he said. The look in his eyes was pure Jackson and pure love for me. *He was proud of me.* I felt a naughty little thrill. He felt it with me and grinned.

Something else, too. There was pain here, but we both knew how to work with it. *Remember how you came to this knowledge when next you face those who think themselves our enemies.* Jackson had become the sort of being who sees the possible futures.

We were guarding the gateway to Portsmouth together. Outside the door were arrayed all the hosts of Hell awaiting only the order to attack. The real enemy behind our human opponents, far away and far too close, metastasizing like a cancer of the event horizon.

The Fallen had been barred from Earth for decades. They'd been barred from the fae-road since the beginning of all beginnings, when the Fae and the Morrigna first walked away from good and evil.

The Walloon and the screaming gold mummy had undone the choice the Fae had made so long ago, when the fairy tales say we all lived in the forest and none of us lived anywhere else. The Fallen would have come screaming onto the fae-road from their endless self-damned void, but something prevented it.

Someone, really. First Jackson alone. Now Jackson and me. Hence our shared pain. I saw no way to turn it into pleasure.

The Fallen were poised far outside Great Bog, far outside Earth, massing to enter the fae-road directly. Where the Claimant probably felt his One Will ought to prevail, as he wanted it to prevail throughout the whole physical universe so that all creation might be uncreated.

I'd released the spirits of the Fae into the *bardo* realm between lives. Were they safe from the Fallen there? Unknown.

Jackson was here in a mysterious emptied condition. We were plagued by radiation and evil's proximity. Jackson had called me. We needed help to make a stand. It was no time to be proud.

We extended an invitation to the elves who aren't really elves:

Ladies and gentlemen, if you're still in the body, your presence is urgently requested. The road around the human worlds is about to rejoin the human condition—unless the Fallen sack and burn it.

We called out to the angel who guards the next world over:

We remember love and light: your first words of greeting to everyone who comes home. We ask you to help these separated Fae brothers and sisters walk on to their next human birth.

Elves began popping up on the fae-road. Scores of men and women formed up shoulder to shoulder with us, something none of us had ever seen. It was pretty impressive.

The radiation's impact abated. Jackson healed himself and me and everyone else. Healing shone through us like morning sunshine through clear glass, like pleasure through our bodies and minds.

Then the angel was there, standing in the gateway to the fae-path and somehow still standing guard over the next world over. His thought was powerful and determined: *Go see to the human beings, children. I'll guard this gate. This war was won long before your first births. I think our enemies will not want to face me again in battle.*

Did I mention how impressive angels are?

Battle planning never takes long for people with joined minds. It wasn't Jackson everybody looked to for orders. It wasn't even the angel.

It was me, little Janjan, who was in charge of this beachhead. I'd seen the predicament the Fae were stuck in. I'd vowed to do something about it. I'd gone ahead and done it. Whatever happened now was on me.

66

Radiohead Sings "Creep" *(Louis)*

And fear not them which kill the body, but are not able to
kill the soul: but rather fear him which is able to destroy
both soul and body in hell. - (Matthew's Gospel)

The Walloon watched the golden statue fly to the fae-road and disappear in the distance. He thought, *What about me?*

As he stepped back onto the path and began to walk, the sands of Louis' body shifted within him. If he lost the mineral body Gold had given him, the Fallen were not present to reconstitute his flesh—assuming they would be *willing* to help him. The terms of the devils' bargain had been changed unilaterally and without negotiations.

The best he could hope for was a demon escort to the humiliation of a new human birth. He would be embodied as a lesser being on the Dark Path, courtesy of the Sisterhood. The Fallen would downgrade him to human raw material, a willing worker. *Food for the Moon*, as the Order expressed it.

Louis couldn't bear the thought of Mother Mariah's loathing as she oversaw his growth from infancy to childhood. She thought her hatred of men was masked, but habitual contempt had distorted her face.

He'd thought to dance nimbly from the power of the Fallen to the power of Gold's mysterious ancient magic. He'd almost persuaded himself to face the agony of the transformation into immortality. Was Gold's offer still available?

Louis had left the protection of entities who used him to further their own ends but despised him. He was now under the aegis of a being whose view of him was merely neutral. Louis had never fathomed Gold's motives. The ancient sorcerer had been too long away from the human condition.

Materialist Magicians are taught to ask, *If you could have whatever you wanted, what would you have?* What did Gold want? By enlisting the mummified sorcerer in the war against the elves, perhaps Louis had only helped Gold learn what he wanted from a world that had become alien to him.

As a practical matter, Louis was dying and Gold was nowhere in sight. He had left Louis to his own devices. Louis felt the presence of human minds somewhere down the fae-road, but no trace of the ancient magus, so powerful, so strange.

Louis had expected to welcome the Fallen as they burst onto the fae-road to claim it for their own. Not to lead their invasion, of course, but to point them at his enemies like a scout. He felt no exhilarating rush of terror, no nearby echoes of the greater evil he served. Had something barred the demons from this dying realm as they were barred from Earth?

With every passing moment Louis grew weaker. What should he do? Find his way back to the doorway Gold had blasted out of Earth? Throw himself upon the tender mercies of the Fallen? The master of Materialist Magician masters had no idea what he wanted.

Irresolute and exhausted, the Walloon sat down to rest again at the side of the road that had once risen to meet the feet of every Fae who walked it. Within his body sandstorms swelled, presaging dissolution. He felt the ache of loss.

The road where Louis sat, which he had once flown through in a smoky spirit body, had gone dead. Something had happened deep inside the fae-path. It seemed unwise to plunge himself into it in his fragile state. What could be worse than being trapped inside solid rock for all eternity? He would go madder than Gold.

Walking toward him along the ordinary-looking byway came Darnand.

When Master Gold flew in the front door of the fae castle, Darnand had run out the back. The traitor looked as lost as Louis felt.

"Master Louis." Darnand greeted his superior with a formal nod. He sounded fearful, as well he should have.

The Walloon considered stopping Darnand's heart, but feared the effort of working that minor magic would accelerate his own demise.

"Darnand," said the Walloon. "Is that a *crucifix* around your neck?"

Darnand nodded and clutched the silver figurine. Had he really put himself under the High Enemy's protection by wearing it to ward against Louis? "I'm dying," he said. "I want to live." His answer was more ironic than he knew.

Louis understood his lieutenant's motives. "Will you go back to the Fallen, then?"

"There's no immortality to be had here. And will you go back to our masters?"

"Once I've rested," the Walloon said.

After a pause Darnand said, "I would be honored if you would allow me to help you off this damnable fae-road and back to Earth."

Louis extended a dark blue hand. Darnand helped the Walloon to his feet.

67

An Exchange of Prisoners

Verily, verily, I say unto you, Except a corn of wheat
fall into the ground and die, it abideth alone: but if
it die, it bringeth forth much fruit. - (John's Gospel)

As Jackson and I stood with our fellow nextworlders at the door to Earth,
two men came walking down the fae-path. One was the stocky guy I'd
seen in Great Bog with Rob. The other had a blue face and blue hands like
a member of Blue Man Group, except with neatly-trimmed dark blue hair
instead of a bald blue head.

The blue man was the Walloon.

The other was Darnand, Rob's captor. He stopped a hundred yards
from the gateway. Indecision. Second thoughts.

The Walloon kept walking toward us.

He walked slowly; moving hurt him. His mind was masked. The forces
of his body were ebbing. His spirit would have to find a new home.

Jerry August left the line of elves and walked past the Walloon without
a word. Louis was no threat.

The Walloon approached the gateway to Great Bog. The elves stepped
aside to let him go. Free will, remember? Killing his body would be

pointless.

Louis stepped off the fae-path into Portsmouth like a very old man with arthritic joints. He lifted both arms slowly above his head in a gesture of appeal: *Help me!*

Something happened in the distant demon-storm. There came a rush of wind and a scream as the Fallen gathered Louis' spirit to themselves. After you get what you want, you don't want it.

The blue sand of the Walloon's body lost all human shape. The ill wind scattered a million million particles around the field. Empty hiking clothes collapsed into the long grass.

–

As if it had been predestined, two men met on the dead surface of the fae-road. Jerry August stood between Darnand and the gateway to Portsmouth a hundred yards away. Jerry wore a dark blue shirt, loose black pants, and soft boots. Darnand wore a 1940s-vintage brown wool suit, a white shirt with no tie, and heavy shoes.

Jerry thought: All he's missing is a truncheon and a Nazi armband.

Jerry was less ordinary than he appeared. He read Darnand's unguarded surface thoughts and saw what kind of creature he was up against. Even here separated from the Earth and its history, the mad black magic of the *Shoah* cast its shadow over the Frenchman.

Darnand had helped send Jews to the extermination camps. Had insisted on the deaths of thousands for reasons of ideology and personal ambition. It made no difference that the Holocaust was powered by the reproductive cycle of an Other World god and goddess. Darnand had chosen to kill Jews of his own free will, insisting they were *life unworthy of life.*

Karma. Jerry's mother was Jewish and therefore so was he—not that parentage mattered to the elves. All her European relatives were dead before she was born, shot and buried or gassed and burned. That line of the family had been obliterated: *Vernichtung.* Jerry's impersonal awareness followed the threads between the past and this moment.

Threads connecting Darnand to the specific deaths of his Jewish ancestors.

The Dark Path had honed Darnand's perceptions. His eyes widened in recognition. Jerome August's name was on the Order's kill list next to his photograph.

"An elf who is also a Jew," Darnand said. "Everything I hate most in one man. Since I shan't be able to kill you, I expect you will kill me now that I am at your mercy, *coward*." He pulled his suit coat aside to free the hilt of his dagger.

Jerry ignored the sneering provocation and the Nazi dagger. "Why would you come here where your masters have no power?"

Darnand grimaced and told the truth. "I thought the Fae lived forever. That is what the *soi-disant* King Robert told me. Once the Fae *did* live forever. But no more, it seems."

Jerry saw Darnand's vitality ebbing rapidly. "You're dying?"

Darnand nodded. "I came here rather than seek out the Sisterhood of the Dark Path to receive my new body."

"'*Receive*'?"

Darnand shrugged. "It's not a gift. The Earth belongs to the Order of Materialist Magicians. We who serve the Brotherhood *take* what we need."

Jerry understood. The Order had tried to help the Old Gods *take* Jerry's body to prolong the earthly life of his old, corrupt uncle Quincy August. That didn't happen the way the magicians wanted.

The demons Darnand served would evict a newborn's spirit so Darnand could have the child's body. Like the Nazi death camps, it was a perversion of the natural order.

"Assuming I don't kill you," Jerry said, "what'll you do now?"

Darnand's body sagged as if he wanted to shrink into the shell of himself like a turtle. "Another conscious rebirth through the Sisterhood, I suppose. It's a horrible experience. Humiliating. I imagine you'll say I deserve that and worse. And the Fallen will torment me for deserting my post. I imagine you'll say I deserve that, too. At the end of my time in hell with the demons, I will be allowed rebirth again—with such scraps of sanity and memory as remain to me."

The Dark Path was a devil's bargain. Given what the Fallen were, the Path of the Materialist Magicians only offered a perversion of something better. Something already given to everyone for free.

Contact with the Fallen eroded people's humanity and made them more malleable. They were left with little will of their own. In Darnand's case, what was left of his free will rebelled against the constraints of being consciously reborn in the body of a helpless newborn. One sniff of the Fallen made every remaining natural human instinct revolt, even Darnand's.

Elflord though he was, Jerry was only human. He was sorely tempted to kill the Nazi collaborator where he stood, a partial payment for so many Jewish deaths. But Darnand's execution would be futile. The man's spirit would be re-embodied soon enough. Deadlier than ever, he'd return to Earth and continue the Order's lunatic work of destruction.

Jerry centered himself in the source of his strength and said, "There's a way off the Dark Path."

"How? If I die, the Fallen will sweep my soul up. Can *a filthy Jew* take me to the world of the elves?" Even in his terror, the Frenchman was still jeering.

Jerry shook his head. "Not me," he said. "I have no power to take you to the next world over, not as you are. You would return to human rebirth. Are you willing to go back to Earth and live as ordinary men do?"

Darnand stared at the unpromising fae-road under his feet. No immortality to be found on it or under it. There was no salvation from what he'd chosen, except to choose differently.

Finally he looked up at Jerry. "Willing? At least a little," he said.

"Good enough," Jerry said. He extended his mind back toward the Portsmouth gateway.

A light began shining in Darnand's mind. It grew until it filled his sensorium and became the vast outer appearance of a creature so unfathomable that all his thoughts went still.

The warrior angel.

Darnand saw thoughts fly like shining birds between Jerome August and the angel. Then it seemed that the angel looked into Darnand, drew his flaming sword, and swung it.

The sword severed Darnand's spirit from his dying body. It severed Darnand from the Dark Path. Untenanted, the body collapsed to the road.

Beside his spirit, Darnand felt Jerry August's mind guiding him on to the great blessing that is human birth. *This way, yes. Now over that way.*

Freed from the body, Darnand's mind was filled with the enormity of all he had done. Every effect of his every action became horribly clear; he had no defense against it. He suffered with each of his victims.

Protected again from the Fallen, his free will was restored. What he chose to do with his next life was back in his own hands.

Darnand's last thought echoed in Jerry's mind: *I am sorry, August. I have spent two lifetimes killing people who meant me no harm.*

Jerry made no response to Darnand, not in words. But standing in the clear light with the angel, he saw that *justice* and *mercy* were two English words for the same thing.

It seemed to Jerry that what Jews call *tikkun olam* was well under way: *to heal the Earth.* He was part of that healing, not in charge of it.

Good enough.

68

It's Not Me, It's You *(Rob)*

What is it men in women do require?
The lineaments of gratified Desire.
What is it women do in men require?
The lineaments of gratified Desire.
- (William Blake, "The Question Answered")

"I'll need a word with the queen in private," Rob said.

Beth saw the nobility in his plain, strong face. Being king hadn't corrupted him, it had made him wiser, more himself. But...

"I feel like all the chaos here is my fault," she said. Seeing that he wanted to comfort her, she went on, "I *know* it's more complicated than that. Be as kind to Moira as you can. I still have to go back to Earth and divorce my husband. *He's* not going to be happy, either. I don't want to hurt Andrew, but I can't stay with him."

Rob gave her a rueful, adult smile and shook his head. He'd grown to manhood in a time when there was no divorce for people of his class. Marriages ended in death. Deserting a wife was as dishonorable as having children with a woman and not marrying her. More dishonorable than deserting the battlefield, something he had on his conscience twice over.

He felt this was another sordid episode in a life that had taken a shameful turn when he first chose to walk with the Fae. "What a mess," he said. "I'll be back soon. I love you, Beth."

"I love you, too," she said. "Go now before I start bawling again."

Rob knew where Moira was. Though they'd never been married in any church, the king and queen of the Fae had been joined together in the power of the fae-road. Even with the Fae now passing into legend, he still felt the green pulse of what had bound him to her.

Moira smiled when he entered the room, until anger replaced her genuine affection. Her first husband, the father of her sons, had left her for a younger woman. Here it was happening again. Moira couldn't fight Rob about the end of their ... *affair*, but she didn't have it in her to be gracious.

"Little Bobbi here has been telling me what she and Janjan and your old friend *Beth* have got up to together," Moira said. "I hope you'll be happy—you and your titless blonde *dyke slut*."

Having learned about twenty-first-century women since Janjan saved his life last year, Rob declined to take the bait. He and Moira were *not* going to have another screaming fight followed by shattering make-up sex that made the fae-path shake. Not this time. Not ever again. Rob put his arms around her and held her stiffened body close until she started crying helplessly into his shoulder.

It's a new beginning for me, he thought. But it's the end of everything she thought she wanted.

"Do you remember when Janjan offered to take me to her world?" Rob said.

Moira nodded. "You said you wanted to stay with *me*. Because I *need* you." She started crying again quietly, real tears from real sadness, pleading with him without saying the words. *If you really loved me...*

He stepped back. "Moira, it's time to go where I belong. You don't need *me*, you need *this*." He meant the fae-road and the privileges of royalty. He gestured at the castle walls around them. "This life we've led is over for everyone now. The Fae will go wherever they can. On to new lives on Earth." He paused. "Will you come to the elves with me?" He knew better than to say *"with us."*

Moira shook her head decisively. "Nay," she said. "I mean *No!* The boys and I will go back to Earth. I'll make the best of menopause and mortality. I'll go back to church and confess my sins. The boys will go back to school—I'll get their father to pull some strings. Life will go on. I suppose I'll forget all about this. Eventually."

"I'll always remember you, Moira. I'll never forget the life we lived. You were a kind and just queen to our fae-children and to their children. You were good to me when I needed a woman's touch to heal me." He knew better than to say *"when Beth broke my heart."*

Moira managed a sad smile. "I wish we'd been married in the Church. Maybe then..." She shook her head. "What am I saying? If the Church knows anything about the fae-road, they think it's the Devil's. You're the best lover I've ever had, Bobby. I loved you as best I could, but we were just playacting at being ancient Celtic royalty. This last year hasn't had much to do with real life."

"You're not going back to your old job, I hope?"

"Earth is as much real life as I can take," she said. "I can't go back to work for the materialists—they'll kill me. Maybe I can work for the Elf Friends while the boys finish school and start their own lives."

Rob knew Moira's children came before him, before anyone in any world. Beth would be his traveling companion to the undiscovered country of the next world over.

He held his arms out again. "Will you hold me for just a minute, Moira?" His face was wet; he wasn't ashamed.

"Oh, darlin', of course I will." She moved into his arms where she'd been embraced so often. She was crying, too. She stroked the back of his head. "I'm going to miss you so much," she said. "We were important here. Even our orgasms mattered."

Rob thought what Moira would really miss was being young and fertile and juicy and full of life. The Morrigna weren't going back to Earth with her, were they?

They let each other go and shared a smile like old lovers do. Even their most passionate embraces had been a substitute for something. Whatever it was, they hadn't found it together.

69

Intermission

The Fallen took the Walloon and left. I'd say they went home, but they *rejected* home when they chose to fall forever. Evil is a spiteful, stupid, *anti*-rational mystery.

We carried Darnand's body into another human world. Out of some sense of the fitness of things, we buried it beneath a mound of stones. Jerry and the angel had done what needed doing for the man's spirit. One by one we touched the cairn and said "Go with God" in our language. The stones glowed with the words and the ground shook.

Darnand was no hero to be buried in honor with his sword. Jerry took the Waffen SS dagger in two hands and spoke a loud command in the Unfallen Tongue. The knife fell onto the bare ground and shattered like a sheet of ice. Let the foeman's blade be broken.

If a high elf had shattered the golden sorcerer's body that way, it would have triggered a nuclear explosion. Meeting magical force with force isn't always the answer. Rock-paper-scissors.

There was no further external threat to the fae-path now that the Fae no longer walked it or swam beneath it. Saving the spirits of the Fae had destroyed their way of life. I didn't regret what I'd done, but I wasn't totally happy about it, either. Every action has consequences.

Beth said the Morrigna were returning to Earth to serve the Lady as Nereids in the oceans. I won't lie, the Lady's old pagan truth called to my heart, or called to something a little lower. I kind of wanted to go a-roving with Cypris, but there were things I wanted even more. I still had promises to keep.

After hugs all around, most of the elves left the fae-path in a flash, heading home and heading back to whatever Jackson and I had interrupted with our Mayday call.

The angel smiled and was no longer visible among us. We'd meet again at home.

That left me and Jackson, Leda and Jerry, Beth and Rob, and Bobbi all standing on the motionless fae-road looking out at Great Bog through the ragged gateway.

Bobbi watched my thoughts. She gave me a hug and said, "See you back at the apartment?"

"Yeah," I said. "We have more battle planning to do, don't we?"

She was relieved that I wasn't going to disappear to go slooting around with the Lady. She shook her head. "C'mon, Beth. C'mon, Rob." She patted her pockets. "Yay! I still have my car keys."

Beth looked from me to Rob and back again. "I have a phone call to make," she said.

"Your husband?" Rob said.

"I'll tell him I want a divorce. I don't plan to get into the details." Beth made a gesture that encompassed Portsmouth, the fae-road, and all of us who stood on it: *who'd* believe *the details?* "That marriage was a mistake. Sending you away was a bigger mistake." She held out her hands to Rob. He took them.

Bobbi, Beth, and Rob stepped off the road and walked back along the path to the park-and-ride.

As she walked away, Bobbi thought to me, *I've arranged with Moira to have some Elf Friends meet her and her sons here in the morning. She's gonna work for the good guys.*

You're the best, I thought back to her.

Don't tease me. There was a smile in her thought.

Jerry August looked at Leda. Together they looked at Jackson and me where we stood with our arms around each other's waists.

"Funny," Jerry said, "there's a statue of Leda and me on the Other World that looks just like you two. So the Old Gods said, and why would they lie to *us?*" There were tears on his cheeks.

Leda's Elvish thought was sharp and clear: *My heart is full right now, dear Janjan, dear Jackson. Our people will sing forever of the things you've done.* There were happy tears on her cheeks, too.

Jerry looked at Leda with love in his eyes and said, *"Greater works than these shall you do, because they go unto the source of all life."* In the way of the high elves, he was both sincere and ironic.

I shook my head in mock indignation. "Will you two get *out* of here?" I said in English. "If you don't mind, I'd like a bit of privacy to boink my husband."

Leda and Jerry laughed. "See you at home," she said. They vanished—pop!

Jackson turned to me with one eyebrow raised. *"'Boink'?"*

"Don't mind if I do," I said, like the little elf-sloot I am.

He might have been a copy of himself today, but he was still hot. Woof.

70

Tammy Wynette Sings "D-I-V-O-R-C-E" *(Beth and Andrew)*

She could softly play the piano, up in her room, and sing: 'Touch not the nettle, for the bonds of love are ill to loose.' She had not realized till lately how ill to loose they were, these bonds of love.
- (D.H. Lawrence, Lady Chatterley's Lover)

Beth called Andrew with a burner phone. At first he was overjoyed to hear her voice. Then he got righteously indignant. Beth led him into a tense, absurdly formal conversation where everything was left unsaid except: *yes*, she'd been kidnapped; *yes*, she'd escaped; *yes*, she was okay; and *no*, she wasn't coming back to Texas.

Andrew wanted to cry; he didn't think that was an option. He wanted to scream obscenities; he didn't think that would help. Instead, he controlled his temper and told her he'd fly north. They could either make peace or end things face to face like grownups. He'd text her his flight details.

He told the company's president, "Looks like Beth is leaving me for good." Regretfully, he asked for a few personal days off. He didn't mention hiring a private investigator or anything Ben had told him. Andrew had told his boss nothing about Beth's disappearance. He didn't mention hiring a divorce lawyer, either. Family Values.

Andrew's mentor favored him with a neutral expression. "Take all the time you need," he said in a tone that conveyed: *Get your personal life in order and come back to work.*

The boss was not unhappy with this development. Beth hadn't made much effort to fit into the company's culture. Which is to say, she hadn't embraced the customs and teachings of their church, particularly the commandment to be fruitful and multiply (or to accept second-tier status and adopt children).

The CEO's wife would be relieved to hear that Beth and Andrew were separating. Beth had stopped trying for the Real Housewives' approval. They attributed Beth's reserved, skeptical manner to an unlikely combination of dogmatic Catholicism and freethinking Yankee libertinism. Logical consistency was not a virtue much celebrated in their denomination.

Texas law makes divorce easy enough. Once both parties sign a few papers, the union is dissolved. Still, a marriage is too important to end over the phone or, God forbid, by text message or email, Andrew and his boss agreed. Texas is a community property state, the CEO reminded him, but careful negotiations can still protect a man from financial ruin. Andrew didn't mention the legal documents he was carrying.

The next day he flew into the little airfield that grandly called itself Manchester-Boston Regional Airport. He rented a car and drove east.

This being tourist season, there was no on-street parking to be had in Portsmouth. He was lucky to find the last spot in the city's parking garage.

As agreed, he met Beth in front of a Market Square coffee shop. He got carry-out coffee for himself and tea for her. In silence they strolled to Prescott Park to talk by the river. With their beverages, they looked like every other young couple, except that Beth had no phone in her other hand. Self-conscious, Andrew put his phone away.

It was a beautiful sunny day. A few puffy white clouds blew slowly across the bright blue sky, heading for England. Andrew couldn't bring himself to talk about the weather.

Parents strolled near the water's edge while their kids ran around yelling happily, playing tag, doing whatever kids find to do. Andrew watched the children. Beth saw the sadness in his face. They were not going to be having kids. No Family Values for them.

"How much of this story do you want to hear?" she said.

Looking at Beth dressed in a worn t-shirt, old jeans, scuffed sneakers, no makeup, no jewelry, and short natural fingernails, made Andrew even sadder. She looked beautiful, even with the long blonde hair he loved now blunt-cut short and parted on one side. She looked happier and more vibrant than she ever had in Texas. Her joy had nothing to do with him or with their life together. *Gonna cut that man right outta my hair.*

Whatever had happened to her wasn't about him.

"Are you ... sleeping with somebody else?" he said. Something he could probably forgive her for eventually. He hadn't answered her question. Or maybe he'd answered it indirectly.

She saw that he was unwilling to face his fear. She'd been there and done that.

"This isn't about sex," she said. That was true, but was also evasive. He wouldn't *want* to hear about her time with the Lady of Cyprus. Or their time swiving with Janjan. Or her time swiving with Janjan and Bobbi. "It's about *love.* I think we loved the idea of marriage more than we loved each other." That was unkind, but was also true. There was no point telling Drew that she and Rob were *spoken for.*

Drew looked dispirited. She wanted to comfort him, but he didn't want the kind of comfort she had to offer. And he wasn't going to comfort her. He didn't want to know what had happened to her.

His voice got hoarse. "I thought we wanted *kids,*" he protested. The wrong way to talk himself back into her heart. Rob had won her love simply by loving her. He hadn't changed for her, just become more himself.

Beth put a hand on his sleeve. "Before I met you, I had a baby." She paused, thinking what to say that wouldn't sound crazy. "My son ... passed on. I didn't tell you. I wanted to pretend it never happened. When we moved to Texas, I thought I'd put my old life behind me. It didn't work out that way."

Beth didn't have to read minds like Janjan did. She could read Drew's face. Her husband was judging her harshly. He was imagining a story to make himself feel better.

He imagined she had something wrong with her that made her infertile. She might have gotten pregnant out of wedlock (shameful) and had an abortion (unforgivable). She might have gotten chlamydia (disgusting) or even had her tubes tied and not told him. Beth watched herself become irreparably damaged goods in Andrew's eyes as he confabulated an unlikely combination of deadly venereal diseases and stillborn bastard foundlings in dumpsters. *What terrible moral failing made a woman deceive her innocent husband-to-be about her slutty past?*

He stared like he'd never seen her before. "Oh," he said. *"Oh!"*

"So if you want a divorce, I won't fight it. I don't want anything from you. No money, no community property, no house. You did all the work, Drew. You earned it, I didn't. I'll be fine. I've got … a new job. If you need me to sign something, I'll be happy to."

Andrew got control of his face. He thought he looked manly and determined. Beth had lived with him long enough to know he was seething.

He unslung his messenger bag briefcase and fished out a file folder. Beth found them a bench in the shade. He gave her a form to sign that said she wasn't contesting his divorce petition. He handed her a pen. She signed her maiden name without thinking about it. She initialed the mistake and signed her married name as well. She had to ask him the date. Her phone was powered off. In her travels she'd lost track of what month and year it was supposed to be.

With today's important legal business concluded, he tucked the papers into his briefcase. She declined to accept a copy for her files. For the first time in her life she *had* no files and no place to put them. *Yay, school's out.*

They stood up. Andrew gave Beth a quick, awkward hug. She would have rested her head on his chest for a moment, but he disengaged from her arms as quickly as he could. Like she might contaminate him.

They hadn't had sex, but Andrew suddenly wanted to take another shower and brush his teeth again. Like she *had* contaminated him.

They found themselves with nothing more to say. *Sudden and swift and light as that the ties gave.*

She held up a hand in farewell. He nodded goodbye. If he said another word, he'd start crying. Real men don't cry, do they?

He left Beth in the park and walked quickly back to his rental car. He drove out of the parking garage without looking in the rear view mirror. He headed for the highway that would take him back to the airport

He couldn't wait to get home and get back to his ordinary Texas life. He couldn't wait to get the divorce finalized. He couldn't wait to start dating again.

Somebody *normal*, for God's sake.

Andrew felt he'd dodged a bullet with his name on it. *A damaged woman* had misrepresented herself to *trick* him into marriage. She signed the documents his lawyer prepared; she didn't bother to read them. He hadn't had to give away half his worldly goods to escape the Whore of Babylon. He'd gotten off easy.

Strangely, he also felt he'd just missed his main chance in life. Like the investigator he'd hired, Beth had something important to tell him. Something weird and life-changing. *How much of this story do you want to hear?*

He was afraid to hear any of it.

He shook his head. New life, no regrets. He didn't want to think about New Hampshire—or Beth—ever again.

It was like the real estate signs he saw around Portsmouth: *Do not inquire within.*

71

Every Man a King *(Janjan)*

This whole escapade started when Aimee and I came down the World Mountain, walked back to Earth on top of the water, and stepped into Portsmouth at the Odiorne Point breakwater.

I met Beth and Rob there. Symmetry.

We come to the next world over at our own pace. Some of us travel there instantly in a moment of danger, like Jackson and I did. Others have to *see* the Invisible Mountain appear in the immeasurable distance outside Portsmouth Harbor. They have to *walk* into the mystery.

I saw Beth's heart. She felt she was walking toward the end of everything. She knew better, but feelings have to be dealt with mindfully. Leah, the old Healer taught me that.

I saw Rob's heart. He was weary down deep in his soul. I marveled that he'd managed to stay in the body and carry that burden around. The weight he bore would have killed me. Instead, Good King Robert had governed the Fae as wisely and well as anyone could. He'd been Queen Moira's consort until their romance came to an end as final as the ending of the fae-road.

Beth chose to love Rob and to let him love her. I wondered what Rob would make of Beth's sexual adventures with the queen of love and beauty—and with Bobbi and me. Would he apply the harsh moral code he'd grown up with in the 1800s, or the happy hedonism he'd learned among the Fae and propounded as their king?

Would he accept elvish compassion and forgiveness?

What would Beth make of a closer approach to the real source of all love and beauty? Would she let her mistakes be corrected by the clear light that shines through the next world over?

Free will makes us unpredictable.

Anyway. I'd do what I could and not worry about the rest. So I held out my hands to Beth on my right and to Rob on my left.

I smiled at each them in turn. "Ready to walk home with me?"

Rob said, "Yes!"

Beth nodded nervously. "Uh-huh."

I whispered Elvish words to surround them in the light Leda had first shown me in myself. The three of us stepped carefully down the huge granite stones of the breakwater. We stood together on the surface of the water, rocking gently in the ebb and flow of little waves, finding our balance.

We put our trust in something that was within us and beyond us, too. As we started walking toward the Invisible Mountain, *surprise!* Its lower slopes appeared outside the mouth of the harbor. We couldn't see how high it might go.

As we walked, my housemates inquired deeper and deeper within. Rob's *mandala* had started him down this path. Beth's time with the Lady made her wonder what she was that such blessings of love and beauty could flow through her.

Ordinary thought and speech became difficult.

"This is really *happening*, isn't it?" Beth managed to say. She sounded happy and scared.

I squeezed her hand to keep her grounded in the here and now. "Huh, you said the same thing the night I climbed into bed with you,"

She started laughing, couldn't help herself. Rob and I laughed along with her. It didn't bother him that his lady and I had pleasured each other. We started laughing *and* crying. Feelings flowed like the tide.

I remembered when the three of us hugged and wept in the kitchen of our Portsmouth house. We'd just left the Fae and their long, long road a-winding. Each of us had different reasons for our sorrow.

This time we were laughing and crying for the same reason. *Forever wilt thou love, and she be fair* only sounds hopeless on Earth. In the next world over there's abundant love and no confusion about truth and beauty.

As we walked on the cold Atlantic water, Rob saw where the water-walking spell came from. His *mandala* had shown him his inner lights. As he inquired within, he saw Beth's lights reflected in his. As Beth's awareness descended below the level of ordinary mind, she saw her own lights with Rob's reflected there.

The same thing had happened to Jerry and Leda when their lives were threatened in the world of the swan god and his goddess. Elves have no powers that aren't also given to everyone.

Hesitantly, Beth and Rob spoke mind-to-mind for the first time.

Beth turned to me and thought, *This is the end of my life, isn't it?* She wasn't being a drama queen. The gravity of the occasion was dawning on her.

One life ends when your new life begins, I answered. "Remember *It's a Wonderful Life?*" I said aloud. "You matter more than you can know."

Rob let go of my hand and took up the spell he'd seen in my mind that allowed us all to walk on the ocean. He looked at me in happy surprise. "You were right," he said. "This is pretty great."

You ain't seen nothin' yet, I thought to him.

Rob walked around and took Beth's other hand. *I want to be holding your hand when we meet the angel*, he thought to her.

Which started her crying again, but happily.

—

When they met the angel, he dried our tears.

I see that you do remember who you are—and whose *you are, dear Janjan*, the angel thought.

Then he thought to Rob and Beth: *Welcome home, dear Robert, dear Elizabeth. This is where your real life begins.*

359

72

The Cynosure of All Eyes *(Janjan, Aimee)*

Let me back up a bit in the interest of full disclosure, ho ho ho.

We were about to step off the Atlantic Ocean and onto the lower slopes of the Invisible Mountain, which is actually the World Mountain that has the human worlds somehow arrayed around it. I don't understand that any more than I understand how the fae-path touches on all those worlds.

A naked elflady came walking downhill to meet us. It was Aimee Amory-Ryun, sleek, and focused, centered and strong, lithe and beautiful.

Jackson had sent her here to be healed of the ancient hidden hurt that made her need pain to pay for her pleasure. She was also on a mission of diplomacy. Daniel had sent her here to negotiate.

In a flash of thought images I shared Aimee's story with Beth and Rob. Even an hour ago they might have been skeptical. Now, standing on the spellbound sea like it was a frozen lake, they accepted what I told them.

In another flash of thought Aimee and I brought each other up to date.

Were we both *spoken for*, still married to our husbands? Yes, thank God. Were we both still aroused by each other? Yes, and thank God for that, too. Aimee, I may have mentioned, looked spectacular without clothes.

But we had things to do. There was no time for dalliance, even though it would have pleased us.

"Hello, Rob and hello, Beth," Aimee said. "Before you come home, I ask you to do a service for our world and for Earth."

"*Anything,*" said Beth, clearly smitten with Aimee, as who would not be. Realizing that she sounded slootier than she meant to—and not wanting to hurt Rob's feelings—she brought his hand to her lips and kissed his palm.

Rob smiled a lover's smile; Beth's kiss aroused him. He didn't stare at Aimee's beautiful naked body, he marveled at the *light* in her. Normal healthy man though he was, Rob found himself yearning for the clear light of the high country.

"Lady Aimee," Rob said, "Beth will speak for herself, of course. But I see plainly that you want only the best for us."

Rob and I stood rocking on the gentle waves, knees flexing like we were riding the subway, waiting patiently. Aimee took Beth's hand and led her along the shore of the Mountain. We heard Beth's voice faintly because of the breeze coming off the land.

Beth called out to Cypris, "*O, Aphrodite...*"

The Lady answered.

Near the two women on the smooth rock where no earthly plants can grow, now there were six women. The four new arrivals only assumed a female form. They stood out upon the water as if they had just risen from the waves. It was the queen of love and beauty and her retainers, the Nereids. Except for Beth, all were naked.

The six held converse for a while in words and in pure thought. Reaching agreement, the Lady's retainers disappeared into the sea.

Beth silently witnessed Aimee's conversation with the Lady. Aimee spoke shining Elvish. Cypris spoke aloud and her meaning arrived in the women's minds colored like roses.

Smiling, Aimee left Beth standing on the rock and took two steps onto the ocean where the Lady stood. Smiling, the Lady took two steps toward Aimee. Each reached out and placed the palm of her right hand over the other's heart.

One unitary life for the Lady since their first shock of meeting, but many lives for the woman who came here now as Aimee. They had loved each other as best a mortal and an immortal can. Each was implicated in the other's ancient hidden hurt; the goddess had pursued and chastened the woman through many lives. It was time to forgive and be forgiven.

"As long as there is an Earth wilt thou be fairest," Aimee said.

"No one here will judge us," said the Lady. "There is no chorus; there are no townsfolk to behold thy naked splendor. I think thou hast come to know better than I where thy love and beauty come from, my priestess, my beloved Phryne."

The two gazed at each other for a long moment and embraced.

"If in thy travels thou shouldest see my son," said the Lady, "say that his mother loves him dearly. Tell him how I see his marriage was the first sign of a change in the world. The transformation that sent all my brothers and sisters away from Earth led thee here to me with thy mind full of elf-light, O Psyche."

"I will tell him," said Aimee. "In our world love takes whatever form is needed. *Eros* and *Agápē* live happily in affection and friendship."

Two very different beings smiled at each other in incomprehension and appreciation. As quickly as she had arrived, the Lady was gone.

Beth and Aimee walked back to Rob and me.

There were tears on Aimee's face, but they were happy ones. All discord left her heart when Cypris touched it.

73

The Home for Wayward Girls (*Janjan*)

We walked from the main road down a narrow dusty lane. Anyone watching from the walled compound might think a kind stranger had dropped us off on the highway.

It was hot and dry. Bobbi and I wore loose pants, t-shirts, and hiking shoes. I'd always thought straw cowboy hats were a city-girl affectation—*Look how cute I am*—but they kept the sun out of our eyes here in the desert.

Wherever we go on Earth, local Elf Friends give us clothes so we can blend in. This mission was about making it safer to be an Elf Friend.

At this stage in her training, Bobbi looked like an Earth girl with a tan. I might have looked like a Eurasian girl to an untrained eye, but the nextworld mark was on me for anyone who knew what to look for. In this part of the country I could pass for Latina, possibly a *Juanita* who anglicized her name to *Jan*, hoping to fit in with tanned white girls like Bobbi. My masquerade would either work or it wouldn't.

Even if someone identified me as an elf and threw me out (or attempted worse), Bobbi would be allowed to stay. Our story was that we'd met at the bus station like a couple of country sloots new to the big city. Our parents, we would tell those who ran the Sisterhood's convent, had forbidden us to abort our pregnancies. We'd be delivering our (fictional) babies and giving them up for adoption.

Cameras: they're everywhere. I saw fisheye lenses high up on the wall on both sides of the tall solid-wood gates.

We got our stories straight mind-to-mind. I pushed the button next to the gate. For a long moment nothing happened.

Finally, a woman's clipped voice from the speaker grid, "Yes?"

"Um, is this the, um, convent?" I said.

"Yes, it is, dear." The voice sounded kinder now. "Can we help you?"

"I hope so, ma'am. My friend and I are kind of ... in trouble?"

"Tsk. Wait there, child. Someone will let you in."

After a long wait, we heard the crunch of footsteps. A young woman unbolted one big door and opened it. She wore sneakers and brown clothing, like a Carmelite nun's habit. My eyes and elf perceptions said she was pregnant, about six months along, mother and unborn doing well.

"Hi, I'm Suzy," she said. "And you are...?"

As agreed, Bobbi spoke for both of us. "I'm Roberta. Everybody calls me Bobbi. My friend Juanita here goes by *Jan*."

We walked the hard-packed driveway to the main house.

Suzy nodded. "So how far along are you?"

We'd discussed this, too. Our story wouldn't stand up to a medical exam, something we'd have to refuse. "I'm probably about a month along," Bobbi said. "Jan doesn't exactly know. Irregular periods?"

I nodded and stared at the ground, embarrassed by this clinical talk.

I know what you're thinking. Elves aren't supposed to lie. True enough, we're not. We're not supposed to kill, either, if there's a better way to protect ourselves. Or steal. Or covet our neighbors' spouses. Or beat them for our mutual pleasure. You get the idea. One more reason it's easier for new elves than for elflords and elfladies to come back to Earth and do what has to be done. I hadn't gone full-elflady yet.

This mission was about protecting Earth from the Sisterhood of the Dark Path. We hadn't known about the Sisterhood until Darnand told us. Now that we knew, we had to act.

It was cool and quiet inside the main building. Thick walls. Clean corridors with worn tile floors. Suzy led us to the convent's office. She knocked on the door twice and opened it.

A formidable woman in late middle age sat behind a big antique dark wood desk. She wore one of those prairie dresses you see the women wearing when the cops bust up a polygamous desert religious cult. Something in the woman's face made my heart sink. I kept my eyes on the floor.

"This is Jan and this is Bobbi, Mother Mariah," Suzy said. "They've come to stay with us if they can."

"Please sit down, girls," Mariah said, indicating two guest chairs. "Thank you, Suzy. We'll see how this interview goes. I'll buzz you shortly." It was her voice we'd heard through the speaker at the front gate.

Suzy left. Mother Mariah studied us closely. I resisted the temptation to look her right in the eye as the elves do, direct and challenging. I kept my gaze averted. I didn't feel any psychic power coming from her, but human beings are transparent to anyone who knows how to look. Elves are even more transparent because we have nothing to hide. Usually.

"How did this happen, Bobbi?" Mariah said.

Don't be a smart-ass, I thought to Bobbi, seeing what was in her mind. She answered with an inner smile of agreement.

"The condom broke, ma'am," Bobbi said. Pretty funny, considering that Bobbi slept only with women. She'd never even seen a condom close up and personal, let alone put one on a man.

"*Disgusting*," Mariah said. "Artificial birth control is an *abomination*," she added. "Sex is of course necessary if the human race is to fulfill the divine commandment to be fruitful and multiply."

Bobbi nodded and stared at the floor as if ashamed. *The crazy is strong with this one*, she thought.

"And what about you, Jan?" Mariah said. "Why is it that you're pregnant?"

I looked at her briefly, said "Raped," and looked back down again.

Mariah exhaled sharply. "Women are better than men and *deserve* better than men. Males are no more than a regrettable necessity in this fallen world. I'm glad you decided not to punish your child for the sins of its father."

I looked up at her. "My mother and father are dead," I said. True, but irrelevant. "I heard … you could help us?"

"That's what the Sisterhood is here for," Mariah said. Her expression revealed neither kindness nor amusement. The smarmy politician's smile made me want to vomit. I looked at the floor before my face betrayed me.

Suzy was summoned back to the office. Bobbi and I had passed muster.

Suzy showed us to the dormitory. Rows of single beds. Whoa, flashback to summer camp. Probably no boys across the lake to fool around with and no surreptitious girl-on-girl fingerbanging in the bunkhouse here, though. No boys and no lake.

And cameras in opposite corners of the dorm.

Bobbi and I were accepted immediately. Once they saw that we deflected personal questions with brief, reluctant answers, the twenty other girls gave us our privacy and went on chattering about themselves.

Some of the kids—teenagers is what they were—had gotten pregnant the old-fashioned way, courtesy of a boyfriend. None were in any position to raise a child, and neither were the teenage dopes who'd impregnated them. Parents who might have been willing to help bring up a grandchild were unable to do so because they were busy working multiple jobs to keep a roof over everybody's head. Everybody was working, in school, or both. Daycare was unaffordable. The state was closing all the clinics they could, trying to make abortion impossible. Adoption seemed the only course of action. It's the fucking economy, stupid.

Word about the Sisterhood spread from girl to girl around the four-state region. The Sisterhood had no internet presence. They didn't need one.

One of the girls had been violently raped by a stranger. Another had been raped by her father. I spent more time with these two kids, not talking, just listening to them. I couldn't use what I knew about healing without revealing what I was, but I could sit and be fully present to them.

After a couple of days, both girls would have followed me anywhere, and I hadn't done more than hold their hands and hear their stories over and over. Like Jackson, I'd developed more presence than I knew in the nextworld high country.

Bobbi and I, supposedly in the first trimester of healthy pregnancies, helped out with the work of the place. There was a lot to do. Cooking, cleaning, gardening, caring for goats and chickens, laundry, picking up supplies from town in the Sisterhood's pickup truck, it all went on from dawn to dusk. While we worked, we listened to what the girls and the older sisters said and how they said it. When people think you're shy or dim, they speak freely around you.

Before I went to the elves, I worried about my personal worth and my place in the world. It's easy to grow up thinking a female human being is just a support system for her uterus. Not that I *accepted* it, you understand, but I was afraid it might be true.

Here we were surrounded by people who believed that stuff about a woman's place and taught it to the girls: *biologism*. Bobbi and I just nodded and smiled uncomfortably when Mother Mariah or a senior sister trotted out the party line.

Why did they pretend to believe a woman had no more value than a broodmare? In service of what?

After giving birth, the young mothers never saw their children again. One of a group of older women bundled the babies off to a separate walled area within the compound; none of us temporary residents were allowed to enter it. They called it *the crèche*, out of British sensibility or irony overload. Some newborns were quickly adopted out. The older women handled that under Mother Mariah's oversight. Rumor had it that money discreetly changed hands, disguised as charitable contributions. The poor birth mothers weren't charged for their stay, of course, and left as soon as they recovered their strength. *Vaya con Dios* (or whoever), *muchachas*.

The Sisterhood raised most of the children in *the crèche*. Rumor said that at the age of seven these kids were driven away in big black limousines in the dead of night. I never saw this happen. Hell, I never saw a single child during my stay. I didn't go looking for them.

About three o'clock in the morning, one girl's water broke. It was Marie, the kid whose father had violated her. Bobbi pressed the dormitory's call button. Suzy and Mariah came running. They hustled Marie off toward the suite of rooms the Sisterhood was pleased to call the Birthing Center.

The rest of us were ordered to clean up after Marie and then to go back to bed. We all nodded agreement like good girls. After Mariah and Suzy left the dormitory, Bobbi and I linked minds and followed them at a discreet distance.

We had a bad feeling about this. It was the hour of the wolf.

We walked in barefoot silence down cool tiled hallways. The three women ahead of us made no effort to be quiet. Marie's contractions were painful and frightening. When she had one, she yipped like a puppy. Poor kid, this was the second-worst thing that had ever happened to her.

The Birthing Center's double doors were open wide. Waiting inside, gloved up and wearing surgical scrubs, was Sister Rachel, a physician's assistant, the Sisterhood's nurse midwife. The girls didn't usually see her until they were close to delivery, so she'd had no opportunity to discover that Bobbi and I had faked our way in here. Rachel would have wanted to examine any girl who had bleeding during her pregnancy. That would have been a problem, but elf women don't menstruate. Girls who developed complications were driven off to a local hospital, and nobody saw them again. So said the dormitory gossip.

Mariah shut the doors behind her. We heard the *thunk* of a bar dropping into place to lock the doors shut.

That can't be good, I thought to Bobbi. She nodded agreement.

Something bad is happening, she thought. *I can feel it.*

74

Rural Free Delivery (*Janjan*)

Our birth is but a sleep and a forgetting...
- (Wordsworth, *Ode*)

We stood in the cool, dark hallway and considered our options. The door presented no obstacle. We could get in, but that would reveal us to be elf spies, not wayward girls.

From behind the thick, barred doors we heard Mother Mariah's voice raised in a chant. It wasn't a prayer. It wasn't English or Spanish and it wasn't Church Latin, either. I recognized that ugly, hateful language. The Walloon had directed a weaponized version of High Aghartic at me in a castle on the fae-path. Last year in Earth time, how long ago it seemed.

We could counter the Fallen Tongue, but speaking Elvish aloud would also defeat our purpose.

I'd learned something from listening to Marie talk about the times her father had raped her. Learned something from sitting there, accepting her story, empathizing with her as I felt her feelings with her. It was something I didn't realize before we met. Listening is a power in itself. You'd think the elves would have drummed that into my head. It's not just my ass that's thick.

Bobbi and I sat on the worn tile floor listening intently. What would two ordinary rebellious Earth girls do if they were worried about a friend? They wouldn't be able to sleep, so they'd stay as close to their friend as they could get. Method acting.

In the operating room (that's really what it was), we read poor Marie's surface thoughts. She'd been given an intravenous sedative that disconnected her conscious mind from what was happening to her body.

I don't know nothin' 'bout birthin' no babies. *Is that normal?* I thought.

No, it's not, Bobbi answered. *At least it's unusual these days.*

Rachel kept an eye on the sedative drip. Her thoughts were professional, cool and detached. Suzy stood by to fetch and carry. She'd done this job before. She was sleepy and a little frightened—not for Marie, but for herself: *Is this what it's gonna be like?*

Mariah's mind walked into a bad neighborhood as she spoke High Aghartic. She was caught in a perverse ecstasy of terror. The terror came from the creatures she invoked. The ecstasy came from the prospect of revenge on the male half of the human race.

There was another, fainter mind-trace in the locked room: the child who struggled to make his way down the birth canal into the world. Being born is harder than dying. This child's spirit came to birth from the land between his last life and this new one, following his karma. Like we all do, again and again, until we wake up and come home. The baby fought to cooperate with his mother's body and to enter Earth through her once again.

Bobbi looked at me in the gloom of the hallway and thought, *What are they* doing *to that kid—and her kid—in there?*

Listen! I answered. The Elvish word meant *focus all your senses.*

Something was coming this way in response to Mariah's invocation. Something *wicked*, in the original, scary sense of the word.

Demons.

We sat still and straight with our minds paused between thoughts. One moment followed another as moments do. We clung to nothing. It was peaceful and restful to sit like that, something I wouldn't have discovered in a million years without Leda and Jerry.

Elves don't mask their minds like magicians. The mind needs no protection; nothing real can be threatened. Centered stillness even makes the body less noticeable.

The Fallen see human beings not by their bodies but by the flame of their desires and the darkness of their sins. Their massed malignant attention passed near without detecting us. It was as if the demon swarm *descended* from above the roof.

That moil of hateful minds wasn't all demons. The fallen creatures who answered Mariah's High Aghartic invocation were an escort, a dishonor guard for the spirit of Louis, master of Materialist Magician masters. The Walloon.

A thunderhead formed around the operating room, under the roof of the convent and within its walls. *Darkness visible* flashed like lightning in the cloud. The malign intelligence of the Fallen fastened on Marie, directed by the guttural syllables escaping Mother Mariah's mouth.

Fastened on Marie's child as his little head emerged from his mother into the air of Earth. Seeking to replace the newborn baby's innocent spirit with the Walloon's dark spirit.

Ironic that the Fallen who loathe all embodied life on Earth hijack human bodies to accomplish their aims.

Bobbi and I surged up off the floor. We stood side by side and spoke a silent invocation with joined minds. The Elvish words given to every new elf by the angel who guards our world. *Remember*, we thought to the child's mind, to the mind of his twilight-sleeping mother, and to the immortal bodiless creatures who assailed him to deflect his spirit from rebirth. *Remember love and light.*

None of the conscious adults in the birthing center perceived the forces contending for the child. Not even Mariah. She employed materialist magic without understanding it. She knew *something* was going wrong but didn't know what to do about it.

Our Elvish thought sent the demons packing. The Walloon's spirit went with them. They lost their link to the building and the people in it.

On the physical level, all that happened behind the locked doors was that Marie's child was born. Rachel and Suzy cleaned the baby up and wrapped him in a blanket. The medication drip was curtailed; Marie was wheeled into a little room on the perimeter of the operating room to wake up at her own pace. In another little room Suzy rocked the baby and fed him some formula.

Bobbi and I stayed on our feet, senses questing.

In the birthing center Mother Mariah said, "The transfer miscarried."

Rachel said, "And the baby...?"

"It's just a baby. An ordinary human child. I felt Master Louis' mind as I spoke the invocation. Then he was ... *gone*."

The nurse shrugged. "That does happen occasionally, doesn't it?"

"It should *not* have happened to the master of masters," said Mariah. "It's easy for you to be casual about this. No one's going to kill *you* for your failure."

As the two women sniped at each other behind the doors, Bobbi and I witnessed an event at the border between death and life.

Our minds had spoken an Elvish command of great power at a crucial moment. In the land between one birth and the next a spirit has no defense against the truth. *Remember love and light* clung to Louis; he had no way to deny the words.

He remembered.

There was no way to escape the clear light of memory shining on his lives in the body. In an agonizing eternal moment, he suffered along with the beings whose lives he'd blighted when he went seeking magical power.

His *bardo* body reached the end of its time in the intermediate state. His will was free. It was time to choose.

Off went Louis' spirit, not to another birth on the Dark Path of the Materialist Magicians, but to the great mercy of ordinary human rebirth elsewhere on Earth. *A sleep and a forgetting*.

The Unfallen Tongue had been a blessing to Louis; it was a curse to the Fallen who had to release him. They *chose* their eternal fall into hell, where there was no memory, no love, and no light.

Bobbi and I tippy-toed back to the dormitory. We'd done what needed doing.

75

When Sisterhoods Meet *(Janjan, Beth, Bobbi)*

I don't believe in the world, not in money, nor in advancement, nor in the future of our civilization... - (D.H. Lawrence, Lady Chatterley's Lover)

I left before sunup the next day.

Bobbi would call if she needed me. She could keep Mariah from using High Aghartic to steal another child's body.

Mariah would be told that "Jan" had decided to go home and keep her baby. It wouldn't be the first time a girl had changed her mind and left the convent. The Sisterhood of the Dark Path was used to dealing with teenagers. They expected some inventory shrinkage.

In an instant I went home to the next world over. My husband was fully himself again, strong and quiet. Just being with him made me better somehow.

And! We had each other – a lot—whenever we weren't doing the other things life had for us to do.

Jackson healed people in the Groves of Healing and taught healing to elves new and old.

I taught Beth things new elves need to know. Leda came back from the highlands to help. The three housemates were back together again, more badass than ever. Elfgrrl Power.

"You were both right," Beth said. "It *is* pretty great over here."

"It's better than 'pretty great'," Leda said, "but I hate to oversell."

"Have you tried the mental sex yet?" I asked Beth. "No wonder it's so popular."

Beth and Leda looked at each other with raised eyebrows, like, *There goes horny Janjan again.* The word they might have teased me with on Earth, "sloot" or one of its nastier synonyms, doesn't exist in Elvish. The Unfallen Tongue has no word for a woman who pursues and gets all the sex she wants. In the next world over it's not just sex, it's also the creative act of lovemaking, which is rightly regarded as a miracle and as nothing special.

"You know the answer to that, Janjan," Beth said. "Don't I *look* happy to you?"

That made me smile. She *did* look happy. She hadn't looked that happy when she was swiving with me *and* the goddess of love and beauty, which didn't hurt my pride. Beth and Rob were good for each other. They pleased each other, mind, body, and spirit and got exactly what they needed. Like Jackson and me, like Jerry and Leda, they were *spoken for.*

"Rob asked me to marry him," Beth continued, "so I asked him to marry me. Will you two and your mates conduct the ceremony before I go back to Earth?"

Of course we will! Leda and I answered.

And so we did and so it was.

There are no bridezillas among the elves. Beautiful Beth and noble Rob wanted to get married naked, so the four of us who conducted the marriage were naked, too. None of us had any secrets from each other, or needed any. And as I've pointed out, I enjoy being naked, maybe a bit more than I ought to—whatever that means. *Yeah, you want some of this?* (Jackson *did* want some of this. He wanted *all* of this; a girl can tell.)

I was happy for the happy couple, of course I was, because they were so happy with each other. Wise and kind and beautiful and strong, both of them.

I was less happy for myself. Yes, Jackson and I were living happily ever after, like couples do here. Being happy doesn't mean you live unchanged forever.

I remembered when I was living in Portsmouth and the doorbell rang. It was Leda. I let her in.

"Beth hasn't come home. I don't know where she is," I said. "I'm so worried." I started crying because I was scared. And also because Leda had rung the damn bell of the house she used to share with me and Beth. Everything had changed. There was a barrier between us that hadn't been there until she and Jerry went and joined the elves. She wasn't our housemate anymore. She wasn't an ordinary human being anymore.

Leda just took me in her strong arms and hugged me. Whatever she saw of my thoughts and feelings, she said nothing. That scared me, too.

Beth, you may remember, pregnant with Rob's fae-child, ended up going to the Fae with him. Leda, who'd gone to the elves with Jerry, came back to Portsmouth to help *me*.

Now we were all elves, all safe at home in the place that was made for us. Jackson and I had gone through a lot. We'd changed. We heard the call loud and clear these days. It made us restless.

Rob and Beth took time alone together for their honeymoon. Then Rob returned to the Groves for the deep rest and healing he still needed. Too many Earth-years among the Fae had wounded and wearied him.

To complete her own healing, Beth took on a mission on Earth. I'd sit in a woven grass hut in Nextworld Portsmouth and be her contact. If she needed me, I'd join her in the instant between one thought and the next.

———

Homing in on Bobbi's mind, Beth traveled elf-fashion from Janjan's side to the main building inside the Sisterhood's compound. Like Bobbi, Beth was new enough to the whole elf business that she looked like a lightly-tanned white girl. Maybe calmer, but only a little older than the pregnant teenagers the Sisterhood existed to exploit.

Beth's confidence was deep and strong, but she still had no clear idea what she was supposed to do. Janjan had grinned and said only, *You'll know what to do when you get there. That's how this works, sweetie.* A classic Janjan assessment.

Beth felt Janjan's mind, shining and quiet. Her friend's invisible presence was a comfort.

Beth appeared in a hallway near the Sisterhood's laundry room. Bobbi hugged her and thought, *Where to?*

Beth said, "Let's go see the head bitch."

Janjan had given Beth a mental map of the Sisterhood's compound. As she and Bobbi walked to Mother Mariah's office, Beth compared the map to the territory.

Beth knocked on the thick wood door. They heard a muffled voice from inside and entered.

Mother Mariah was sitting behind her desk. She was wearing reading glasses and writing paper checks to pay the Sisterhood's bills. Out of vanity she snatched off the glasses and stuck them in a drawer.

Like it's shameful to grow old, Beth thought to Bobbi.

Well, it's unnecessary, but not shameful, Bobbi thought.

"Remember me, Mariah?" Beth said.

At first Mother Mariah *didn't* remember. She hadn't seen Beth since the first ceremonies at Odiorne Point when the Children of Venus invited the goddess to appear through the priestess, her earthly vehicle. The woman who stood before Mariah's desk bore little resemblance to the pale, drugged sacrifice the Order offered the Old God in California. When the Lady shone through Beth, Mariah had seen only Aphrodite. How could this glowing woman be the shallow girl the goddess had bound and borne away with her?

Mariah saw women in terms of how the Sisterhood could use them. Individuals didn't matter. A woman's youth and beauty served her womb, just as flowers are the sexual organs of plants.

"I see you have deserted the goddess," Mariah said. "Just another faithless little whore, after all."

Beth and Bobbi exchanged a look. Mariah hadn't tried to summon the police or call the Order for help.

Beth shook her head. "Not exactly. Would you like to meet the Lady? You can *ask* how well I served her."

Mariah said, "The question is whom do you serve *now*?"

Beth and Bobbi didn't answer. The nextworld signs were there for anyone who looked closely.

Mariah's eyes widened. "I see the *elves* have infiltrated my Sisterhood." She pressed a button on the desk phone, picked up the handset, and waited. And waited.

"If you're calling the Walloon, he won't be answering," Bobbi said.

"He laid his body down. He's not on the Dark Path anymore. His spirit couldn't enter the poor child you selected for him."

Mariah reached into her desk drawer. Before she got the revolver out, Bobbi was standing next to her. She pushed the drawer shut on Mariah's wrist.

Mariah *hissed.*

"Leave the gun in the drawer," Beth said. "You're not going to hurt us, Mariah. We won't hurt you unless we have to."

Mariah slowly put her empty hand on the top of the desk next to the silent phone. Bobbi used her knee to shut the drawer.

"What do you people *want?*" Mariah said.

"You can't continue what you're doing here," Beth said. "We're giving you a chance to choose differently."

"Sooner or later the Order will kill me." Mariah's voice was full of old grief and rage. Beth saw how badly one man had hurt Mariah before puberty and how other men had hurt her worse afterward.

"You won't *be* here," Beth said. "You'll be somewhere safe. All you have to do is help us."

Bobbi moved a careful step away from Mariah's side to give her space to think.

Mariah looked between Beth and Bobbi several times. Finally she said, "I'm listening."

A little willingness is all it takes, Beth thought to Bobbi.

"There's another sisterhood that can help," said Beth. "They'll come talk to you."

O Aphrodite... she thought. As she thought, she inquired within the place from which she'd called the goddess in the fae castle. *I think this woman is your worshiper more than she knows. Will you meet with her?*

A silence in Beth's mind that filled with the Lady's thought: IF SHE WISHES TO BE MY SERVANT, LET HER SPEAK TO THOSE WHO CAME ASIDE TO SERVE ME.

Smelling of ocean, long hair twined with seaweed, the forever-young Morrigna appeared in Mother Mariah's desert office surrounded by the Lady's rosy light. Really, they were Nereids now, though they kept the names they'd taken as deities of the fae-road before human history began.

Smiling, Badb, Macha, and Anann regarded Beth and saw her for the moment touched by the same light that shone in the three of them. Beth knew whatever love and beauty she possessed came not from any Old God, but from the source of life itself.

"The Lady sends her greetings," said Anann.

"Please give her my love," Beth said. "The Lady Janjan greets you and your mistress through me." Beth shared the light of Janjan's mind with the Morrigna. The Nereids bowed formally. Beth bowed on Janjan's behalf.

"She who could have been queen of the Fae was wiser than we knew to refuse the throne," said Anann. "The fae-path is dead."

"We live in the seas of Earth now," said Badb. "Despite our labors, I fear they too may die."

"When the seas die, the Earth will die soon after," said Macha. "And all the men and women on it. Not until then will Cypris depart—and we with her."

Beth felt alarm, an emotion she'd thought was forever behind her. The Earth was dying. What could she do?

For the first time, Janjan spoke in Beth's mind to steady her: *Just do what you can here and now, my sister.*

Beth thought, *I will.*

Mother Mariah sat stunned behind her desk as Beth and the three demigoddesses discussed what might be done to help Earth.

Sensing a shift in Mariah's emotions, Beth moved to her side and put a gentle hand on her shoulder. Mariah put her hand on top of Beth's. Tears ran down her face.

Beth caught Mariah's thought. The Sisterhood had other Dark Path convents scattered around the Earth, Beth told the Nereids.

"If you would serve the Lady," Anann said to Mariah, "will you travel with us to these other places where women work to end life on Earth? Together we will bring the Lady's love and beauty to those who most need it."

Mariah's tears stopped, but she still clung to Beth's hand. Beth was no mere human being, but she was more human than the three sisters who'd appeared in her office. Mariah was more frightened than when the Fallen drew near during the body-stealing invocations. Along with that, she felt hope.

"I will," Mariah said. "I *will* go with you."

Macha nodded. "What's been done can be undone. The past never returns, but it doesn't have to."

The sisters drew Mariah to her feet and encircled her with their arms. Their dresses clung to their supple bodies, smelling of brine and open sea. Surrounded by light the color of roses, the four set out for another Sisterhood compound. They grew smaller and smaller until they disappeared.

Bobbi and Beth looked at each other, surprised.

"That went better than I expected," Beth said.

"Yeah, great," said Bobbi, "now *we're* in charge of this place and all the poor girls who came here."

"We need help," Beth said.

Bobbi picked up the phone and started making calls.

The elves and the Elf Friends would get the Sisterhood off the Dark Path. Sisters who refused to renounce the Fallen would be allowed to leave the compound. Free will. Sisters who chose to stay could continue helping the girls who really needed their help. Those girls were still pregnant, still stuck in poverty, and still unable to care for kids themselves. What a world.

At least Beth could fix one thing that had gone wrong on Earth. *Just do what you can here and now, my sister.*

76

Too Wonderful to Realize (Janjan)

Emily: Take me back —up the hill —to my grave. But first: Wait! One more look. Good-bye, Good-bye world. Good-bye, Grover's Corners....Mama and Papa. Good-bye to clocks ticking....and Mama's sunflowers. And food and coffee. And new ironed dresses and hot baths....and sleeping and waking up. Oh, Earth, you are too wonderful for anybody to realize you. Do any human beings ever realize life while they live it—every, every minute?
Stage Manager: No. (pause) The saints and poets, maybe they do some.
Emily: I'm ready to go back.

- (Thornton Wilder, *Our Town*)

I was restless. My work was finished on wonderful Earth and in the wonderful world next to it. I'd found the meaning of *my* life while I was living every, every minute of it. Love and light, remember?

Jackson was restless, too. He turned over the Groves of Healing to Rob and Beth. In going through deep healing with Jackson, Rob discovered that he and Beth shared that gift.

We said *until we meet again* to everyone face-to-face or mind-to-mind. Not because we were dying or going to our graves.

Where we were going was the opposite of the grave.

Sometimes the elves who aren't really elves travel instantly to their nextworld destinations. More often they walk there like people do on Earth. Today it pleased us to *fly* upcountry, hovering just above the ground we loved so much. *God bless the ground*, the poet said.

We loved where we were; we were going somewhere even more wonderful. I'd met Jackson there when he came back to the flesh. Daniel and Aimee were somewhere up here on walkabout, as were Jerry and Leda. Jackson and I were going higher and further than any of them.

What was it like to travel that way? I can tell you that our breath was twined around Elvish spells at the center of our bodies. I can tell you that our minds were joined. I can tell you that we shared more-than-sexual pleasure with each breath we took. *Just like this. Yes, and like this also.*

We remembered everything in all the lives that had brought us to this moment. We were deep in love for each other and for everyone. We were surrounded by light that showed us how all things had been created out of love to be shared with all beings.

This was what the angel who guards the next world over had promised, come now to fulfillment.

If you could have whatever you wanted, what would you want?

Jackson came to the elves looking for his deepest, truest power. I came here looking for my deepest, truest pleasure. True power and deep pleasure turned out to be the same true, deep thing, no irony, just simple fact.

If I could have whatever I wanted, I wouldn't want anything I didn't already have.

Seeing that everything I could possibly want had been freely given me, I thought:

Bobbi, my sister, I see you running along behind us. Tell our story when you go back. Know that I love you and wish you every happiness. From where I sit now I see you walking toward joy.

Where I sit on Jackson with my legs wrapped around him. Yum. Whatever is going to happen to us is going to happen soon. I am finally so ready for this.

I don't know if I'll be back, Bobbi. But know that I am always with you. Ha! Just like Josh said.

Jackson and I find ourselves in an embrace that goes on and on. Waves of orgasm break upon us, inside us.

Oh, Jackson, yes, please. Come with me, come inside me. I love you.

I love you, Janjan.

And he speaks to me, in me, without words, of his love. His body holds my body as our spirits entwine.

So much love. So much light, wave after wave of it. Am I coming or going?

In our inner distance I see the ninth and greatest wave approaching from deep in the ocean of clear light.

And then? Two of the Many caught the wave and rejoined the One.

If you love your mate, leaving your mate behind is like abandoning your own body. If you love your freedom, going back to the flesh curtails that freedom dramatically.

What if you and your mate let the body go *together*?

The All, the everything. The Tao. The Mind of God. Whatever we call the love which so powers pleasure that there's no end to it.

Like Richard Round said, I have good news and I have no bad news.

[...]

77

Postscript *(Bobbi)*

He who binds to himself a joy
Does the winged life destroy
He who kisses the joy as it flies
Lives in eternity's sunrise

- (William Blake, "Eternity")

Because I'd loved Janjan not wisely but too well, my mind followed hers as she floated upcountry with Jackson. Because I'd been in her mind and body and she'd been in mine in the way of nextworld lovers, it was hard to let her go. Even though I knew we'd never be *spoken for* by each other.

Okay, fine. I know it sounds pathetic and stalkerish and it's a violation of the elves' unspoken code, but I know where Janjan and Jackson went because *I followed them in person*, okay?

Followed along behind them on foot, remembering everything that had happened, wanting to bring Janjan's account of her life to a conclusion that would make sense to our friends on Earth.

That's what I told myself.

So I ran along behind them at a brisk pace, until I saw them find exactly the right place. A place that must have satisfied some high-elf sense of the fitness of things.

I watched discreetly from a stand of trees as they dropped their robes to the ground. Upon those coarse, humble robes they sat like king and queen of the universe, wrapped around each other. She sat in his lap and he was inside her. With minds full of bliss they sat, their beautiful bodies rippling with the intensity of joy.

There was no room in me for envy. I saw something astonishing.

As they'd dropped their robes, they dropped their bodies, too. Their physical forms just *went away* in all directions at once. They flew together into a final freedom I wasn't ready for.

I was happy for them. I felt a joy unlike anything I'd ever experienced; I knew enough to let it fly wherever it would.

Yes, I was crying. Who could see such a thing and not be moved?

I saw Janjan and Jackson go, not into the sunset, not into extinction, but into *eternity's sunrise.*

Eventually, I knew I'd follow them. I was ready for the high country, but I had things to do back on Earth.

Heading gradually downhill on foot, I followed my intuition around the World Mountain. *I see you walking toward joy.* I might have cried for myself a little bit. *I am always with you.*

Jesus Christ, Janjan, first you harrow fae-hell, and now *this?*

Naturally, she didn't answer. If I wanted to talk to her now, I'd have to go where she went. I cried some more for myself at that thought, even though it was good news. Like Janjan said, there's no bad news in this world.

By the time I recovered my composure, I found myself on a flatter part of the mountainside. I saw a hut of stone and wood, roofed with woven boughs. Standing at the open door of the little house was a woman whose mind shone like sunlight on the great river.

It was Leah. She'd been Healer to all the elves for uncountable years of nonlinear time. Her white hair had now grown darker. Her eyes that had been weary were now bright. Living closer to the source of all life gave her new life.

Of course. Of course it did.

Leah smiled at me. "I think perhaps I've been waiting for *you,*" she said. Elves don't flirt, not when they're at home.

I felt an enormous sense of things fitting together. The fitness of things.

I smiled at her. "I think I've been waiting for you. I have things to do back in Portsmouth, though."

"They'll wait," Leah said. "We have all the time we need. Shall we bathe together in the spring? I hope you like older women."

"I like *you*," I told her. As I said the words, I saw how true they were. How inevitable this all was. I was for her, she was for me: *spoken for.*

So come to us when you can, dear Elf Friend. Come to the next world over, either with your lover or alone.

Forever wilt thou love, and she be fair. Or he. It's all good.

To quote Janjan, my friend forever, my sometime lover, savior of the Fae, leader of men and women:

If you live in the present moment, you don't worry much about the future. Naturally you still remember the past that brought you here. The process of cause and effect continues invisibly in our every thought and action. I mean, even among the elves who aren't really elves, things change. Sometimes things change dramatically.

Fairy tales often end with And they lived happily ever after. *"Ever after" is the tricky part. "Forever" means different things in different time streams.*

[digitally signed],

Bobbi

—

PPS: Bobbi's manuscript was uploaded to a Canadian server for the Elf Friends' website, *When Is an Elf Not an Elf?* Shortly thereafter, another anonymous denial-of-service attack took the server offline. Just because you're paranoid, doesn't mean someone isn't watching you.

I hereby attest that Bobbi logged in properly with her unique password, posted in accordance with our terms of service, and then logged out.

Her story sounds as legitimate—and as improbable—as everything else on our website. I love the elves I've met, but I don't understand them, not even a little. They try to help the Earth, so I help them. What else can a man do? Why is light given to those in misery, and life to the bitter of soul?

[digitally signed],

GrouchySkeptic1, Elf Friend and system administrator

About the Author

David Barnette is a lifelong resident of Portsmouth, New Hampshire, where he lives with his wife Judy. He is a graduate of Portsmouth High School. After graduating from Syracuse University, he served with the U.S. Navy in Vietnam. After working many years as a federal civilian employee, he now writes full time. He is available for readings and is happy to talk to groups large and small.

Dedication and Acknowledgments

This book is dedicated to my family. I'm grateful for you.

I also want to acknowledge my debt to C.S. Lewis and to Father Malachi Martin, SJ. I'm sure they'd both be properly horrified by what I've done with all I learned from them.

My sincere thanks to Elizabeth Barrett for her editorial recommendations. Any remaining narrative infelicities are entirely my responsibility.

www.ingramcontent.com/pod-product-compliance
Lightning Source LLC
Chambersburg PA
CBHW051520250626
47156CB00001B/167